Praise for Emily March

"Feel-good fiction at its finest."
—Susan Wiggs, *New York Times* bestselling author

"A brilliant writer you'll love."
—Susan Mallery, *New York Times* bestselling author

"Emily March's stories are heart-wrenching and soul-satisfying."
—Lisa Kleypas, *New York Times* bestselling author

The Getaway

The Getaway

A Lake in the Clouds Novel

EMILY MARCH

FOREVER

New York Boston

Forever
Hachette Book Group
1290 Avenue of the Americas, New York, NY 10104
read-forever.com
twitter.com/readforeverpub

First edition: September 2022

Forever is an imprint of Grand Central Publishing. The Forever name and logo are trademarks of Hachette Book Group, Inc.

The publisher is not responsible for websites (or their content) that are not owned by the publisher.

Library of Congress Cataloging-in-Publication Data

Names: March, Emily, author.
Title: The getaway: a Lake in the Clouds novel / Emily March.
Description: First edition. | New York: Forever, 2022. | Series: Lake in the
    clouds; 1
Identifiers: LCCN 2022019472 | ISBN 9781538707371 (trade paperback) |
    ISBN 9781538707395 (ebook)
Subjects: LCGFT: Love stories. | Novels.
Classification: LCC PS3604.A9787 G48 2022 | DDC 813/.6—dc23
LC record available at https://lccn.loc.gov/2022019472

ISBNs: 9781538707371 (trade paperback), 9781538707395 (ebook)

Printed in the United States of America

LSC-C

Printing 1, 2022

For Mary Lou
You know why.
And, for Molly
Because books and dishes and red sparkling shoes.

Part One

One

New Braunfels, Texas

THE DINING ROOM TABLE sat dusted and polished, an empty canvas awaiting that first brush of an artist's paint. A classic Queen Anne double-pedestal style in solid mahogany, it sported a nick here and a scratch there, wrinkles on the old grande dame's timeless face.

Standing in the dining room doorway and gazing at it, Genevieve Prentice recalled the Sunday morning more than thirty years ago when the table became part of her life. Her smile turned bittersweet. She'd been out of milk and down to one diaper for eighteen-month-old Jake. With her husband out of town on business, she'd loaded her toddler into the minivan for an emergency grocery store run.

She'd spied the estate sale sign posted at an intersection on the way home and turned into the old, established San Antonio neighborhood on a whim. Arrows led the way to a large Victorian house with turrets and towers and dormers. Ornate spindles and gingerbread decorated the wide, wrap-around porch. A rope swing hung from a thick branch of a century-old pecan tree in the front yard. It was Genevieve's dream house. *Someday,* Genevieve thought. *Someday David and I will live in a home like this.*

Genevieve often shopped garage sales, being a young stay-at-home mom whose husband was struggling to get established in his career. Ordinarily, estate sale offerings were priced beyond her budget. She knew she wouldn't be able to afford anything in this historic home, half-price Sunday or not.

Nevertheless, it was fun to dream. She removed Jake from his car seat, propped him on her hip, and headed inside.

She'd oohed over the wicker on the porch and aahed at the Oriental rug in the entry. The secretary in the parlor made her yearn. The bookcase in the library gave her the wants. But when she walked into the dining room and spied the table and chairs, Genevieve pulled up short.

Her mouth went dry. Her heart began to pound. It was love at first sight.

She wanted this table. She *needed* this table.

It would become an heirloom. Not something that came down from his family. Not something that came down from her. It would be *their* family heirloom. Hers and David's. It would be the centerpiece of their family life.

She'd bought the set on the spot.

It was Genevieve's first and last spur-of-the-moment furniture purchase. The table came with a matching sideboard, eight chairs, and two table leaves, which created a problem since their little family occupied a small, two-bedroom apartment at the time. She'd rented a storage unit and hired a couple of high school boys with a pickup truck to move it for her, but to say that David was unhappy with her decision was an understatement.

And yet, she'd never regretted buying her dining room

table. Then and now, it stood as a symbol, a promise, and a dream of that which mattered most to her.

Family.

The passage of more than thirty years had not changed that. If anything, family mattered to her now more than ever. After David died, her family gave her a reason to go on living. It gave her life meaning and a purpose. She'd devoted her life to her family. The family that she'd built with her husband for the fifteen years before his sudden death, and then on her own for the eighteen years since that tragic event, would be her legacy when she was gone.

When she was gone.

Genevieve unconsciously lifted her hand to touch the still-tender incision on her right breast. She willed herself to keep her thoughts off the dark path along which they'd wandered way too often in the past weeks. When the door-bell rang, she was glad for the distraction. She glanced through the dining room's large picture window toward the street, where a dry cleaner's delivery van idled at the curb. She detoured into the kitchen to grab some tip money from her purse, then answered the door.

Instead of the sandy-haired teen who usually delivered her dry cleaning, she discovered her third-born child carrying her linen delivery. "Hey, Mom." Lucas Prentice sailed into the house. "I swiped these away from Sam hoping to score his tip."

"Dreamer." She waved the teen to the door. "Perfect timing, Sam. I'm just about ready to put the linens on my table."

"Good deal."

As she handed the young man cash, a gust of wind swirled across the lawn and sent dried sycamore leaves skittering up onto the porch. Genevieve groaned. "That darned tree. I've

swept the porch twice already today. I wanted everything
neat and clean for Thursday, but my lawn guys can't get out
here to deal with the leaves until Friday." She glanced over
her shoulder. "Lucas, could you...?"

"I can't stay, Mom. I have a date."

The teen piped up. "My brother and I could do it in
the morning if you'd like. No school tomorrow, and I'm not
scheduled to work. We could use some Christmas money."

Genevieve didn't hesitate. Sam and his younger brother,
Nathan, lived four houses down from her, and they'd often
done odd jobs for her in the past. They were good, hard-
working kids. "Wonderful. You're hired."

They settled on a rate and a start time, then the teen
promised, "We'll have your yard looking good for your
Thanksgiving guests, Mrs. Prentice. Are y'all having a big
crowd again as usual?"

Genevieve's smile hitched just a bit. "We're a little smaller
this year."

"Smaller can be good. More pie to go around. A person
can never have enough pecan pie."

"Good point."

He waved a good-bye, and Genevieve moved quickly to
shut the door when another cloud of leaves threatened to
invade. "This is a surprise. What brings you by?"

"Just in the neighborhood." Lucas kissed his mother's
cheek, then held up the linens. "Where do you want these?"

"The coat closet, please. Your timing is good. You can
help me with the table."

"Sure. Sorry about the leaves, though Sam and his brother
will probably do a better job."

"No probably about it. You never had the patience to get
them all."

Lucas hung the dry cleaning in the closet, then followed his mother into the dining room and took a position at one end of the table. "So what's the theme for this Thanksgiving, Martha?"

"Martha?" Genevieve grasped the table opposite her son, and they tugged, opening the extension table wide.

"Stewart."

Genevieve sniffed. "I'm no Martha Stewart."

Lucas strode to the short hallway lined with custom built-in cabinets that connected the kitchen with the dining room and served as a butler's pantry for Genevieve's dishes. He opened the cupboard where the table leaves were stored. Lifting one, he said, "I'll agree that you don't pile decorative pillows on the beds or set out guest towels that people are afraid to use."

"And the only books on my coffee table are those I happen to be reading." Genevieve watched with an eagle eye as her son carefully placed the first leaf.

"True. But, Mom, you gotta admit, you do get your Martha on in the dining room." Lucas returned to the butler's pantry for the second leaf.

That was true. Genevieve loved to set a pretty table, and holidays were her specialty. She usually spent weeks planning her theme, colors, centerpieces, and linens. She'd taken a course in floral arranging at the local junior college and learned calligraphy because she'd wanted her place cards to shine. She often went so far as to change the artwork on the walls to complement her table.

"So what is it? Your theme?"

Genevieve studied her son as he placed the second leaf into the slot in the table. Between this unusual surprise visit and the out-of-character question, she knew something was up. Lucas didn't care about decorations. He was a typical thirty-year-old bachelor. His idea of home decor was matching paper plates. After they closed the table around the leaves, she responded. "Why do you ask?"

He shrugged and gave his dark hair a toss and that crooked little smile that invariably reminded Genevieve of her younger brother, Mark, whom they'd lost to pancreatic cancer six years ago. Her heart gave a little twist. Another seat at the Thanksgiving table that wouldn't be filled this year.

"Just curious."

Just delaying, if she knew her son. And she knew her son. Well, no sense trying to rush him. He'd get around to sharing whatever had brought him home when he was ready.

So, Genevieve returned her attention to her canvas. Last year she'd gone with a sleek, contemporary look with her decor using muted colors—sage, vanilla, stone, and wheat. She'd loved the way it had turned out. However, with all the turmoil churning the family seas, she wanted tradition with a capital *T* this year. That meant earth tones—brown, russet, gold, and shades of green. Mini pumpkins would add a pop of color. Place cards this year were black-and-white photographs in small crystal frames. She had spent weeks searching through her albums for just the right photos.

She had a message to send to her children this year at Thanksgiving, though she wanted it to be subtle. In her home, holidays were a time for fun, fellowship, and fantastic food. Drama wasn't welcome, especially not at the holiday table. Her kids were all bright people. They wouldn't miss the point she was making—that they needed to count their damned blessings.

Beginning with the one that was their family.

"I want my table theme to be a surprise, Lucas." She wanted all four of her children to be there to get the meaning of her theme in person at the same time. Her offspring hadn't gathered together since last Christmas, not because of jobs or distance or life commitments, but because of stubbornness and temper and the inability to ask for or offer forgiveness.

Genevieve's patience with it had run out.

Lucas shoved his hands in his back pants pockets. "Well, Mom. About that. I, um, well. I, um, I wasn't actually in the neighborhood. I came by because, well, even though this would be a lot easier to do by text, I need to be an adult about it."

Genevieve went still. She knew. At that moment, she knew what he was going to say.

"Mom, I'm not going to be here on Thursday."

"Lucas," she warned. "You are breaking my heart."

"No, Mom. Don't." He raked his fingers through his hair. "Just don't. It's better for everyone if I just stay the hell away on Thursday."

A dark storm of emotion rolled inside Genevieve. She was sympathetic and angry and frustrated and hurt and torn and dozens of other feelings she couldn't put a name to at the moment. Her heart bleeding, her throat clamped around a knot of pain, she willed back tears. Then, without responding, she turned and retrieved the protective table pads from the cabinet.

Lucas continued, "I thought about making up some excuse. I thought about calling and saying I was sick at the last minute, but I decided to be honest with you."

Well, she'd taught her children to value honesty, hadn't she? Somehow, though, she couldn't help but feel her lesson was being used against her now.

"Mom, I'm not ready. I need more time. It's just too soon."

She managed, barely, to keep her tone calm. "It's been almost a year."

He shrugged. Rather than defend himself further, he took the heavy pads from her hands and placed them on the table. Genevieve wanted to snap at him. She wanted to slap at him. She wanted to send him to his room without any supper. However, even though he acted like a child, he was an adult, so all she did was radiate disapproval. Like a nuclear bomb.

For all the good it did. Of her four children, Lucas was the least bothered by her disapproval.

Having delivered his news, he prepared to beat a hasty retreat and offered up something he expected would soften her up. Under other circumstances, it might have worked. "I have to go. Like I mentioned, I have a date. She's a nice girl, Mom. Might be something there. I think I might bring her to Sunday dinner sometime soon."

Oh, you think so, do you? Well, you might just find the restaurant is closed.

"I love you, Mom."

"You're breaking my heart, Lucas," she repeated.

"I'm doing the best I can."

No. No, you're not.

He hugged her, kissed her cheek, and left, shutting the door behind himself with a firm thunk.

Genevieve stood in her dining room, staring at her dining room table for a long moment. Her pulse pounded. Her chest hurt. Her breaths started to come in shallow, angry pants. She felt a storm coming on, and she knew only one thing to do.

She pulled her phone from her pocket and called her sister.

Two

JAKE PRENTICE WAS HAVING a bitch of a day.

As managing director of Bensler, International, a global architecture, planning, and design firm headquartered in Austin, Texas, he handled crises and emergencies daily. The job played to his strengths. With a natural affinity for languages, he was fluent in four and could get by in another three. He possessed an engineer's mind for detail and a salesman's gift for gab. He knew how to listen, delegate, and motivate, and his talents had helped him climb the corporate ladder at a rapid pace.

Jake had learned to take charge at the age of fifteen, the day his father dropped dead in front of him while the two of them changed the outboard motor oil for Jake's little aluminum fishing boat purchased with his lawn-mowing money. As the eldest of the four Prentice siblings, Jake had stepped up and stepped into his father's shoes to the best of his ability. In this family role, he had developed discipline as well as mediation, organizational, and decision-making skills, not to mention the ability to see through bullshit.

His brother, Lucas, was otherwise known as King Bullshit and Emperor Pain-in-the-Ass. The idea of sitting down to break bread with him on Thursday was about as appetizing as liver and onions. Jake despised liver and onions. Right now, he had a similar opinion about his brother, too.

And just think. His reward for surviving two full days of hell here at the office was that he got to spend Thursday with his little brother. Oh, joy. Let the angels burst into a heavenly chorus.

"Just shoot me now," he muttered, then reached into his desk drawer for the antacids. Maybe he should look at Thursday as his penance for the sins he was committing today.

Jake looked at the stack of folders on his desk. Twelve on the right, sixteen on the left. He wasn't even halfway through the pile. Twenty-eight employees whose lives and livelihoods he was in the midst of disrupting, two freakin' days before Thanksgiving.

At a knock on his office door, he glanced up to see his admin. "Mr. Franklin would like to see you in his office, Jake. Right away."

Great. Could this day get any better?

"All right, Jason. Thanks." Rising, he reached for his suit jacket and slipped it on. "Would you call HR and give Amanda Wilson a heads-up that our break has been extended? Tell her you'll give her a buzz when we're ready to resume the bloodletting."

His assistant gave him a sympathetic smile. "Yes, sir."

Jake popped another antacid before leaving his office. He strode briskly down the hallway past the elevator to the stairway, where he climbed the flight of stairs to the C-suite level. His boss's door was open, and his executive assistant was with him. Paul Franklin sat behind his desk, phone to his ear, speaking Mandarin. Jake rapped on the threshold. Paul waved him into the room and motioned Jake to take a seat.

"Coffee, Mr. Prentice?" the assistant asked quietly.

The last thing Jake needed was more acid. His stomach was already sour from the morning's events. "Club soda would be good. Thanks."

Jake settled down to wait for his boss to finish his call. Experience during the past six months since Franklin took over from Jake's retiring mentor had taught him that he could be sitting here for some time. His new boss liked his little power trips. Never mind that Jake had eight days of work to pack into the next two. He had files to read. Letters to write. Lives to ruin.

Playing the game, Jake sat without fidgeting. He pasted on a smile and turned his mind to his upcoming ski trip. He had a flight out of San Antonio headed for Taos Thursday evening. He intended to be on the slopes bright and early Friday morning. He'd need the strenuous exercise after the frustrations of this workweek and a holiday dinner with the fam-damn-ily. It might be the only thing that prevented him from stroking out.

Finally, Franklin ended his call. "Prentice. Sorry to keep you waiting."

Yeah, right. "No problem. What's up?"

"I understand you have involved yourself in the layoffs? Calling the employees into your office to deliver the news?"

Inside, Jake stilled. Considering he'd had to make the call as to which twenty-eight people had to receive pink slips, then yes, he would say he was involved. "I'm making personal notifications, yes, along with a representative from HR."

"Bad idea. That's what department managers are for. Not an effective use of your time."

Jake worked to keep the anger rolling through him off his face. "They're part of my team."

"Delegate, Prentice. At your pay grade, you need to delegate such tasks. But that's not why I called you in here. We have a problem in Dubai."

As Paul Franklin outlined the problem that had developed on the other side of the world, Jake wanted to groan. He knew where this was heading. He was accustomed to grabbing his go bag and heading for the airport at a moment's notice, but it was two days before Thanksgiving.

His mother would have his hide.

She'd always been a little intense about holidays. They had family traditions for every holiday, even those that didn't count as major ones. Seriously, while growing up, Jake had not known of another kid who was expected to spend Presidents' Day with his parents. Sure, it always had an educational component, but Genevieve Prescott invariably made it an event.

After Dad died, it only got worse. Mom's intensity ratcheted up about seven notches. Understandable, considering. The heart attack had come out of the blue, and she'd been lost for a little while. Jake had recognized even then that the holidays had saved her because focusing on cupids and shamrocks and fireworks and witches kept her from losing her grip entirely. Holidays, because they happened damned near weekly, helped her keep it together for her kids.

Unfortunately, nineteen-and-a-half years later, she still tried to keep as tight a grip on the family as ever. He wished she'd let loose a little. Then, perhaps the family growing pains wouldn't be as painful.

Painful didn't begin to describe the results if Jake canceled on his mother for Thanksgiving dinner at this late date. But, on the other hand, he wouldn't have to break bread with Lucas and pretend to make nice. That, at least, would be one lone bright spot in this craptastic day.

Sure enough, his boss wound down his lecture by saying, "We need you to go to Dubai. I know it's unfortunate timing due to the Thanksgiving holiday. Still, luckily, you don't have a family you need to please."

Tell that to my mother, asshole. Jake smiled and said, "I'll be happy to make the trip, Paul. I'll try to get a flight out tonight."

"Good. Get this fixed, Jake, and get back here ASAP. I want you at the board meeting next Tuesday to present our restructuring plan."

Our plan? Not hardly. It was Paul Franklin's plan, top to bottom. Jake had proposed a completely different scenario that would have saved ten of these twenty-eight jobs being eliminated today. "Sure, boss."

"Good. Glad we're on the same page here." Franklin rose and extended his hand for a handshake in dismissal. "Have a good trip, and remember to delegate."

Jake fumed his way back to his office, where he found a baker's dozen calls had come in while he was gone. News of the layoffs had gotten out, and the jackals were circling.

He popped another antacid, asked his administrative assistant to call Amanda with a fifteen-minute heads-up, and then book his trip. "Get me on the late flight if you can, Jason. I'll need every minute here this afternoon. First, though, get Bob Mason on the phone, please."

He'd ask Bob to gather the information he needed for Dubai. Ordinarily, he'd do that task himself, but he'd been told to delegate, hadn't he? But he'd be damned if he'd pawn the layoffs off on someone else.

The conversation with Bob went fast, and Jake had seven minutes before Amanda was due. Just enough time to call his mother. As a rule, Jake preferred to tackle unpleasant things first and get them over with. Yet for some unknown reason, he simply couldn't force himself to punch in her number or scroll to her name in his contacts list and connect the call. So what was he waiting for?

He killed six-and-a-half minutes. Wasted them in frozen idleness. He was shocked when Amanda knocked on his door and forced him to admit that he was afraid to call his mom.

Okay, he'd save that unhappy business for last. He'd totally chicken out and call Mom from the plane. Maybe even send a text.

"You okay, Jake?" Amanda asked as she took the seat off to his right that she'd occupied earlier this morning.

"I'm fine." He could use a drink, but that would have to wait until he was on board his flight. "Who is up first?"

Amanda checked her files. "Tess Crenshaw."

Tess Crenshaw. The most talented designer in the department. Hell, maybe the entire company. She'd been a valuable team member for three or four years, worked hard, worked smart, and deserved a promotion rather than a pink slip. Jake liked her very much. Could this day get any better? "Ask her to come up."

꜀ᴌ✦

Tess Crenshaw was having one of the best days in her professional life.

Driving toward downtown on I-35 after making a

presentation in Georgetown, she imagined she was driving a gleaming fire engine red Porsche 911 convertible instead of her boxy six-year-old white Kia sedan. She would gun her engine and weave in and out of the heavy traffic with the skill of a Formula 1 driver.

However, since Tess wasn't in a Porsche convertible, she settled for rolling down the driver's side window of her Kia and pretending she was in a sports car. And since she was fantasizing, she decided to go all out. She'd be a tall, slender blond with supermodel cheekbones wearing designer clothes and big sunglasses.

In reality, she was a short, curvy, natural redhead with freckles, whose pragmatic nature sent her shopping at Macy's for her work clothes and Target for her casual attire. She used her signal every time she changed lanes, chased points with the strategic use of credit cards, and made a grocery list from which she seldom deviated. Though sometimes her sweet tooth got the better of her, which was when the basket gremlins assumed control of her shopping cart. Invariably they'd tug it down the candy aisle toward the chocolate-covered mints.

But maybe…fingers and toes crossed…things were about to change. Maybe someday soon, she'd have the means to justify a serious splurge. Like, perhaps a spa day? Designer sunglasses?

A mortgage?

Tess giggled like a schoolgirl.

The downtown skyline rose in front of her, and her gaze found the forty-story building that housed Bensler, International. She couldn't wait to get back and share the news about this morning's meeting.

She'd worked her fanny off on the design for the renovation

of the historic Baker Hotel in San Antonio, and she'd totally rocked the presentation. As a result, the clients had all but told her that Bensler would be awarded the contract. Even better, they'd requested she review the plans for a current project in Louisiana and make a proposal for a new hotel in Nashville on the drawing board.

It couldn't have gone any better, and the timing was perfect, with her annual review coming up in less than ten days. Today's events were guaranteed to snag her an exceptional rating. Surely, the promotion she'd worked so hard to earn was within reach. And the Christmas bonus!

As Tess moved to the right-hand lane to take the downtown exit, she released another little giggle. If this year's bonuses were comparable to last year's, she should have enough saved for a good down payment. A promotion would give her the confidence to contact a real estate agent. She could be in a house by spring!

Her own house. Because she'd been a foster kid shuttled from house to house to house since the ripe old age of six, Tess had made home ownership her number one goal. She wanted a lawn to mow and walls to paint and windows to drape. She wanted to hang Christmas lights from her roof and a poinsettia wreath on her very own front door. To have it so close within her grasp was a heady feeling and the first step on the road she longed to travel—having a family with whom to share said house. Mortgage, matrimony, and maternity. The three M's. Tess's most cherished dream.

She was sitting at a traffic light on Lamar Boulevard thinking about hip roofs when her work cell rang. "Good afternoon. This is Tess Crenshaw with Bensler, International. How may I help you?"

"Hello, Tess. This is Jason, calling for Jake Prentice. He'd like to see you as soon as possible. Will you come up to his office, please?"

Tess's heart gave the *ka-thump* that it always made when she knew she would see Jake Prentice. She had a little crush on her boss's boss's boss. Nothing would ever come of it, of course. Jake was a consummate professional, as was she, and workplace romances were verboten at Benşler. Nevertheless, she enjoyed the little buzz she got whenever he said her name in that smooth, sexy voice of his. Maybe it wasn't exactly politically correct for a contemporary professional woman, but what did it hurt to have a private, not-a-secretary-but-a-designer-boss fantasy from time to time?

"Sure. I'm not at the office right now. I had a presentation up in Georgetown this morning, and I'm on my way in. I'll come straight there if that works? Probably about fifteen minutes?" That would give her time to stop in the ladies' room and comb her not-quite-a-convertible hair.

"Yes, that will be fine. I'll let Jake know you're on your way."

The light turned green, and Tess proceeded toward her office building's garage, her excitement about the day escalating. She wondered what this meeting was about. The Baker Hotel, maybe? Jake was a hands-on manager. He might well have known that her presentation was today. Either way, since she'd mentioned it to his admin, he was bound to ask how it went. She'd get to share her news. "Bonus, here I come," she murmured. Maybe she should spend some time on Realtor.com tonight.

A few minutes later, she pulled into an empty parking spot and shut off her car. As was its habit, the engine knocked a few seconds before shutting down. She gathered her purse and briefcase and exited the car, headed for the garage elevator. It took real effort not to skip.

Tess rode the elevator to the thirty-second floor and ducked into the ladies' room. She brushed her hair and was touching up her lipstick when the restroom door opened and a woman wearing a smart red suit whom she vaguely recognized but couldn't place stepped inside. Tess smiled at her, they exchanged hellos, and the woman disappeared into a stall. Tess wiped a smudge of rust-colored lipstick from her tooth, gave her reflection one last scan, then exited the restroom. Excitement hummed in her veins as she walked down the hallway toward the corner office where Jake's assistant sat at his desk. "Hi, Jason."

Jason Perdue offered Tess a reserved smile. "Hello, Tess. You can go on in. He's ready for you."

"Thanks." Tess approached the open doorway and spied Jake Prentice standing at the window, his face in profile. Her heart did that pity-pat thing.

He was tall, six-three at least, maybe six-four, with thick, wide shoulders that broadcast "athlete." Quarterback, in fact, Tess knew. He'd played ball for Rice University. He wore his thick, dark hair short and parted on the side—clean, classy, and classic. His nose was thin and straight. His face, all angles and planes. His eyes—oh, those eyes—were a fathomless shade of green that, when focused on a woman, on Tess anyway, invariably left her tongue-tied.

Today he wore a suit in charcoal gray, a white shirt, and a red tie. Tess didn't know men's fashion designers, but she'd bet everything he wore was either custom-made or from an exclusive shop. He could have stepped off the pages of *GQ* magazine.

Tess's crush grew a little bit bigger. She couldn't wait

to tell him about her presentation. Knocking softly on the doorsill, she said, "Jake?"

He looked her way. "Come in, Tess."

His gaze was serious and unsmiling. Okay, that was unusual. Jake Prentice always had a friendly smile for his employees.

He gestured toward the chair across from his desk. "Have a seat. We're waiting for another person to join us. It'll be just a minute before we get started."

"Oh. Okay." She took a seat where he had indicated, tucking her purse beside her.

"Would you like coffee? Water?"

"Water would be great. Thanks."

He strode over to a credenza, where he filled a glass with ice water from a pitcher. She smiled brightly up at him and reached for the glass as he approached with it. As was her luck, her butt cheek knocked her purse from the chair. Of course, its contents spilled. Tess felt her cheeks blaze with heat as Bensler's managing director smoothly bent, scooped her lipstick and tampons back into her bag, and handed it to her.

She wanted to pour the water over her head and drown herself. Instead, she pretended the incident had never happened and said, "I talked a lot during the Baker Hotel presentation this morning, so I'm thirsty."

"Ah. So that was this morning? I didn't realize. Thought that was next week."

"The client moved it up. He's taking an extended Thanksgiving holiday and wanted to make his decision this week."

"I see. Well, how did it go?"

"Fabulous!" The word burst from her lips, and Tess allowed her excitement to bubble forth. "They loved the design, Jake. I am ninety-nine-point-nine percent sure that we're going to win the project."

She launched into a detailed account of what had transpired during her morning meeting. Halfway through her narrative, it slowly dawned upon her that Jake's reaction wasn't what she'd anticipated. Where was his pleasure? His enthusiasm? His approval?

Nowhere that she could see. In fact, his reaction to her Baker Hotel coup could best be described as a grimace. What the heck? This wasn't the Jake Prentice she knew, the team leader who encouraged and supported, and who was always there with pats on the back. Instead, the more good news she shared, the unhappier he looked.

Unsure of herself now, Tess cut to the end. "They told me they'll call with their decision by close of business tomorrow."

"Did they now? That's good. I'm not surprised. I reviewed your design, Tess. It's excellent."

"Thank you."

So where was her "Atta girl"? Why did he look as if someone had just stolen his puppy? Tess awkwardly smoothed a nonexistent wrinkle from the emerald green skirt of her favorite presentation dress and puzzled over his reaction.

Jake cleared his throat. "Tess, I need to...oh good." He waved someone into the room. "Here's Amanda."

Tess watched the woman in red from the restroom walk into the office, a folder in her hand. Jake said, "Do you know Amanda Wilson?"

Upon hearing the woman's last name, her identity clicked. Amanda Wilson from Human Resources. Tess had met her last year at the Christmas party. Why is someone from HR—oh.

Tess's eyes went wide. Her gaze flew to Jake's suddenly stony countenance.

Oh. Oh no. I don't believe this! Tess's world came crashing down.

I'm about to be fired.

Three

JAKE DIDN'T WANT TO fire Tess Crenshaw.

He respected her talent and work ethic more than any person on his team. Over the past year or so, she'd become his go-to person when creativity mattered. And now the irony of this timing. Dammit, somebody should have clued him into the minor detail that she was making the Baker Hotel presentation this morning. If she did win the contract...hell.

It was all about the numbers. Damned numbers and metrics were the only things that the higher-ups allowed him to count. He had fought to keep her. Of the twenty-eight pink slips he was giving today, hers was the one he'd battled against issuing the most.

He'd miss her. The team would miss her. Bensler would miss her. She made a difference at the company in a host of different ways. Not only did she work hard and produce fabulous results but people liked her. She didn't ruffle feathers. She pitched in to help even when she wouldn't get credit for doing so. And she never missed a chance to volunteer when the company sponsored a civic event. The woman had a heart as big as Texas.

Jake liked that about her. He liked a lot of things about her. The fact was he'd had a thing for Tess Crenshaw for a while now, even though he'd worked hard to ignore it and went to great lengths to hide his attraction from her. Tess had been part of Bensler's Tokyo project, which Jake had personally overseen until its completion last spring. As a result, the two of them had spent a lot of time together. The woman did it for him on many levels. He'd have asked her out long before now if he wasn't her boss.

Of course, he wouldn't be her boss after today, would he? No corporate dating policies to worry about any longer. He'd be free to ask her on a date.

Yeah. Right. Like she'd date you after you fire her. That ain't happenin', Prentice. Just get this over with.

He cleared his throat and folded his hands atop his desk. "Tess, there is nothing easy about this. I'm not allowed to say very much, which is something I find appalling. Suffice to say that—"

Knock. Knock. Knock. "Excuse me, Mr. Prentice. You have a phone call."

"I'm busy here, Jason. You know that."

"Yes, sir. I do. However, it's one you've told me always to put through."

Oh hell. Mom.

Another thirty-four-year-old corporate executive might hesitate to give his administrative assistant a similar instruction, but Jake took his family responsibilities seriously. In the eight years that he'd worked at Bensler, his mother had called precisely three times. Alarmed, Jake rose, saying, "If you'll excuse me for a moment, Tess. Amanda."

He exited the office, closing the door behind him. Quietly, he asked, "My mother?"

"Yes. She's quite upset. Something about Thanksgiving and last-minute cancelations."

After slumping in relief, Jake immediately stiffened. "You didn't call her about my trip, did you?"

"No, sir. This isn't about you. I believe she mentioned your brother, Lucas, and an empty seat at the holiday table."

Lucas. What the hell had he done now?

"Do you want to take the call here?" Jason asked. "Want me to clear your office?"

He hesitated, debating what action to take. Holidays were Mom's special thing. If both her boys missed Thanksgiving, she'd be devastated. Guess he could contact his brother and ask why he was pulling this BS on Mom.

No. That would be a waste of time. Lucas wouldn't answer his call. Besides, Jake would rather cut off his left nut with a rusty knife than phone his brother.

What he should do was go back to his boss and refuse the trip. He should demand that Bensler send a substitute overseas.

A substitute. Huh. Jake rubbed the back of his neck. Maybe…no. That was a stupid idea. Totally inappropriate and unprofessional. And yet…

He couldn't fire Tess. She'd just won the Baker contract.

He *wouldn't* fire her, dammit.

So what would it hurt to float the idea? He met his admin's questioning gaze. "Please tell my mother I'm in an important meeting, and that I'll call her later."

"Yessir."

Jake turned and reentered his office, interrupting small talk between Amanda and Tess about the flooring in the

Baker Hotel. Ignoring the underlying tension in the air, he took his seat and said, "Sorry for the interruption. Like the saying goes, when it rains it pours, and today my rain gauge is overflowing. Tess, your news about the Baker has provided the only break in the clouds. Thanks for the rays of sunshine."

"I'm glad I could help."

Jake drummed his fingers on his desktop. He should tell her congratulations and send her back to her department. Tess's pink slip would go to Scott Parker instead. Scott Parker, expectant father. Jake closed his eyes. *I'm going to drink my way across the Pacific.*

Amanda said, "Jake, I think we should proceed."

Probably so, but when this meeting ended, he'd have to call his mother.

His mother. Jake leaned back in his chair, folded his hands across his belly, and focused intently on Tess. It was a crazy notion, but what would it hurt to ask? "Now, Tess, as I recall, you are a member of the Bensler Giving Back Team. Correct?"

"Yes."

"Did you volunteer to help serve a Thanksgiving meal at the homeless shelter this year?"

"Yes, I did."

"So your family isn't having a gathering? You're not going away for the holiday?"

"No, I'll be here." With a short, unreadable smile, she added, "I don't have a family that gathers."

Oh. Jake had grown so accustomed to thinking of his family holidays as burdens that he'd never stopped to con-sider the alternative. Despite all the Prentice family warts, he was lucky to be a member of the family. Uncertain how

to respond, he replied with a neutral, "I see. Well, I'm proud
of the way our company supports the community. It's great
of you to contribute and volunteer your time, especially on a
holiday weekend."

"I'm glad to do it."

"You like representing Bensler?" Out of the corner of his
eye, Jake could see the HR rep frowning. Tess looked confused
by the direction the conversation had taken. Smart girl.

"I do. I love my job. This is a great company, and I'm
proud to be part of the team."

"Good. Good. I'm glad."

Amanda from HR shifted in her seat and shuffled her
papers. Jake ignored her, focusing intently on Tess. "What
if Bensler could use your volunteer services in a different
arena on Thanksgiving Day? Would you be interested?"

"I'm happy to help wherever I'm needed. Do you want the
entire Giving Back group?"

"No. No. Just you. There's a place for you at a particular
table. You'd be filling in for me, and you'd be a perfect fit with
the company. They're honestly very nice people." That was
true. Lucas wouldn't be there. "I think you'd enjoy yourself.
Here. Let me write down the address." Jake removed a note-
card from his desk and scratched out an address in his bold
handwriting. "You don't need to take anything, but if you're
the type who prefers to bring a dish, a pie is always appropriate. Doesn't matter what kind. Can never have too much pie.
You'll be doing me a real favor. Just go and represent Bensler
and me. She'll be expecting you, and I promise you, she'll be
happier to see your pretty face than my old ugly mug."

"I will, of course. Will I be serving, like, at the shelter?"

"Oh no. You'll be a guest." He leaned forward encourag-
ingly. "At my mother's house."

Amanda Wilson grimaced and closed her eyes.

"Your mother's house," Tess repeated. "I don't understand."

"Paul Franklin is sending me to Dubai. I leave tonight. That leaves an empty spot at my mother's table, and since Bensler emptied it, I figure it's Bensler's place to fill it. Want to represent the company?"

Tess's chin dropped. "Is this a joke?"

"No. Yes. Sort of. Mom is a great cook. You love her cookies, don't you?"

"This is totally inappropriate, Jake," Amanda interjected. "Especially under the circumstances."

"What circumstances?" Tess asked.

Jake hastened to say, "There are no circumstances."

"Your position is being eliminated," Amanda said simultaneously, her voice kind but all business, typical HR, as she handed Tess the folder that contained the paperwork detailing the package she would receive. "You've been out of the office and busy with your presentation this morning, so perhaps you haven't seen the e-mail from corporate announcing the workforce reduction."

When Jake spied the tremble in Tess's hand as she accepted the manilla folder, all the frustrations of the day, hell, the past few months coalesced and propelled him to his feet. He reached across his desk and snatched the folder out of her hands. "No. I'm putting a hold on that."

"A hold?" Tess stared at him for a long moment, betrayal in her gaze. "What? Until after your mother's Thanksgiving dinner, I presume?"

"No. One has nothing to do with the other. Look, I've decided I want to take another look at things. Crunch some numbers. But I'm pretty sure today's developments change the order of things."

"Jake, you need to be careful here," Amanda cautioned. "Employment law—"

"Her job isn't being eliminated. The dinner request was a joke, albeit a poor one. Are you going to sue us over turkey and dressing, Tess?"

She folded her arms and studied him with a long look. A spark of temper had replaced the betrayal. Lifting her chin, she asked, "Cornbread or white bread?"

For the first time all day, he felt a tiny bit like smiling. "Mom is third-generation Texan."

"Cornbread, then." Tess drew a deep breath, then exhaled in a rush. "Okay. No lawyers."

Damn, but I like this woman. I want her on my team. Jake looked at Amanda and arched a brow. "Will you excuse us, Amanda?"

"Jake," she said with a warning in her tone.

"Please."

The HR rep rolled her eyes, gathered up her files, and exited his office. She didn't slam his door behind her, but she shut it firmly.

Jake dropped back down into his chair. "I'm sorry, Tess. This is not exactly my most shining managerial moment. The fact is that you are a talented and valued member of my team, and I don't want to lose you. The numbers I was given to work with are brutal. I believe this reduction decision is shortsighted and will bite Bensler in the butt in the coming months. I've argued myself blue in the face over it, but in the end, I had to work with what I was given."

He wanted a drink. If these were the old days, he'd have a bottle stashed in his desk drawer. If they were the good old days, he'd have a bar cart in his office. "However, the Baker contract is a big deal, and it does alter the landscape. It'll change your numbers, and that shuffles my list."

"Your layoff list."

"Yes."

"How many people are getting the ax?"

"From our team?" He dragged his hand down his jaw. "Twenty-eight."

"Whoa." She slumped back in her chair. "That's a huge layoff."

"A bloodletting." He drew in a deep breath, then released a heavy sigh. "Bottom line, I'm not eliminating your job today. Let's just pretend this little meeting never happened."

Tess stared at him for a long moment. "Taking the Baker contract into account, is the number still twenty-eight?"

He looked away, focusing on the photograph of the sunset from the deck of his grandfather's lake house. No matter what Lucas said, Jake had loved the Lonesome River Ranch. "Probably, yes."

"Who will lose their job if I keep mine?"

"Scott Parker."

"Jake, his wife is about to have a baby. Their third!"

"I know. Believe me, I know. Look, your designs are better than Scott's, but he's topped you on bookings for the past three years, and he has seniority. You've been catching up, and bringing in the Baker will put you ahead for this year. I can justify bumping you ahead of him."

"Amanda Wilson would kill you for telling me all of this."

"As well she should. This is totally inappropriate. I seem to be on a roll." He gave a little laugh and added, "Maybe I'll get lucky, and she'll whisper in Paul's ear, and he'll fire me before I have to call my mother and tell her I'm going to miss Thanksgiving."

"Your mom is going to be that upset?"

"Oh yeah. My brother has already canceled on her. I assume that both of my sisters will be there, but having a fifty percent offspring absentee rate will break her heart. Holidays are a huge deal to her, and I hate to disappoint her. She's really a world champion mom."

"You've talked about her often, and she's a legend around our department because of the homemade cookies she's sent every month. I was sorry I wasn't in the office to meet her in August when she delivered them personally rather than sending them through you."

He gave her a hopeful smile. "Well, now's your chance. She'll host a fabulous holiday meal. She always does. It's her thing. You'd have a great time. Seriously."

"Thank you, but I think not." Tess licked her lips, smiled crookedly, and reached for the file on Jake's desk. Rising, she brought the conversation back to the matter at hand. "Have Scott take over the Baker. He'll do an excellent job."

"Tess—"

"The Baker deal isn't signed, sealed, and delivered yet. The way I see it, nothing has changed. I'm still lucky number twenty-eight."

Jake opened his mouth to argue, but then he shut it. Technically, she was correct. However, they couldn't forget the client. "You made the presentation. You were the driving force behind the design. The Baker people will expect you."

"They'll be fine with Scott. He's good. I'm sure you took the Baker project into consideration when you made your layoff list. Right?"

Jake shrugged. "I planned for Scott to make the presentation."

"That was the right decision, Jake."

When he'd made it, yes. And when he'd second-guessed it. When he'd forty-fifth-guessed it. It had been the right decision for Bensler anyway, and making those decisions was why Jake earned the big bucks.

He also understood that Tess Crenshaw had made her decision in part because Scott's wife was about to deliver baby number three. Because Tess possessed that Texas-sized heart rather than cold-blooded ambition.

Of course, he hadn't mentioned her heart size in the reference letter that he'd written and included in her file, because not every prospective employer would consider that a plus. But Jake had sung her praises in every respect that mattered. He hoped it would help her get another job. A better job. Something she loved. Something that made her sparkle and shine like she'd sparkled and shined when she'd walked into his office half an hour ago.

"Tess?" With her hand on the doorknob, she turned and met his gaze. The wounded look in her eyes sank another knife into his own heart. Jake honestly didn't know if he'd survive twenty-eight of these today. "Good luck."

She surprised him with a plucky smile. "Good luck to you, too, Mr. Prentice. Happy Thanksgiving."

Oh hell. I've got to call Mom.

Four

GENEVIEVE HAD A HANDFUL of constants in her life. Every morning the first thing she did was to pop her thyroid pill and set the timer on her phone for thirty minutes. The moment the blissful chime sounded, she took her first sip of blessed coffee. Every day, come hell or high water, she took her walk. She preferred her two-mile route outdoors through the neighborhood, but on bad weather days, she joined the mall walkers. More important than coffee and exercise, each day, often more than once, Genevieve talked to her sister on the phone. Their calls lasted anywhere from two minutes to two hours.

Helen was Genevieve's elder by six years, the middle kid in a family of five, and the first girl. Ten years old during the tumultuous Summer of Love in 1968, Helen had watched the evening news each night with her parents, and the seeds of her rebellious, flower child ways had been planted during that time. By the time of America's Bicentennial, while Genevieve played four square and rode horses at Camp Fire Girls summer camp, Helen was sneaking out of the house to smoke pot and sleep with her long-haired boyfriend.

The sisters weren't particularly close growing up, but Helen had always been a good big sister. She was the person Genevieve called when a disaster happened—like when she'd lost her winter coat in junior high school—and she dreaded telling Mom. Helen had asked Genevieve to be one of her bridesmaids when she'd married her first husband, an honor that sent her fifteen-year-old baby sister over the moon. And of course, Helen always had Genevieve's back in any confrontation with one of their brothers.

In return, Genevieve did her best to be a good sister to Helen. She supported her through each of her miscarriages—four of them—and all of her divorces—three of those. She ran interference with their parents whenever they got sideways with Helen—not an unusual occurrence. Helen was the most intelligent of the five Bennett progeny and the most professionally successful, having won a full-ride scholarship to the University of Texas and then to Georgetown law. However, her very traditional parents never understood Helen's dreams. They were great parents. Helen and Genevieve and their brothers all loved them dearly. But the elder Bennetts had been old-fashioned people. The generation gap was a big one. Times and the changing roles of women in society were something they never grew comfortable with.

So, they didn't recognize Helen's accomplishments within the family to the extent they should have. Helen wouldn't call out them on it. Genevieve had, and Helen appreciated her sister's efforts.

The sisters' relationship changed forever when David died. To this day, Genevieve didn't think she would have survived that terrible time without her sister's steady shoulders to lean upon. Helen had requested a three-month leave of absence from work and taken a short-term lease on an apartment half a mile from Genevieve's house. She showed up every morning at 7 a.m. to help get the kids off to school.

For a woman who had partied her way through her youth, Helen was far from a poster child of a saint, but that's exactly what she'd been for Genevieve. "Not a saint," she'd said when Genevieve had expressed the thought. "A sister."

Today she was the dearly beloved sister whom Genevieve couldn't get on the phone when she needed to talk. Shoot, not even Jake had been able to take her call. Jake always took her calls.

Attempting to distract herself from fretting over family strife—at least until she could whine to Helen about it—Genevieve went to work building her centerpiece. She smoothed a table runner embroidered with autumn leaves atop the beige tablecloth and arranged the sprigs of rosemary she'd cut from the bushes in the backyard earlier this morning. Slowly, she began to find the joy that the task of decorating her table ordinarily brought her. As she retrieved her Fitz and Floyd harvest figurine candleholders from the butler's pantry, she hummed the Prentice family classic Thanksgiving song—an old Motown sixties tune, "Mashed Potato Time."

She was engrossed in her task and didn't notice when the car pulled into her drive, so the sound of a knock at her back door startled her. She set down the candleholders and headed toward the kitchen. The door opened, and a familiar voice scolded, "Genevieve, how many times have I told you not to leave your garage door open and your door unlocked during the day?"

Delight washed through Genevieve as her sister sailed

into her kitchen wheeling a colorful Vera Bradley suit-case. "Helen!" Genevieve exclaimed. "You're here! You're early!"

"I know. I wasn't tired last night when I got to Amarillo, so I drove on to Wichita Falls. I got an early start this morning."

"I'm so glad. I've been trying to call you. Oh, Helen. I'm so glad you're here."

The sisters embraced, and Genevieve caught a whiff of Cashmere Mist, Helen's signature Donna Karan cologne. The scent swirled around inside her until it found and filled that part of her heart that needed family, her first family, the family who shared history that wasn't Prentice.

Helen was it, the only one of them left.

Tears stung Genevieve's eyes, and she hugged her sister a little tighter. Helen Bennett McDaniel was tall, lanky, brilliant, and still lovely in her early sixties. She had mossy green eyes, fair skin, and she wore her auburn hair in a sassy, short style that suited her. She'd never had children of her own, but she'd loved being the adored favorite aunt of Genevieve's brood.

Helen stepped back. Keeping hold of her sister's hands, she gave her a long once-over. "You've always been a tiny thing, but you've lost weight. You okay?"

"I'm fine." Genevieve blinked away her tears. "I'm fine. I'm just happy you're here, so happy to see you. It's been too long."

"Honey, you visited me in September."

"Well, September was forever ago!" Genevieve blew out a heavy breath and added, "I'm not dealing well with your retirement."

"No?" Helen drawled. "I hadn't noticed."

Genevieve smiled sheepishly as her sister continued, "You need a haircut and highlights. Don't tell me you've decided to go gray!"

"No, my hairstylist has been out with the flu. I'm going in first thing in the morning."

"Good. You had me worried. Not as worried as I'd be if I arrived to find you sans makeup, but…"

"Hey, I might just surprise you and follow your lead. Go all mountain woman natural."

"You go out in public without your foundation? Now that would be a sea change."

"Maybe I need a sea change," Genevieve grumbled.

Helen arched a brow. "I sense a story there, but first, I've gotta pee. Which bedroom am I in?"

"The downstairs guest room."

"Perfect. I love the morning light in there."

"You go get comfortable, and I'll put the coffee on. We can have a chat and catch up. I want to hear all the latest gossip about life in Lake in the Clouds, Colorado."

"Perfect. I do have a couple of stories I've been waiting to share."

Helen didn't take long to freshen up. The coffee was brewing, and Genevieve stood inside her walk-in pantry transferring a variety of homemade cookies from tins to a plate when she heard her sister exclaim, "Oh, I'm in time to help with the table! Hurray!"

Genevieve grinned as she exited the pantry to see her sister standing at the entrance to the dining room. Helen glanced over her shoulder, her green eyes shining. "You're pulling out the Pilgrims this year. Going old school. I love it."

"Wait until you see my place cards. Old school on steroids."

"Cool." Helen eyed the plate and then strode over and

snagged a ginger cookie. She took a bite and closed her eyes. "Oh my. It's like going home, isn't it?"

The ginger cookies were their mother's recipe, a soft cookie made with blackstrap molasses, cinnamon, and cloves in addition to ginger. It had been one of the regulars in the cookie rotation in their home when they were growing up. Their dad had a serious sweet tooth, and Mom had made two cakes and three batches of cookies each and every week.

The neighborhood kids loved to play at the Bennett house after school, having declared Mrs. B as the queen of after-school snacks. For their part, the Bennett sisters often lobbied for after-school snacks at other children's houses, where, sometimes, exotic things like chips were to be had. Doritos and Fritos and Cheetos, oh my. Mom had only purchased boring old potato chips.

Warmed by the memory, Genevieve said, "I have chips and salsa and Fritos and bean dip if you'd rather salty over sweet."

"Fritos and bean dip!" Helen let out a maniacal laugh. "Let the Thanksgiving splurge begin. Cookies and coffee are perfect for now." Licking cookie crumbs from her fingers, she gave her sister a wink. "Let's save the chips for the after-school snack."

As usual, the Bennett girls were on the same page.

"You want to sit in the kitchen or in here?" Genevieve asked.

"Honestly, I need to move around. I've spent too many hours in the car the past couple of days. We can visit while we set the table, can't we?"

"Absolutely." Genevieve set the cookies on the sideboard buffet, then returned to the kitchen, where she poured two mugs of coffee. "Half-and-half or the real deal?"

"You have cream?" At Genevieve's nod, Helen said, "Calories don't count at Thanksgiving, right? Give me the good stuff."

Moments later, Genevieve handed a mug filled with lightened coffee to her sister, who took a sip and then sighed with pleasure as she stood staring up at the packed shelves of the butler's pantry. "My new friends think I'm weird."

"Your old friends think you're weird, too," Genevieve replied because that's what sisters do. But then she asked, "Weird in what way?"

Helen twisted her lips and jerked a thumb upward. "I talk about my dishes like they were my children. Getting rid of everything but Mom's china was the hardest part of downsizing for me. By a mile."

Genevieve instantly understood. "I don't know that I could do it, Helen."

She and her sister shared a passion. They both loved dishes, and until Helen retired and moved to Colorado eighteen months ago, they'd both owned multiple sets. They'd used them and enjoyed them.

Both sisters' gazes rose to the cabinets. Genevieve kept her everyday pottery in the kitchen, but the butler's pantry displayed her wedding china and Christmas china. Over the years, she'd added Thanksgiving- and Easter-themed salad plates and serving dishes. She had small plates with hearts for Valentine's Day, shamrocks for St. Patrick's Day, and jack-o'-lanterns for Halloween. Jake teased her with the claim that she'd never met a tidbit plate she didn't like.

And then, there was her mother's Haviland. She and Helen had split the set when they lost Mom, and Genevieve had supplemented her half with pieces she'd found on eBay. Yes, she'd gone overboard and become a little too addicted to Internet auctions. However, it had come in handy to have service for forty-seven when Willow married nine years ago.

They'd used the china at the reception for the bridal party and family tables in remembrance of Willow's beloved Nana. Genevieve had needed to borrow only three salad plates and two bread and butter plates from Helen. Seriously, that bridal party had been way too large, but the room had been breathtaking. Seeing her mother's china on the tables at her daughter's wedding reception had touched Genevieve's heart in a deeply personal way she didn't have words to describe.

Well, she had a handful of words. Yearning. Regret. Sorrow. Loss. Grief. Gratitude. Satisfaction. Bittersweet joy.

"What dishes are you using on Thursday?" Helen asked.

"My wedding set. I seriously considered using Mom's, but I think it's still too soon for Willow. Mom's dishes are her wedding dishes, after all." And Willow's husband, Andy, had passed away only a little over a year ago.

"Ah," Helen murmured. She linked her arm with Genevieve's, standing beside her offering silent support—just like she had the afternoon before Willow's wedding.

Genevieve had been a ball of nerves that afternoon as she'd ducked into the reception hall to give everything a once-over before heading to the church for the ceremony. She teared up easily as a rule, but on her daughter's wedding day, she'd remained dry-eyed. Placing the photographs of her parents and her husband at the remembrance table hadn't brought on the waterworks. Neither had buttoning Willow's gown. Even when Genevieve gave Willow her beloved diamond drop to wear—David's fifteenth wedding anniversary present to her, which he'd gifted to her a week before his death—Genevieve hadn't so much as gone misty. That had taken Mom's china.

She'd taken one look at the china gracing the tables at the reception and gone to hundred-year-flood tears in a tenth of a second.

She'd come darned close to ruining her makeup at a point when it was too late to fix. The wedding coordinator had offered her a tissue and a calming smile while throwing Helen a helpless look. Then, like now, Helen had known what to do. Genevieve's sister understood the dishes. She was the only one alive who did.

It was something that Genevieve had tried to impress upon her children in recent months, though she didn't think any of them had listened. As one aged, memories of youth and the experiences of events shared by siblings took on a new significance and importance. In other words, the older Genevieve got, the closer her childhood seemed to be.

Events of the past few weeks had her thinking about her childhood all the time.

Genevieve lifted her gaze and focused on the Haviland platter. She stored it up high, but their mother had kept it within easy reach at her and Helen's childhood home in Wichita Falls, Texas. They used it almost every week for Sunday dinner. The family would come home from church to the savory aroma of beef roasting in the oven. Helen's job was to set the table, Genevieve's to clear. Mom washed the china by hand, and armed with flour sack dish towels, both girls dried and carefully returned the pieces to the china cupboard.

Their brothers got off scot-free with dinner prep and cleanup, but then, those had been different times. The boys mowed the lawn and had paper routes. Give Genevieve a dish towel over a push mower any day.

"Willow still thinks it's horrible of me to give Jake and Lucas a pass when it comes to washing china."

"Yeah, well, Willow wasn't there the day poor Gary dropped the gravy boat, was she?"

As was their habit at the mention of sixteen-year-old Helen's seventeen-year-old boyfriend's trying-to-be-helpful fumble, both women made the sign of the cross. Then they laughed.

Genevieve leaned back against the counter, took another sip of her coffee, and observed, "Sometimes when I open this particular cabinet, I swear I catch a whiff of rump roast."

"If that is the case, then somebody around here is a spectacularly poor dishwasher."

"Or dish dryer," Genevieve shot back. It was an old family joke. Their mother's sister used to repeat it every holiday when the women did dishes following the meal. "How long has Aunt Grace been gone now?"

"Oh, I don't know." Helen paused and thought a moment. "Has to be close to twenty-five years."

"More than that, I think. I wish she was here to make the gravy this Thanksgiving. Nobody made gravy like Aunt Grace."

"That's because she put bourbon in it."

Genevieve turned a scandalized look her sister's way. "She did not!"

"Come on, Gen. Why do you think she and Mom giggled so much while they cooked?"

"I knew they enjoyed their toddies, but..."

"They are why we started enjoying our cocktails while we prepare our Thanksgiving meals."

"True." Gen's lips twisted in a crooked smile.

Helen gave Gen's arm a squeeze, then her tone turned matter-of-fact. "Maybe it would be good for you to use the Haviland on Thursday. Rip the bandage off. Make a new memory with it. Honestly, since Willow won't be here, you and I are the only people likely to make the connection to the wedding."

Genevieve stiffened. "Excuse me? What did you say? Willow isn't coming for Thanksgiving?"

Helen's eyes rounded. "She didn't call you?"

"No."

"That little…" Helen huffed out a breath. "She said she'd call you."

"She didn't." A wave of emotion so big and dark and deep rolled over her that Genevieve thought she might just drown. Willow hadn't called her mother, but she had called her aunt Helen to tell her she wasn't coming home. That she wasn't bringing her children home for Thanksgiving as planned.

Lucas was bad enough. But Willow? Genevieve's lungs hurt. Her heart hurt. The scar on her breast even hurt. She needed to sit down.

Helen muttered a curse. "That girl is officially on my shit list now. She promised she would call you the minute she hung up with me."

"What's her excuse this time?" Genevieve asked softly.

"She has to work on Friday. Her boss won't let her off."

She scoffed. "And you believed that crock of cranberries?"

Helen shrugged. "It's what she said."

"I don't believe it for a second." Genevieve brought up her hand and rubbed the back of her neck. "Lucas dropped by this morning. He's not coming, either. He doesn't want to be around his brother."

"Oh, Gen." Helen covered her mouth with her hand.

"Thursday is just going to be a grand old time, isn't it? You know, I was counting on the children being there to dispel the tension. Even without the war going on between the boys, we'll have Brooke to deal with. She's angry at the world these days, no real surprise considering the man she married."

"Not-so-good-old Travis. Do you expect him to join us on Thursday?"

"Yes." Genevieve shot the word like a bullet, then set down her mug with a bang and added, "Forget the coffee. How about a Bloody Mary?"

"I can drink a Bloody Mary, though maybe we should get the china down from the cabinets first."

"Screw the china. We might just eat Thanksgiving dinner off paper plates this year. Come on, Helen. Let's make drinks and sit out back and ogle the golfers on the number three tee box. You can tell me all about Happy Acres."

"It's the Mountain Vista Retirement Community. And I'll mix the cocktails. I've become quite the Bloody Mary pro since I joined the Tuesday Morning Book Club. Do you have celery?"

"This close to Thanksgiving? Of course I have celery." Five minutes later, Genevieve carried a tall Bloody Mary out to the backyard. She left her cell phone inside and didn't hear it ring.

Twice.

Five

AMANDA FROM HR WAITED nervously for Tess outside Jake's office. Tess visited with her briefly, went over the paperwork for the generous severance package, and apparently reassured her enough that she didn't call security to have Tess escorted immediately from the building. Instead, Tess went to her department, where her boss had a banker's box waiting for her. He told her they were calling it the Bensler Thanksgiving Massacre. No one was quite sure just who the turkeys would turn out to be—those who got the ax or those who stayed. She appreciated his effort and thanked him for being a good team leader, then she cleaned out her desk and said her good-byes. She managed to keep it together until she left the building.

Barely.

She was scared.

Security was important to her. Security meant everything. That's what happened when you never had a father and your mother died when you were six, and adoptions fell through because of do-gooders doing bad things.

Oh crap oh crap oh crap oh crap. She was out of work. Laid off. Unemployed. Jobless.

What was she going to do?

"It'll be okay," she told herself as she retraced her steps from an hour ago—or was it a year ago—through the garage. "Everything will be okay."

It would, truly. She had savings. Bensler had offered a more than generous settlement. She dug in her purse for her key fob as her temper spiced the soup of fear and grief sloshing around inside. She added, "After all, I don't have a mortgage to worry about."

She jabbed the button to pop open the trunk. Now the tears she'd managed to stave off began to flood her eyes, and she furiously blinked them away. Tess didn't necessarily cry when she was sad, but she couldn't hold them back when she got angry. She hated it.

She was angry now. Furious. Not at Jake. She'd have made the same decision as he if their positions were reversed. She wasn't even all that upset with Paul Franklin, though she disagreed with the direction in which he was leading the company. He got his marching orders from the Board of Directors. This was corporate life.

No, Tess was angry at her old nemesis—call it fate or bad luck or destiny—she didn't know or care. Whatever the name of this force sitting behind the wheel of her life bus, it needed to find another blasted vehicle to drive! Seriously, hadn't she had enough?

Abruptly, her anger drained, leaving her sad and scared and—the worst part—lonely.

Too often lonely. Story of her life. Because she'd focused on work, her social life did, too. Almost all her friendships revolved around work. That had been something she'd hoped to change once she had a home. She'd planned to establish herself in the neighborhood, to volunteer for the schools or Little League teams or dog rescue groups and expand her circle. She hadn't figured she'd run out of time. Would her friendships survive once the common bond of Bensler had been severed?

Maybe, but probably not. She'd seen it happen in the past when someone moved on from Bensler. Face it, more often than not, work friendships were just that. Once the commonality of work was removed, the friendship languished.

"Well, it doesn't have to be that way, does it?" she murmured, reaching deep within herself to find a glimmer of positivity. She set the banker's box that her immediate superior had given her for her personal items into her trunk and told herself she shouldn't give up before she even got started. She might have missed out on having the since-childhood lifelong friend she craved, but she was still young. She could meet someone today who would still be her friend in fifty or sixty years. It could happen. She just needed to open herself to the possibilities.

"Tess? Tess, wait!"

Jake. She swallowed a groan. *Now what?* Had she dropped another tampon? Could this day be more humiliating?

She knew better than to dream that Jake Prentice might be the friend she craved. Fate had never been that kind to her.

She did *not* want him to catch her with tears in her eyes. She had left his office with the perfect parting shot. She'd been so proud of it! Now he was going to ruin it by catching her crying. Why couldn't he leave her be? What was he doing here in the garage? Didn't he have more lives to ruin today?

"Tess, hold up."

Grrr. She closed her trunk, pasted on a closed-lips smile, and turned to face him. "Hello again."

"I'm glad I caught you. I tried your phone, but..."

"I'd already turned it in."

"Yeah. Ron had it. He answered when I called. He told me you'd just left the department."

Tess waited. She was seeing another side of Jake Prentice today. Ordinarily, he was calm, cool, and collected. The ultimate professional. She'd watched him make presentations and work deals in high-stakes circumstances and never break a sweat. Today, the man was shaken. *Well, welcome to the club.*

"Did I leave something behind in your office?" *Besides my career. My pride.* "My breath mints, maybe? They rolled out of my purse?"

"What? Oh no. No. I have something I want to give you." He pulled a card from his jacket pocket and handed it to her. His card—the second one today—with a name, the name of a firm, and a phone number scrolled on the back. "I thought of Steve after you left the office. I gave him a call and told him a little bit about you. He'd like to hear from you. I know you'll be thinking about the big shops. You'll be a prize for whoever you choose to work with, but before you make your decision, I think you should reach out to Steve. It's a small boutique firm, but they do some awesome projects that would be right up your alley."

"Oh." Tess stared down at the card in her hand. He'd done this? He was in trouble with his mother and on his way to catch a flight halfway across the world, but he'd taken time to job hunt for her? He really was a superior supervisor.

He's not going to last much longer working for Paul Franklin.

"Thank you, Jake. This is really nice of you to do. I've

heard the buzz about Innovations Design. I will look into this. I appreciate your help. A lot. Thank you."

He nodded. "Good. Good. Well, glad I caught you. I was afraid if I waited until after I got back from my trip, you'd already have a job."

"It's Thanksgiving, Jake. Nobody's hiring this week."

He gestured toward the card in her hand. "You don't know that. Think positive, Crenshaw. I'm a big believer in the power of positive thinking."

"Oh really?"

"Yeah. So putting my money where my mouth is…and since it's the week of making mouths happy…how about reconsidering that Thanksgiving dinner invitation? Gobble gobble?"

Tess couldn't believe she was doing it, but she laughed. "I take it you haven't spoken with your mother yet?"

"No, she didn't answer her phone."

"Ah. I appreciate the effort, but I'm still going to pass."

"Oh well. I had to try." He started backing away. "I'd better get going. Plane to catch. People to ruin. Good-bye, Tess. I've enjoyed working with you. I hope we'll get to do it again someday."

"I'd like that," Tess replied. She meant it.

When she slid behind the wheel of her car a few moments later, her tears had disappeared. The anger was gone. The fear was banked. She might even have had a little glimmer of excitement flickering in her heart.

At that moment, she actually felt sorrier for Jake than she did for herself. After being head executioner at the Bensler Thanksgiving Massacre, he had to break the heart of his world champion mother and travel halfway around the world for the job.

"Sucks to be you today, Jake," she murmured as she started her car. It sounded like his mom's day wouldn't be any better, which was a real shame. Tess really liked the woman's cookies.

I wonder if her turkey is as good.

~~✦~~

Genevieve and her sister sat in chairs set around the gas-fueled fire pit at the center of Genevieve's backyard living space. It was a beautiful spot with a swimming pool, spa, and outdoor kitchen separated from the golf course by a simple iron fence. They sat silently sipping their cocktails, watching the golfers, while Genevieve stewed about her eldest daughter.

She loved all her children deeply, and in her heart of hearts, she believed she loved them equally. Differently, but equally. Each child was special to her in their own way, each similarly a trial.

But of the four, Genevieve had always been closest to Willow. She'd been a mama's girl from the day she was born, and that hadn't changed until Genevieve made what she'd come to refer to as her Great Misstep. Helen called it her Royal Eff Up.

Genevieve hadn't liked the man Willow chose to marry. She hadn't liked him the first time Willow brought him home to meet the family. Something about Andy Eldridge had felt squirrelly to Genevieve. He raised her hackles and her protective maternal antennae. Then, in one of her top ten instances of poor mothering, she hadn't taken her time to carefully choose her words, and she'd been too blunt. Willow reacted by digging in her heels, and they'd argued.

For many months, Genevieve had thought that her daughter continued to date Andy to spite her rather than out of a desire to be with him.

Time had proved Genevieve wrong. Andy won her over. Genevieve recognized that she'd been wrong, not just about Andy, but about the way she'd try to helicopter parent her college-age daughter. She'd apologized to both Andy and Willow numerous times and did her level best to make it up to them. Andy let bygones be bygones. Willow said she had. Nevertheless, except for a handful of precious occasions, mother and daughter had never again enjoyed the closeness they'd once routinely shared.

Genevieve mourned it.

She didn't understand why, over a decade later, Willow couldn't move on. Unless something else was going on here. Something Genevieve didn't know her daughter well enough anymore to know. That possibility broke her heart.

She'd polished off half of her Bloody Mary before she summoned the energy to ask Helen, "Did Willow tell you why she's willing to go to such lengths to avoid me? I've been widowed, too. I understand what she's going through. I can help her. It tears me up that she won't let me help her."

Helen shrugged. "I don't know what to say, Gen. She didn't tell me anything that made sense."

"I hate that she's keeping the children from me."

"Oh, honey. I know it probably feels that way, but I don't think that's what she's doing. I think she's, well, lost."

Genevieve blinked back tears. "I miss her. I miss the kids. Outside of my regular FaceTime with the children, I'm lucky to speak with Willow three times a month. Do you think she's still holding the Andy thing against me? It's been over ten years! I don't believe what I did was unforgivable. Do you?"

"No. Clumsy, yes. Understandable, yes. Unforgivable, no."

"Words have such fearsome power. I can't change what I said or how I acted, but I apologized. She knows how sorry I was, I am. I tried to make it up to them both. I wish she'd find some forgiveness in her heart. She needs to forgive. That goes for her brothers, too. What is wrong with my children, Helen? Why can't they forgive and forget and move on?"

"Oh, honey. That's a good question."

"I want to bang their heads together and shake some sense into them. Where did all this coldness and anger and hate come from?"

"Love, that's where. These wounds in your family are deep because the battle was waged between people who deeply love one another."

"I don't know. I'm beginning to think they're not just deep wounds. They are fatal ones."

"No. They just need more time to heal."

"Well, tick-tock. I'm getting old." Genevieve took a crunchy bite from her celery stick. "The sands of my hour-glass might run out at the rate they're going. I'm draining pretty darn fast. Feel like I'm down to my last few grains."

"Nah. Your hourglass has plenty of sand left in it. You can't go anywhere until you go to Salzburg with me."

Genevieve smiled and gave her sister a sidelong look. Helen sang the first line of the first stanza of "Maria" from *The Sound of Music*. Genevieve followed with the second. Helen continued with the third, spilling a small portion of her drink when she used both hands to illustrate curlers in her hair. Genevieve giggled her way through the last line of the stanza and would have stopped there, but Helen was on a roll.

The sisters sang the entire song and finished the final

note with their glasses raised and an arm draped around each other's shoulders. On the tee box, a foursome of fifty-something-year-old men clapped. Helen sprang to her feet and took a bow.

"We need a refill," Genevieve said, using it as an excuse to slink, embarrassed, into the house.

Helen followed her, laughing. "You know, you and your talk about sand running out. We don't have an excuse for not taking that trip we've promised ourselves all of our lives."

"Not our whole lives." Genevieve dumped the ice from her glass and from Helen's into the sink, then carried them to the freezer for a refill. "I was twelve when we watched *The Sound of Music* together the first time it was shown on TV."

"Whatever. Long enough." Helen played bartender, mixing a second cocktail for each of them. "Inside or out?"

Genevieve considered. The foursome should be done hitting their tee shots by now. "Out."

Moments later, they'd resumed their seats. Genevieve took a long sip and tried to recall the last time she'd done any day drinking. She couldn't.

Oh, yes she could. It had been the middle of September when she'd called Willow and mentioned making a trip to Nashville. Her daughter had asked her not to come. Genevieve had poured a glass of scotch after that particular phone call.

"I must have done something to upset her when Andy died and it stirred up all of the old hurts. But I haven't the first clue about what I did wrong."

Her sister, because she was her sister, picked up the thread of the conversation. "I assume you've tried asking Willow?"

"Of course. Half a dozen times. She denies there's anything

wrong. Inevitably after I ask what's going on, she'll make an effort to call a time or two, but then it's soon back to radio silence." Genevieve folded her arms and added, "I can't believe she didn't call me about Thanksgiving and left you to do her dirty work."

"Well, I remember something you said to me dozens of times after David died. People grieve in different ways on their own timelines. With that in mind, perhaps you should cut her some slack."

"I do. I have been. I went to Tennessee when Willow asked me to, stayed for as long as she asked, left when she asked, didn't return because she asked me not to return. But grieving doesn't give you a free pass to throw manners out the window or treat those who love you with complete disrespect. Willow has the right to grieve however she wants, but I have the right to be hurt when her actions wound."

"Fair enough."

"I'm concerned about her mental health."

"She talks to Brooke, doesn't she? Brooke has been out to see her."

"She has." That both reassured Genevieve and made her feel worse. It hurt her feelings.

The sisters sat in silence for a bit, sipping their drinks and watching another foursome tee off. Then Genevieve gave her head a shake. "I can't think about this anymore. Tell me about life in Lake in the Clouds. What new and exciting things have you been up to?"

"Well, I'm thinking about going back to work."

That popped Genevieve's brooding balloon. She sat up straight and turned a shocked gaze toward her sister. "Whoa, whoa, whoa. You're what? The woman who literally burned her briefcase on her last day of work?"

"I gave it a Viking funeral. Work is probably not the best descriptive term. I'm done practicing law. This is more of a project. There's a piece of property up for sale that is calling my name. Raindrop Lodge and Cabins Resort. Look."

Helen pulled her phone from the pocket of her sweater, navigated to the photos, and handed the device to Genevieve. "It's a fixer-upper, which is the part of the project that I find appealing. Look at the property, Gen. It's right on Mirror Lake. The mountain views are breathtaking—beyond gorgeous. Unfortunately, pictures don't do it justice."

"You are full of surprises, sister. I thought your retirement goal was to kick back and relax and read your way down your to-be-read pile."

"It is. That's what I'm doing, and I'm enjoying the hell out of it. But I'm finding that I'm a little bored. I need a project. I know that's something you understand."

Genevieve did understand. Projects were her wheelhouse. She always had one or twelve going. She scrolled through the photos. "I love the bones of the lodge."

"Me, too. The interior has a lot to work with, too. I wish I'd taken photos of the inside to show you. You could give me some ideas. There's a huge stone fireplace that takes up one entire wall. It's fabulous. And there's an awesome antique bar the owner said originally came from a saloon in one of the mining towns in the area. It's a hodgepodge of styles and needs a total makeover, but I can see the possibilities. I've already picked out a couple places for clocks. You know me and cuckoo clocks."

Genevieve smiled. "Now I get it. This isn't a potential business concern. It's a reason for retail therapy."

"I like to shop. Retirement should be about doing things you like to do."

"You're right about that." Genevieve handed the phone back to her sister. "So if you buy this place, you'll oversee the renovation? Will you flip it when that's done?"

"Probably. I don't see myself as an innkeeper. It's possible I could keep it and hire someone to run it. I met the nicest woman who owns a small resort in a town a couple of hours away from Lake in the Clouds, and she's offered to mentor me through the process. Next time you come to visit, I'll take you to Eternity Springs to meet her and see her place. She started out by renovating a Victorian mansion and opening a B and B. She's added all sorts of amenities over the years. Some of the cutest cabins. One is built like a castle. Very Disney-esque. The spa is first class. It's a wildly successful boutique resort."

"That sounds right up my alley. I like spa trips even more than you like cuckoo clocks." Genevieve stirred her Bloody Mary with the celery stick, took another sip, and then said, "Your voice rings with enthusiasm when you talk about this lodge, Helen. I think you should go for it."

"I might. I just don't know. It's a big project, and I'm a little afraid that I'd be biting off more than I can chew." Helen gave her sister a considering look and said, "You know, Gen, Raindrop Lodge would be a good sisters' project."

Surprised, Genevieve reared back. "Project? Helen, our biggest sisters' project was the fund-raiser for your dog rescue group. That was a project. This would be a commitment."

"Okay, then. A sisters' commitment. Seriously, Genevieve, I'm thinking you could use something new and exciting yourself."

"Yes, like an antiquing trip. Or a sisters' trip to Europe. I think you're right. We really should go to Salzburg and do *The Sound of Music* tour."

"Yes!" Helen pumped her fist. "And if I do purchase the lodge, we can go antiquing while we're there. I'll buy clocks! I say we take the trip no matter what I decide about the resort."

"That does sound lovely."

"Let's put it on our calendars. Let's do it now." Helen rose from her seat. "I don't want you to weenie out on me."

"I won't weenie out."

"I know because we're going back inside right now so you can get out your calendar."

Genevieve knew how difficult it was to argue with her sister when Helen spoke in that tone of voice. The best way to stop this train would be to tell Helen about the biopsy, and she'd wanted to wait until she had the results to do that. Otherwise, all her sister would do was worry. "I'm not ready to commit to something as big as our sisters' trip today. How about we start with that visit to your innkeeper friend's place?"

"Deal. But we book it today."

Genevieve stood and led her sister indoors and upstairs to the bedroom she used as an office. Ten minutes later, they had reservations for two nights in December at a place called Angel's Rest Healing Center and Spa.

Less than a minute after Helen ended the call to Eternity Springs, Genevieve's landline rang. She glanced down at the number on the screen. "It's Willow."

"I'll be downstairs." Helen gave Genevieve's hand a comforting pat then exited the room.

Genevieve realized that she didn't want to talk to her daughter. She wanted to let the call go to voice mail. But that would only prolong the inevitable.

That wouldn't do, either, so bracing herself, Genevieve answered the call. "Hello, Willow."

"Hi, Mom."

Willow's voice sounded tense and subdued.

"Am I calling at a good time?"

The photo of a welcoming Victorian mansion with porch rockers and a darling angel's wing logo disappeared from Genevieve's monitor as she closed her web browser. She rose from her seat and stepped toward the window that overlooked her backyard and the golf course beyond. "I always have time to talk to you. You know that."

"Yes, I know."

"How are my blessings doing?"

"The kids are fine. Drew's class is doing a program at school this afternoon. He has a speaking part so he's been running around the house repeating his lines for days."

"Oh, how fun. Wish I could be there to see it. Promise you'll take a video of it and send it to me."

"I will."

"And Emma?"

"She's good. She's decided her favorite thing is to wear a Tupperware bowl on her head."

"You used to do that, too."

"I did?" Willow hesitated, and Genevieve sensed she was working up to drop her bombshell.

Genevieve could let her off the hook and tell her that Helen had already provided the heads-up, but her own heart was too bruised for her to want to make this easier for her daughter. So she waited, her gaze following the progress of a red squirrel climbing the trunk of the huge cottonwood tree just beyond her property line.

"Mom, I need to tell you, I'm sorry, but I can't…we can't…" Willow exhaled a heavy breath, then said, "We won't be there for Thanksgiving."

"So I understand. Your Aunt Helen arrived about an hour ago."

Willow whispered a curse. "She's earlier than I thought."

"Yes, it was a lovely surprise. She couldn't wait to join our family for the holiday."

"Mo-om."

Maybe Genevieve was being a bit passive-aggressive, but she couldn't help herself.

"Look, Mom, I'm sorry to disappoint you. I know how much the holidays mean to you. I know that you've been hoping that everyone could put aside what happened with the fight about the ranch and Poppy's will and be a family again, but the bottom line is that this is not a good time for me and the children to come to Texas. I need to put my family first."

"Why is cutting yourself off from *our* family best for you? Can you explain that to me?"

"I'm not cutting myself off."

"Aren't you?"

"I need time, Mom. When I promised to come to Thanksgiving, I thought I was ready. I'm not. We're not. Maybe next year."

"So you are ruling out coming home for Christmas for sure?"

"I'm taking the kids to Disney."

Disney. They're going to Disney for Christmas. "I thought we were going to take them over the Presidents' Day holiday." Together.

"They can go again."

But it won't be their first time. Genevieve had long dreamed about taking her grandchildren to Disney World for the very first time. And Willow knew that!

Being brutally honest, Genevieve could understand why her daughter might want to skip family time this holiday season. This ongoing war between Lucas and Jake made get-togethers tense and unpleasant, and none of them looked forward to spending time with Brooke's husband. While she expected everyone to be on their best behavior, Genevieve had prepared by buying two extra bottles of antacids.

But a Disney trip at Christmas? That was a jab at Genevieve that had nothing to do with Willow's brothers or her sister's bad marriage. It was cruel, and it made Genevieve want to curl up in a ball and cry.

Instead, Genevieve stiffened her spine and squared her shoulders. She turned away from the window and spoke in a brisk tone. "All right then. We will miss you. Please give the children my love. I hope they'll FaceTime as usual on Saturday morning. I need to let you go now. Helen and I are putting the holiday table together. Bye."

"Mom—"

Genevieve disconnected the call, returned the phone to its base, then swiped her eyes with the heel of her hand. Head held high, she walked downstairs to find her sister standing on the step stool in front of the baker's pantry shelves. Genevieve met Helen's compassionate gaze, pasted on a smile, and said, "Well, that was a kick in the balls."

"I'm sorry, honey."

Genevieve shrugged. "It is what it is. So I guess you've decided it's table time?"

"Yes. I figured you needed a little dish therapy right about now. Are you using chargers this year?"

"Yes, those russet-colored ones on the third shelf."

"How many?"

"We'll be only five this year. The two of us, Brooke and Travis and Jake."

"Seriously? What about neighbors and friends from church? You always invite a crowd, Genevieve."

"Not this year, I didn't. I really wanted a family affair this year. I thought that maybe without other guests to serve as a buffer, my kids might actually talk to one another."

"Or else it would be the most awkward holiday meal in history."

"Prentice family history anyway," Genevieve agreed. "Still, I thought it was worth a shot." Sadness settled over her like a raincloud. This would be the smallest Thanksgiving gathering she'd hosted in, well, longer than she could recall.

Helen handed down the chargers and then moved on to Genevieve's wedding dishes, a Leclair Limoges pattern in ivory porcelain with swirls and scalloped edges bounded in gold. As Genevieve set dessert plates next to dinner plates and bread-and-butter plates on the buffet, she observed, "My counselor says I need to give the kids time, to trust in the foundation of the family we built."

"That sounds like good advice."

"For someone in her forties, maybe, but I stare sixty in the mirror every morning." Her thoughts once again strayed to the biopsy, and she added, "I don't have an infinite amount of time. Sands through the hourglass, remember."

"Oh, stop it. This isn't a soap opera."

"Wanna bet?"

"You're still a spring chicken."

"I'm an old mother hen with a brood of troublemaking chicks. I am out of patience, Helen. I'm so angry with them. All four of them."

"Why?"

"Because this battle of theirs is damaging our family and they don't care."

"Now, Gen," Helen chastised as she descended the step stool. "They care. You know your children love you, and I'm sure they love each other."

"Well, apparently, love isn't enough for them to stop acting like eight-year-old children and fix what's wrong." Genevieve picked up the chargers and began placing them around the table. "And since they're adults, I can't scold them and send them to their rooms. I can't threaten to ground them or take away their allowance if they're mean to their siblings again. I certainly can't fall back on my favorite go-to: Mind me because I'm the mom, and I said so. No, I must measure my words and respect their independence and accept the fact that they are adults who make their own decisions."

"True. That's what one does when one's children grow up."

"I like being the boss better."

"Most people do." Helen picked up the dinner plates and walked around the table, setting them onto the chargers. "Look, Gen, you raised your children to be independent. You did a great job. Be proud of them."

"I am proud of them. You can be proud and pissed at the same time, you know. The bottom line is that they are destroying my family over petty jealousies and childish re-taliations and the inability and/or desire to find forgiveness in their hearts. I taught them better than that. Did they not listen at all during those Sunday mornings in church and Sunday school?"

"As I recall, Jake couldn't keep his eyes open in church."

"He was Pavlov's dog. That boy sat down in a pew and

started to snooze. That's why I always made sure he sat next to me within reach of an elbow jab."

Genevieve sighed, then lifted the stack of bread-and-butter plates. "It's true that they've hurt one another, but that's what siblings do. That's family. No one has done anything unforgivable, so why can't they put it behind them and move on? I've always taught them the importance of family, but they don't seem to care about that now."

"They care. They're just wrapped up in themselves right now. That's normal for young people their age."

"Well, I'm tired of it. It's gone on way too long." Genevieve thought of Willow and her two grandchildren at home alone in Nashville. She thought about stressed-out, overworked Jake with his need to control everything and everyone in his world. She thought about lost and angry Brooke with her wreck of a marriage. And then there was Lucas—hotheaded and cluelessly insensitive despite his good heart. Ordinarily, Lucas had excellent instincts, but her family was still reeling from the chaos and destruction caused by the one time he let his hormones rule the day.

Genevieve met her sister's gaze and declared, "They are making me miserable."

"Now, Genevieve."

"It's true, Helen. They say time heals all wounds. What nobody mentions is that, in Chicklandia, while healing in the henhouse is happening over here—" She jerked one thumb to the right. "Over there—" She gestured left with her other thumb. "You might have a coyote nipping at the chicken wire. If he sneaks inside, you have bigger problems than pick-a-little talk-a-little in the brood. Soon you're off to the great chicken coop in the sky, and you won't be around if the family foundation finally does its work."

"That might have been a reference to *The Music Man*, but I'm not certain. I don't know that musical nearly as well as I do *Sound of Music*. What I do know is that this metaphor has gone off the rails. You've lost me."

"*Cheep. Cheep. Cheep.*" Genevieve groaned, closed her eyes, and massaged her temples with her fingertips. "It doesn't matter. I don't have to make sense. I'm an adult, too, you know."

"Is this where you start acting like an eight-year-old?"

"I might. I just might. I can pout with the best of them."

"You're telling me, sister. Perfected the whine, too, as I recall. I'll admit I was glad when you gave that up. Never cared for whiners."

"Me, either." Genevieve paused a moment, then asked, "Am I whining?"

"Afraid so, yes. A little bit."

"I'm regressing. Sorry. This is what they're turning me into—a whiny child. Next thing you know, I'll look into the mirror, and instead of staring at sixty, I'll look like one of my kids."

"That could be a good thing, Gen. Your kids are all very attractive. I wouldn't mind being a whiny bee if I could look thirty years younger. Silver linings, you know?"

Genevieve laughed. "You're determined to kick me out of my mood, aren't you?"

"Yep. You gotta let it go, Gen. For your own sanity, you need to listen to your therapist and let it go."

"Which therapist? You or the vodka or the doctor I see twice a month on Tuesdays?"

"Sounds like you have the perfect team. No sense leaving anybody out." Helen gestured toward the cabinets. "Waterford?"

"Yes. Water and wine goblets." Genevieve opened the drawer in the buffet, which held her silver chest. She removed the heavy box, set it atop the cabinet, and flipped up the lid. She'd inherited her grandmother's silver, while Mom's set went to Helen. Lifting a knife, Genevieve traced its delicate curves and thought about her grandmother.

"Now there was a steel magnolia," she murmured.

"Hmm?" Then Helen identified what Genevieve held in her hand. "Ah, Nana. Yes. Stronger than the both of us put together."

Frideborg Brunzell had immigrated to the United States from Sweden at the ripe old age of sixteen. She'd arrived in America alone with less than fifty dollars in her pocket. She'd won a job as a housekeeper for a family in New York, married and buried her first husband, remarried, and moved to East Texas to farm cotton with her second husband. She'd borne Genevieve's grandfather twelve children, only eight of whom survived to adulthood. Her husband died of a heart attack after learning that their eldest son had perished at Normandy Beach on D-Day. Genevieve's mother had been Frideborg's youngest.

"Nana would tell me to suck it up, Buttercup."

"Not in those exact words, but yes, she would."

"She'd do it in that Swedish-Texan drawl of hers." Genevieve's lips spread in a smile as she used the polish cloth tucked inside the silver case to give the knife a buff.

Helen laughed. "And she'd end her sentence with 'yah?' Every sentence was a question."

Genevieve was smiling as she set silverware beside the plates on her table, thoughts of her grandmother and mother drifting through her mind like dandelion fluff in spring. "What I wouldn't give to have one more holiday meal with

Mom and Nana. And David and Dad, of course, but Mom and Nana would be in the kitchen helping us cook."

"That would be grand, wouldn't it? I like to think that they're here with us in spirit, at least. Using their dishes and silver gives them a seat at the table with us."

"It does, doesn't it?" Genevieve carefully placed a salad fork next to the dinner fork at the plate where Brooke would sit. "Since my girls would be happy using paper plates on holidays, my spirit is liable to end up spending my Thanksgivings and Christmases packed away in an attic."

"At least you'll be in one piece. I gave most of my things to Goodwill. No telling where all my stuff ended up. My spirit's going to be dashing hither and yon all over the Metroplex."

"Hither and yon, hmm?"

"I tell myself it's a blessing in disguise because at least I'll get my exercise. Want to keep my girlish ghostly figure."

Genevieve laughed. "Speaking of blessings, it's time I recall mine and remember why you and I are setting this table today. Thanksgiving is the time to count our blessings and give thanks. You are right. I've whined enough. I need to channel my inner Disney princess and let it go."

Helen began humming the tune to the popular song from Disney's movie *Frozen*. Genevieve continued setting her Thanksgiving table with a lighter heart and a smile on her face.

She'd just placed the final fork when a familiar tone played on her cell phone. "That's Jake returning my call from this morning. At least I can count on him not to cause holiday drama."

She picked up her phone and connected the call. "Hello, honey."

"Hey, Mom."

"I'm sorry I bothered you on a workday. Nothing to worry about. I just had a little pre-holiday meltdown. No big deal. Lucky for you, Aunt Helen arrived early and talked me off of the ledge."

"Oh. Good. Aunt Helen's there? Now?"

"Yes."

"That's good. That's really good. I'm so glad."

Genevieve's stomach sank to the floor. She knew her eldest. She knew that tone. Something was wrong.

Six

WAS TESS ACTING OUT of character? Well, an apt comparison would be Santa skipping the Macy's parade and asking the Grinch to fill in for him. So yes. She really didn't have a clue why she was doing what she was doing.

Maybe because she was curious. Maybe because she was grateful. Maybe, just maybe, because she wanted to give Jake Prentice a reason to call her when he returned from his trip to Dubai.

It was a beautiful home, a two-story Victorian style, painted a happy yellow, with a big wraparound porch. Tess was surprised the street in front of it wasn't already packed with cars, but then it was still early. She had planned it that way intentionally.

If Tess had had her own big family Thanksgiving holiday to attend, she'd go early and stay late.

She parked her car and switched off her engine. She popped her trunk, then got out of the car and walked to the rear, where she unzipped her Yeti cooler, revealing the carefully packed, precious cargo inside. "Perfect."

If she'd had to bake three to achieve one of such perfection, well, nobody needed to know that, now did they? Besides, she'd had nothing better to do yesterday.

She lifted her apple pie from the cooler and, rather than risk a mishap, left the trunk open. She approached the house, admired the golden mums in the flower beds, and smiled at the turkey sentries on either side of the front door, hearing the echo of Jake's voice saying, "Gobble gobble."

Tess rang the doorbell. About half a minute passed before a woman answered the door.

Genevieve Prentice. Tess had googled her. *Jake has her eyes*, Tess thought, that same beautiful shade of green with a fit-for-a-crown gemstone quality to them. She was petite, slim, and wore her hair blond in shoulder-length, feathered layers. Dressed in jeans and a harvest gold sweater, she was one of those women who looked put together, something Tess aspired to but never managed to pull off. "Mrs. Prentice?"

Visibly startled now, she said, "Yes?"

Up to that point, she'd probably thought Tess was lost and going to ask for directions. "My name is Tess Crenshaw. I work for your son, Jake. Well, I take that back. I *used* to work for Jake. I got laid off on Tuesday."

"Oh. Oh dear." Jake's mother's gaze flicked down to Tess's hands. "That's not a pie bomb, is it?"

Tess laughed. "No. It's a simple apple pie. You may already have one for your Thanksgiving feast today, but Jake assured me that you can never have enough pie."

"Not so simple. It's a beautiful pie. I love the leaf shapes on top of the lattice crust. You made it?"

"I did. For you." She handed it to Jake's mother.

"Well, thank you so much." Genevieve accepted the gift,

stepped backward, and opened her door wider. "Please, come inside."

"No, I can't. I have a packed schedule today. But I wanted to personally thank you for the delicious cookies you sent to our department at Bensler, drop off a pie, and tell you what a really nice guy your son is. He was a great boss."

"Yes, well, he is very bossy. It's always lovely to hear compliments about my baking and my children, so thank you. Though I'll admit, I'm not sure why you went to the trouble of making a pie. A note would be nice, too."

"True, but this is my little way of helping Jake be with his family today. He was torn up about having to make the last-minute trip overseas."

Tess didn't miss the flash of pain that crossed Genevieve Prentice's face. Poor Jake. Bet that phone call was a killer. "He was trying desperately to come up with a way to make up for it. Too desperately. In the middle of firing me, he tried to talk me into coming to your Thanksgiving dinner in his place."

"He what?" Judging by her tone and the look in her eyes, Jake's mother wasn't pleased.

"I know. Ridiculous, isn't it? He about gave Bensler's HR person a heart attack." Tess tried to lighten the awkward moment, and from the start of a smile on Genevieve's face, it looked like it worked.

"Of course, you would have been welcome. I ordinarily do have a crowd for Thanksgiving. Usually, my children give me a heads-up if they've added someone to the guest list," Genevieve replied.

Tess had the sudden sensation that she'd inadvertently stepped into a minefield. Maybe this pie wasn't such a good idea, after all.

Quickly, she got to her point. "Well, Jake wasn't think-ing straight at the time. He had a lot of things going on Tuesday. This is what I wanted to say to you. It was an especially challenging day at Bensler. Jake considered it his responsibility to conduct the layoffs personally, while others at his level delegated the ugly task. In the midst of it all, the trip came up, and while he was dreading having to call and disappoint you, he took the time and made an effort to do a real kindness for me. He went above and beyond, Mrs. Prentice, and I start a new job with a small group called Innovations Design on Monday. It's a job I don't believe I could have landed on my own, and it's one I think I'm going to love. It's a job that could be life-changing for me."

Genevieve Prentice's eyes filled with tears. "Well, that is quite a testimonial, Ms. Crenshaw, was it?"

"Yes. Tess. I'm Tess."

"Well, Tess. I thank you. I needed to hear this today, more than you can possibly know. You are right. Jake *is* a good man. All of my children are good people. Maybe that needs to be enough."

Okay, that was a strange comment. "I'd better run. Like I said, busy day. I hope you enjoy the pie, Mrs. Prentice."

"I'm sure we will. Thank you again, Tess. This was terribly thoughtful of you. I do love apple pie, and this looks delicious. I can't wait to try a piece."

Tess gave her a bright smile. "I'm counting my blessings. That's what today is all about, right? Happy Thanks-giving!"

Happy Thanksgiving. Yeah, right.

Genevieve stood at her dining room window, watching the young woman return to her car.

"What was that all about?" Helen asked, coming up behind her.

"I'm not really sure. It was a girl who worked for Jake."

"A woman, Genevieve. You can't use 'girl' anymore."

"Why?"

"It's sexist. It's insulting."

"I totally disagree. I consider it a compliment. David always called me his number one girl."

"I remember that," Helen said with a smile.

"I like being referred to as 'girl.' It makes me feel young. Now that I think about it, instead of a grandmother, I want to be a grandgirl. I'm going to tell Drew and Emma that's what I am, and that's what they can call me. It's still America, and this is Thanksgiving, even if none of my children are here to break bread with us. A friend of Jake's brought us a homemade pie to symbolize his being with us at our Thanksgiving feast. Such as it is."

"He made her do that?"

"No, she did it on her own."

"That's weird. What kind of pie?"

"Apple."

"Awesome. Apple pie goes good with pizza."

"It's not weird. It's sweet."

"How so?"

"If this was a regular Thanksgiving and not the Thanksgiving from hell, then I would put this pie on the buffet with the other pies, and when we served dessert, I would think of Jake specifically. It was generous and unexpected. Sweet."

"Hmm." Helen moved beside Genevieve and gazed out the window. "Where is she?"

"She just climbed into that white Kia."

"I can't see her. Is she a looker?"

"She's pretty. Curvy. Gorgeous blue eyes."

"Trying to get on the boss's good side."

"Nope. He fired her on Tuesday."

"Oh. Maybe we should pass on the pie. Might be poisoned."

"He got her another job. It's a thank-you pie. She's counting her blessings because it's Thanksgiving."

"Better than counting calories."

"I'm not doing either. Not today."

"You don't have to. It's a holiday. Calories don't count, and you get one day to wallow. Tomorrow, it's back to eating healthy, and no more feeling sorry for yourself. Right?"

"Right. Tomorrow it's a new diet. A new attitude."

"You go, grandgirl."

"I am a grand girl, and I think I want a piece of pie. Do you want a piece of pie?"

"Now? Before dinner? You'll spoil your pizza."

Genevieve snorted. "Nothing spoils pizza. I'll have room for pie after pizza, too. Brooke doesn't know what she's missing. None of them do."

"Their loss, our gain."

"Do not use the *g* word, Helen. Remember, calories don't count on Thanksgiving."

Helen nodded solemnly. "Amen."

Seven

January
The Feast of the Epiphany

GENEVIEVE PULLED THE TRIGGER on the fire starter stick, igniting the small flame. Leaning over her dining room table, she lit the candles in her centerpiece. She had thirteen of them: a tall taper in a porcelain Easter bunny candlestick by Lenox, a stubby round one in a Fitz and Floyd candleholder with Santa and his reindeer, a taper in a crystal heart etched with the word *Mom*, a votive in a china Cupid, two birthday candles in metal American flags, a three-wick candle in a ceramic Uncle Sam, a taper in a ceramic witch, and votives in five turkeys.

Her children should begin arriving at any time now. Following this year's Thanksgiving debacle and after three near sleepless nights, Genevieve had made a momentous decision. On Black Friday—never let it be said that she didn't do symbolic—she'd done something she'd refrained from doing for a very long time. She'd phoned each of her children—even the one on the opposite side of the world— and put down her foot. She'd laid down the law by playing the mom card, demanding their presence here today—no excuses tolerated or allowed.

At the sound of footsteps descending the stairs, she called, "I'm in the dining room."

Moments later, Helen joined her. She studied the dining room table for a long moment before shaking her head. "That's quite a hodgepodge. You've stumped me on the theme."

"It's every holiday we've celebrated together."

"Hmm. No birthdays?"

"That's what four of the turkeys are for."

"Cold-blooded, Gen." Helen folded her arms and sighed. "You have too many holidays."

"Maybe so, but we made a lot of memories."

"What good do they do you now?"

Genevieve smiled sadly. "That's an excellent question, sister. What good are all of those memories? Ten years ago, they gave me joy. Two years ago, they gave me bittersweet joy. Today, all they give me is the bitterness and pain. Sort of like family gatherings."

Helen took hold of Genevieve's hand and gave it a comforting squeeze. "Courage, hon. It won't always be like this."

"I know. Because I can change my attitude. I *must* change my attitude. I'm so angry with my children, and it's poisoning my soul. That's why we're here. I'm going to lance the boil."

"Are you going to tell them about your biopsy scare?"

"Yes. I'm going to be completely honest with them. No biting my tongue today. They certainly never bite theirs, and I'm tired of that being a one-way street."

Just then the two women heard the slam of a car door out front. "That's my cue," Helen said. "I'll be waiting at the nineteenth hole. Text me if you need reinforcements."

Genevieve followed her sister to the kitchen. "I will. Don't drink all the vodka before I get to the clubhouse bar. I'm sure I'll need a Bloody Mary or twelve."

Helen squeezed Genevieve's hand and then slipped out the back door as a quick rap sounded on the front door. It opened, and her eldest's voice called, "Mom?"

"I'm in the kitchen." She picked up her whisk and began stirring the gravy.

Genevieve wasn't at all surprised that Jake was the first of her offspring to arrive—almost ten minutes before the specified two o'clock. That's the way he rolled. Jake arrived first—always. Lucas showed up last—always. Willow and Brooke traded out spots second and third.

Genevieve glanced over her shoulder as her son entered the room. She almost dropped her utensil into the gravy. He looked terrible.

Maternal instincts urged her to set down her whisk, set aside her own concerns, and insist that he share whatever burdens he carried. Genevieve resisted them, reminding herself of how the Prentice family had gotten to where it was today.

He came over and kissed her right cheek, then gave her a one-armed hug. "Hey, Mom. Something smells good. Turkey?"

"Yes."

"Excellent. I was hoping for turkey since I missed Thanksgiving. What can I do to help?"

Tell your brother you love him when he arrives. Tears stung Genevieve's eyes, but she blinked them back. *No. Do not do that. Start that nonsense now, and this will be over before it starts. You have to be strong.* "Nothing. It's all ready."

"All right. I brought wine." He removed a bottle from

the tote bag he'd carried inside and showed her the label. It was one of her favorite pinot noirs. It would go lovely with the turkey.

"Should I open it? Pour you a glass?"

"Open it, yes, please. We will need two bottles, I'm certain. However, I don't need a glass right now. I already have a drink."

Jake gave her a sharp look. Genevieve lifted her chin. Yes, she was drinking alone. What did it say that she needed fortification before a gathering of her clan?

Jake carried his tote to the wet bar off the great room, where he found a corkscrew and opened the wine. The clink of ice into a glass suggested that he'd chosen the harder stuff, too. "Like mother, like son," she murmured.

Bet a dollar every last one of them had had at least a swig of liquid courage before today's gathering.

Jake glanced toward the staircase. "Is Willow upstairs? I'm looking forward to seeing her."

"No. She and the children are staying with Andy's parents this trip. I believe Willow and Brooke plan to arrive for dinner together."

"Seriously?" Jake took a moment to digest that surprising bit of news. His sister always stayed here at the house when she came home from Nashville. "Mom, what's going on here? What's this all about?"

"We are going to have a family dinner. All of us, together."

Jake's jaw firmed in the familiar way that telegraphed the terrier, dog-with-a-bone aspect of his personality that his siblings—and frankly, sometimes Genevieve herself—found so annoying. As a boy, the character trait had contributed to his success in everything from academics to athletics, and she was confident it helped him today in business. Personal relationships were another kettle of fish.

Jake attempted to manage everybody. He was the cattle dog trying to herd the family in the direction he wanted. He'd been doing it since his father died. She'd appreciated the help in the beginning, and truth be told, she'd probably depended upon him too much. But his siblings were adults now who wanted to blaze their own trails. Jake needed to take a rest. Bensler paid him to manage. The Prentice family did not.

There was a lesson in there for Genevieve, too. In the wake of the Thanksgiving debacle, while doing some hard, hard thinking, she'd recognized it. Today, she was doing something about it.

Whatever he planned to say was interrupted when the front door opened, and his sisters stepped inside. Genevieve's heart twisted as she took a good look at her girls. Willow was thin, too thin. She must have lost twenty pounds since Andy's death. She had circles beneath her big green eyes, and her cheeks were hollow, her cheekbones pronounced.

Brooke looked...angry. Nothing new there.

Genevieve waited while Jake greeted his sisters, and then she gave them each a hug and thanked them for coming. "Like we had a choice," Brooke said, her tone teasing, but the look in her eyes sending the message that she meant what she said.

Genevieve smiled serenely at her youngest child, then asked, "How was your trip, Willow?"

"Fine. It was fine. Mom, why are we here? Why didn't you want the children here?"

Brooke interjected, "Or Travis? Mom, are you sick?"

"Actually, I'm hungry." Genevieve glanced up at the clock on her oven. She could always count on Jake being ten minutes early—and Lucas being ten minutes late. "Jake, you can pour the wine now if you would, please. Willow, will you call Lucas and ask about his ETA?"

She'd no sooner finished her sentence than the back door opened and her younger son entered the house. People who didn't know the Prentice brothers well sometimes mistook them for twins, so closely did they resemble one another. However, Lucas had his father's brown eyes, while Jake's were green.

"Hey, Mom," Lucas said, walking over to kiss her cheek— the left. Of course, he'd choose the opposite cheek from the one his brother had kissed. It was the story of their lives. "Are you having problems with your garage door opener? It wouldn't open for me."

"I've changed the code."

"Seriously?" He gave her a crooked grin. "You trying to lock me out?"

Genevieve dodged answering by opening the oven door, and Lucas turned to greet his sisters. A moment later, Jake entered the kitchen from the dining room carrying an empty bottle of wine. The temperature in the kitchen seemed to drop a dozen degrees as the brothers' gazes met. Neither one of them smiled. Neither one of them spoke. Genevieve let the oven door bang shut.

Into the awkward silence, Willow played peacemaker by asking, "What can I do to help, Mom?"

"Dinner is ready. If you'll each grab a serving dish from the buffet and bring it in, I'll dish up the hot things." Genevieve bumped up the heat under the gravy, then began pulling items from the oven, where they'd been keeping warm.

Brooke entered the kitchen from the dining room carry-ing a vegetable bowl from the Christmas china and the

Halloween gravy boat. Shock wreathed her face. "Mom? What's up with the table?"

Willow brought in the melamine Stars and Stripes platter from the set of outdoor dishes that Genevieve had brought home from her late father-in-law's lake house, which was part of the Lonesome River Ranch property. "Paper plates? We're eating off paper plates? In the dining room?"

Lucas brought in the platter from Genevieve's wedding china. "I must be seeing things. You cannot possibly have a television hanging on the dining room wall where the landscape oil painting belongs? What about your no TV during meals rule?"

"All in good time, children," Genevieve responded. "All in good time."

From the corner of her eye, she noted the first interaction between her sons when Lucas shot his older brother a hard look and mouthed, "What the hell?"

Genevieve ignored them all. With the serving dishes filled and carried to the table, she indicated that her offspring should take their seats. She asked Brooke to say grace, then directed plates to be filled. No one spoke as they passed serving dishes clockwise. Once everything had made its way around the table, Genevieve took a sip of her bourbon and began. "I want to preface this by telling you that mothering the four of you has been the joy of my life. I love you all, and I know that all four of you love me very much, too. That said, it's been over two years since our entire family sat down at this table together. The one event we did have was fraught with tension and passive-aggressive comments and behavior. I will not tolerate that today. That's why I've planned something to mitigate the problem."

She clicked the television remote, which she had left beside her plate. An image flashed on the screen. Genevieve watched the faces of her progeny as they viewed the photo that she had chosen to be the first in her presentation.

It was Genevieve's favorite candid picture of her four children. A three-year-old Brooke sat in her highchair with cherry pie smeared all over her face. Eight-year-old Jake was feeding her, flanked by six-year-old Willow and four-year-old Lucas. Brooke grinned happily at her brothers and sister, who all had their heads thrown back in laughter.

Now, twenty-six years later, four expressions told the story of their family. Genevieve spied yearning on Brooke's face and grief on Willow's. Lucas appeared wounded, and Jake...his expression was stony. Defensive. And yet, Genevieve was his mother and knew him well. He couldn't hide his wistfulness from her. Good. She had their attention. *So far, so good.*

Now, onto the next step. Genevieve said, "Lucas brought up my no television during dinner rule. Do you recall the one time when that rule was suspended?"

"Family movie night," Willow said.

"Yes. We ate pizza in front of the TV, watched our home movies, and laughed together. Once upon a time, this family loved to be together."

"Mom—" Jake began.

Genevieve held up her hand, signaling silence, and continued, "I considered serving pizza today, but I had that on Thanksgiving. Honestly, I missed the turkey and dressing, and it's ridiculous to cook a turkey for one. So, today we're having a mashup of family movie night and holiday dinner. Feel free to share your comments, observations, and memories about the events you'll see."

Her kids exchanged a look with one another—even Lucas and Jake momentarily suspended their civil war. Genevieve read their expressions easily. They were wondering if she'd lost her mind. Pizza on Thanksgiving? Paper plates in the dining room? *Just wait, kiddos.*

She took a bite of stuffing and hit play on the remote. For the next half hour, her family watched videos interspersed with photographs of their childhoods. Genevieve had thought long and hard about her presentation, and she'd spent many hours reviewing her photos and videos. She'd actually made two videos. One included images of their father. This one did not. She had a point to make.

She definitely had their attention. Both girls got tears in their eyes a time or two while watching. The boys actually shared a laugh once. They cleaned their plates, the girls ate like birds and everyone took refills of wine.

A chorus of giggles coming from the television signaled that part one of her Prentice Family Chronicles was drawing to a close. The final photo in the video, one of this house, the home in which they'd grown up, their family home, in springtime, appeared on the screen.

Jake cleared his throat. "Well, that was certainly a trip down memory lane."

And that memory road led to today's dead end. Time for the next act to begin. Genevieve cleared her throat, summoning their attention. "I put together that movie to remind you of our functional family in contrast to this dysfunctional mess we have today. Now, I have a question for you. If I were to die today, what word or phrase would you put on my gravestone?"

"Moth-er," Brooke protested. "Don't talk about that."

Lucas went suddenly still. Jake's mouth flattened in a

grim line. Willow asked, "Mom, is something wrong with your health?"

"Something is wrong with my heart." Genevieve moved her paper plate to the side and folded her hands in front of her. "It's broken."

Brooke threw her napkin onto the table and stood. "No. I'm not doing this. I can't deal with this. My therapist told me to avoid—"

"Sit down, Brooke. Today is not about you. Today for a change, my needs, wishes, and desires come before those of you and your siblings."

Well, that certainly shocked them. Like clockwork, her children's chins dropped. Lucas raked his fingers through his hair. "What the hell, Mom?"

Genevieve gave Lucas a quelling stare, then met the gazes of each of her offspring in turn. "Now, back to my grave-stone. Who wants to go first?"

There was a long silence.

"Someone go first. What word or phrase would you put on my gravestone were you making the decision today?"

Jake, being Jake, took it as his cue. "Beloved Mother."

Her eldest's response sapped some of the tension from the moment, and Genevieve couldn't help but smile. Leave it to Jake to lead the way. She nodded in his direction. Then, honoring birth order, she turned to her elder daughter. "Willow?"

After a moment, Willow said, "Our Family's Heart."

Genevieve liked that one, too. She smiled at Willow, then turned to her younger son. "Lucas?"

He gave a faint example of that roguish grin of his. "How about 'There goes the neighborhood.' Or, 'She made a great meatloaf.'"

Typical Lucas. Genevieve chuckled. "Let's pretend you wanted to be serious."

He shrugged. "Family first, last, and always."

She nodded, a lump growing in her throat. It was a phrase she'd repeated often when the children were growing up. "Brooke?"

"I don't understand why you're doing this." Her youngest released a long, heavy sigh. "What Lucas said. You're all about family."

Bingo. "And that right there is the reason why we're here today, Brooke. I am all about family. Since the day your father and I married, I've dedicated my life to the health and happiness of this family. After your father died, I doubled down and always, *always* put your needs first. Would you argue against that?"

All four of her children shook their heads.

"Being your mother has been fulfilling in so many ways, but now that you're adults, the job has changed. It's time I acknowledge that and make a change. Did it ever occur to you that I had needs of my own? That I had wishes and dreams that I put aside because they would have interfered with yours? I loved your father deeply, and I was devastated when he died, but I was only thirty-nine years old. Did it ever occur to you that I might have liked to remarry?"

Her children's expressions ran the gamut from surprised to shocked, and then Genevieve took it farther than she'd originally intended. "Or that I would have liked to have had a regular sex life, at least?"

"Mom," Jake said. "Please."

"Please what? Bite my tongue? Like I've been biting it for the past three years while you and your brother have staged a civil war that has ripped this family apart? Because

I've always, *always* tried to remain neutral in your wars. Invariably, you both are wrong, and you both are right. In that respect, this battle is no different from the time you dropped your brother's baseball cards in the bathtub, Jake. No one is innocent here or blameless."

Brooke broke in, defending her brothers by pointing out, "Poppy did the most harm with the provisions of his will. He set this whole mess up with the way he had us vote on whether or not to keep the ranch. Just because the legal advice Lucas's ex-girlfriend gave him turned out to be—"

"Stop. Poppy bequeathed a small fortune to each of you! It's the epitome of ingratitude to complain about how he went about it. Besides, he expected you all to be able to act like adults, and a few unfortunate clauses in the documents shouldn't change that. Sadly, he was wrong."

Lucas and Jake opened their mouths to add their two cents, but Genevieve knew that she would lose control of the moment if she allowed anyone else to have the floor. She held up her hand, palm out, and cut to the bottom line of that particular argument. "I'm done biting my tongue. I'm done, period. I will not subject myself to another holiday season like the one that ends today on the Feast of the Epiphany. That's why I've summoned you all here now. I like the symbolism. We're sharing the feast of my personal epiphany."

Willow and Brooke looked at Jake, their eyes silently imploring him to do something. Lucas scowled and rose to take a piece of pie off the sideboard.

Jake cleared his throat, then cautiously spoke. "Mom, we all understand why you're upset about Thanksgiving, but—"

Genevieve was unable to hold back the sarcasm dripping from her tongue, as she interrupted. "It's so reassuring as a mother that I raised children who are all bright enough to understand that I'd find you all bailing on Thanksgiving at the last-minute upsetting."

"I didn't bail," Brooke defended. "You uninvited me."

"Only after you complained about the menu."

"Pizza, Mom?"

"You love pizza. You don't like turkey."

"Travis loves turkey."

"Travis is a turkey," Lucas muttered.

Brooke shot him a glare as Jake drew in a deep breath and tried again. "Thanksgiving was bad all around. I know I feel terrible about it. But as far as Christmas goes, three of the four of us were prepared to be here Christmas Day, Mom. You were the one who decided to spend Christmas with Aunt Helen."

Lucas added, "Yeah. We thought we were having our Christmas today. My gifts are in the car. But you don't even have a tree up, and we're eating off paper plates."

"Excuse me, but the sooner you stop interrupting me, the sooner you'll understand why we are all here."

"You're being mean, Mom," Brooke accused.

"Yes, well, I'll own that. I'm feeling mean. I'm feeling combative because I've been living in a combat zone since you all went to war. You all are apparently free to be mean and combative in this family. Why can't I?"

"Because you're not like that, Mom," Willow said. "You're, well, Mom."

"True, but I'm Genevieve , too. It's time you all realized that. Like I was saying, this holiday season changed things for me. I did a lot of thinking and exploring and talking with my therapist."

"You see a therapist?" Willow asked.

"I do." Genevieve met her daughter's gaze. "I recommend

it. And her. My doctor makes telehealth appointments, and she's taking new patients. I'm happy to give you her information."

Turning her attention back to all her offspring, she continued, "Anyway, it shouldn't surprise any of you that I have been devastated by what's happened to our family since your grandfather's death. I've spoken to each of you—or tried to speak to each of you—about the situation on numerous occasions. More often than not, you shut me out or shut me down. Dr. Rose told me I needed to be patient, to trust in the foundation of the family I built. To trust that, beneath all the anger and hurt, you still love one another and care about each other and will someday find your way back to one another. I've tried to heed her advice, but it's been three years."

Genevieve pointed toward the Thanksgiving candlesticks. "Three Thanksgivings." At the flag platter. "Three Fourth of Julys." At the Christmas oval vegetable bowl. "Three Christmases. Recently, circumstances drove home the point that I'm not guaranteed a fourth."

"Oh God!" Brooke covered her mouth with her hands. "That's what this is about. It's what I've been afraid of. Your cancer is back!"

"No. However, I did undergo a lumpectomy the week before Thanksgiving."

Jake leaned forward. "Mom, why didn't you tell us?"

"I intended to once I received the results. They came the day before Thanksgiving." She let her pause say it all. Each one of her offspring winced.

"The tumor was benign, thank God, but it was the clichéd wake-up call for me. Life is short. You'd have thought your father's death would have driven this lesson home for me, but I think I was so busy trying to keep it together and get you guys raised that I never stopped to think about me. I had time in November and December. I realized I don't want to waste another Thanksgiving or Christmas or National Puppy Day or Thursday. I want to enjoy each and every day I have left. I want to *live* each and every day I have left."

She paused to sip from her water glass. Then, she sipped her bourbon again, gathered her courage, and continued, "However, the road of self-discovery revealed some hard truths that need to be faced, by me and by each of you. I think you'll agree that after your father's death, I devoted all my energies to the four of you, to what was portrayed in the photographs and videos we just finished watching—the Prentice Family. I'm proud of the job I did. I was damned good at it. Now I'll admit that the life insurance Dad left us lightened the burden but being Mom for the four of you was still a daunting task. However, I rocked it. The four of you are proof of it."

She paused and looked each of her children in the eyes in turn. "I'm so proud of each of you. You are good, generous, caring people, and that's why it pisses me off so much that you are such assholes to one another and, as a result, to me. I taught you better."

"Did Mom just say 'assholes'?" Brooke softly asked her sister.

"Yeah. And 'pisses,'" Willow responded.

"Because I did teach you better, I think Dr. Rose is likely right. You will someday realize that you need to grow up and get over it, that family matters, that this family matters. But my hard truth is that I can't control 'someday.' I can't control you, and it's time I stop trying. I need to let go."

"You do tend to hold on hard," Lucas observed. "Your expectations are a heavy burden sometimes."

"You are absolutely right. I don't want to be a burden to you. I depend upon you all too much. It's not your responsibility to entertain me or give purpose to my life or be my emotional support. As you all have mentioned repeatedly, you are adults with lives of your own to live. It's time—past time—I begin living mine. I need to do that living outside of this family. So today, I am announcing my retirement as the Prentice Family CEO."

"Is that supposed to be funny, Mom?" Brooke asked.

"Oh jeez." Jake closed his eyes and rubbed his temples with his fingertips. "I am so tired of drama."

"Yeah, well, welcome to my life," Genevieve snapped.

Willow folded her arms defensively. "What are you saying, Mom? You sound like you're quitting us."

"Well, I will always be your mother. I can't quit that, nor would I want to. But recent events have shown me that I have to make changes in my expectations." With a nod to Lucas, she added, "Burdensome that they are. What I am doing is reimagining my role. It's time I allow myself to be more than your mom and your father's widow. It's time I figure out who I'm going to become now that I'm ready to make changes."

"How much did you have to drink before we arrived?" Lucas asked.

Genevieve ignored the question, picked up the television remote, and clicked the play button. An image of their two-story Victorian home in the full bloom of springtime appeared on the screen. Glorious pink azaleas, puffy white geraniums, and the purple wisteria that Genevieve had painstakingly trained to drape the wood-rail fence. A bittersweet pang of regret pierced her heart as she gazed upon the swing that hung from the branch of the old pecan tree.

She remembered the day that David had hung that swing as though it were yesterday.

"When your father and I bought this house thirty-two years ago, it was a dream come true. We intended to raise our family and grow old together here, but God had a different plan. After we lost Dad, I considered selling the house and starting over somewhere new but decided that you four needed the stability of this home. I believe that was a good decision. It was the right decision for the time, but like the song says, 'The Times They Are a-Changin'.'"

She advanced the video, and the screen filled with a photo of snow-capped mountains reflected on the surface of a crystalline lake. "Life is short. In order to live, I need to let go. I need to let go of my dreams of picture-perfect family holidays. I need to let go of my worries and expectations regarding your relationships with each other. I need to let go of the past and look to the future."

Genevieve took one last sip of her bourbon. Here it was. The moment of truth—where her hard truth's proverbial rubber met the road. She clicked the remote again, and the photograph she'd taken on Christmas morning filled the television screen. "With all that in mind, I decided that my future is here."

Brooke read the sign aloud. "Raindrop Lodge? What is Raindrop Lodge?"

"It's my new project. My new challenge. It's a lakeside tourist resort on the outskirts of my new home in Lake in the Clouds, Colorado. Aunt Helen and I bought it. We will refurbish it and then either flip it or operate the resort for a season or two. The property has tons of potential."

"Wait." Jake held up his hands, palms out. "You invested in property? You didn't talk to me about it?"

"I did." She clapped her hands together, clasped her fingers, and smiled at him. "And guess what? I don't have to consult with you before making decisions."

"C'mon, Mom."

"Here's your hard truth, Jacob Alan Prentice. You are not your father. It's time you figure out just who you are."

Jake's chin dropped as if she'd just struck him with a roundhouse punch.

"Whoa." Lucas whistled. "Brutal."

Genevieve decided to kill the pleased gleam in her second son's eyes. "Ya think, Lucas? Since I'm being brutally honest, I might as well share this. The words 'I'm sorry' are two of the most powerful words in the English language. Use them."

His chin lifted pugnaciously. "So you *do* blame me for the changes Poppy made to the will!"

Genevieve refused to respond. She had said all she was going to say about that.

Lucas was nothing if not persistent, and he opened his mouth to argue with her, but Brooke spoke first. "What do you mean, your *new* home, Mother? What about this one?"

Genevieve hesitated. She was well aware that she could have gone about this in a kinder, gentler manner. The pre-Thanksgiving, always-caring-and-concerned mother who wanted more than anything for her family to be a happy, loving unit certainly would have attempted to soften the blow. Well, that Genevieve didn't live here anymore. She'd thrown in the towels. Packed them into a box labeled "Garage Sale" because Thanksgiving had opened her eyes.

Her kids didn't want what Genevieve wanted.

They didn't want the family ties that bind. They wanted to live free and to war with each other at will.

Well, let them. Genevieve finally understood that this family wasn't *her* family. It was *their* family. Her children were adults, so now their votes counted the same as hers did. Trying to hold on to something that didn't exist anymore was killing her. She had to stop. She *was* stopping. She was done. D.O.N.E. done.

She smoothed the napkin in her lap, then met her children's gazes. "I sold the house."

Jake winced. Lucas scowled. Willow gasped and repeated, "You sold the house?"

"Our house?" added Brooke.

"Technically, it's my house, and yes, I sold it. Closing is on the twentieth. The estate sale starts a week from Thursday. That's another reason I called you all here today. You have until then to take anything you want from here. I've taped names on the backs of any items I promised to any of you in the past. If no name is on something in particular and more than one of you want it, well…" Genevieve shrugged. "Your grandfather's attempt to divide the ranch didn't work. I'm not even going to try. Be adults or fight it out among yourselves like you've been doing for the past three years. It's your problem, not mine."

Genevieve lifted her napkin from her lap, wiped her mouth, then rose and picked up her paper plate. "I've already taken everything I want out of here."

As she turned to leave the dining room, headed for the kitchen, Willow's troubled voice followed her. "Mom, wait. Please, just wait. I'm so confused. Aren't estate sales for when someone dies?"

"Ordinarily, yes, but estate sales do so much better than moving sales or garage sales. Unless you all take much more than I expect you want, the estate company I hired will have plenty to sell to make it worth their while."

Tears welled in Brooke's eyes. "But...you can't do this, Mom."

"Nothing is done that can't be undone," Jake added, his tone soothing. "Contracts can be broken."

"I don't want to break the contract."

"You're doing this to hurt us!" Brooke accused.

Genevieve paused and considered the charge. "No, I'm really not. This isn't about the four of you. It's not about our family. I'm doing this for me, and it would be nice if I had your support. Like I said at the beginning of dinner, I love you all. That hasn't changed. It will never change. But it's time that I love myself a little, too."

She gave her stunned offspring a sympathetic smile. "Now, I have some errands to run. I cooked, so I'd appreciate it if y'all will clean up before you leave."

She was halfway through the butler's pantry when Willow spoke up, a hint of heartache in her tone. "Mom? You said you've already taken everything you want to keep? What about your dishes? What about this furniture? What about the dining room table?"

Genevieve stopped and turned around. Emotion welled up inside her, and went tight in her throat. She pulled her phone from her pocket and snapped a photo of the moment. Her kids. Her dishes. Her dining room table.

Her life. Her old life. She could add it to the video as an epilogue—and then turn the page. End the chapter. Close the book.

Then, start something new. While there's still time.

While there's still life.

Well, Genevieve, it's time to let go. Time to let go and

live. Discover who you're going to be now that you're finally growing up.

Genevieve met her elder daughter's gaze and smiled. "I'm not taking them with me, Willow. I'm done with dishes and dining rooms. I'm packing light for this next stage of life."

The trick, of course, was leaving her baggage behind.

Part Two

Eight

March
Austin, Texas

JAKE SHOVED OPEN A street-level door at Bensler, International and strode out onto the sidewalk. He turned north and walked away from the office as fast as his legs would carry him. Rage had been building inside Jake all morning. Really, all week. No, all month. Hell, all year.

Truth be told, he'd been on a slow boil since Halloween.

That's just from work. Add the family BS to the pot, and well, he was a pressure cooker building toward the blow.

Bensler was in the midst of yet another "workforce reduction." He hated that term. "Bloodletting" or "massacre" said it so much better. Jake had spent the morning firing people again. He couldn't believe he was singing this song, second verse, so soon. And for what? To make a buck? Money he didn't need? Doing a job that somewhere along the way turned from something he'd enjoyed and excelled at to work he despised? Why was he doing this?

Maybe because the one pleasure he got out of all this was being a constant thorn in Paul Franklin's side.

He told himself that the way to look at the entire debacle

was that he'd saved eight jobs this week. Originally, they'd wanted him to lay off fifteen. He'd pared the number down to seven by whittling his budget to the bone in other areas, and he'd referred all seven to strong opportunities at other firms. Hell, he was beginning to feel like a recruiter.

The lunch break hadn't come nearly soon enough.

Get through this day. You just have to get through today. Today is the worst of it.

Without conscious thought, his steps carried him to the edge of downtown and the hole-in-the-wall Mexican restaurant that had long been a favorite. He might even order a beer to go with his chile relleno to help him get through this afternoon.

Jake took three steps inside the restaurant, headed toward a customary seat at the bar, when his gaze fell upon the figure of a man already seated there with a basket of chips and a glass of tea in front of him. Jake froze midstep. Lucas.

His brother hadn't seen him. Once, not long ago, Jake would have sat down beside him and poured out his troubles. Lucas would have gladly shared the burden and his advice. Jake always listened to his brother's opinions. Lucas had lots of opinions. It had been a source of frustration to Lucas that Jake so often listened to what he had to say but then made a different decision.

Jake subconsciously shifted his position, putting a potted ivy between himself and his brother's line of sight. It was the first time he'd seen Lucas since that crazy day at Mom's house in January. Lucas had left not long after their mother's departure, dramatically telling his sisters to divide up the spoils, that he wanted nothing, that his siblings had already denied him the only thing he'd ever desired or requested—the Lonesome River Ranch.

"Drama queen," Jake muttered, watching Lucas sip his tea.

What should Jake do? He didn't have the mental energy for a confrontation today. Neither did he want to turn tail and leave. Jake was no coward who surrendered the battlefield.

Probably his best plan would be to forget sitting at the bar and go directly to a table. He should act like he'd never seen Lucas and give his brother the same opportunity.

Plan in hand, Jake shifted his body weight, took a step forward, and stopped. Lucas picked that moment to slide off the bar stool. He said something to the hostess and gestured toward two people who stood in a doorway beneath a sign proclaiming "Restrooms." Two women.

Brooke and Willow.

Jake blinked hard and looked again. His jaw literally dropped. Yes, the two women were definitely his sisters. Willow was in town? She'd made the trip from Nashville and didn't bother to tell him? Lucas, Willow, and Brooke took seats at one of the round tables in the dining room of the Mexican restaurant. Why? Jake's heart all but stopped as a possible reason occurred. Was somebody dead?

No, he immediately realized. All three of them smiled as they accepted menus from the server. They wouldn't be smiling if somebody was dead. This looked like a simple lunch. A family get-together. A weight settled over Jake, and he lifted his hand and rubbed his chest. Damned if this didn't hurt.

"Sir?" The hostess moved in front of Jake, blocking his view of his siblings. "How many in your party?"

I'm alone. He hesitated, then gave the woman his pleasantest corporate smile. "I'll take that seat at the bar, after all. First, though, I need to say hello to some folks in the dining room."

Jake wasn't sure what he wanted to say to his brother and sisters, so he decided to let them start. He stood behind the empty fourth chair at the round table, casually gripped the chair's back, and waited to be noticed. Brooke was the first to look up from her menu. Her smile faded. Her eyes went wide. "Oh."

Alerted by her tone, Willow and Lucas both glanced at her, then followed the path of her gaze. Anger flashed in the stare Lucas turned on his sisters. "Somebody want to explain this?"

"I didn't invite him," Brooke defended.

Guilt clouded Willow's eyes as she met Jake's gaze, but she responded to Lucas's charge with an explicit denial. "I didn't tell Jake we were meeting."

Jake smiled his corporate shark's grin. "Oh, and here I assumed my invitation to today's soiree simply got lost in the mail. After all, in a city of one million people, you chose to meet in a restaurant that's within walking distance of my office. Why else would you do that if not to make it convenient for me to attend?"

Lucas folded his arms. "It's my favorite Mexican food place downtown."

"Mine, too," Jake fired back. Lucas had known that, of course. He had to have been aware of the possibility, however slight, that Jake might choose Mexican food for lunch today. Had the idea given his brother a thrill? Probably.

Brooke piped up. "I chose the restaurant! It's mine and Travis's favorite Mexican place, too."

"Too bad everybody wasn't in the mood for sushi today." Jake considered pulling out the chair and taking a seat but decided against it. Standing, he occupied the high ground. "So, since I didn't get the invite, what's the plan? Should I expect one of you to pay a call at the office this afternoon to present whatever proposal you've put together? If you're all coming, I'll book a conference room. Or will I simply be hearing from your lawyers?"

Brooke groaned and buried her face in her hands.

"Jake," Willow said, his name part protest, part plea.

Lucas said nothing, only pasted on that familiar smirk that invariably managed to get under Jake's skin.

Judging he'd made his point, Jake reached into his pocket for his wallet. He pulled out a handful of bills—enough cash to pick up the tab for four in a five-star restaurant—and tossed them onto the table. "Lunch is on me."

Jake pivoted and headed for the exit. Outside, blue sky and sunshine had disappeared behind a bank of gray clouds promising rain. He felt the first spatter of raindrops at the exact moment he heard Willow call his name. "Wait, Jake. Please."

He should stop and let her talk to him. Let her explain. But if Willow ran after him, there was a good chance that Brooke would follow. The streets of downtown Austin weren't the place for the Prentice family episode of *Jerry Springer*.

But dammit, he wouldn't run from her. Abruptly, he stopped. His heart pounded like he'd run a marathon as Willow hurried up to him. "I'm sorry. I know this looks bad, like the three of us are conspiring against you, but I want you to know that I wouldn't do that to you, Jake. This was a fact-finding trip, that's all."

Jake set his mouth into a grim line. Fact-finding, huh? Undoubtedly another one of Lucas's schemes. Everything always came back to Lonesome River Ranch.

Jake met his sister's worried, guilty gaze. She wanted his reassurance, his absolution. She wanted him to pat her on the head and tell her that it was okay that they'd gone behind his back.

That's what she expected him to do. It's what Jake always did. He took care of her. Of things. He solved problems. That's what he'd been doing three years ago when he discovered that Lucas's lady lawyer love had wormed her way into his grandfather's good graces and talked him into restructuring the Lonesome River Ranch Trust that formed upon his death. Hell, it's what he'd been doing since the day that Dad dropped dead at his feet. Jake had tried to take care of his family. He'd tried so damned hard.

Willow's eyes were the same green as his and Mom's, and as Jake stared into them, he recalled a moment of that scene in January.

"Here's your hard truth, Jacob Alan Prentice. You are not your father. It's time you figure out just who you are."

Okay, then. Maybe she was right. Maybe it was time he started listening to his mother. He wasn't his father. The family wasn't his responsibility. It wasn't his job to soothe his siblings' psyches or protect their financial interests. Why try so damned hard? For what?

They really weren't much of a family anymore, were they?

Was that the conclusion that Mom had reached? To hell with all for one and one for all? It's now every man for himself in Prenticeworld?

Maybe so. Maybe so.

So, Jake responded to his sister in a way that neither one of them would have expected. Shrugging, he said, "Whatever."

Then he walked away.

Jake didn't get lunch before returning to the office. He took a long walk around downtown. Actually, it was more of a march, close to a jog, he walked so fast, his strides fueled by a jumble of dark emotions. Betrayal, hurt, fury, confusion, and grief spiced the primary ingredient—anger.

He was due back at Bensler at 1 p.m. for the first scheduled bloodletting of the afternoon. His phone started ringing at ten after the hour. He silenced it. Jake didn't want to talk to the office. He didn't want to talk to anyone. So he didn't.

Ordinarily, when Jake went on long walks, he spent the time thinking, making plans, and problem solving. Right now, he put one foot in front of the other, his mind on auto-pilot. The heat had him loosening his tie, and at some point, he stripped it off and stuck it in his pocket. The muggy, warm air foretold the thunderstorms forecast for the after-noon. It had that tornado weather feel, which was fitting. Storming inside and out.

He paid no attention to his direction and was somewhat surprised to find himself walking along the river. The Col-orado ran particularly green today. When he spied a turtle sunning itself atop a fallen log along the bank, he stopped and watched. A metaphor about a turtle hiding its head in its shell hung just beyond his grasp. Maybe because a turtle wasn't right. Maybe it was the ostrich with its head in the sand. Except that was an animal myth. He'd seen it on National Geographic Kids when he was babysitting Emma and Drew for Willow.

Jake abandoned the metaphor effort, and his gaze drifted along the opposite riverbank to the development beyond. It snagged on a fire station. The building wasn't new or innovative, but it brought a different fire station to mind, that sweet little volunteer fire station built last year outside the small Texas Hill Country town of Redemption down in Enchanted Canyon. The Innovations Design project.

Innovations Design, Tess Crenshaw's new employer.

Jake pulled his phone from his pocket and, ignoring the multiple missed calls, texts, and voice mail notices, scrolled through his contacts list to Tess's name. Hmm. He only had her personal number. He lifted his gaze back to the fire station across the river. A moment later, he pulled up another app on his phone.

The Uber arrived within minutes. Jake climbed inside the car, vaguely aware that his actions were completely out of character and made little sense. It didn't seem to matter. Fifteen minutes later, in what had once been a residential neighborhood but was now primarily commercial space, he climbed the porch steps of a 1920s cottage. He rang the doorbell beside the simple brass plate that read "Innovations Design."

Moments later, footsteps approached. A college-age woman answered the door wearing black slacks, a crisp white shirt, and a friendly smile. "Good afternoon. May I help you?"

"I'm hoping to see Tess Crenshaw. Is she available? I don't have an appointment. My name is Jake Prentice."

"If you'd like to come inside, Mr. Prentice, I will certainly see." She opened the door wide and gestured toward the room that had once served as the home's living room. "May I offer you something to drink?"

He realized he was thirsty after his long walk. "Water would be great."

"I'll be right back." True to her word, she brought him a bottle of spring water and a glass filled with ice before climbing the stairs to the second floor.

Jake chugged half the bottle of water down before pouring the rest in the glass. He'd no sooner settled into a seriously comfortable club chair than he heard footsteps on the stairs. Two sets.

He set down his water glass and rose.

Tess breezed into the room as bright as sunshine. She wore a solid yellow sweater over a yellow polka dot sundress. She looked good. She looked great. She sparkled, her blue eyes shining and her smile wide and warm.

"Jake!" she said, extending her hand for a handshake. "This is a lovely surprise."

"I was in the neighborhood. I, um..." He faltered. Jake didn't know exactly what he wanted to say, so he delayed. "The pie. Could I get the recipe for your pie for my mom?"

Tess frowned in confusion. "My Thanksgiving pie?"

"Yes."

"Your mother already has that recipe. She asked me for it in the thank-you note she sent me after Thanksgiving."

"She did? How did she know how to reach you?"

"She sent it here. I told her you helped me get a new job here."

Oh." Jake rubbed the back of his neck. "Well, shoot. Guess your recipe will not be part of her Mother's Day gift then."

"You're already planning her Mother's Day gift? Six weeks early?"

"Yes-no. No. That's a lie. I'm not here because of pie. I needed to see you."

Her gaze grew guarded. She gestured for him to take his seat. She perched on the edge of a chair beside his. "What about?"

Again, he hesitated. He must have looked troubled because she asked, "Is there a problem? Something with one of my old projects? The Baker Hotel?"

"No. Not at all. Everything is fine in that respect. I'm just wondering, are you happy, Tess? Here at Innovations?"

"Why?"

Frustrated, he said, "Because I'd like to know."

"Okay. I *am* happy. I love it here."

Jake nodded. Good. That's good. "Tell me about the job."

Her brow furrowed as she studied him, but rather than ask the questions he read in her gaze, she responded to his request. "It's challenging. I've been so busy I've hardly had time to breathe. I spent most of January and February traveling, visiting job sites, and familiarizing myself with the firm's projects. Steve wants all of our associates to be knowledgeable about our work. As far as the job itself goes, it's a perfect fit for me creatively. I'm working on some fabulous projects. And the people, well, we're like a family."

Jake nodded. He took a sip of his water and thought about what she'd said. It was the deepest bit of thinking he'd done since he saw his siblings open their menus earlier today.

"What is this all about, Jake?" When he took a sip of his water rather than respond, she teased, "Did you come to offer me my old job at Bensler back?"

He almost spit out his water. *Hell, no.* "I like you too much to do that to you, Tess. Honestly, I think I just wanted to know that my judgment wasn't off base, that sending you here had been a good call."

"Sending me here was an excellent call. It's the best thing anyone has ever done for me professionally."

"Good. Okay. Good." He sent down his glass and stood. "That's what I wanted to know. Thanks for your time, Tess. I won't take any more of it."

She walked him toward the door, her expression a mix of curiosity and confusion. "It was nice to see you, Jake."

"You, too." He hesitated, not quite ready to leave but not sure what the hell he was doing.

She waited a moment before filling the void by reaching toward a basket that sat atop an entry table and handing him an Innovations Design branded koozie. "Take a koozie. Summer is just around the corner. You can never have enough koozies."

"True. Thanks." He stuck the koozie in his jacket pocket. Then, without thinking about it because, after all, he wasn't thinking today now, was he, he asked, "Are you with anyone, Tess?"

"With anyone?" she repeated. "Um, perhaps you should define that a little more clearly."

"Seeing someone. Together with a guy. A couple."

She smoothed a wrinkle he couldn't see from her skirt. "No, I'm not."

"I'd meant to call you after the holidays, but then my mother ran away from home, and life got crazy."

"Your mother ran away from home?"

"Yeah. Long story. Maybe I can tell it to you over dinner sometime?"

"I'd like that. Only, I'm leaving tomorrow for a stretch of traveling. I'm afraid I'll be away the better part of the next six weeks."

"Maybe some of the crazy in my life will settle down by then." Jake doubted it, but miracles did happen. "I'll call you."

"I'd like that."

With the receptionist looking on, Jake gave Tess's hand a professional handshake. Then because he had all but asked her out in front of the receptionist, he leaned down and gave her cheek a friendly little kiss.

Tess's cheeks flushed prettily. Her sparkle notched up another degree.

Jake departed Innovations Design with a sense of having taken a step forward. Along what road, he couldn't say because he didn't have a blessed clue where he was headed. The one thing he did know was that he was going to listen to his mother.

It's time you figure out just who you are.

He Ubered back to the office and walked in to find his admin in a near panic. "Jake! Am I glad to see you. Are you all right? All hell has broken loose around here. When you went MIA, HR confiscated the employment files from your desk and turned them over to the department heads."

"All of them?"

"Except for Stephanie Watson's."

Jake nodded. He wasn't surprised. He was Stephanie's direct supervisor. The only other person who could do the honors with Stephanie was Paul Franklin.

"Mr. Franklin wants to see you as soon as you return," his admin continued.

"I imagine he does." Jake shrugged. "I have a couple things to take care of first. Sorry for the grief I caused you today, Jason. It won't happen again."

"No problem, Jake. I'm just glad you're okay. I was worried. It's not like you not to answer your phone or miss meetings."

"Yes, well, today was an unusual day. I know it's been tough. Why don't you knock off early? Go hit a happy hour. You look like you can use it."

"You sure?"

"Positive."

Jason beamed. "You don't have to tell me twice. Thanks, Jake."

"Thank you, Jason. You've always been a terrific assistant,

and excellent help when I've needed it." Jake gave the younger man's shoulder a collegial clap, then went into his office. He spent less than five minutes composing two e-mails, which he saved in his draft folder. Next, he picked up his phone and dialed Stephanie Watson's extension. "Stephanie, it's Jake. Could I see you in my office?"

There was a moment of silence before his colleague returned a resigned, "Of course. I'll be right there."

After disconnecting the call, Jake crossed the hall to the conference room, where he knew that supplies had been stored. Grabbing what he figured he needed, he returned to his office and went to work. When Stephanie rapped on Jake's open door a few minutes later, Jake stood staring at the Lonesome River Ranch sunset photograph hanging on his wall. "Come on in."

"I guess my number is up," Stephanie said, attempting a brave smile that she didn't quite pull off. "Honestly, I felt lucky to have survived the Thanksgiving Massacre."

Now that he'd made a decision, Jake was ready to act. He cut straight to the chase. "Do you want this job, Stephanie?"

"Is it going to do me any good to want it if I'm on the layoff list?"

"This isn't about today's layoffs. I'm not talking about your current job. I'm talking about my job. Do you want my job?"

Stephanie obviously took it as a corporate trick question. "One always strives toward advancement. Your job is the next one up the ladder, so of course, if there were ever an opening, I would hope to be considered for the position."

"That's what I wanted to hear." Jake pulled up his draft e-mails, hit send, then rose and walked out from around behind his desk. "Have a seat."

Stephanie started to sit in one of the visitor's chairs, but Jake stopped him. "No, behind the desk."

"I don't understand."

"I'm throwing you to the sharks. I should probably ask for your forgiveness, but you just told me you wanted the job. Be careful what you ask for, Stephanie." Jake shrugged. "Of course, it's always possible that Franklin will override my decision due to the circumstances and go in another direction, but he's not a fool. An ass, but not a fool. You are the best person for the position. You'll have sixty days minimum to prove you can do this job, more likely ninety. One piece of advice. Keep Jason. Give him a raise. He's the best assistant I've ever had, and he'll be invaluable through the transition."

"Wait a minute," Stephanie said, bracing her hands on the desk and leaning forward. "I'm sorry. You're going to need to spell this out for me. I came up here thinking my job was getting guillotined, but you're telling me what exactly?"

"I'm promoting you to managing director."

Now she sat back hard in the chair, a shocked expression on her face. "There's only one managing director in our division. That's your job."

"I quit."

The words sounded strange on his tongue. He couldn't think of another time in his life that he'd actually spoken those two words together. Not since his dad died anyway.

I quit.

Huh. Two little words. The impact of saying them aloud rolled through him like the surf at Waimea Bay. Damned powerful. *I quit.* He wondered if this was similar to how his mother had felt on that Sunday dinner in January.

"You quit," Stephanie repeated, her tone filled with

disbelief. "You're leaving Bensler? Oh my God. You are! You have a box!"

Jake glanced at the banker's box that he'd loaded with his personal items while awaiting Stephanie's arrival. It held only a few things—some plaques for awards he'd received that he didn't give a flip about, a nice pen, an engraved business card holder, and a letter opener a former girlfriend had given him. The box also contained a football and the tee he'd used for its display.

Jake had been awarded the game ball for leading his underdog team to a come-from-behind victory over the big bad University of Texas Longhorns his senior year. He'd displayed it in his office as a reminder of life lessons more than a glory days trophy. The game ball was a tangible representation of what drive and perseverance, and belief in oneself, can accomplish.

He picked up the football from the box. The leather felt cool to the touch, stiff and worn, the ball deflated. He spun it in his hands, noticed the roughness of the seams and laces.

I quit.

He didn't give a damn about the ball any longer. He gazed down at the contents of the box. Baggage. That's all it was. A box with a lid and handholds instead of a zipper and wheels. He didn't need any baggage. His gaze shifted to the framed photo of the Lonesome River Ranch sunset still on the wall. Baggage didn't need him. He was traveling light.

I quit.

Former quarterback Jake Prentice tossed the ball to his replacement. "It's all yours now. Good luck."

Then he turned and walked out the door, leaving his baggage behind.

That's what he tried to tell himself anyway.

Nine

May
Lake in the Clouds, Colorado

STANDING AT THE JEWELRY counter with shopping bags at her feet, Genevieve stared at her reflection in a mirror. She gave the earring dangling from her lobe a tap, setting the hammered metal ovals swinging. She liked the jangling sound they made. The weight was surprisingly light for something so big.

"I don't know, Liz," she said to the shopkeeper. "I do like them, but maybe something a little bigger? A little more eye-catching? What do you think, Helen?"

"Those earrings are so not you."

"You're right." Genevieve gave her head a shake and sent the earrings swaying. "I'll take them."

Her sister rolled her eyes and moved to another jewelry case. "Come look at these, Gen. They're perfect for you."

"I'll bet you're looking at the jade clusters, aren't you?" asked the shopkeeper. "They match her eyes."

Genevieve wandered down to the next jewelry case and eyed the earrings her sister pointed out. They were lovely, something that a year ago she'd have jumped at. Today, she wrinkled her nose. "I've worn jade forever."

"You didn't bring any north."

"North" was the shorthand she and Helen used to refer to events surrounding the sale of her home and belongings and the move to Colorado. Genevieve shrugged. "That's an interesting necklace there on the end."

"Which one?" the shopkeeper asked.

"The pink one. The big flower."

"Oh, for heaven's sake," Helen scoffed. "It's like a Georgia O'Keeffe painting. You are too old to hang a vulva around your neck, Genevieve."

Genevieve gave her sister a withering glare. "Hey. I'm not the one who's getting Medicare Advantage flyers in the mail on a daily basis. I suggest you keep that *O* word to yourself."

"Ouch. Harsh, sister."

Genevieve smiled warmly at the shopkeeper. "I'd love to try on the necklace."

Helen closed her eyes, sighed, and shook her head. "I've created a monster."

"Look at those topaz bangles, Helen."

"Ooh. Love."

To the shopkeeper, Genevieve said, "She's been a bangle girl from way back."

Twenty minutes later, the sisters exited the boutique. Helen carried two bags. Genevieve toted five. "Want to drop those off at the car before we go to lunch?" Helen asked.

"That would be great."

"You just have to promise not to dawdle and detour and fill up your arms again before we get to the Bear Stop Café. We don't want to be late for our appointment. Besides, I'm hungry."

"I promise. I won't. I'm hungry, too. I need to refuel for afternoon shopping."

"Allow me to repeat, I've created a monster."

Genevieve smiled and swung her shopping bags. It was a gorgeous spring day, sunny, with only the barest hint of a breeze. She lifted her face toward the sunshine, happy to feel the warmth on her skin. She'd enjoyed burrowing in during January and February, but she was ready for spring. Ready for change.

As they approached her sister's car, Helen hit a button on her key fob, and her trunk lid glided open. Genevieve deposited her bags in the car. "Remind me. What's the skinny on the when and where of all of our meetings today?"

"We have three. Our lunch meeting is at noon at the Bear Stop Café with Danny Ayers."

"The banker."

"Yes. The two o'clock is at the lodge with Granite Mountain Construction."

"Oh yes. Mr. Chiseled Jaw. Ross Hopkins. Granite is the perfect name for his company, don't you think? Hold on a minute." Genevieve dug through her bags for the necklace she'd just purchased and slipped it on.

"Oh, for pity's sake." Helen rolled her eyes. "You are pathetic. He's young enough to be your son."

Genevieve gave a nonchalant shrug. "If I'd been a child bride. Ross is forty-six years old."

"You googled him?"

"I asked him."

"When did you talk to him? You didn't have a meeting with him without me, did you?"

"No, of course not. I ran into him at the cycle shop when I bought my snowmobile." She paused a moment before adding,

"He's been divorced for six years. He has two children, boys. Eighteen and twenty-one. They're both in college."

"Mm-hmm."

"Oh. And I told him I go by Vivie."

Helen dropped her bags next to her sister's. "You what?"

Genevieve lifted her chin. "Well, I've been thinking about it. I think the name suits the new me. Genevieve is old-fashioned. Genevieve lived in a two-story Victorian and had fine china for every occasion, china which she regularly used and washed by hand. She had a landline. She preferred speaking over texting as a means of communication. Vivie, on the other hand, is modern. Contemporary."

"MCM maybe."

"Excuse me?"

"Midcentury modern."

"What are you trying to say, Helen?"

Helen glanced around. "Never mind. We are on a public street. Let's not make a scene."

Genevieve folded her arms and kept her feet planted. "I'm not making a scene. I'm asking a question."

"And I'll answer your question when we're not in full view of the beauty shop. I don't want to get the third degree when I go in to get my roots done on Thursday."

Genevieve glanced toward the large plate glass window of Salon in the Clouds, where she spied at least one avid observer. "Fair enough. Good point. What about the third meeting?"

"It's at the lodge at five o'clock."

"That's with Independence Construction? The Throck-morton guy?"

"Yes. Zach Throckmorton. After all the trouble his dad gave us over the contracts on our purchase, I can't imagine we'd do business with him. We are probably wasting his time and ours."

"Probably," Genevieve agreed. "However, he went out of his way to separate himself from Gage Throckmorton when he contacted us and asked for the opportunity to bid."

"True." Helen shut the trunk. "Guess we shouldn't hold sins of the father against the son."

"We absolutely should not."

A horn beeped, and the sisters glanced around to see Helen's next-door neighbor stopped at a red light across the street. They waved hello, then continued their walk toward the Bear Stop Café. Genevieve absorbed the hustle and bustle happening along Main Street, and pleasure filled her. She loved her new home!

Long ago the citizens of Lake in the Clouds had made it a priority to preserve the town's history and heritage. As a result, many of the structures in the town's central business district and surrounding neighborhoods dated to the small town's silver-mining origins. When Helen first told Genevieve she was moving to a Colorado mountain town with a population of less than 10,000, she'd said Lake in the Clouds was a mash-up of Tombstone and Mayberry plunked down in the middle of Vail.

Genevieve considered it to be an apt description. The place had an Old West flavor with small-town values and friendliness and location location location. It had been a perfect fit for Helen, and so far, so good for Genevieve, too. Aka Vivie.

Genevieve would have bought one of the Victorian mansions off Main Street. Vivie had purchased a sleek, high-tech contemporary halfway up a mountain out of the valley away from town.

She'd found it wonderfully empowering to be free of the past when it came to decorating. She'd chosen clean, modern lines and some innovative materials in her furnishings. Her new dining room table was made of metal and acrylic and she loved it. Her dinnerware, of which she had one set, was hand-painted porcelain she'd picked up from a modern art gallery in Aspen.

Every so often she did feel a pang of nostalgia for the Victorian house and her discarded possessions, usually during those moments of self-doubt when she second-guessed her decision to sell everything and move to Colorado. In those moments, she felt the absence of her dining room table like a missing limb. But the doubting days didn't come along too often, and she liked this new person she was creating.

That person was happy to be here today, and today was all that mattered. She was taking things one day at a time. Right now, she was going to soak up the sunshine and pleasure in the purple pots of pansies brightening the doorways of the shops. She'd savor the scent of springtime on the air. She'd sing along with the birds.

She might just go wild and crazy and order dessert with lunch.

At the Bear Stop Café, a hostess showed them to a table on the outdoor patio. As soon as they took their seats, their phones rang simultaneously. Helen dug in her purse. Genevieve noted her caller and said, "It's Ross."

"This is Willow's ringtone," her sister informed her.

Genevieve groaned. "She's calling to check up on me?"

"Probably. It's her day. The girls alternate."

Helen finally located her device and tugged it from the depths of her bag as Genevieve thumbed the green button on her screen. "Hello?"

"Vivie? This is Ross Hopkins."

Vivie. Genevieve let the name float across her mind like a summer cloud. It was the first time someone other than she had used it. *Hmm. Not sure I like that, after all.* "Hi, Ross."

He sounded harried. "Hey, listen, I got called to a job site in Panther Valley this morning, and I took the road over Dickerson Pass. The sheriff's department has the highway completely shut down for a wreck. I'm running about an hour behind. Could we push our meeting back until three? Does that work for you?"

"I believe so, but let me check with Helen. She's on another call. I'll phone you right back after I speak with her."

As Genevieve disconnected, she heard her sister say, "A cougar. Yes. Your mother. She's on the prowl, Willow."

"Oh, for crying out loud," Genevieve muttered, then smiled her thanks at the server, who arrived with a bottle of champagne, two glasses, and a note.

Helen arched her brows and gestured for Genevieve to read the note. "A contractor. Yes. I know. I know. Maybe it's something in the water. No, she's not smoking weed."

Genevieve scanned the note. The banker was standing them up.

"Hey," she said aloud. "Pot is legal in Colorado, so I could do it if I want, but I decided not to surrender my high moral ground. I've lived this long without doing any drugs. For a girl who was a teen in the seventies, that's saying something. If you can tear yourself away from gossiping with my daughter for a moment, we have a decision to make."

"Hold on a minute, sweets, would you, please?"

Genevieve explained the contractor's traffic delay and the banker's last-minute cancellation. The sisters settled on a plan, and Genevieve dialed Ross Hopkins to okay the hour delay. When she disconnected her call, Helen was wrapping up with Willow.

"I will. Of course. I'll ask her." Helen offered Genevieve her phone. "Want to say hello to Willow, Gen?"

Genevieve shot her sister a narrow-eyed glare but kept her hands folded in her lap as she cheerily called, "Hello, Willow."

Helen rolled her eyes before saying a simple good-bye to Genevieve's daughter. "So a champagne apology from old Danny. At least he cancels with class. Wonder what his real reason is for standing us up?"

"You don't believe he has a stomach bug?"

"Not for a minute. Based on gossip I overheard while you were in the dressing room trying on that orange skirt you bought, I think he's home doing damage control. I'll bet his wife got wind of his affair."

"His affair?"

"Uh-huh. With a nail tech who is younger than his daughter."

"And we are doing business with him, why?"

"As far as I'm concerned, we're not. I only heard about it myself last night. That said, I wanted to listen to his pitch today and discuss everything with you this afternoon. I knew if you heard about the nail tech, you'd cancel lunch or dump his tea in his lap, and I want information before we kick him to the curb."

"Hmm." Genevieve set down her glass. "I don't think I want to drink his champagne. We shouldn't be day drinking anyway. We have business meetings this afternoon."

"Aw, Gen. That's really good champagne. And it's not *his* champagne. It's our champagne. He gave it to us."

"And we can give it to somebody else."

"Oh, all right. But to make it up to me, we get to go back to the shoe store on Second Street before we meet Mr. Mountain out at Raindrop Lodge. Deal?"

"You're going to buy those yellow sandals after all. I knew it. Deal."

The sisters studied their menus, placed their orders, and Helen relayed the news that Willow had shared during the call, details about Emma's new vocabulary words and Drew's scout troop. Genevieve already knew most of it. She kept in contact with her children via text messages and e-mail, and she still enjoyed FaceTime calls with the grands at least once a week. However, she wasn't ready to take phone calls from her children.

She still needed to keep a degree of separation between herself and her offspring. Four months into her big move, the ground beneath her feet remained a bit soft. She had yet to find her footing. She wanted to wait until she'd found her balance in her new life before she opened the door too wide to her old.

The thought brought her back to the midcentury modern crack Helen had made out in front of the hair salon. "So, Helen, midcentury modern? Seriously?"

Helen shrugged and sipped the iced tea she'd ordered. "*V* is for vintage, *Vivie.*"

Yes, I definitely don't like it. "No, it's not."

"Sure it is." Helen mimed winding an antique crank telephone. "Ding. Ding. Ding. Hello, 1970s? Genevieve Bennett calling. I burned my present to the ground, and now I'm peddling backward trying to recapture my past."

"That's not what I'm doing," Genevieve protested. "I'm moving forward. Actually, I'm leaping forward."

"Off a cliff maybe." Helen returned to her fantasy phone

call. "What year was it that I went to summer camp, and I told everyone my name was Farrah?"

Genevieve scowled at her older sister. In 1976, every girl she knew wanted to be Farrah Fawcett. "You're fixin' to tick me off. I was twelve years old."

"I always know I've touched a nerve when your Southern starts to show. Look, if you don't want to hear my answer, then don't ask the question. You know I always shoot straight."

That was true. Unfortunately, right this minute she would prefer a little reassurance over target practice.

Genevieve sipped her water. Maybe Helen was right. Maybe she had headed in the wrong direction since her move to Colorado. And yet, in her heart of hearts, she didn't believe that. Why did Helen? Maybe it was time to ask. She set down her glass. "Fine. Regale me with all of your infinite wisdom, O sister mine."

"We'd still be sitting here come Labor Day if I attempted to do that."

"Of course. How silly of me. How about you hit a few of the highlights?"

"I can do that," Helen said lightly. Then she totally changed the tone by reaching across the table and giving her sister's forearm a squeeze. "Here's the deal. I think you did something bold and brave by moving to Colorado, Genevieve. I'm very glad you made the choice. However, you have done a lot in a very short amount of time. I think you should pause and take a breath before you make any more big life-changing decisions."

Genevieve wrinkled her nose. "What do you think I'm going to do? Run off and marry the contractor?"

"I don't know what you're going to do." Helen sat back

in her chair hard. "That's what worries me. You still have plenty of adrenaline sloshing around in your gas tank, but your GPS is all out of whack. I'm afraid you took a wrong turn at a crossroads."

"I have time to explore the side roads before I commit to a route."

"That's just it. You're not exploring. You're trying to back up."

Ordinarily, Helen was better with her metaphors than this. "I'm not following you."

"Vintage. Midcentury modern." Helen punctuated the phrases with a dramatic little flourish of her hand. "The period when you were young, and life lay ahead of you. I get why the past is attractive, Gen. Barring the unforeseen, the road headed that direction is longer and therefore more attractive. I imagine it feels safer to you, but it's not. I promise you it's not. Honey, the past is not the track to Happytown. You need to turn your little choo-choo train around before you derail."

Genevieve scowled at her sister. "Did you have a Bloody Mary morning? You are not making a lick of sense."

"Well, neither are you. I'm worried about you, Genevieve. If you jump the tracks, I'll be responsible for the wreck, and then I'll be a wreck, too!"

Genevieve folded her arms and studied her sister. This was so not like Helen. What was she missing?

Wait a minute. "You talked to Willow a few minutes ago. You said the girls alternate. Do you talk to one of my daughters every day?"

"Yes."

"The boys?"

"No. They only call occasionally now."

"I see. How long has this been going on?"

"Well, my phone rang the first time as you were walking to meet me at the clubhouse that Sunday. They all called me most days through the end of January. I finally convinced the girls to go to the alternating schedule the week before last."

Those blasted troublemakers. "They can't get to me, so they did an end-around. Oh, Helen. I'm so sorry. You should have told me. I'd have put a stop to the harassment."

"I can handle my nieces and nephews. Besides, it's not harassment. It's caring and concern. They are worried about you."

"I know. But also, I'm the shiny distraction." Genevieve smiled up at the server, who arrived carrying a tray with their order. Once their salads had been served, she continued, "Here's the deal, Helen. As long as they are fretting about me and my problems, they're not working on their own. They're *not* working on their own, are they? Has any of them done anything about—no."

Genevieve stabbed lettuce with her fork and repeated, "No. Never mind. Pretend I didn't just ask that question. It's their lives. I'm letting go. How is your salad?"

"It's really good."

"Let's change the subject. I'll get indigestion if we continue to talk about my children."

Her sister laughed. "Good idea. I picked up a second juicy piece of gossip at the boutique while you were in the dressing room trying on that yellow dress."

"Oh yeah? Spill."

They spent the rest of their meal discussing the budding romance between Helen's condominium's maintenance man and the local librarian. They split a piece of chocolate cake for dessert and added a large tip for the server to the banker's tab. As the sisters left the restaurant, Helen's cell phone rang. She checked the number. "It's Jake."

"My Jake?" At her sister's nod, she added, "I thought the boys didn't call you."

"They call. Just not every day."

Genevieve rolled her eyes. "Let it go to voice mail."

"I think I will."

Genevieve's pleasure in the day had dimmed as she retraced her steps across Lake in the Clouds and brooded. "This is unacceptable. It's one thing for my children to drive me bonkers, but it's something else entirely for them to do it to you."

Helen sighed. "I've given you grief for not talking to them, but I'm beginning to understand why you declared the moratorium. Have they always been this involved in your business?"

Genevieve huffed a laugh. "But they're *not* involved in my business right now, are they? I haven't allowed them to be involved."

"True. That's the problem."

"According to my children."

"Yes."

"Which has made it your problem."

"Yes!"

"You should stop answering your phone, Helen."

"They might start paying calls to Colorado if I do. In-person calls."

"Oh." Genevieve's eyes went round. "Oh dear. You're right. Continue to answer your phone, Helen."

Helen smirked.

Genevieve went through the motions of shoe shopping,

but she had lost interest in the activity as she continued to dwell upon the problem of her children. She should have known that they'd be sneaky, go around her back, and pester her sister. Had she been in their shoes, that's what she would have done. While she was tempted to fire off a group text telling them all to butt out, she recognized that wasn't the right thing to do.

Her children loved her. They worried about her. While mother hen labored to let go, her chicks' natural inclination was to hold on.

Her actions had shocked them, but for the most part, they'd handled the situation well. They hadn't tried to have her declared mentally incompetent or have her committed— not that she knew anyway. She needed to give them credit for honoring her wishes regarding phone calls and visits. That said, Helen wasn't their personal intelligence agent. They'd used her as such long enough. Genevieve just needed to figure out the best solution for the problem.

"You see anything you like?" Helen asked as she accepted a package from the sales clerk.

"No, not really. Though I've realized I should probably buy a pair of work boots. I expect I'll be spending quite a bit of time out at the lodge during the renovation."

With that, talk shifted to business. They headed out to Raindrop Lodge a little early, their conversation focused on Ross Hopkins and Zach Throckmorton and the upcoming interviews. They were a full month behind the schedule they'd planned in December when making the decision to buy, owing to a few minor snags and one substantial road-block in the acquisition process.

The title hadn't been as clean as the owners had led them to believe.

Like so much of the land around Lake in the Clouds, Rain-drop Lodge and Cabins Resort had been built on land once owned by the sprawling Throckmorton Triple T Ranch, land with some sticky strings attached to it. In effect, the ranch remained in control of development in Lake in the Clouds similar to the way a home owner's association did in Texas. Long story short, Genevieve and Helen had needed the current Throckmorton family Grand Poobah, Gage Throck-morton, to sign off on their purchase of the property.

He'd been out of the country and incommunicado for much of the time, but unwilling to delegate decision-making responsibility. That led to one problem after another. Genevieve had finally managed to communicate with him through an e-mail exchange that, unfortunately, devolved into somewhat of a squabble. The man managed to push Genevieve's buttons, and she'd come close to spoiling the deal. In fact, she'd thought she'd blown it following one par-ticular late-night exchange. Instead, to her surprise, papers had unexpectedly and without accompanying explanation arrived from the attorney's office okaying the sale. Curious, but not about to look the proverbial gift horse in the mouth, Genevieve had dropped a handwritten thank-you note into the mailbox on the way to the closing a little over two weeks ago.

She had yet to meet Gage Throckmorton in person, though she'd heard he'd made an appearance or two in town during the past week.

The sign marking the turnoff to Raindrop Lodge came into view on the right, and seeing it, Genevieve frowned. "We haven't heard back from the graphic artist about the logos, have we?"

"No, not yet."

"Hmm. I'll reach out to her when I get home to my computer. I'm anxious to see what she's come up with."

Helen gave her sister a sidelong glance. "Well, who are you, and what have you done with Vivie? You've certainly shifted into business mode all of a sudden."

"I know. Maybe I listened to my big sister's lunch lecture."

"Seriously?"

"Stranger things have happened." Genevieve smiled and shrugged. "Honestly, I did listen. You have a point. Maybe in my, shall we say, enthusiasm for change, I went a little too far. I don't need to reinvent as much as I need to renovate. Vivie isn't necessary. I just need to spruce Genevieve up. I've done a lot already—new home, new furnishings, new wardrobe—but it's time I get professional. No more goofing off. I haven't been holding up my end of our deal, and I owe you an apology for that."

"Now, Gen, that's not true."

"Yes, it is. You did almost all of the heavy lifting when the glitches on the sale happened, and I let you. Not only that, I almost tanked the entire deal by getting snippy with His Highness. That was wrong."

"I worked thirty years as an attorney, Genevieve. That sort of stuff was my wheelhouse."

"Well, I'm going to do better. Also, running interference between me and my brood certainly was never anywhere in your job description. There's no reason you should have to do it in retirement. It's past time I put a stop to it, and I will."

"How?"

"Well, I don't know for sure, but I'll think of something."

Helen smiled. "Have I told you lately how proud I am to be your sister? Hey, look. There's Ross's truck. Did we lose track of time? Are we late?"

Genevieve spied the pickup parked in front of the lodge. "It's only two forty, and that truck is maroon. Ross drives a white truck. I hope we're not going to start having trouble with trespassers. We might need to consider hiring a security service."

Helen suddenly braked to a stop. "If it's a trespasser, he sure is a bold one. Look over at Cabin 1. There's smoke coming from the chimney. Somebody strung a hammock between two aspen trees. I see a Yeti on the front porch and fishing gear beside the door."

Genevieve glanced toward Cabin 1 just as the door opened and a figure emerged from inside. A man.

Helen said, "That's one scary-looking dude. Get my gun from the glove box."

"You have a gun? Since when? You said you'd never own a firearm!"

"That's before I moved to the mountains. Bears frighten me. So do scraggly trespassers coming this way. Get my gun, Genevieve. Now."

"You don't need to be afraid of him," Genevieve said, a grim tone to her voice. "Be afraid of me."

Helen gaped at her sister as Genevieve released her seat belt and flung open the car door. She sprang out of the auto and advanced on the bearded figure. Her voice simmering with temper, she demanded, "What in the hell are you doing here?"

Jake Prentice opened his arms. "Hi, Mom."

Ten

HE OBVIOUSLY WASN'T GETTING a hug.

Jake's welcoming smile slowly died as he gawked at his mother and the…thing…hanging from around her neck. She'd changed her haircut. Her hair color, too. Moreover, something was different about her makeup and her clothes were all…flowy. He'd never known his mother to wear flowy clothing. Dangling earrings and that thing around her neck? *Who are you and what have you done with my mother?* He knew better than to voice the thought, of course, so he said, "Hi, Mom."

She didn't look particularly glad to see him.

Aunt Helen emerged from the driver's side of the car. "Jake? Is that really you behind that beard?"

He scratched at the thick pelt of whiskers. He hadn't touched a razor since the day he'd walked away from Bensler three weeks ago. "Hey, Auntie."

Helen's gaze scanned him up and down. "I can't remember the last time I saw you dressed in something other than a suit."

His mother interrupted. "Is somebody dead or bleeding?"

It was an age-old question, one to which she already knew the answer. Jake wouldn't have greeted her with a smile if his visit heralded bad news, and both of them knew that. "No, ma'am. Not that I know of."

She whirled around and headed back toward the car. After a few steps, she stopped. "No, I'm not dumping this on my sister, too." Glancing over her shoulder, she said, "Helen and I have a business meeting up at the lodge shortly. You and I will speak afterward. Watch for our visitor's arrival and departure, and then I'll expect you at the lodge. Helen? Shall we go?"

Mom spared Jake not another glance as she returned to the car and climbed into the passenger seat. After sending a little shrug toward him, Helen joined her sister, and the Honda crossover she drove continued toward the lodge. Jake stood staring after them, rubbing the back of his neck. That went well.

He had known she might not be thrilled to see him, but he hadn't expected outright rejection. Apparently, time and the Colorado winter hadn't chilled her temper as much as he had hoped.

Jake busied himself stacking wood for a campfire, and with every log he placed, his annoyance grew. This wasn't right. She shouldn't have gone off on him that way. They'd left her alone for more than four months. He wasn't doing anything wrong by checking on her.

"Glad you want to speak to me, Mom," he muttered. "I have a few things to say to you, too."

The sound of an approaching vehicle reached his ears, and he glanced up to see a white truck headed in his direction. As it passed, he read the logo on the side panel aloud. "Granite Mountain Construction."

Okay, then. A contractor. He'd wondered why he hadn't seen any sign of renovation activity around the place when he'd arrived late last night. Last he'd heard from Brooke, who had heard it from Aunt Helen, the project was going well. Admittedly, Jake hadn't spoken with anyone in the family about Raindrop Lodge in a while, but he'd had no reason to think the project had never begun.

He'd come to Colorado to see how his mother was doing. He'd wanted to view the progress of her project. However, unlike his sisters, he hadn't really been worried about her. Once he'd moved beyond the shock of her decision to move to Colorado, he could see how it might be a good thing for her. His mom had really missed Aunt Helen. While he wished she would have made her move in a less spectacular manner, he'd heard her when she spoke that day in January. This was how she'd needed to make the break. She'd said the things she'd needed to say. He'd heard what she'd said concerning the family.

He just wasn't sure yet how he felt about all the things he'd heard about himself. *You are not your father. Who are you?*

Jake shook off the memory and moved around to the side of the cabin, where he had a better view of the lodge. He watched the contractor's truck stop and a long-legged man climb down from the cab. Mom and Aunt Helen descended the wide front steps of Raindrop Lodge to greet him. The guy shook Aunt Helen's hand.

He gave Jake's mom a hug.

Jake decided the time had come to break his business meeting moratorium. He headed for the lodge.

His first thought upon entering the building was that his mother had made a huge mistake. The interior pictures of the lodge that he had found on the Internet had not

shown the extent of the neglect. A second glance caused
him to think that this might be exactly what his mother
needed. She'd always been a project-oriented person. He
could see her sinking her teeth into a renovation like
this one.

Jake followed the sounds of voices and found the trio in
the lodge's kitchen. The two women fired off rapid instructions while the man took notes on a yellow pad. Mr. Granite
Mountain Construction saw him first. He wasn't quite able
to hide the flash of dismay that crossed his face, and Jake
instantly grew suspicious. Did he view Jake as a competitor?
A competitor for what? Or whom?

Mom saw him and scowled. "Jake, we just got started."

"I know. I thought I'd take the meeting with you."

"That's not necessary."

He extended his hand toward the contractor and yanked
his managing director's smile out of mothballs. "Jake
Prentice."

"Ross Hopkins." Light dawned in Hopkins's eyes while
the two men exchanged a firm handshake. "Prentice. You're
related to Vivie?"

Vivie?

"My son." Mom's voice sounded anything but pleased.
"He's visiting from Texas. It'll be a brief visit." She tore her
gaze away from Jake and smiled sweetly at her contractor.
"He has a demanding job."

Vivie. Thrown completely off his game, Jake took a moment
to form a response. "Actually, I don't. I quit my job."

Now it was his mother's turn to stand around looking
dumbfounded. As she so often did, Aunt Helen played savior
and stepped into the fray. "Ross is one of the contractors
we're considering for our renovations. Jake, you're welcome

to tag along while we discuss our vision, but you need to keep your lips zipped. Your opinions are neither solicited nor desired."

"But I can—"

"Jake, those are the terms."

"Okay. Got it."

Aunt Helen shifted her stare to Mom. "I think that's about all we had for the kitchen. Let's show Ross the guest rooms now, shall we?"

Jake shoved his hands into his pockets and trailed after the trio. For the next forty minutes, he busied himself biting his tongue. Only a supreme effort at self-discipline kept him from adding his two cents about everything from the lighting upgrades the contractor suggested to the way he shortened Jake's mother's name.

He did manage to piece together a few details about the renovation delay from the conversation that took place around him. He was curious about this Throckmorton fellow and the hold his family maintained on the land around here. Too bad the Prentices couldn't have done a similar thing with the Lonesome River Ranch. Maybe some of their family drama could have been avoided.

By the time Ross from Granite Mountain Construction took his leave, Jake had a list of questions a mile long to ask his mother. Top of the list was Vivie. However, cooling his heels during the contractor meeting had given him time to think rather than simply react, so he waited to take his cues from his mother.

It proved to be a good decision. As soon as the door to Raindrop Lodge closed behind Hopkins, she turned and walked toward him, her big green eyes soft with concern, her arms open wide. Mom was ready for her hug.

Jake closed his own eyes and gave himself a moment to bask in the warm comfort of his mother's embrace. He murmured in her ear, "I've missed you, Mom."

"Oh, Jake." She had a bit of a hitch in her voice as she said his name. She squeezed him a little tighter, then released him and stepped back. "You quit your job? Honey, what happened? Are you all right? You're not sick?"

"I'm okay. I'm fine. I'm not sick."

"Did you move to a new firm?"

"No. It's a long story. How are you?"

"I'm good."

"You're different."

"How so?"

"Well, for one thing...Vivie?"

She waved that away. "That was just something I tested. I'm not sticking with it."

"Your hair is longer."

"So is yours. A beard, Jake? I didn't think you liked wearing a beard. You always said whiskers made your skin itch."

He shrugged. "I've been testing, too."

"Talk to me, son. Tell me about your job and why you're here."

He nodded. "I will, but it's a bit of a long story."

"We have another contractor meeting at five," Aunt Helen piped up. "Do I need to cancel it?"

"No," Jake said. "It's not *that* long of a story, but I could use a beer while I tell it. I have Shiner in my cooler and wood stacked for a campfire. How about we do this in front of my cabin?"

"That would be the one in which you are trespassing?" Aunt Helen drawled.

"Yep." He winked at her. "Cabin 1."

"I could use a beer myself," his mother said. "I trust you have more than one?"

Jake's eyes widened. He'd seen his mother drink beer maybe twice in his entire life. "I have a six-pack."

"Don't suppose you have any champagne?" Aunt Helen asked. "If I'm going to day-drink before a business meeting, I might as well go all out."

"No, sorry."

Mom shot her a glare. "It's one beer."

Aunt Helen gave an innocent shrug, then suggested, "Why don't y'all head on down to the cabin so Jake can get that fire going ASAP? I need to visit the ladies' room and return a quick phone call. But don't spill any of the beans before I get there. I'll be quick, I promise."

Mother and son shared a look, and Jake said, "All right, Auntie."

During the five-minute walk down the hill to the cabin, which he'd found unsecured upon his arrival late yesterday, Jake and his mom made small talk. She asked him when he'd left Austin and how he liked driving a pickup compared to his BMW. He asked her if she'd enjoyed the snow as much as she'd anticipated and whether or not she'd read the recently published novel in a fantasy series they both read. They discussed their plot predictions until Jake succeeded in getting a nice little campfire blazing.

Gravel crackled beneath Aunt Helen's tires when she pulled up in front of the cabin. Jake carried two rocking chairs from the porch to set around the fire for the women. He passed out a round of Shiner beer, then took a seat on the camp stool included in his own gear and prepared for the inquisition. He would have liked to quiz his mother first, but he knew he'd be wasting his breath.

She crossed her legs, folded her hands, and asked, "Well, let's hear it."

He went with his fastball, a pitch he honestly didn't know he had until he threw it. "I'm trying to figure out who the hell I am."

Her brow wrinkled. It obviously blew by her.

Jake could take comfort in that since he'd damned sure surprised himself. "You had some hard things to say along with Sunday dinner in January, Mom. I've been chewing on them."

"I didn't tell you to quit your job!"

"That's true. You didn't. Quitting was all my idea, and I'm glad I did it." Jake quirked a grin. "It's the one thing I'm certain about today."

"So tell us what happened."

He did, beginning with the layoffs and ending with his resignation. His mother, being his mother, zeroed in on one particular piece of the story.

"The pie girl? You're still seeing the pie girl?"

"I haven't been seeing Tess. We never dated."

"Why not?"

"She was my employee."

"That's a lousy excuse. You fired her six months ago."

"Yeah, well." Jake shrugged. He hadn't dated anyone in the past six months. "She's been traveling a lot with her new job."

"That's a shame."

Yes, it was. The bigger shame was that he hadn't known about it until she'd told him.

In the relatively short Uber ride from her office to his, he'd examined his recent romantic life and realized he hadn't had sex in over eight months. He was thirty-four years old, and his libido was MIA. Or would that be MII—Missing in Inaction? Whatever, it was AWOL, and he hadn't even noticed. How sad was that?

To his relief, quitting his job appeared to have fixed the problem because he found himself thinking about sex often. Come to think of it, he thought about Tess Crenshaw quite often these days, too. Maybe he'd give her a call soon, see where in the world she was at the moment. Tell her his news.

"So what have you been doing since you quit?" Aunt Helen asked. "It's been, what, two weeks? Have you been playing a lot of golf?"

"Almost three." Jake hesitated. He'd rather not tell them, but he'd never been able to lie worth a damn to his mother. "Haven't played golf. Mainly, I've been binge-watching TV."

Mom asked, "You've been doing what?"

He shrugged. "I finally watched *The Wire. Breaking Bad. Game of Thrones.* A few other shows. Now I'll have something to contribute during pop culture discussions for a change."

His mother and aunt shared an incredulous look. Aunt Helen said, "You binged? But you don't watch TV."

"I did for the past couple of weeks. I realized when I was starting the sixth season of *Friends* that I needed to get out of the house."

"I can't believe you watched *Friends.* You didn't want to watch *Friends* when you were growing up."

"That's because Willow and Brooke were so into it. I couldn't admit to liking it. Anyway, that's when I decided it was time to make a trip to the mountains. So here I am. That's enough about me. Tell me about you. Fill in the deets you haven't shared in any e-mails. I want to hear all about life in Lake in the Clouds."

His mother lifted the Shiner to her mouth and studied him while she took a slow sip. Jake had a pretty good idea about what was going on in her head right about now— the same things that had launched her out of Aunt Helen's car when she first saw him earlier today. Mom had flat out told all four of her children that they needed to wait for an invitation before they came to visit her.

Well, they'd all waited. They'd all worried. They'd respected her wishes.

They'd given her since January.

Now she was deciding whether to read him the riot act for showing up uninvited or give him a pass due to the special circumstances that had led to his visit.

If she went the riot act route, he was ready to fire back. He hoped it wouldn't come to that.

She lowered her bottle. "Life is good. I'm settled in the new house, and I've met some lovely people. Making friends. Staying busy. We're looking forward to getting started on this project."

Whew. "It's a great property, Mom. The views from here are spectacular."

"I think Raindrop Lodge has a lot of promise."

"So this meeting today with the contractor, I take it you haven't already hired him?"

"No. We invited three companies to bid on the contract."

"You know, I'd be happy to look over—"

"Thank you, but no." His mother stood up. "Helen and I have this project under control. In fact, we should get back up to the lodge. Our five o'clock appointment will be here soon. You should run into town, Jake. The tourist center on the square downtown is open until seven. They have a pamphlet that lists all the outdoor amenities of the area, but

I recommend you check out the trails on Granite Mountain. I know you'd enjoy hiking the alpine trail. You'd need to get an early start, but tomorrow's weather forecast is perfect for it. I did one of the easy trails in December, and it afforded me an excellent opportunity to think and reflect."

"I don't know, Mom. I'd be afraid I'd go home and give away all my furniture."

"Very funny." She handed him her empty beer bottle. "I'm free for dinner tomorrow night if you want to plan that. Send me a text once you figure out your schedule. How long were you planning on staying, Jake?"

"Well, that's open-ended at the moment."

"I see. Well, you're welcome to stay here until Helen and I leave on our trip. I'm glad you came this week, because next week you'd have missed us. That would have been a shame."

"A trip? Where are you going?"

Aunt Helen watched her sister closely as she tipped her bottle of Shiner to drain the final sip.

"Europe," Mom said, both her smile and her tone bright as the sunshine reflecting off the surface of the lake. "Salzburg. We're off on the *Sound of Music* tour we've promised ourselves since we were girls."

Aunt Helen swallowed her Shiner wrong and started to cough.

Eleven

St. Pete Beach, Florida

TESS SAT IN HER pajamas on the balcony of her beachfront hotel room, sipping a cup of chamomile tea. The soft rolling rumble of the surf as it washed ashore provided music for the evening. Light from the three-quarter moon reflecting off the water painted the masterpiece for her eyes.

It was late, and she had an early morning. She should go inside and get to sleep, but she didn't have the self-discipline to call an end to this last night she had in Florida. She loved Texas. She loved Austin. Despite all that city life had to offer, what was missing were moments like this where Mother Nature fed the soul.

She heard a faint ding that signaled an incoming text on her phone. She ignored it until she realized it could be an alert about tomorrow's flight from the airline. Maybe a flight delay. Checking now might mean an extra hour's sleep in the morning. "Hey, a girl can dream, can't she?"

She unfolded from her chair and then picked up her

phone from beside the bed where she had it plugged into the charger. She read the text first. Are you available for a phone call?

Not the airline obviously. Her gaze rose to the contact at the top of the screen, and her eyes bugged. "Jake Prentice?"

Why would Jake Prentice want to call her at—Tess glanced at the bedside clock—eleven seventeen Texas time on a Tuesday night?

Only one way to find out.

She carried the phone back to the balcony, took her seat, and texted back. "Yes."

Twenty seconds later, her phone rang. Jake. "Hello."

"Hey."

"This is a surprise."

"I'm not catching you at a bad time? You are somewhere you can talk?"

"I am. Actually, I'm sitting on a beachfront balcony watching the moonlight play on the Gulf of Mexico."

"Oh yeah? You down in Galveston? Or Port A?"

Port Aransas, Tess knew. "No, I'm looking in the other direction. I'm in Florida. St. Pete Beach."

"Nice." Following a moment's pause, he added, "Guess I should apologize for the late call. It's after midnight there."

"No need to apologize. I wouldn't have responded to your text if I wasn't awake and happy to talk. What's up?"

"I'm actually staring at the moonlight on water, myself tonight, and I got to thinking about you. I wanted to thank you."

"Thank me," she repeated. "For what?"

"Listening to my ramblings last month. I went back to the office and quit."

"Quit what?"

"My job. I gave it to Stephanie Watson. Now I'm in Colorado keeping warm at a lakeside campfire."

"You quit Bensler? Seriously?"

"I did."

"Wow. It was obvious something was up that day you stopped by my office, but I didn't believe you'd actually quit. Where did you move to? Barton's?" She named Bensler's chief competitor.

"No. I didn't go anywhere. I'm not working. I'm taking an extended vacation while I decide what to do next."

"In Colorado."

"A place called Lake in the Clouds. My mother moved here after Christmas."

"She moved? As in permanently? She sold that gorgeous Victorian?"

"She did." Jake told Tess the story of Epiphany Sunday at the Prentices'. "Since I had time on my hands, I decided to pay a visit and check out her new world."

"Wow. When y'all make a decision, you go all in, don't you?"

Jake laughed. "I guess we do. Maybe that's part of the reason why it takes us so long to make up our minds to act as a rule. I think my mom simmered for years before she blew. I know I'd been unhappy at Bensler for a while."

"I'll bet you can tie it to Paul Franklin's start date. You gave his changes a fair shot, Jake."

"I did. I have no regrets about leaving. So tell me about your job. What are you doing in Florida? When are you going home?"

Tess told him about the pitch she'd made to the city earlier that day and the four-day conference she'd attended in Orlando that had ended on Sunday. "I'm getting a little tired of the traveling, to be honest. It's a lonely way to live. I fly home tomorrow morning, but I'm not in Texas long. I'm actually headed up your way next week. I have three days of meetings in downtown Denver."

"Oh yeah? Are you free for dinner? I'm driving my mother and aunt to the Denver airport. I'd love to take you to dinner."

"Oh, well, sure. That would be nice. I don't have any dinner plans yet. What night will you be in town?"

"You know, I'm not exactly sure when their flight leaves. What night are you free?"

"Tuesday or Wednesday or Thursday. I'll fly home on Friday. I quit taking evening flights after getting stuck overnight in airports twice in February. Which reminds me, I need to book my return flight."

"You don't have a return flight?"

"Not yet."

"Don't book one. Come up to Lake in the Clouds for the weekend, let me show you around. In fact, you should tack on a few days of vacation. Recharge your batteries."

Tess gave a little laugh. "Oh, I can't do that."

"Why not? There's a ton of stuff to do. Hold on, I have a pamphlet around here somewhere."

Tess heard some creaks and shuffles and thunks, then he continued, "It's too dark. I can't find it. But there's fishing and hiking and climbing and biking. Four wheeling. White water rafting. Birding. Parasailing."

"I'm not going parasailing."

"Chicken."

"You already said birding."

He laughed. "I'll check with my mom tomorrow about their flight and get back with you about dinner, all right? Promise you'll hold off on booking your flight?"

"Well..."

"Great," he said, as if her "Well" had been a "Yes." "Now, it's getting late in Colorado, so it's really late in Florida. I should hang up and let you get some sleep. I'll call you tomorrow. What time is your flight?"

"Early. I land in Austin at noon."

"Ouch. I'll call tomorrow afternoon. Good night, Tess. Sleep well. Safe travels."

"Good night, Jake."

Tess lowered her phone from her ear and stared at her recent calls screen in wonder. Yes, it really said Jake Prentice. And he'd really asked her out to dinner. Dinner in Denver. And then he'd invited her to spend the weekend with him in the mountains.

Nothing about the invitation had made it sound like a business dinner. Maybe it was a thank-you dinner. He'd said he'd called to thank her. But the call had sounded like more than a simple thank-you. They'd talked. That parasailing and birding exchange had felt like flirting to her. So maybe the invitation was a date. Except he hadn't called her planning to ask her to dinner. It was just a coincidence that they were both going to be in Denver at the same time. Yet he was making an effort. The Denver Airport was a long way from downtown. She thought she could legitimately consider this a dinner date. On Tuesday, Wednesday, or Thursday of next week in Denver. With Jake Prentice.

If he didn't ghost her and actually called her tomorrow and set the date like he said he would. He could ghost her. This could have been a late-night drinking call.

He hadn't sounded like he'd been drinking.

Well, she'd find out tomorrow. Tess glanced at the time and winced. No, later today. This afternoon. Either he'd call, or he wouldn't. Either she'd have a dinner date in Denver next week, or she wouldn't.

She drifted off to sleep with a smile on her face and visions of *GQ* Jake floating through her dreams.

~*~

Genevieve set her alarm for the first time in forever since she had to do some research before making a call to her travel agent. Luckily, Helen had proven to be Johnny-on-the-spot last night with the travel wish list folder she kept on her phone. Following their meeting with Independence Construction, the sisters had been able to sketch out a broad itinerary of where they wanted to go. When Helen dropped her off last night, Genevieve had promised to have arrangements made by the time they met the third and final contractor candidate at Raindrop Lodge this morning at ten.

She'd spent two hours on the Internet checking websites, making lists, and every so often, giggling out loud. They were going to do this. She and Helen were going to Salzburg. No dilly-dallying. No more maybe next year. No scheduling around doctor's appointments or volunteer commitments and absolutely no having to be home to bake a cake for someone's birthday. *Just call me Ms. Spontaneous.*

This was so not her. Not the old her, anyway. And the new her, well, she was still a work in progress, wasn't she? But somehow, making this spur-of-the-moment decision felt like a much bigger change than the hairstyle and jewelry. Spontaneity was an internal change, where the hair and house were external. Inner change wasn't something one bought off the rack.

"Progress," she murmured. "Baby steps, but steps."

Of course, her children would argue that selling the
house and moving to the mountains were the opposite of
baby steps, but then her children didn't understand. In all
honesty, how could they? She was still trying to figure it all
out herself.

But she'd be doing that figuring while singing "Do-Re-
Me" in the Alps! Grinning, Genevieve pulled her address
book from her desk and flipped to the page listing her
travel agent's contact information. Before she could dial the
number, Helen called. Genevieve put her phone on speaker.
"Good morning."

"Genevieve, I had the wildest dream. I dreamt you told
Jake that you and I are going to Austria next week."

"Aren't you Ms. Comedy Central this morning?"

"Maybe. I just need you to reassure me that you didn't
sleep on it and change your mind."

"I didn't sleep on it and change my mind. In fact, the more
I think about it, the happier I am with the timing of the trip.
It gives Jake a deadline to leave town."

"As thrilled as I am about jetting off to Salzburg, you
don't need to leave town in order to get your son to do the
same. I doubt Jake is planning to take up residence in your
basement, Genevieve. He's not the type."

"Nor is he the type to quit his job and grow a beard and
play Goldilocks in a mountain cabin without an invitation.
But I'm not worried that he'd outstay his welcome. I'm
worried that if he hung around Lake in the Clouds very long,
I'd start to worry."

"About what?"

"Take your pick. Jake's job. Willow's secrets. Lucas's
dashed dreams. Brooke's marriage. If I start to worry about
one thing, I won't stop. It's like eating vanilla wafers. You

say I'll just have one, maybe two. First thing you know, half the box is gone. This letting-go business isn't as easy as it seems, Helen."

"I never thought it was easy, honey."

"It was easier when I was angry. Now that the red haze is starting to clear, well, it'd be easy to dive into the cookies. I've worked too hard to blow my diet at this point. Jake is an adult. It is his life. These are his decisions to make, and he'll make them—without me worrying about it. Which brings up another point. The trip isn't just about Jake. It's my girls and those daily phone calls. They have to stop pestering you, and I know how to make it happen."

"An eight-hour time difference?"

"That will be a big assist in breaking that habit. I'll also ask them to stop when I call them tonight to tell them about our trip."

"Oh, Genevieve." Approval rang in Helen's voice. "I'm so glad."

"I'm stronger now. I'm ready."

"Good for you."

"Now, enough about my kids. I'm thrilled at the idea of finally seeing Salzburg, Helen. It's a great time for us to go. Whichever contractor we choose is going to need a little time to work our project into his schedule. This will be downtime for Raindrop Lodge. Plus, we can go antiquing while we're there and legitimately write part of the trip off of our taxes."

"I do like the idea of that, and I'm not arguing against Austria. Not at all. I can't wait. I just wanted to make sure you weren't having second thoughts this morning so that my high-flying hopes didn't go splat against the cliff face of Granite Mountain."

"No second thoughts. Now let me get off the phone, so I can book our tickets before I speak to my son again. If he asks me any more questions about the trip and you're not there to deflect, he'll know I was travel planning on the fly."

"Will do. See you at ten thirty."

Genevieve reflected on her conversation with her sister, spent some time on the phone with her travel agent, then showered and dressed. She stood in front of her closet for a few more minutes than usual, debating which version of Genevieve she wanted to be today. She hadn't missed Jake's surprise yesterday at the changes she'd made to her look. Maybe she should dress a little more conservatively today. It might reassure him and help ease him on down the road.

Yesterday she'd felt like celebrating spring when she'd pulled clothes from her closet. Today she had nuns on her mind. Humming "Climb Every Mountain," she decided on black jeans, a black long-sleeved chambray shirt, and a sleeveless puff vest in snowy bright white that she would shed as the weather warmed. She donned her black hiking boots and finished tying the laces just as her travel agent called with the happy news that their flights, hotel, and most important, *Sound of Music* private tour guide were booked. Genevieve and Helen would depart a week from Thursday. Their return remained open-ended.

Excited about the trip and chastising herself for putting it off for so long, Genevieve paid little attention to her surroundings as she stepped outside to water the flowers that she'd planted over the weekend in two large pots she'd placed on either side of her front door. Everyone had told her she was foolish to put out annuals this early here in Lake in the Clouds, but for Genevieve, spring wasn't spring without pots of geraniums on her front porch. She'd put a frost alert app on her phone and planted her flowers. Guess now she'd have to sacrifice her geraniums to the vacation gods or hire a neighbor kid to tend to them.

Her mind on the upcoming travels, Genevieve picked up the end of the garden hose. She turned the spigot, then adjusted the spray head to achieve an appropriate stream of water pressure and set about tending her flowers. She and Helen would probably be a few weeks early for prime flower season in Austria, too. Not that it would matter. Salzburg was bound to be beautiful any time of year. She wondered if it had a rainy season.

Genevieve's thoughts drifted to the scene in the movie when a thunderstorm sends the frightened Von Trapp children scurrying to Maria's bed. Genevieve was softly singing about raindrops on roses and kitten's whiskers when a male voice spoke directly behind her. "I like crisp apple strudel myself."

"EEK!" she squealed, whirling toward the noise.

Water from the hose in her hand soaked the blue chambray shirt of a stranger who frowned down at himself and said, "Well, *that's* not one of my favorite things."

She had to look twice to assure herself that this wasn't Kevin Costner straight off the set of the television show *Yellowstone*. He had the hat, the worn blue jeans, the scuffed boots. The chiseled cheekbones and sky blue eyes. The entire movie star package.

So why was a celebrity look-alike sneaking up on her porch before 9 a.m. on a Wednesday morning in May?

"I am not going to apologize. You frightened me."

"I apologize, Ms. Prentice. I didn't mean to sneak up on you. I got distracted. You have a lovely singing voice. If you will spare me a few moments of your time, I need to speak with you."

Genevieve held the water hose at the ready. As defensive weapons went, it was better than nothing, though she didn't know why she'd need a weapon on a sunny spring morning in small-town Colorado. She glanced toward the street, where she saw an extended cab pickup truck parked in front of her mailbox. His, obviously. She took a cautious step backward toward her front door.

Her tone a little sharper than normal, she asked, "Have we met?"

His brow furrowed. He appeared confused. "You don't know me?" At her blank look, he continued, "Well…apparently you don't."

At that, his lips lifted in a slow grin. Genevieve looked a third time to make absolutely certain he wasn't Kevin Costner.

He stuck out his hand. "Gage Throckmorton. We exchanged a few e-mails about the Mirror Lake property."

Out of habit more than anything, she accepted his handshake. Then his words finally pierced the mush in her mind.

"Oh. Oh!" She released his hand, all but snatching it back, saying, "The sale has closed. It's too late now. Don't try to tell me there's a problem now!"

"There is no problem." He held up his hands, palms out. "I just need to talk to you. I have a favor to ask, and I need to do it somewhere away from prying eyes. In this town, that can be a difficult place to find. Will you invite me inside, Ms. Prentice?"

"I don't know."

"Will you at least put down your weapon?"

"My what?"

He gazed pointedly toward the water hose.

She didn't know that she wanted to do that. She didn't feel

all that kindly toward him. Gage Throckmorton had been a thorn in her side for weeks. She wouldn't turn him away, but she wasn't going to be too hospitable. "Do you know what time it is?"

He shot his cuff and checked his watch. "Nine sixteen."

"I need to leave here in forty-five minutes." Sighing heavily, she motioned him inside. "There's a powder room beneath the stairs with towels you can use to dry your shirt. There's a coffee bar in the kitchen. Make yourself at home. I'll be in when I finish watering my flowers."

"We're going to have a freeze tonight."

Genevieve's smile was pure saccharine. "I plan to light smudge pots like they do for the orange groves in Florida."

His lips twitched with a grin, but he nodded and stepped into her house.

Genevieve took twice as long with her flowers as she needed. A favor? Gage Throckmorton wants to ask her a favor? Of all the nerve!

What could he possibly want?

It probably had something to do with yesterday's meeting with Independence Construction. Was he going to bribe her to give his son the contract? Was he going to threaten her in some way? Zach Throckmorton had impressed her last night. He'd gone out of his way to assert his independence from the Triple T Ranch operations.

And yet his father wanted to speak with her away from prying eyes. Hmm. Well, this should be interesting. She might need to teach the man a lesson about letting go. Not that she was much of an instructor. Perhaps they could discuss a twelve-step group.

Genevieve inhaled a bracing breath of crisp mountain air and stepped into her home.

Twelve

HE SAT AT HER kitchen table with a mug of steaming coffee in front of him. He'd removed his blue shirt and wore only a plain white undershirt. She glanced toward the laundry room, where she heard the sound of her dryer running.

"You told me to make myself at home, Ms. Prentice," he explained.

"That I did." She crossed to the coffee bar and made herself a cup. "Call me Genevieve. Or Gen."

"I'm Gage." While she waited for it to brew, he said, "Nice views from this spot on the mountain."

"Yes. That's one of the main reasons why I bought this house. It fits the name of this town. It's like living in the clouds." She brought her coffee to her table and took a seat across from Gage Throckmorton. "So what is this all about? Why show up at my house out of the blue at daybreak? If you had something important to discuss with me, why didn't you e-mail me or phone me to make an appointment?"

"I'm a rancher, Genevieve. It's calving season. This is the

middle of the day for me. I didn't call or e-mail because apologies should be made face-to-face."

"This is about an apology?"

"That's part of it, yes. The first part. I need to apologize for the, um, misunderstanding we had during the approval of the Mirror Lake property. I handled that whole thing poorly."

Genevieve folded her arms. "Misunderstanding? You tried to play raptor and swoop in at the last minute and destroy our deal using fine print so tiny that a gnat with twenty-twenty vision couldn't read it, and you used a four-year-old bully's justification for doing so. It was big-city business hidden by small-town camouflage, and it would have worked were my sister not a legal eagle herself."

"Whoa. You've been storing that one up, haven't you? Your sister is one smart cookie. I'd try to hire her, but I understand she's retired."

"Something tells me you're not very experienced when it comes to making apologies, Mr. Throckmorton."

"Gage." He sighed. "Yes. You're right. I'm making a hash of this, aren't I? All right, then. Allow me to start over. I am sincerely sorry for the way I treated you and your sister during your purchase of the Raindrop Lodge property. It was poorly done. I regret it. I apologize for my actions and for the unnecessary stress they caused you. If at this time you believe the check for damages, which was conveyed to you at closing, isn't sufficient, I will be happy to take another look at the numbers." He paused a moment, then asked, "Was that better?"

"Yes. The money bordered on overkill, though."

"Oh yeah? How come?"

"I've done my research on you. You're not a man to give

away money for no good reason. The fact you're dangling more now adds the scent of desperation."

"Dang it." He sighed and closed his eyes. "I knew better. I have lost all faith in my own instincts of late. It's these kids of mine. I can't seem to do anything right where they are concerned. They make me doubt that the sun rises in the east and sets in the west."

Kids? Genevieve was intrigued. She couldn't help herself. She took a sip of her coffee, then asked, "Kids?"

"My children." He muttered words beneath his breath that she couldn't hear but thought were probably curses. "I don't do this. I never talk about private, personal matters. Of course, you live in a small town, and your dirty laundry hangs on the line in the backyard for everyone to see, but it's not my way to call attention to it with words. In this particular case, that practice of mine has only made things worse, so I guess I'll just lay my dirty laundry out here on this pretty table of yours. Figuratively speaking, of course. I'm rude, but not disgusting. Is that all right with you, Gen?"

She shrugged. "You've already involved my clothes dryer, so we have a theme. Go for it."

He tossed back a sip of coffee as though it were a shot of whiskey, then said, "The Raindrop Lodge property had been on the market for a long time with little serious interest ever shown in it. As a result, certain people who were passionately entrenched upon opposing sides of a local issue had been able to avoid confronting the problem. Your offer changed the paradigm, and my family went to war. My interference in your deal was part of my attempt to bring an end to the Throckmorton family feud."

Family feud? The man was speaking her language.

"Unfortunately, I not only treated you and your sister

poorly, I made my own family matters worse. As of today, my family is estranged from one another. The only thing my three children agree upon is that they want nothing to do with me."

"Oh, Gage."

He gave her a wry smile. "They're a hardheaded bunch of pups. I say they take after their mother's father. She always said they take after me."

Genevieve glanced down at the worn, simple gold band on his left hand. "Is she taking sides in the feud?"

The wry smile turned bittersweet. "Only from afar, I'm afraid. We lost her last summer. It'll be a year in July. Breast cancer."

It took conscious effort for Genevieve not to lift her hand to her own breast. "I'm so sorry. You have my sincere condolences."

"Thank you. We wouldn't be having this problem if she were still with us. She'd have busted heads and whipped everyone into shape. My wife took care of these types of things when they came up. We are all lost without her."

"How long were you married?"

"Thirty-six years."

"I won't offer platitudes. I hated it when well-meaning people did that to me. I will offer a bit of advice. I learned the hard way that a deceased spouse's shoes can become a destructive pair of heels in a family. Do yourself a favor and get rid of them ASAP, rather than try to fill them. My husband has been gone for two decades now, and my family is still, well, picture a litter of pups fighting over a worn leather slipper."

He shot her a droll look. "Gee. Appreciate the effort to cheer me up."

"My point is that if you honestly did what you thought was best in the situation, then you shouldn't beat yourself up."

"It's an age-old problem. Develop and change, or don't and die. Unbeknownst to me, my son-in-law had been working on a big-money development plan for Lake in the Clouds with a partner who discovered that ancient clause and blanket approval policy in the family trust documents. When they found out you had a contract on Raindrop Lodge, they wanted the sale stopped. As you know, I was out of touch..."

Yes, and why he had to go to Nepal to climb mountains when he had perfectly good mountains here in Colorado, Genevieve couldn't begin to guess. At his age, too!

"And by the time I got word, our veto window had technically elapsed. Stupidly, I tried to help, thinking that it was just one piece of property. A *great* piece of property. I figured we'd secure it first, and then we could tackle the bigger development issue on the backside. The fallout of my getting involved was a family meeting full of shock and betrayal and anger and pain, where pro-development and anti-development factions went to war. That's where we are now."

"Wow. You've reminded me that I'm not the only one with family drama. So, Mr. Throckmorton, I accept your apology. What is the favor you wish to ask?"

He set down his mug, folded his hands, and leaned forward, staring at her intently. "I have gone Switzerland in World War Throckmorton. I am strictly hands-off. That said, I don't think it violates policy to mop up earlier blood spills."

"And Raindrop Lodge is a blood spill."

"Yes, and it doesn't need to be. That's the favor. I

understand that Independence Construction is going to bid on your project. I want you to know that Zach was very deliberate in the name he chose for his construction business. He runs it completely on his own. I have no stake in the business. I have no say in the business. The only reason I know that my son is in the running for your project is because we use the same dentist. I broke a tooth on the same day he had a routine exam, and the hygienist is a pro at extracting information from patients. She's not hesitant to share, either."

"What dentist do you use?" Genevieve asked. Forewarned was forearmed, after all.

He shared the name and continued, "Look, Genevieve. You and I didn't exactly start off on the right foot. I can understand why you would not want to have anything to do with me or mine. That's fair. But Independence Construction isn't mine in any way, shape, manner, or form. Zach intends to succeed on his own merit. He shouldn't fail because of me."

"I'm not sure what you want from me."

"I'm asking that you don't hold my actions against Zach when you evaluate his bid. Let him win it or lose it on his own merits."

Genevieve sat back in her chair. "That's not really a favor. That's being fair."

"Yes, but be honest, Gen. Were you predisposed to be fair to Zach?"

"Maybe not in the beginning, no, but he is a good salesman. He talked his way into a meeting with Helen and me, and he made it very clear that the only tie between the two of you is your last name."

Gage Throckmorton winced. "Ouch."

Her dryer buzzed. He made to rise, but Genevieve moved quicker. "No, I'll get it."

Allowing a stranger into her laundry room implied an intimacy that left her uncomfortable. She removed the shirt from the dryer. A quick scan showed the wet spots had dried. It was warm and soft and smelled faintly of bubblegum. Instincts honed by three decades of motherhood had her checking the front pocket. Yes, gum. Two or three pieces, still in the wrappers, thank goodness. They were soft and melted but not a mess.

She folded the shirt, then carried it to the kitchen. "Did no one ever teach you to check your pockets before doing laundry?"

His brow furrowed. "What?"

"Gum." Genevieve opened her freezer door and set the shirt inside.

He grimaced. "I forgot all about that. Stuck 'em in for my grandson. I'm scheduled to pick him up after school today, so I had to come prepared. We have bubble-blowing contests."

Genevieve grinned at the idea of that. "How old is your grandson?"

"He's six. A first-grader. Bubble-blowing is a recent skill he's acquired."

"That's an important life skill."

He nodded.

"So, World War Throckmorton, to use your term, doesn't include grandchildren?"

"I just have the one. Nicholas. I call him Scamp. His parents have been good about not using him as a weapon." He opened his mouth as if he were going to say more, but then he shut it. "Do you have grandkids?"

"Two. A boy and girl. They're Drew and Emma and live in Nashville."

"That's a long way from Lake in the Clouds."

"It is, though my number of visits won't change from when I lived in Texas. Technology is the savior here. I don't know how I'd bear it without FaceTime and Zoom. I'm able to stay abreast of their day-to-day activities fairly well, but I do envy you having your grandson local."

"Scamp is in Durango. That's more local than Nashville, certainly, but I don't know that I'm any better off than you. It's a custody situation, and while it's good right now, that can change on a dime. Grandparents have to dine on what scraps we are offered."

"You are right about that." Genevieve opened the freezer door, checked his shirt pocket, and decided the gum could use another minute or two of cold. She glanced at the clock on the oven door and confirmed that she was okay on time.

"So, back to Independence Construction," he began.

Genevieve interrupted. "I'm afraid you made a mistake there, Gage."

He went still. "Why is that? My argument wasn't convincing?"

"It was. That's not what I'm talking about. I do not promise Zach's company the project, but I will promise him a fair shot. We decided to give him that yesterday after we met him. He really did do a great job selling himself."

"So what's the problem?"

"Your truck parked in front of my house before nine a.m. this morning. You came here in an attempt to meet me away from prying eyes, right?"

"Yes."

"Do you know who lives catercorner to me?" Genevieve opened the freezer and checked the shirt pocket.

He nodded. "The Jenkinses. Bill and Linda. They own the hardware store in town."

Judging the gum to be safely solid, she removed the shirt from the freezer and emptied the pocket. "You want these, or will you get more before school lets out?"

"I'll get more. What about the Jenkinses?"

Genevieve tossed the gum in her trash can. "Their middle son, Mark, is married to a woman named Sarah."

"Sarah Jenkins. I know. They have a boy Scamp's age. They played T-ball together last summer and…oh. Sarah's sister."

"Yes, your favorite dental hygienist." Genevieve carried his shirt back into the laundry room, where she tossed it into the dryer to heat up for a few minutes.

"Well, just hold on. Linda isn't a gossip. Why would she say anything? It's not like my truck was parked here overnight. That would stir up a hornet's nest for sure because I don't…I haven't…it's way too soon."

Was he explaining, Genevieve wondered, or warning her off?

Gage huffed a little laugh and added, "I guess if I wanted to take WWT nuclear, I could start dating. That'd do it."

"I have four children. The oldest was fifteen when their father died, so I waited five years before I began dating again. In the Prentice family, the explosion skipped atomic bombs and went straight to hydrogen."

Gage shook his head and repeated, "Too soon."

"Your problem isn't Linda, Gage. It's yoga."

"Pardon me?"

"Sarah and her sister pick up Linda and take her to the

nine-a.m. yoga class on Wednesday mornings. They drove by right as you stepped inside my house."

Gage groaned, propped his elbows on the table, and buried his face in his hands. "I don't suppose you waved to Linda before I arrived here this morning?"

"No."

"Great. Just great. You're the beautiful new widow in town. I'm the lonely widower whose kids aren't talking to him. We'll be the scandal of the year by lunchtime."

Beautiful? Genevieve couldn't help but smile as she pulled his toasty warm shirt from the dryer. "We will be fine as long as you and I get our stories straight and have them at the ready when asked. Because somebody will ask, and we'll both be asked and our answers compared. It's a small town."

"This is ridiculous. I didn't do anything wrong. It's just that I promised Zach long ago that I would stay far, far away from Independence Construction, and I recently made a big production about remaining neutral in WWT. My kids wouldn't view my having had this conversation with you as cleaning up my mess. They'd see it as breaking neutrality. Thank you," he added when she handed him his shirt. "Excuse me."

Gage strode from the kitchen, and moments later, Genevieve heard the powder room door shut. She tried to consider the problem at hand, but her thoughts kept drifting back to "beautiful new widow in town." He'd said it so off-hand. What a nice little goose to her ego! She'd be glowing about this one for a while.

It made her want to help him.

Gage returned to the kitchen wearing a scowl on his face and his dry shirt neatly tucked into his jeans. "I swear, some-times I think I would have been better off limiting myself to raising cows and horses and taking kids off the board entirely. I don't have a clue how to spin this conversation, Genevieve."

"I do. We don't spin it. We have a different conversation entirely."

"About what?"

"I have a glimmer of an idea, so let me ask you a few questions to see if I can flesh it out. Did your wife have any special interests here in town? Any clubs or organizations that were especially near and dear to her heart?"

Genevieve could tell by the look on his face that he wanted to know why she asked, but he displayed patience. "She wasn't a clubby sort of woman, but she gave money to everyone who came calling for it. Except for political organizations. She didn't like politicians."

"What about hobbies?"

"She liked to cook. She loved the outdoors. She was a movie buff. Loved old movies. Classic Hollywood films." His expression turned wistful, and his voice thickened a bit as he added, "I had a theater room built onto the house as soon as they became a thing."

"Oh yeah? Huh." Genevieve glanced at the clock again. She needed to leave here in about ten minutes. "Was it widely known? This love for old movies that she had?"

Gage considered the question a moment, then nodded. "Yes, I believe so."

"What did she think of musicals?"

"Oh, she loved musicals. Rogers and Hammerstein especially."

"So she liked *The Sound of Music*?"

"Very much. She was a big Julie Andrews fan."

"Excellent." Genevieve beamed at Gage and picked up the

coffee mugs from the table. "In that case, allow me to quickly summarize the conversation you and I had this morning. I happen to have a passion for old movie theaters, and I've seen too many torn down or fall down due to neglect. A couple of weeks ago, I noticed the For Sale sign in The Strand downtown in Lake in the Clouds. I got my Realtor to show it to me."

"You did? A friend of mine owns that building."

"I imagine you are friends with almost everyone who owns property in town. Anyway, our story is that after our skirmish involving Raindrop Lodge, I wasn't going to get my heart set on anything without knowing if your trust would exercise your veto and rip the rug out from underneath me. This morning we talked about the possibility of my purchasing the theater and renovating it to show classic movies. I share your wife's interest, Gage. Next week my sister and I are leaving on a European trip that includes a *Sound of Music* tour and a ride on the Orient Express between Paris and Vienna. I'm thinking about decorative items I might purchase while I'm in Europe if this project is a possibility."

"But you haven't even begun the lodge renovations," he protested.

Genevieve waved that away. "Doesn't matter. You wouldn't give me the okay because you're Switzerland, and you're not about to jeopardize that. However, the idea caught your fancy because of your wife's love of classic movies, and you had a counterproposal for me. We are going to consider a partnership."

"We are?"

"We are. You want to rename the theater to—what was your wife's name?"

"Emily."

"The Emily. Or Theater Emily. Or The Emily Theater at Lake in the Clouds. Whatever you like. Anyway, this is what we talked about this morning, and we're both going to think about it while I'm away. If I run across appropriate memorabilia while I'm in Europe, I'll likely buy it. I can always have a themed cabin or guest room at Raindrop Lodge."

"The Emily," Gage repeated, a smile ghosting on his face. "I like it. She would have liked it."

"Good." Genevieve brushed her hands. "My work here is done, and you need to leave because I do, too. We are meeting with another contractor shortly."

"Oh yeah? Which one? Doesn't really matter. He's not gonna be as good as Zach."

Genevieve rolled her eyes and walked to her front door, which she opened. Gage Throckmorton smirked and strode through the house toward the entry, where he picked up his hat from the table and placed it on his head. He shook Genevieve's hand. "Nice doing business with you, Ms. Prentice. Give your sister my regards."

"Oh, I'll do that."

"Good." He tipped his hat. "Safe travels, Genevieve. I hope you enjoy your trip."

"Thank you. I'll tell Switzerland you said hello."

She shut the door behind him and quickly gathered up her purse, keys, and notebook with all the travel arrangements so she could share the details with Helen. When she backed out of the garage, she wasn't listening to her *Sound of Music* sound track. Instead, she listened to the original soundtrack album of the motion picture *The Bodyguard* starring Kevin Costner. While Whitney Houston sang "I Will Always Love You," Genevieve pictured the grief on Gage Throckmorton's face as he spoke about his Emily. She'd wanted to tell him that it would get better, that time truly did ease the pain.

Mostly. Never completely. Even after almost twenty years, a wound on her heart remained raw from the loss. "Oh, David. I do miss you."

She sometimes went days without thinking of him. Every now and then, she might even go a week. Other days, she thought about him almost constantly. She'd hear a song that reminded her of him or see something that triggered a memory. Or Lucas would grin. He had his father's grin. And Jake, oh, Jake was David down to a T.

Jake, you are not your father, she'd told him. That was true. Just barely. Especially now that he'd hit his mid-thirties. The way he'd looked yesterday with the beard? Helen hadn't been around that one winter when David grew the beard. Jake could have been his clone.

What would David have thought about her great getaway? He probably would have demanded, "What took you so damned long, Gen?"

Grief. It was such a compound, complex animal. She wouldn't call it an emotion. Actually, "monster" was closer to the right term.

On the car stereo, Whitney sang about bittersweet memories. Genevieve decided that "monster" indeed was an apt term. During the first weeks and months following David's death, she'd known to expect its appearance. Getting through her days had been like touring a haunted house at Halloween. You knew the monster waited just around the corner, ready to leap out and scream and frighten you to tears. But as time marched on, one exited the haunted house, climbed into the minivan, and merged back onto life's highway. That's when the monster grew sneaky. It started hiding behind bushes and lurking in the shadows ready to leap out and call "I'm ba-ack" when you least expected it.

Grief concealed itself beneath an unmarked speed bump that would tear up your chassis if you weren't a careful driver.

Genevieve laughed at herself and said aloud, "You are terrible at metaphors, Genevieve Prentice."

Genevieve thought of Gage Throckmorton and his Emily and his family's WWT. She thought about her own children and the loss of their beloved grandfather, which had precipitated the Prentice family estrangement and her own flight from everything. She thought of David, her first love. Her only love. Her lost love.

She didn't need bad metaphors to define grief. It wasn't that difficult. It wasn't difficult at all. Whitney Houston summed it up in one sentence in the title of this song. Well, actually, Dolly Parton because Dolly wrote the song.

"I Will Always Love You."

Thirteen

JAKE WORKED THE LINE on his fly rod, setting the Woolly Bugger gently onto Mirror Lake. Ripples disturbed the placid surface that reflected a robin's egg sky against snowcapped mountain peaks. Sunrise this morning had been a burst of pink, rose, and gold rays streaking across the sky above and reflected in the glassy expanse of the water stretching out before him.

Standing beside the lake, being part of the moment, Jake had felt small and insignificant, and at the same time, bigger than himself. Which made no sense and fit right in with the rest of where his head was right now. Nevertheless, despite having been skunked as far as fish were concerned this morning, he was glad he'd rolled out of bed in time to be part of the sunrise.

Sunrise. A new day. New beginning. *I'll get this figured out. I always do.*

The morning's gentle breeze whipped across the water, carrying aromas from the campgrounds farther up the lake. Bacon. Jake's stomach answered with a gurgle, and he decided to make this his last cast. A big breakfast sounded appealing.

He headed back to the cabin, changed into his running clothes, and headed out for the diner on the highway, approximately three miles away. He ordered bacon, eggs, and hash browns, then let the waitress and another customer talk him into an order of biscuits and gravy on the side.

He waddled back to the resort property in plenty of time to shower and dress for the appointment at ten thirty.

He probably shouldn't horn in on his mother's meeting this morning. He knew she didn't want him there, and she'd get snippy with him. However, since he was here, what did it hurt? In for a nail, in for a hammer, right? He hadn't opened his mouth during the first two interviews. He didn't plan to in this one either unless she asked for his opinion. Or if he saw them making a huge mistake—something he didn't expect.

Both his mother and his aunt were smart, savvy women, which was why he hadn't disregarded his mother's wishes and traveled to Lake in the Clouds in January as his sisters had wanted him to do. Mom's flight to the mountains might have been out of character, but Aunt Helen was a rock. Jake knew the family could count on her to be there for Mom with whatever support Mom needed.

In hindsight, he recognized that his mother had been a little lost without her sister ever since Helen retired and moved to Colorado. Mom's decision to move shouldn't have caught the family by surprise the way it had. Of course, she'd told them in no uncertain terms why she'd decided to do it. Now that he'd blown up his own life, the "how" of her effort was beginning to make sense to him, too.

For Mom, a decision this huge had required an equally

huge commitment. She'd had to fix it so that there was no turning back.

She'd darn sure succeeded there. Hell, she'd even walked away from her precious dining room table.

He wondered how she'd taken the news from the estate sale company that it, along with all her dishes, had been included in the sales inventory. Had it been the arrow in the heart as his sisters claimed?

It had turned out that the disposal of family heirlooms had been the lone subject on which the Prentice siblings could agree since their grandfather's death. To a person, they figured that Mom would come to regret her decision to give away everything that once had mattered to her so much. They also saw no reason to go through the hassle of dividing things up just to turn around and return them to Mom in a not-to-distant future.

So once the estate sale company had valued everything, they'd pooled their money—equally—and purchased anything one of them believed Mom would want when she came to her senses. It was all in a climate-controlled unit in a storage place Lucas owned.

One thing on Jake's to-do list while in Colorado was to decide if the time was right to tell her about the storage unit. He didn't have a good feel for that yet. What he did feel better about was the potential of the Raindrop Lodge and Cabins Resort property.

Admittedly, he would rest easier once they hired the contractor, and Jake could feel confident that the person knew what he was doing. He'd been impressed by the first two candidates. Might as well check out the third. Mom might not like it. She'd probably get snippy with him, but face it, that's what she would expect him to do. He'd been checking out her hires for almost twenty years.

It all started when Mom contracted with an unethical roofing company to do work on the money pit that had been their Victorian home six months after his father died. As a rule, Mom had good instincts about people and made good hiring decisions, but these crooks had taken her for thousands and thousands of dollars. After that, as a precaution, Jake had made it a habit to do a deep Internet dive on the companies she planned to hire. When he'd discovered potential red flags, he'd let her know. That process had worked for them for years, but lately, his efforts seemed to chafe her. Mom had grown independent.

Now, there was an understatement.

She was a thousand-watt digital billboard for independence. She'd always been courageous. Always honest and steadfast and generous and kind. Mama bear protective of her loved ones. She had a huge heart, those good instincts, and she was smart. But the independence was new. Jake was both frightened and fascinated by the change in his mother.

He'd missed her these past months. He'd come to Colorado because he wanted to talk to her, to share his big professional news, and perhaps ask for her advice. He wanted to get to know this new Genevieve Prentice. He wanted her to know that he'd heard her and accepted the challenge she'd thrown down at their dining room table. Although he hadn't realized it himself until he'd said it.

I'm trying to figure out who the hell I am.

He was surprised to hear a horn honk outside his cabin as he tied the shoelaces on his boots at a quarter past ten. A glance out his window revealed his mother's idling car.

The driver's side window slid down as he hurried outside. "What's up?"

"I saw your truck was here, so I assume you're planning to come to this morning's meeting. Want a ride?"

"I'm welcome?"

"I'm stubborn, but I hope not stupid. Since you're here, and you are going to show up at the meeting anyway, we might as well take advantage of your expertise." She gave a little laugh and added, "You've been developing your remodeling skills since you were eight years old, after all."

Jake snorted. He'd never live that one down. He'd only been trying to help the day he'd decided to start his mother's car and pull it into the garage. He did that. He'd pulled into the garage. Over his dad's golf clubs. Over the lawnmower and through the wall into the kitchen. Luckily, he'd missed clipping the water heater by an inch and a half.

His father had done most of the repairs himself, primarily to have Jake work side by side with him. It was supposed to be punishment. Turned out to be one of the best times Jake ever had with his father, one he treasured to this day.

He climbed into the passenger's seat and told Genevieve about his morning as they drove the short distance up to the lodge. "The sunrises are glorious here. I'm glad you've been able to experience them. You should come enjoy the sunset at my new place this evening. Would you like to join me for dinner? You could bring your stuff and stay there if you don't want to roll out of bed and fish in the morning."

"I would love to have dinner at your new place, Mom." He could make sure she had room for the dining room table and all the dishes. "Thanks for the invitation."

She shifted into park and switched off her engine. "I'll

rescind it and kick you out if you try to butt in during our meeting today."

"Hear you loud and clear, Mom."

She nodded and exited the car. They walked toward the lodge's front steps, but she stopped him with a hand on his arm. "Honey, I wasn't very welcoming yesterday. I'm sorry about that. I am glad to see you."

"That's okay, Mom. I showed up uninvited. Actually, specifically not invited. I anticipated worse."

"You did?"

"When you lay down the law, Mom, you mean it."

"It didn't stop you from coming."

"That's because I'm not here to check up on you."

"Oh really?" she drawled, her tone dripping with doubt. "Why did you come?"

He had a dozen reasons rolling through his mind, but he voiced the one at the top of the list. "I came for a hug."

She chastised him with a look. He drew a cross over his heart with his index finger. She sighed and laughed and gave him another hug. "Oh, Jake."

The third contractor candidate wasn't as impressive as the first two, and his reluctance to commit to the start date Mom and Aunt Helen required should his bid be accepted eliminated him from their consideration. With business mostly out of the way, talk turned to their trip.

"Wait a minute," Jake said, lifting his head from the scope of work document he'd been studying. "Durango to Dallas? You're not flying direct out of Denver?"

"No. The flights were better out of D/FW."

Well, okay. Guess he didn't really need to take his mother to the airport to make the drive to Denver. When he'd first awakened this morning, he'd wondered if he'd dreamed the phone call where he'd volunteered to drive three hundred miles one way for a date with Tess Crenshaw. But by the time he threw his first cast out over Mirror Lake, he knew that the dinner date with Tess was at the top of his certainty list.

Unfortunately, the list contained only two items at the moment, the second one being paying a visit to the local hardware store. That he intended to tackle later today. After listening to a steady drip, drip, drip in the shower of Cabin 1 for the past two nights, he had a shower head to replace. While he was there, he just might go wild and buy new toilet parts, too.

But hey, at least he had a list. It was a start.

"So do you see anything we forgot?" Aunt Helen asked when he'd finished reading the final page of the stack of papers that she'd given him.

"No. You've done a great job."

"Templates rule. Now we wait for bids. In the meantime, I have an appointment to get my hair done I'd best toddle along to. What's on your agenda, Jake?"

"I'm not sure. Mom? Are you free?"

"I can be. What do you have in mind?"

"I picked up a flyer at the tourist center. I was thinking about making the drive up to Inspiration Point. I'd like to see that waterfall. Would you care to come with me?"

"I'd love to, but I'd need to be back by two thirty to meet the drapery installer at the house. That should give us plenty of time, though."

"Sounds good," Jake said.

"I take it the drapes for the guest bedroom finally came in?" Aunt Helen asked.

"Yes. Thank goodness. If, fingers and toes crossed, the installer shows up this afternoon and nothing is wrong with the drapes, I am officially and forever done with Lina Perez."

"Hallelujah. I am so sorry." Aunt Helen explained to Jake, "The interior designer I recommended to your mother proved to be the world's biggest flake."

Mom nodded in agreement. "She has a good eye, but her work ethic isn't worth squat. I don't think she'd recognize the truth if it bit her in the butt. We're going to need to find someone else to work with going forward. But that's a problem for another day. You and I can pick up a picnic lunch on our way out of town, if you'd like. There's a nice spot to eat up there. It's perfect weather."

"Works for me, Mom."

Forty minutes later, a bell chimed as Jake walked into Cloudwiches sandwich shop to pick up the order his mother had called in. She remained in the car, answering a question for Ross from Granite Mountain Construction regarding the bid he was preparing. Inside the restaurant, conversation hummed with the lunchtime crowd. Customers occupied almost all the inside seating, and three people stood in line to order. A tall, gangly teenager wearing a T-shirt with the shop's logo on the front bussed the tables. He nodded at Jake, then asked, "Are you Jake Prentice?"

"I am."

"Thought so. Your order is ready. You can pick it up in the back." He nodded toward the doorway leading into a kitchen and added, "My grandmother wants to meet you."

"Okay. Thanks." Jake walked into the kitchen to see a woman of about Aunt Helen's age standing at a worktable. She had long red hair worn in a neat braid and turned curious amber eyes his way. "You're Jake?"

"Yes, ma'am.

"Aren't you a handsome young man! Welcome to Lake in the Clouds. I feel like I know you already, you and your brother and sisters. I'm Virginia Higgins. My condo is one floor up from Helen McDaniel's, and your mother and I are in the same belly-dancing class. We're like a small family here in Lake in the Clouds."

Belly-dancing class? Jake really didn't need that picture in his head. Well, better than a pole dancing class, he guessed.

"I just adore Genevieve. She told me the two of you are making an unscheduled trip up to Inspiration Point this afternoon when she called in your order. I filled a cooler with some drinks to send along with the sandwiches." She glanced toward the front of the shop, then waved him closer and lowered her voice. "My husband and I hiked the north trail out of the point the day before yesterday, and it was fabulous. It's Triple T land, but Gage Throckmorton allows locals access. Tell your mother that I said the two of you should make the hike today. The snow is all but gone. It's spectacular and not too challenging for someone as athletic as your mom. She'll want to use the walking sticks she keeps in her Land Rover. I stuck a map in with your sandwiches. Some trail mix, too. You'll work up an appetite."

Jake had no idea whether or not his mother would want to go hiking today, but he was game. Besides, Virginia Higgins wasn't somebody he wanted to cross. "Thanks. I'll tell her."

"I hear she and Helen are headed to Europe next week. That's exciting news. I can't believe neither of them mentioned it to anyone before now."

"I gather making the trip has been a last-minute decision. Although it's something that they've talked about for as long as I can remember."

"Well, good for them. They're good people. We are lucky to have them in Lake in the Clouds."

"We miss having them in Texas."

"I'm sure you do. They're going to do great things out at the Raindrop, though I worry a little bit about the finished product now that your mother's gotten crossways with Lina Perez. They'll have to hire a designer from out of the area. I know Lina can be a trial, but at least she'd be able to talk Helen off the ledge about the cuckoo clocks. And now that she's going to Europe and going antiquing in Bavaria, why, I'm afraid what she'll bring back to Colorado for the Raindrop."

Cuckoo clocks. Jake winced. Yes, Aunt Helen did veer strangely out of character when it came to cuckoo clocks. From what he recalled, it had something to do with her first husband.

"Well, that's a worry for another day." Virginia gestured toward a table where a paper bag sat next to a soft-sided cooler. "You and your mom enjoy your afternoon. Take the hike. Take a nap. Sit and reflect. Talk to your mother. Reach out to your brother. Call a friend. The cell reception up there is excellent. Inspiration Point can change your life."

"In that case, we'd better get going." He reached into his pocket for his wallet. "Do I pay at the register?"

"Nope. Lunch is on the house. Your mom picked up drinks after belly-dancing class last week, and I owe her. Tell her we're even now."

"All right, I will. Thanks. It was nice to meet you." Jake picked up the sack and cooler and exited Cloudwiches. He stowed the picnic supplies in the back of the car and slid into the driver's seat as Genevieve was finishing up her call. A different call, he realized, when she spoke his younger sister's name.

He arched his brows and looked at her. She shrugged. "I spoke to you. Didn't seem right to continue the silent treatment with your siblings."

"Good. That's good." Jake started the car and shifted into reverse. Ten minutes later, he was navigating his mother's new Land Cruiser up a twisting, two-lane mountain road. She sat in the passenger seat and answered his questions about life in Lake in the Clouds. He'd already had a general picture of her world from the group e-mails and photos she shared with the family every week, but today she added layers. Having seen Aunt Helen's condo and met the ancient waitress with the beehive hairdo at the diner this morning in addition to Virginia Higgins, he was able to appreciate some of her stories even more than before.

She sounded happy. She sparkled when she shocked him by admitting to buying a snowmobile, and she glowed when she talked about new friends that she'd made in a quilting group.

"Quilting, Mom? You always claimed to hate anything to do with needles and thread."

"I did. I know. I was wrong." She gave a long sigh and added, "I've been wrong about a lot of things. There is something beautiful about taking scraps from the past and piecing them together to create something entirely new. I find it appealing at this time in my life. Not that my work is beautiful. I can't sew a straight line for the life of me, and I prick my finger a lot, but I am learning. Now, enough about me. Tell me about you. I want to hear about you."

Jake thought about Tess. "Well, I haven't taken up quilting, Mom, but I do have a first date on my calendar next week with Tess Crenshaw. She's a scrappy thing, too. I wouldn't be averse to creating something new with her."

His mother's spine snapped straight, and she whipped her head around to pin him with a look filled with yearning, excitement, and delight. "A baby? You want to have a baby?"

Jake almost ran off the road.

~~⚶~~

Tess didn't have to go into the office on a travel day, but it was on the way home from the airport, and besides, she wanted to keep busy. Otherwise, she would sit and twiddle her thumbs while waiting for her phone to ring.

If it rang. If Jake had not awakened and had second thoughts this morning. If he even remembered calling her. He hadn't sounded stoned or drunk last night, but Tess wasn't an expert on stoned or drunk. She could have missed it.

She didn't think she had missed it. She believed he'd been sober and sincere when he had asked her out to dinner. On a dinner date. A date. With Jake Prentice. *Me*.

Holy guacamole.

So to pass the time until her phone rang or didn't ring, she went into the office. She was seated at her desk riffling through her drawers looking for a nail file when her boss walked past her door, stopped, then backed up. "What are you doing here?"

"Hey, Steve. Nice to see you, too."

"You know what I mean." He came into her office and sprawled in one of the two visitor's chairs. "We missed you around here. Didn't expect to see you until tomorrow. How was the flight?"

"I had a talker next to me."

"Oh, Tess. I'm so sorry. I'd rather have a crying baby than a talker."

"I know. You've said that many times. I thought about you often on the flight. The woman seated next to me was on her way to see her first grandchild. She was very excited. It's a little girl. Charlotte Elizabeth. Seven pounds three ounces. Cute baby."

"Did you drink?"

"No. I thought about it, but my car was at the airport."

"Tess, airplane talkers are why God made headphones."

She laughed. "Honestly, I didn't mind. I actually walked out with her because I wanted to witness the big moment and meet the baby myself. It was sweet."

Her boss shook his head. "Just when I think you're all business, you up and surprise me. Is your biological clock ticking? Do we need to plan for that around here?"

"You can't ask me that, Steve. I'll report you to HR."

"We don't have an HR department. We're too small."

Then, because travel fatigue combined with a restless night loosened her tongue, she spoke a truth she ordinarily would have kept to herself as a relative newcomer to the firm. "We are not too small. We're all creatives. I adore you, Steve, and I've learned so much from working with you. Your instincts are fabulous, and your design skills are inspired, but management is not your strong suit. Long term, for this firm to grow and thrive, you need to bring in someone whose skill set is better suited to management than yours. You are a fabulous managing partner, but what Innovations needs to grow to the next level is an experienced CEO."

He scowled at her. "If I was a better leader, I guess I would fire you for being impudent."

"No, you'd promote me for identifying a problem."

"No. You'd get the promotion for *solving* the problem."

Tess's gaze drifted to her phone. The idea that had

been simmering in her mind since yesterday bubbled to the surface, tugging her in two distinctly opposite directions. Goals. Tess had her goals, ones she'd defined years ago and devoted herself to achieving. She would achieve them. The goals were attainable.

But then there were the dreams. Dreams were lovely, ethereal hopes, wishes, and desires. Hard work couldn't make dreams come true. That took luck and angel dust.

Tess's life had been woefully lacking in angel dust.

She'd be a fool to reach for a dream when a goal was in sight. She needed to keep her eyes on the ball. On the goal. On the achievable, the attainable.

"Okay, how about you put your money where your mouth is? Not only will I solve the problem, but I'll also turn the problem on its head. My solution will double our profits within six months, guaranteed."

Steve folded his arms and settled back in his chair. His mouth twisted in a crooked, challenging grin. "Oh yeah?"

"Yeah."

"Just how are you going to do that?"

"See, here's the negotiation part, Steve. For this to work, I need two things." She ticked them off on her fingers. "An executive package suitable to attract an industry whale and, when I land him, a partnership for me."

Now he laughed. "A whale, huh?"

"Get me the package to present to a candidate and a written partnership contingency offer for me."

"You sound awfully confident, Ms. Crenshaw. Who would—" He broke off abruptly. His eyes rounded, then narrowed. "Jake Prentice stopped by here to see you not long ago. What do you know?"

"I'm not going to betray any confidences, Steve."

"Did he ask you about joining us?"

"No. Not at all. That I will say. The subject has never come up."

"But you think...whoa, Tess. All kidding aside, do you honestly have reason to think we could get Jake Prentice to move to Innovations?"

Goals. Dreams. Angel dust. Tess's heart gave a little twist. "I think with the right incentive, yes, we could."

Steve dragged a hand across his chin. "Jake would be a game changer. He's exactly who we need around here."

"I know."

Her boss pushed to his feet. "I'll talk to Chris and Justin. How quickly does this need to happen, do you think?"

"I'll need the offer in hand when I go to Denver next week. He's planning to be there, too." *I hope. If he ghosts me, I'll really be the fool.*

"Prentice is attending the Denver conference? That's unusual."

"No, he's there on personal business, I believe. We're going to have dinner if we can make our schedules work."

"I see. Well, make it happen. Clear your calendar. Cancel the conference if that's what it takes. Take all the time you need. I've gotta go talk to the guys." He paused at the doorway and met her gaze. "If you pull this off, Tess, you'll have earned the partnership."

Take all the time you need. I can do more than dinner. "I know. I want Innovations Design to be a huge success, and I want to be part of it. It's my goal."

"I'll touch base with you after I talk to the others." He gave her a salute, then left her office.

Tess sat back hard in her chair. The sinking in her stomach was not dismay. It was not! She could not mourn something she'd never possessed. It would have been a long shot under any circumstances. It was one dinner date. If he'd had any genuine desire to date her, he'd had plenty of time to ask her out in the past six months. She shouldn't kid herself.

Besides, Jake Prentice might make a great fantasy, but who's to say she'd even like the reality?

It was a legitimate question. How many times in the past had she gone out on a first date with high hopes only to be disappointed? More than she wanted to remember, that's for sure. It was possible that were she ever to get to know Jake on a personal basis, she'd experience something similar.

Tess opened a new file on her computer and began to make notes for her recruitment pitch. If she only managed a bullet list of five points before logging into her favorite department store's website in order to shop for a dress for her dinner in Denver, well, that was a business activity under the circumstances, wasn't it?

Then why was she looking at fun and flirty styles rather than something professional?

She ordered three dresses and two new pairs of shoes from the department store and then surfed to a specialty retailer. She spent over an hour on that site researching outdoor gear. When she checked out, her shopping cart looked like one of her Black Friday hauls.

Jake called at a quarter past three Texas time. Tess drew a deep breath, licked her lips, then answered. "Hello?"

"Hi. Did you make it home safe and sound?"

His warm, friendly voice made her smile. "I did. Well, I'm back in Austin anyway. I decided to stop at the office and dump some files since it's on the way home."

"So you're sitting at a desk?"

"Yes."

"That's too bad."

Tess frowned. "It's a nice desk. In a nice office. In a very nice building."

"I know. Well, I know the building is nice. I haven't seen your office but you were watching moonlight on the Gulf last night, so I couldn't claim bragging rights. Today I can. You should see where I'm sitting, Tess. It's spectacular, a place called Inspiration Point, and it's aptly named. I'll bring you up here if you visit Lake in the Clouds next weekend. Is that going to work for you?"

Tess closed her eyes. So it was happening. He'd called. He hadn't ghosted her. The invitation hadn't been rescinded. *Why did you go and open your big mouth to Steve?*

Because you're a realist, that's why.

But do you have to be real right away? Can't you go with the fantasy for a little while?

That would be stupid. However, that didn't mean that she shouldn't go to Colorado and present her proposal carefully. At the proper time. Toward the end of the visit. However long that visit may last.

"I believe so, yes. I spoke to Steve, and I can get some time off."

"Great. That's awesome. You will love this place, Tess. Right now, I'm sitting on an outcropping of rock overlooking a valley that is green with spring. I can see the whole of Mirror Lake, which is gorgeous. It's as blue as..."

When he didn't immediately complete the sentence, Tess clutched her phone a little more tightly. He wasn't about to say "your eyes." Surely not.

Her eyes were arguably her best feature, prominent and thickly lashed, and a nice color of blue. Ever since boys started taking notice of her, when a guy went searching for a compliment, he'd invariably roll out something about her eyes. Tess wasn't complaining. Praise was always lovely to hear, and she sincerely appreciated kind words from anyone. However, if she'd heard her eyes compared to sapphires or a crystal lake or the ocean or the sky once, she'd heard it dozens—maybe even hundreds—of times.

She'd never heard it from Jake Prentice.

She realized she really wanted to hear Jake Prentice compliment her eyes. She wanted him to tell her that the gorgeous blue lake in Colorado he described reminded him of her gorgeous blue eyes.

Jake's hesitation ended when he declared, "Mirror Lake is as blue as the sleeves on the Dallas Cowboys Cheerleaders uniforms."

Oh. Startled, she laughed, more at herself than at him. "Geez, Prentice. What sort of simile is that?"

"It's a perfectly good one! I drew a vivid picture of beauty with my words, didn't I? Who could argue that a Dallas Cowboys Cheerleader isn't a vision?"

Tess shook her head. This was not the same Jake Prentice who was her boss's boss's boss; that was for certain. He never would have said something like that. "Well, if you're getting away from natural descriptives, I might be more impressed if you said Mirror Lake was as blue as Zac Efron's eyes."

"See, that's what I get for trying to be unique and not sounding like I was using a line from my repertoire. I could have said, 'Mirror Lake is a gorgeous sapphire blue like your eyes,' but I didn't."

Oh! Tess moistened her dry lips. "Because that would sound like a line from your repertoire."

"Exactly. Never mind that it's the truth…"

She closed her eyes and grinned.

"…and as a result, the most obvious comparison to pop to mind when I'm talking to you. It would sound like I'm hitting on you, and I'm not. I wouldn't do that."

"Oh." She opened her eyes and slumped back in her chair.

"My mom is close to being within earshot. We've been hiking together. I don't think she's listening, but just in case, I'm not going to hit on a woman where my mom can hear me do it. That's just wrong."

Oh. She straightened back up.

"Look, I've invited you to spend some time with me at Lake in the Clouds. I'm not going to scare you off by acting like a creeper the moment you say yes, you will join me."

Oh!

"However, now that the subject has been introduced, I probably should go ahead and address it. I want you to know that there are no expectations on this end, Tess."

Oh. She rose to her feet and walked to her office window.

E-I-E-I-O. You are losing your wits, Tess Crenshaw.

"Hopes, maybe," he continued. "Okay, hopes definitely. But primarily, I want to spend time with you. I want to explore Lake in the Clouds together with you. I want to sit here at Inspiration Point and talk with you."

Two short little words bubbled up inside her and escaped before she had the good sense to suppress them. "Why me?"

This time, his hesitation dragged on longer than it had before the Cowboys Cheerleaders comment. Finally, he said, "You'll think I'm dodging the question, but I'm not. I don't have an answer that will make any sense. See, the only answers I have right now are that I want to change the leaking shower head in the bathroom in the cabin I'm staying in and spend time with you. So fair warning. My head is not on straight these days, and I have a feeling that you are the person who can properly adjust the fit."

"Let me repeat. Why me?"

"I don't know. I'm hoping our time together in Colorado will lead to an answer."

Tess propped a hip on the windowsill and stared out at the skyline of downtown Austin. "All of a sudden, this trip feels more important than a vacation."

"I'm sorry. My bad. See, I told you my head isn't on straight. Tell you what, I hereby declare a moratorium on all heavy talk until you are sitting beside me here looking down at Lake in the Clouds."

"'Looking down at Lake in the Clouds' makes it sound like you are up very high."

"We are. The elevation at Inspiration Point is ten thousand one hundred twenty-three feet. So what night do you want to have dinner?"

"You tell me. What works best for you?"

"I'm at your disposal. Turns out that Mom is flying out of Durango, so I'm free to meet you for dinner whichever day of the conference best suits your schedule."

Tess pursed her lips and considered this bit of news. "What other business do you have in the city?"

"Nothing of note, but I can find things to do until your conference ends. I haven't been there in quite a few years."

"So you don't need to go to Denver? You're just making that drive to have dinner with me?"

"And to bring you back to Lake in the Clouds."

"That's ridiculous. I googled it. It's, what, a four-hour drive?"

"That's not a big deal."

"But you don't need to go to Denver," she repeated.

"No, but—"

"Neither do I," she interrupted, taking the plunge. "I'll play hooky and skip the conference. It's not anything very important. I'll fly into Durango, and you can pick me up there. Will that work?"

"Yes. Absolutely yes. Mom leaves on Wednesday. Want to come in then?"

"I can do that. And the return? On Sunday?"

"If you want. Or leave it open ended."

Tess allowed a full fifteen seconds to tick by before she said, "We haven't even been on one date, Jake."

"Not officially, no. But we've known each other for, what, five years? Six? We spent a lot of time together. We've traveled together and attended the same social events. Be honest, Tess. The attraction was always there, humming beneath the surface. Dare I mention the team-building event last spring when I walked you to your cabin?"

"It was dark," she defended. "The coyotes were howling."

"Yeah, well, so was I. You know how close we came to kissing good night at your cabin door."

"We both acted professionally."

"By the skin of our teeth."

"You were my boss. Actually, my boss's boss's boss. It would have been beyond stupid."

"You're right. So we stepped away from the ledge. But I'm not your boss any longer. They have coyotes in Colorado, too."

"Do they?"

"Well, I imagine so. I'll google it and see. I know they

have mountain lions. Bears. I'm not your boss's boss's boss now, Tess."

"You haven't been so for six months. You haven't called. Have you been seeing someone?"

"No. Life has been complicated with family drama and work trauma in the aftermath of the Thanksgiving Massacre. It wouldn't have been fair for me to force my black mood on you or anyone."

"So the drama and trauma are over now?"

"For me they are. Come to Colorado, Tess. I'm not your boss. You are not my employee."

But there's a possibility that you could join Innovations Design. We could work together again. Only, as partners this time. No HR regulations against kissing your partner.

"No strings. No expectations. Though I'll warn you up front. I'm going to want a good night kiss."

What time are the flights? A smile of anticipation fluttered on Tess's lips. How many times had she fantasized about kissing Jake Prentice? Too many to count. "So you're telling me that, in addition to coyotes, mountain lions, and bears, there's a wolf in Colorado, too?"

Jake made a howling noise in reply. Darned if it didn't cause a shiver to race up her spine, a shiver that had nothing to do with fear.

Her voice sounded husky to her own ears as she told him, "I'll hold off booking a return flight."

Fourteen

A BRIGHT RED CARDINAL swooped from the branch of a cottonwood tree and perched atop the wooden signpost that read "cabin 12" as Genevieve approached with a wagon filled with fresh linens, toiletries, flowers, and a fruit basket in tow. Helen followed behind her pushing a housekeeping cart loaded with a broom, a wet mop, a dust mop, trash bags, paper towels, and cleaning supplies. As the wheels rattled over the rocky ground, the bird flew off.

Genevieve opened the door, tugged her wagon inside, then turned to assist her sister in lifting the cart over the doorjamb. The cabin smelled just a little bit musty, so the first thing Genevieve did was open the windows over the sink in the kitchenette and in the bedroom. Then she and her sister each pulled on a pair of long yellow rubber gloves and prepared to go to work.

Jake had invited a woman to visit. Not just any woman, but the Thanksgiving pie woman. The Bennett sisters' interest had been piqued with a capital *P*.

This was the sort of thing Lucas did all the time, but

Jake—no. He rarely brought women around his family, even if it was only an hour overlap in flight times at the tiny airport in Durango, where one can't exactly count on not being noticed. In that respect, this one probably shouldn't qualify, but something about his attitude when he told her of Tess Crenshaw's visit set his mother's antennae quivering. This was no casual visit.

"I don't know, Helen," Genevieve said, scanning the interior of the cabin with a critical eye. "Maybe we should have gone with Cabin 7, after all."

"No. This is good. It has the best view, and it's closest to Jake. Let's face it. She probably won't spend any time here."

"Do you think?"

"Of course I think. She'll be with Jake. They're vacationing together. Although after we do our thing, Twelve will be more much comfortable than One. Jake is neat for a guy, but he's still a guy, and he hasn't done anything to make his cabin cozy. No, they'll likely sleep here."

Genevieve's thoughts veered away from her son's sleeping arrangements. As his mom, she was very interested in his love life, but she'd just as soon not think about his sex life.

In fact, why was she thinking about his love life at all?

"Vacation, shmacation!" Frustration rolled over Genevieve like a tidal wave. "If Jake is on vacation, he should make a better effort at it. All he's done since our trip up to Inspiration Point is work. He's replaced three cracked sinks, set two new toilets, relocated a family of raccoons from Cabin 4, and patched the leak in Cabin 9's roof!"

Helen shrugged. "Let's not look a gift handyman in the mouth."

Genevieve folded her arms and snapped. "It's classic takeover Jake!"

"Whoa." Helen braced her hands on her hips and frowned at her sister. "A minute ago, you were excited about sprucing this cabin up for Tess Crenshaw. What tripped your trigger?"

To Genevieve's shock and dismay, tears suddenly pooled in her eyes. *Good heavens, what is the matter with me?* Jake was trying to help, and it wasn't his fault that she was so...so...discombobulated. *Wow, where had that old word come from?*

The past, that's where. Sighing heavily, she tugged a yellow glove from the housekeeping cart and pulled it onto her left hand. "Oh, Helen. I'm a mess. I feel like I'm backsliding. It unsettles me."

"Backsliding?"

"Yes!"

"I don't understand."

"Look at me, Helen. Jake casually mentions he's bringing a girl home—to a place that isn't even actually his home, I might add—and what do I do? I immediately drop all of my own business—my lodge-related work and my trip preparations and my social obligations—and I grab my sister and tug her along and prepare to dive into...into..." She made a sweeping gesture toward the cleaning cart. "Cobwebs!"

"We shouldn't find many cobwebs. The cleaning service was here on Saturday."

Genevieve ignored that and continued, "I couldn't sleep last night, and do you know what I did? Was I researching the Swiss Alps? German museums? French restaurants? No! I was shopping on Amazon! For cabin curtains!"

"Oh dear."

"I came to my senses, thank goodness, and canceled the order."

"I should hope so. Amazon doesn't have same-day delivery

in Lake in the Clouds. If you wanted curtains here, we should have run by the general store. I think Lisa Bodine stocks some curtains that would fit these windows."

"No! That's the problem! Seriously, Helen. What am I doing even thinking about curtains for this cabin? It. Is. Not. My. Job! It's not my business. What are we doing here at all? We pay someone to clean Raindrop. Why are we here with the cleaning cart this morning when we're leaving for Europe in less than twenty-four hours? We should be packing and watering our plants and stopping our mail. We should be double-checking our passports and our medicines and that we've notified our credit card companies of our travel plans."

"Yes, but we've already done all that. We're both ready to go. We're ready early." She slapped her hands against her cheeks in feigned shock. "Us ready early. Imagine that."

The Bennett sisters were always ready early. It was their MO.

Genevieve resisted the oh-so-mature urge to stick out her tongue at her sister. Barely. "Don't you see, Helen? I'm supposed to be letting go, not hanging curtains!"

"Honey…honey…honey. Calm down." Helen picked up the bucket and carried it toward the sink. "We're not here this morning because of curtains. If you stop to think, you'll see that."

"I'm too agitated to think. Give me a hint."

Helen sighed dramatically. "Mom? Our little blue book?"

"Oh. Yes." Genevieve immediately made the connection. Emily Post's etiquette book. She and Helen had learned it from cover to cover. Their mother had made sure of it.

"You and I own Raindrop Lodge and Cabins Resort. We are not open for guests. We had no intention of hosting guests.

Nevertheless, Tess Crenshaw will be our guest. Of course, we are going to make sure that her room is as comfortable and welcoming as we can possibly make it. Mother will come back from her grave and whack our heads with Emily Post if we do anything less. You are not backsliding, Genevieve. Our reason for being here has nothing to do with letting go and everything to do with basic hospitality rules."

Relief washed over Genevieve. "Oh. That's right. You're right."

"Of course I'm right. I almost always am. Now, get in that bathroom and get to work."

"Aye, aye, Captain." Genevieve gave her sister a yellow-rubber-gloved salute and disappeared into the bathroom with a sponge and a spray bottle.

The spruce-up didn't take long. They made the bed with fresh sheets, placed the fluffy white towels and fragrant toiletries in the bathroom and the kitchen linens in the appropriate drawers. Helen set out the fruit basket and wrote a welcome note, while Genevieve arranged the flowers, a sunny bouquet of yellow daffodils, purple irises, and white roses. They finished up a little before ten, and Genevieve took one last look around.

Number 12 was a one-bedroom, one-bath log cabin with a rock fireplace and a kitchenette, furnished simply with a drop-leaf table and four chairs for dining, a sleeper sofa, and a bentwood rocker. The bedroom had just enough room for a queen bed and a single nightstand with a lamp. In an effort to take Cabin 12 from "rental" to "guest house" status, yesterday Genevieve had dropped off a hand-crocheted afghan, a small rug to place before the fire, and pillows for the sofa. She'd also stocked the refrigerator with staples. Clean and neat, the cabin looked welcoming. "I like these cabins."

"I do, too."

"We probably won't need to tear them down."

"I wouldn't vote for that, no. Now, Cabin 11 might need to go, but that's a special case, what with the leaky roof and the fire damage and the animal infestation. We knew that when we bought the property."

"I should probably thank Jake for the work he's doing."

"I don't see what it would hurt."

"I hope she's comfortable here. She's a city girl. I hope she's prepared for the quiet and solitude of Mirror Lake."

"Well, if we get more dead week partyers at the campgrounds across the lake like we had last week, quiet and solitude might be hard to come by."

"Those college kids were a rowdy bunch," Genevieve said, wincing at the memory. "From what I heard at the beauty shop yesterday, we're lucky nobody drowned."

"She'll like it here. She's going to be with Jake."

Genevieve shut the door and followed her sister up the path toward the lodge, where they stowed the housekeeping cart and wagon. Then they went looking for Jake. They found him with his head beneath the sink in Cabin 5, a wrench in his hand and curse words flying from his mouth.

Genevieve felt a rush of love roll through her. She shouldn't be so hard on him. He was, after all, just like his father. Genetics was a difficult thing to overcome.

⚜

By the grace of God, they didn't all die.

Having grown up on the edge of the Texas Hill Country, Jake knew better than to swerve to avoid a deer when one darted out in front of your car. Unfortunately, the driver of the oncoming car in the opposite lane didn't get the memo. Instinct and lack of training caused that guy to jerk his wheel, which sent his car careening into Jake's lane. Jake had no choice but to swerve at that point and run off the road to avoid a collision.

He gave thanks to the Almighty and the Ford Motor Company that no one in his King Ranch pickup suffered any injury. The same couldn't be said for his truck, which suffered a blown tire, a bent wheel, and possibly a bent axle when they'd bounced off that boulder.

The truck wasn't going anywhere.

When he relayed the information to his passengers, his aunt Helen observed, "I love you, Jake. But if we miss our flight, this wreck will have caused a casualty after all because we're going to have to kill you."

"No one is missing their flight." Jake picked his phone up from the console. Thinking they might have a shot, he checked Uber. *Yes!* A car was ten minutes away. He quickly ordered it.

His mother said, "I'm grateful we insisted on leaving as early as we did."

Yes, everyone should have a four-hour window at an airport where it takes five minutes to clear security. "I am, too, Mom."

Twenty minutes later, he waved the women off in a car that was big enough for the two of them and their luggage but not for him. Jake considered that a lucky break. He tipped the Uber driver well and then settled back to wait for the tow truck to arrive, and once that task was handled, he got an Uber for his own ride to the airport.

Unfortunately, he had to wait significantly longer than he would have liked. As a result, Tess's plane had already landed by the time he hurried into the small Durango-

LaPlata County Airport. He spotted Mom, Aunt Helen, and Tess seated around a table in the airport's lone restaurant right away.

Tess wore her hair up in that casual knot she'd worn most workdays at Bensler. Her big blue eyes sparkled as they focused on Aunt Helen. Her full lips were painted cherry red and stretched into a smile. A fierce sense of gladness swept over Jake to see her here in Colorado, even if she was sitting at a table with his mom and his aunt. All three women had martini glasses in front of them. All three women were laughing.

He had the sense that he was the butt of the joke.

The instincts that Jake had been following lately told him to pivot and go the other direction. Fast. Of course, those same instincts had put those three women here together, so this was a moment of his own making. "Be the ball, Danny," he muttered beneath his breath, quoting *Caddyshack* because, well, that's what guys do.

"Everybody made it, I see," he said, striding into the restaurant with a casual confidence that was all show. He walked over to Tess, leaned down and smiled into her eyes, and then gave her a friendly kiss on her cheek. "You look great. I'm so glad you decided to come."

"I'm glad to see you, too," she replied. "I understand it's been a challenging trip."

"A little more excitement than I'd anticipated." He met his mother's gaze. "I was glad to get your text saying that y'all had made it okay."

"I'm glad we don't have to kill you. We didn't pack our guns."

"She packed everything else, though," Aunt Helen piped up. "Sit down, Jake. Tess was just about to tell us about the time that your team played an April Fool's Day prank on you. I guess it involved balloons and shaving cream?"

"Oh jeez." He sighed, waved to the bartender, and called, "I'm going to need a beer, please. Whatever local microbrew you recommend."

He sat and spent the next twenty minutes listening to the women in his life tell embarrassing stories about him.

The women in his life. Well, now, that was the question at hand, wasn't it?

Finally—thankfully—Mom announced she and Aunt Helen needed to proceed through security and go to their gate. By that time, the two women were on hugging terms with Tess, so they all embraced and said good-bye. Then Tess stepped aside while Jake said a more private farewell to his aunt and his mother.

He hugged Aunt Helen. "Watch out for her, Auntie. Check in with one of us regularly, or folks back here will worry themselves sick."

"I will. We will."

He kissed her on the cheek before turning to his mother. "Mom, you two have fun. Go climb every mountain. Follow all the rainbows. Twirl across the meadows. Sing to the nuns. But if you get arrested…"

Her eyes glistening, Mom repeated the Prentice family refrain, "Don't call me."

"Seriously, I hope you have the trip of a lifetime."

"Thank you. I'm planning on it."

Aunt Helen interrupted. "Let's go, Genevieve. A line is beginning to form at security." She extended the handle of her carry-on, tossed back what was left of her drink, then picked up her purse and stared meaningfully toward her sister.

Jake glanced toward the TSA entry to see a whopping

seven people in line. "Yep, you'd better go." He gave his mom one more hug. "Love you, Mom. Enjoy the Alps."

"Love you, too, Jake. Enjoy the Rockies."

He stepped back and met Tess's gaze. Was that a wistful look on her face? "I plan on it."

"I'm sure you do." Mom retrieved her things, then followed her sister toward the security line. Tess called after them, "Thanks for the drink! Next time is on me!"

The women smiled, waved, and moments later, disappeared from sight. Jake let out a heavy sigh of relief. "Now I can finally breathe."

"Difficult day?"

"Oh yeah." He gave his head a shake, then added, "I'm sorry I wasn't here to meet you when you arrived."

"No problem. Your mother and aunt were waiting for me, and explained what was going on."

"Let's pretend that was me." He took her hands in his and smiled down at her. "Welcome to Colorado, Tess."

Then, without thinking, and to his surprise, he leaned down and brushed her lips with his. It was a friendly hello, appropriate for public spaces. When he stepped back, Tess met his gaze with a teasing glint in her own. "Saying good night already?"

"I was aiming for your cheek. Guess I missed. Or else you moved. Did you move?"

"No. Not intentionally anyway. I intend to go slow here, Jake."

"Okay. That's fine." He allowed a little bit of wickedness to enter his eyes as he added, "I'm good with slow."

Her answering smile was wry. "I'll just bet you are."

Before he could continue the flirtation, a familiar voice intruded on the moment. "I told you so, Genevieve."

Jake jerked his gaze toward the TSA lines. His mother and his aunt stood on the other side, finger-waving at him. "I left my bag of snacks," his aunt called. "It's beside my chair in the restaurant. Is it still there?"

Tess giggled and went to get it. "Yes, it's still here."

"Thank goodness." Aunt Helen breezed through the exit and met Tess to retrieve it. "A girl can't head off to Europe without her Fig Newtons." She kissed Tess's cheek and rushed back toward the TSA agent, waving. "Ciao! Don't forget to practice safe se—"

From the far side of the security line, Mom interrupted, "Helen!"

Jake grimaced and asked Tess, "Is your bag in the restaurant, too, or did you check it?"

"I checked it."

He grabbed her hand and pulled her in the opposite direction. "Then let's get it and get out of here while we still can."

Tess laughed, almost running to keep up with Jake's long strides. "I think I've been hugged and kissed more in the past forty-five minutes than I have in the past year."

"We Prentices are a demonstrative lot."

"I love your mom, Jake, and I adore your aunt, too. You don't know how lucky you are."

Something in her voice clued him to the fact that this was not an offhand remark coming from Tess. Jake took a moment to formulate a response. "Yes, I know. They've been rocks all of my life. Not that sometimes they don't roll down the hill and flatten me."

Tess shrugged. "What are rocks for?"

"They taught me to jump out of the way when they get to rolling, that's for certain. But enough about them." They reached the baggage claim, where a sky blue carry-on stood against the wall behind the customer service booth. "I take it that's yours?"

"Yes."

She retrieved it from the attendant, and Jake led her outside to where his Uber driver waited, running up the tab Jake had been happy to pay to have a car waiting. He opened the car door for Tess and asked the driver to pop the trunk. He deposited her bag next to his small overnighter, then climbed into the backseat next to her and instructed the driver to head for their destination. Then Jake turned to Tess and smiled. "All right. You ready to get this party started, Ms. Crenshaw?"

"I didn't come dressed for a party, Mr. Prentice. I thought we were off to Small Town, Colorado."

"Oh, we are. But we are taking the scenic route." He reached for her hand and gave it a squeeze. "As glad as I am not to make the long drive to Denver, this whole thing started because I invited you out to dinner. I had intended to take you out to a very nice meal in the city, and after asking around town, the best Lake in the Clouds has to offer isn't what I want for our first dinner date. I knew of an excellent restaurant here in Durango, so it seemed to me that the stars have sort of aligned. A college friend of mine has a vacation home here, and he's offered it to us for tonight. The plan is to explore Durango today and drive to Lake in the Clouds tomorrow. Does that work for you?"

"Sounds great."

Fifteen minutes later, their driver dropped them off at the address Jake had provided, a modern condominium on the edge of downtown. "This is really nice," Tess said as she followed Jake into the fourth-floor unit and looked around.

"It is. I stayed here last winter on a ski trip. Purgatory is a short drive away. Do you ski?"

"No. I've never had the opportunity. I've always wanted to learn to waterski, too."

"Well, we'll have to fix that. Not on Mirror Lake, though. It's comfortable for swimming if you're a polar bear, and besides, motorboats aren't allowed."

"Good. I'm a wuss when it comes to cold water." Tess glanced at the window and observed. "What a great view."

"A convenient location, too. We're within walking distance of most of the attractions downtown and the restaurant where we have reservations tonight." Jake deposited her suitcase in a bedroom with a king-sized bed. He gestured toward a closed door and added, "Each bedroom has a private bath. Yours is through there. Want to meet me on the balcony for a glass of wine in five or ten minutes? We can plan what we want to do before dinner?"

"Sure."

Jake hesitated, feeling unsure of himself. Up until now, the whole running-on-instinct thing had been working well enough, but these were uncharted territories. "Tess, I'm feeling about as sure on my feet as a newborn colt here. Am I doing this right?"

She offered a hesitant smile. "I'm not sure what you're asking me."

"Well, technically, this is our first date, but we are way past first date questions and activities. We know each other very well in some respects, but in others, we are strangers. I'm trying not to overthink it because that's my new mantra, but I need a little bit of direction, or I'll drive myself crazy. I'm shooting for date one point five today. Does that sound about right?"

Her slow smile was filled with delight. "Probably, but a little definition would help."

"Maybe we can work on that over our wine here in a few minutes," he suggested.

"Sounds good."

Jake nodded, then turned and headed for his own bedroom and bath. When she joined him on the balcony ten minutes later, he had a nice pinot grigio chilling in an ice bucket and a charcuterie tray and small plates sitting on a cocktail table.

"All right, either you are a magician, or you did some planning ahead."

"It's from a shop down the street. My buddy who owns this place has an arrangement with them, so we would have the fridge stocked when we arrive. I remembered you were a fan."

"Nice." Tess accepted the glass of wine he poured for her, then she added food to one of the plates. "I'm a cheese and olive hog, and I freely admit it. Fair warning, Prentice. Get what you want off that tray now because you snooze you lose."

Leaning against the balcony railing, Tess breathed deeply, then exhaled in a rush. "Oh, the air smells so clean and fresh. I love the beach, and Texas is home, but nothing compares with mountain air."

"I know." Jake popped a pepperoni into his mouth. "The view is nice from here, too. So about today."

"Date one point five."

"Yeah. We have dinner reservations at seven. Between now and then, I thought you might like to wander around downtown, check out the shops and the galleries. There are a couple museums all within walking distance. If we want to go somewhere a little farther afield, we can always order an Uber."

"That sounds like a perfect afternoon, Jake. So why the uncertainty? What needs defining?"

He swirled the wine in his glass. "You're a coffee drinker, right?"

"Yes."

"Have you ever tried to give it up?"

She wrinkled her nose. "Once or twice. I wasn't very successful at it."

"Well, you've probably noticed that I am by nature a problem solver."

"No." She slapped her cheek dramatically. "Managing Director Jake Prentice solves problems? You must be kidding."

He gave her a droll look and continued, "*Former* managing director. So problem solving, planning, taking charge, hell, call it being bossy if you're one of my siblings—it's like my morning coffee, and I'm trying to give it up. Since I quit the job, I've been going with the flow. I got in my truck one day and ended up in Colorado. I'm very happy that I did. Last week, I wanted to call you, so I did. I asked you to dinner because it sounded like an excellent idea at the moment. It was. Same thing with inviting you to Lake in the Clouds. It's all been spur of the moment, which is so not how I roll as a rule."

"You regret it?"

"Not one iota. But I just want to be honest and upfront and make certain that you have your eyes wide open because if you're expecting the Jake Prentice you saw at the office for the past five years, you're going to be sorely disappointed. I told you on the phone that my head wasn't on straight. That hasn't changed. I promised no expectations or heavy talk until we're in Lake in the Clouds, and I want to hold to that. I want a nice, fun first date today, but we have that pesky point-five thing to deal with."

"Right. So point-five?"

"It's the whole first kiss thing. I totally screwed that one up by going with the flow."

Frowning, Tess took a long sip of her wine.

"I've already kissed you three times."

"You have not!"

"I kissed you at your office and at the airport when I first got there. That's two."

"Those were cheek kisses. Cheek kisses don't count."

"Don't they?" Jake frowned. "They have to count some-where. I know without a doubt they're not allowed on the coworkers' list. Acquaintances is definitely not a go. Cheek kisses for friends are even iffy in this day and age. We almost need to be family or in a relationship for that to be acceptable. Which brings us to the third kiss. "

"The one your aunt interrupted," Tess clarified.

"Yep. It wasn't a cheek kiss, but it dang sure wasn't a proper kiss. Here's where going with my instincts got me into trouble. I shouldn't have kissed you in public, where I couldn't make it a proper one. It's just that I've been dreaming of getting my lips on yours for a while now and, well, instincts. So I didn't give you a proper first kiss. I don't even want to think about kiss number four because if I stay in instinct mode, I'm seriously going to move too soon. I'll take it too far because, again, the wanting my lips on yours thing, and I think today should be casual and—"

"Oh, for crying out loud." Tess reached up and slipped her hand behind his neck. She went up on her tiptoes as she pulled his face down toward hers. Tess's mouth captured Jake's in a thorough, instinctual, and definitely not-so-proper kiss.

Luckily, Jake had used the plastic outdoor wineglasses because at some point, both his and Tess's hit the ground.

It was the hottest first—or maybe fourth—kiss he'd ever had.

Tess ended it, which was a good thing, because had the decision been left up to Jake with the whole instinctive business going on, well, they'd have likely ended up in one of the bedrooms.

Stepping back, she said, "Okay then. I'm not sure how much of that carrying-on you were doing was teasing, but either way, that first kiss is out of the way now. You can quit fretting over it."

"I like your style, Crenshaw."

"I'm pragmatic."

"I know." He caught her hand and brought it up to his mouth, and gallantly kissed her knuckles. "You're also brilliant and creative and a ridiculously hard worker. But there's still so much I don't know about you. I want to change that. I want to learn about your childhood and your family and whether you played sports in school or marched in the band or did both. I want to know what music you listen to and what your favorite foods are. I want to know where you're ticklish."

She bent and scooped up the wineglasses, then picked up the cheese board. "I played softball. No band. I have eclectic tastes in music, but I probably listen to classic rock most often. Perhaps it's time we checked out the shops and galleries you mentioned."

"I think that's a good idea." He waited a beat and added, "Where are you ticklish, Tess?"

Heading inside, she tossed a sassy look over her shoulder that made him want to howl. "Slow down, Prentice. That one stays on your learn-about-me list."

"Fair enough." He picked up the wine bottle and followed her, saying, "I'm looking forward to discovering all the answers."

Fifteen

THE LAST TIME TESS faked it this well, she'd played Rizzo in her high school drama club's production of *Grease*.

She'd been a nervous wreck from the moment she'd walked off the plane. When Jake's mother called her name at the airport security exit and explained his delay, she'd relaxed a little. The conversation and the midday martini helped calm her nerves even further. She'd just begun to feel even-keeled when Jake strolled in looking like a rugged hottie outdoorsman in jeans and a long-sleeved cotton shirt that complemented his green eyes. At that point, her heart had started to flutter. When he'd brushed her lips with a kiss in the airport, an entire flock of butterflies took flight.

She'd captured them and caged them and told them to settle the heck down. What helped her more than anything was Jake's almost boyish insecurity and uncertainty. That had bolstered her confidence in a way nothing else could have done and had given her the nerve to act on her own instincts when it counted.

She'd kissed him. She'd acted on their longstanding, unspoken mutual attraction by going up on her tiptoes and planting a wet one on him. She'd given him her best, too. No hesitation. No holding back.

He'd almost melted her knees.

Free of the need to hide her reaction to Jake, Tess found the afternoon exploring Durango's attractions to be a joy. They poked around antiques shops and wandered through specialty stores. Jake bought a wrench in a hardware store. Tess purchased a novel in a bookstore and cheese in a gourmet market, and they both indulged in dessert in a bakery. They toured the railroad museum and visited three art galleries, after which they sat in the park by the river and argued art preferences until Jake caught Tess in a yawn.

"I saw that."

"Saw what?"

"The yawn. You need a nap. It's the after-brownie sugar crash. Or maybe I need a nap because the car-accident-on-the-way-to-the-airport stress finally caught up with me. Why don't we return to the condo for some downtime? We can rest up and get our second wind so we can argue about something new through dinner?"

"All right. I confess I do like my naps." Tess scooted off the picnic bench, where she had been seated while making her case for modern art. "What will we argue about over dinner?"

"I dunno." Jake reached for her hand and laced their fingers. "Do you have a preference?"

"I'll think about it."

Except she didn't think about it because the large hand holding hers captured all of her attention. She recalled sitting beside him at the office discussing a design and watching those long fingers curl around a pencil and confidently sketch. Then, his nails had been tended, his skin smooth and unmarred. Today, she noted scratches and scrapes and felt a callous against her palm.

He'd been working with his hands. Out in the sunshine, judging by his tanned skin. Earlier, he'd told her he'd been doing some tasks for his mother at the lodge, and Tess had assumed he'd meant computer work of some sort. Something managerial. Apparently, she'd been wrong.

Or maybe he'd been playing hard. Climbing perhaps? Hadn't he mentioned going climbing in the Sierras while on vacation a year or two ago? Today he'd talked of fishing for trout early in the morning at the lake where his mother's property was located. But fishing didn't tear up a person's hands, did it?

She could have asked, but she found she didn't want to break the relaxed, comfortable silence between them as they strolled hand in hand back to the condo. She'd ask him tonight at dinner. Maybe they could argue about the best flies to use to catch a rainbow.

Jake walked her to her bedroom door, where he gave her a long, sweet kiss. Stepping away, he spoke in a husky voice. "Sweet dreams, Sprite."

She floated toward the king-sized bed and flopped backward onto it. Sprite. Not "honey" or "darlin'" or "babe." Not an endearment. Nothing at all wrong with endearments. She liked endearments. But Sprite was a nickname. Jake had given her a nickname.

She'd always wanted a boyfriend to give her a nickname.

She couldn't say why. She'd just wanted one. She remembered that she'd almost asked the guy she dated her sophomore year in high school to give her a nickname but changed her mind upon recognizing that asking for one wouldn't satisfy the desire.

Sprite. She liked it. Check that little box.

Laughing at herself, Tess rolled over on the bed and found a pillow for her head. Perhaps she would take a little nap. Maybe she would dream of Jake wearing a high school letter jacket. Or giving her his senior ring. Giving her a promise ring. Did kids still do that?

She knew they still had a prom. She'd wanted to go to prom, but that hadn't been in the cards for her. Not the foster kid who was bounced from one placement to another because she had just enough blood-related family to ensure that the system worked against her rather than for her. She'd missed out on so much.

Sprite. Sprite Crenshaw. Maybe she'd start using that at work. She could put it on her business cards. She could see it now. Sprite Crenshaw, partner.

No. She didn't want to think about that today. The subject of jobs could wait. Today was a dream-date day, and she was going to enjoy every minute of it.

She dreamed she wore a silver Disney princess dress while slow dancing with Jake in a high school gymnasium.

After her nap, she indulged in a bubble bath and spent extra time on her hair and makeup. She donned her favorite of the new dresses she'd bought during last week's online shopping splurge, switched necessities from her larger purse to the small bag she'd brought, slipped on her new shoes, and exited her bedroom.

GQ Jake waited for her on the balcony.

As dinner dates went, it ranked so far beyond number one in Tess's experience that it deserved its own list. The food was excellent, the service, first-rate. The company made

Tess giddy. Dinner conversation centered around standard first-date get-to-know-you questions. They discussed those favorite foods and music questions Jake had mentioned earlier, and with her dream fresh on her mind, Tess told stories about her high school drama productions. That led to talk about musicals and then his mother's trip to Europe.

"She and your aunt were as bubbly as champagne when they explained why they were there to meet me," Tess said. "After they got past the part of complaining about you, that is."

"I'm surprised they ever made it beyond that subject."

Tess smiled and shook her head to the server, who'd offered to top off the decaf coffee she'd ordered with dessert. "It was your lucky day when Uber came to Durango, Colorado. That's for sure. I would have hated to be you if they'd missed their plane."

"I'd have chartered a plane to fly them to D/FW Airport myself if that had happened. Believe me, I'd already begun making a contingency plan."

"Oh, I definitely believe that. You might be going with the flow these days, but in a crisis, your instincts are going to be to plan."

"You think?"

"It's who you are, Jake. You're a planner, a manager. You're a leader." She picked up her coffee, took a sip, then spoke to him over the cup. "That's why the job at Bensler became impossible for you once Lee Trammel retired and Paul Franklin came on board. Unlike Lee, Paul wouldn't let you lead."

"I should have fired myself in November in that first round of layoffs. I hung on way too long."

"That's because you're not a quitter. It comes with being

a great leader. I think that's why…" Tess stopped herself. "Never mind."

"That's why, what?"

"We've drifted into serious talk. I thought we were going to stay away from that today."

"You're right. But I'm going to file this away and take it up later. You've made me curious."

The server approached the table and asked if they needed anything more, and after confirming with Tess, Jake requested their check. The evening air was downright cold, and Tess had chosen fashion over warmth with a cashmere shawl as her only outer garment. Ever the gentleman, Jake removed his suit coat and draped it over her shoulders. "Shall I get us a ride?"

"No. We don't have far to go, and I'm happy to walk off my meal."

Nevertheless, she was chilled, and her feet were freezing by the time they walked the four blocks back to the condo. When Jake suggested they finish the evening with brandy before the fireplace, she couldn't think of anything that sounded better. Well, anything acceptable under the current first-date policy.

Back at the condo, he flipped the switch on the gas logs and asked her to choose the music as he saw to their drinks. Moments later, Tess sat with her legs tucked up beneath her on the sofa with a soft throw across her lap when Kenny G's saxophone began playing softly in the background.

Jake groaned as he handed her a snifter of brandy and sat beside her. "You're just mean."

She giggled. It was one of the music choices they'd discussed at dinner. Jake was not a saxophone fan. "Don't worry. Frank Sinatra is coming up next."

"Okay then." He snuggled farther into the down-filled cushions and draped his arm around her. "This has been a nice day."

"Yes, it has. A very nice day." They sat in companionable silence for a time. Frank was halfway through "Summer Wind" when she said, "So tell me about Lake in the Clouds. How does it compare to Durango?"

"Hmm. If Durango is Austin, Lake in the Clouds is Dime Box."

"Dime Box? Is there a town in Texas called Dime Box?" Jake nodded, and Tess said, "I've never heard of it."

"And there is my point. Honestly, I haven't done a lot of exploring since I've been in town. Mostly I've been hanging out at the Raindrop working on repairs around the cabins."

"I thought your mother said a construction firm was set to start repairs next week? She warned me it might be busy."

"They are renovating the lodge, which is the main structure on the property, but the resort also has fifteen individual cabins. They're not in bad shape, but they need some basic maintenance. That's what I've been doing. Simple handyman stuff."

"So you're a well-rounded tool man, then. Good with a hammer as well as a calculator?"

"I can hold my own when it comes to power tools. When we were kids, my brother—" Frowning, he broke off abruptly. "Anyway, the cabin we have for you has new fixtures in the bathroom and a new kitchen sink. Mom and Aunt Helen went over yesterday and spruced it up. The cabins are rustic, definitely a different style from this, but I think you'll be comfortable there."

"I'm sure I will." With a wistful note in her voice, she added, "I can't imagine your mother and aunt creating anything that isn't lovely."

"I don't know about that. I'm a little worried about the lodge, to be honest. If you'd heard what I heard on the drive to the airport..." Jake gave an exaggerated shudder. "You're a designer, Tess. What they were saying would have given you nightmares. I'm not kidding. I halfway expect FedEx to begin delivering cuckoo clocks by the middle of next week and the employment application to carry a lederhosen warning."

When Tess laughed, he drew away from her until she met his gaze. "You think I'm kidding? Just wait until tomorrow evening when we stop by Aunt Helen's house to feed the cat. You'll see. I love her to death, and when it came to lawyering, she had some of the sharpest shark's teeth in the ocean, but her taste in decorating—no. I thought Mom would keep her in check, but I swear, Mom sounded almost as crazy as she did today."

"You are feeding your aunt's cat while she is away?"

"Just tomorrow. The neighbor who is going to cat-sit is away on vacation herself. She'll be back the day after tomorrow and will take over."

"So what else is on the agenda for tomorrow?"

"I dunno. No plans beyond driving back and cat duty." He snuggled her against him. "Do you have any preferences?"

Tess rested her head against his shoulder. "What are my choices?"

"Well, let's see. We will be back by lunchtime, so we will have all afternoon. Lake in the Clouds is centrally located for a number of day trips, which is good, but after we've spent the morning driving, I'm guessing you'd prefer to stick close to town and do something a bit more active. Am I right?"

"Definitely."

"In that case, there's a couple of trailheads at Mirror Lake. We could do a hike. Raindrop has a couple of decent mountain bikes available for us to use. We can always explore the town, but that'll take about twenty minutes tops. We can rent four-wheelers and go bounce around to our heart's content on those. There's white-water rafting nearby, but I think we would have needed to book today for tomorrow afternoon. We can go kayaking or canoeing on Mirror Lake, and of course, there's always fishing. We will need to get you a fishing license. We'll pass a place on the way into Lake in the Clouds, where we can stop and take care of that. Any of those things catch your fancy?"

"All of the above," she replied.

He stroked his thumb idly up and down her arm. "We'll play it by ear, then. Sound good?"

"Very good." She sipped her drink and snuggled a little closer. When he nuzzled her hair in response, she recognized that the warmth stealing through her had little to do with the liquor and everything to do with the man.

Jake's voice was a low, soft rumble as he said, "Lest I forget to mention the amenities for when we're feeling lazy, I hung a couple of brand-new hammocks in a pair of prime spots. One is between two big old shade trees out in front of my cabin. Gorgeous view of the mountains."

At some point, he must have set down his drink because the hand that had been holding his snifter pushed her hair away from her ear and neck. His thumb stroked her bare skin from her earlobe to her collarbone.

Tess shivered.

Softly, he continued, "The other is down by the lake, back in this little inlet. Very private. And your cabin, Number 12, has a porch swing that faces west and the lake. Perfect place to watch the sunset."

"That sounds very nice, too." Tess tilted her head away in subtle invitation.

"It is. Unless the campsite across the lake has a bunch of rowdies, it's peaceful and quiet out there at sunrise and sunset at Raindrop Lodge and Cabins Resort. We're unplugged, you know. At the moment anyway."

"No Internet?"

"No Internet." His lips skimmed butterfly kisses over her skin.

There. I'm ticklish there. "That's divine."

"Yeah. I think so. You can always..." His tongue traced the whorl of her ear. "Tether."

"What?"

"To your phone. To get Internet. Or you can go up to the Sunshine Diner on the highway if you need more than what you can get on your phone. The diner is the Lake in the Clouds version of Starbucks. Better coffee, too, if you ask me. I recommend the waffles."

"I'll have to try them."

"Yeah." Jake reached over, plucked her brandy snifter out of her hand, and set it aside. He pulled her onto his lap and resumed his kisses, working his way toward her mouth.

"Tess?" he asked, his tone husky, his lips hovering just above hers.

"Hmm?"

"I would be remiss if I didn't also mention the rainy-day activities."

He worked his way to her mouth, and his hands started

to roam. They spent the next few minutes, or maybe hours, communicating without words. When they came up for air, Tess gasped out. "Jake. Have you, um, checked the forecast?"

"Well, see, my First Date Policies and Procedures Manual states I don't check my phone."

"I've noticed that. I approve."

"And like I said, we don't have Internet back at Raindrop, so I'm not up-to-date on what the forecasters are calling for. That said, our name is Raindrop Lodge. I'm pretty sure my *Farmer's Almanac* calls for a chance of rain every day."

"You think so, do you?"

"Yeah. I do. I hope so. Need the rain. *Really* need the rain. Maybe I could do a dance." He captured her mouth again, sent her head spinning and her blood sizzling again. They both were breathing heavily when he lifted his head and asked, "What do you think?"

It would be so easy. So very, very easy to say yes.

She wanted so very badly to say yes.

Tess licked her lips and said, "I think I'd better say good night now."

He groaned softly. "Yeah. Sorry." He rolled off her and onto his feet. "I got carried away."

"Hey, I was right there with you. It's been a dry spell for me." She accepted the hand he offered and allowed him to pull her to her feet. "Thank you for today, Jake. It was the nicest first date I've had in, well, forever."

"Same here. I'm really glad you came to Colorado, Tess. I'm looking forward to tomorrow and the rest of the trip."

"Me, too." She went up on her toes and gave him a quick kiss. "Good night."

"Good night."

Just before she disappeared down the hallway to her bedroom, Tess stopped and turned around. "Jake?"

"Yeah?"

"I'm counting on you."

"Counting on me?"

"Make it rain."

Sixteen

THE FOLLOWING MORNING JAKE picked up his truck from the repair shop, where it was ready as promised, and then he returned to the condo for Tess and their bags. They were on the road by nine.

It turned out that Tess was one of those travelers who liked to stop at every scenic overlook and historical marker along the route. Following a stop at a mountain pass summit, Jake wryly observed. "At the rate we're going, the trip back to Lake in the Clouds will take longer than my trip there—bent wheel and axle and all."

"We don't need to stop anymore," Tess said.

"I'm just kidding you. We are in absolutely no hurry. Go with the flow, remember? Stop and smell the Douglas fir. I haven't done enough of that in my life. It's why I'm here in Colorado now."

Once they'd returned to the car and proceeded on their route, Tess said, "Jake, about stopping to smell the Christmas trees. I think—"

He interrupted. "Wait. You're a real tree person? Not a fake tree?"

"Well, yes."

"I'm surprised. You're a decorator."

"What does that have to do with anything?"

"Color-coordinated trees." He said it with a sneer. He couldn't help it.

Tess laughed. "You have an opinion about Christmas decorations, do you, Prentice?"

"On trees I do. Yes, I do." A smile flirted on his lips. "You should have seen the battle royal in my family the year my sisters convinced Mom to buy new decorations for the tree. Everything had to be burgundy and gold." He shuddered.

"I take it you and your brother didn't approve?"

"No! I'm a traditionalist when it comes to Christmas trees. They banished all of the ornaments we made in school. That's heresy, I tell you. Heresy!"

Tess folded her arms and studied him, a knowing expression on her face. "So what did you and your brother do?"

Approaching a hairpin mountain curve, Jake spared her only a quick sideways glance. "What makes you think Lucas and I did anything?"

"The gleam in your eyes is flashing like the Las Vegas strip at midnight."

Jake remembered the precise moment Lucas came up with the plan. His lips twitched. It was always Lucas. "My sisters both belonged to some club in town. Don't remember what it was exactly. A service club of some sort. For the Christmas party, everyone went caroling, then came back to our house for food and fellowship. Mom chaperoned during the caroling, so while they were gone, my brother and I took the opportunity to add some decorations to the tree."

"Not the school ornaments, I'm guessing?"

"Nope. Underwear. Gold and burgundy bras and panties."

Tess gasped in horror. "You raided your sisters' dresser drawers?"

"No! We would never have done that." Jake tried to sound affronted, but his smile belied it. "We bought new ones at the mall store. Let me tell you, it was one of the more embarrassing moments in our lives up to that point. We started at Victoria's Secret, but the sales clerk chased us out. Had to go to five different places to get enough. Gold was hard to come by, but we found a sympathetic clerk at the slut store, and she fixed us up."

"The *slut* store?"

His cheeks flushed crimson. "Well, I wouldn't call it that now, obviously. That's just what everybody called it back then."

"That's awful. Just awful. You were teenagers, I assume? Teenage boys are the worst. What did your mother do?"

Jake's smile turned wistful. "Mom was horrified. But looking back, I think she saw it for what it was. See, that was the first Christmas after our father died. We had five grieving, emotional wrecks in that house who all had to power through the holidays the best way they knew how. For the girls, it was to change everything. For Lucas and me, it meant keeping a death grip on the way things used to be. Mom was caught in the middle."

"Did she punish you?"

"The next day—no, the next day was Sunday. We had to go to church service—twice. And then Monday, with our sisters watching, Mom took us to the bank and made us draw out fifty percent of our savings accounts. Then she hauled our butts to Walmart, where we used our money to buy underwear—men's, women's, and children's—which we then took to a homeless shelter and donated."

"Oh, that was inspired," Tess said, her voice ripe with admiration. "I do love your mother."

"I know," Jake said. "Me, too. On the way home from the shelter, we stopped at the grocery store and bought a little Charlie Brown Christmas tree for the upstairs game room. It was our territory. The girls rarely went in there. We went traditional tacky red and green complete with all the old ornaments on that one."

"What did she do the next year?"

"From then on, we had two trees. The pretty one and the tacky one. What about you? What special traditions did your family have at Christmas?"

Tess didn't immediately respond, and when Jake spied the turnoff for Inspiration Point up ahead, an idea distracted him. Maybe they should stop and check that scenic spot out today rather than retracing their steps another time. He wouldn't mind getting out and stretching his legs at this point in the trip, that's for sure.

He glanced down at his passenger's feet. Boots. She was dressed for hiking. He made the executive decision and took the turn.

Tess didn't appear to notice their change in direction. Though her gaze looked outward, her thoughts obviously turned inward. "The thing about special traditions is that in order for them to develop, one needs an element of repetition involved. I seldom had that when it came to holidays."

Holidays. Right. "Your family wasn't big into holidays?"

She laughed without amusement. "My family wasn't big, period. I don't guess I've ever shared my family woes with you, have I?"

"Not that I recall. I'd like to hear them."

"It's not a happy story."

Jake darted her a quick glance. The warning note in her tone clued him in to the fact that it wasn't a simple story, either. "I want to know you."

"You want the long or short version?"

"We're in no rush."

She picked up her water bottle from the console and took a sip. "My first seven years were mostly normal. At least, I thought so at the time. I remember being happy early on. My mom was a single, teenaged mom originally from somewhere back East. She never would say exactly. Her parents threw her out after she got pregnant with me by a guy she met at a party, a summer beach party. She said there were a bunch of college guys there, and she swore someone put something in her drink because she didn't really remember much that happened. She thought the guy's name might have been Trent, but she couldn't be certain."

"People suck," Jake muttered.

"Some do, for sure. Anyway, she was a good mother. She kept me fed and clothed and a roof over our heads. She worked at fast-food joints, primarily McDonald's, and studied for her GED when she found time. The lady downstairs watched me while Mom worked. She had four kids already, so one more didn't really make much of a difference. Everything changed when Mom met Gary."

Jake couldn't miss the bitter note in her voice when she spoke the man's name.

"They got married. He introduced her to drugs. It went downhill from there. I was six when my brother, Brandon, was born. It was…terrible. He was born with severe mental and physical disabilities, which basically meant he'd never be able to care for himself. Gary hung around maybe two months after Mom brought the baby home. She overdosed before Brandon's first birthday. She died."

"Ah, hell, Tess." Jake reached across the console and rested his hand on her knee. "That's terrible. I'm so sorry. Where did you go?"

"Into the system. Gary was still MIA, but he had just enough family to screw things up for a time. His parents did some wishy-washy decision making regarding Brandon, and since he and I were related, I was part of it. Different state agencies got involved, which meant different opinions and experts and judges. It was a mix of well-meaning people and people who couldn't have cared less about Brandon and me, but who wanted the win."

"I swear, so many things are broken about the way we deal with children in need."

"The state finally tracked down Gary when he landed in jail in Florida. He signed away his parental rights to Brandon—no surprise there—but it made the legal side of things easier. I was nine when we were placed in with a really nice foster family. The Millers were just great people. They had two biological children, but I swear, they didn't treat me any different than they did Lisa and Scott. We'd lived with them for two-and-a-half years when Cerise—she was the mom—got pregnant again. Twins this time."

"They sent you back?" Jake asked, his stomach sinking.

Tess shook her head. "Not exactly. They asked our case-worker to begin the process of finding a permanent place for Brandon. He was profoundly disabled. He would never walk or talk. The Millers had been clear from the beginning that they couldn't adopt Brandon, and everyone understood that. They were fine with that. The Millers were willing to take care of my brother as long as they felt they could manage him themselves, but Brandon's condition deteriorated, and it was too much."

"A lot for anyone to handle, much less a new mother with twins."

"Exactly." Tess's voice went wistful. "But they were going to keep me. They began the adoption process for me."

Jake's heart twisted. "Oh, Sprite."

Tess shrugged and sighed. "See, here is where policy and procedure bit my butt. Keeping family members together trumped everything. Somebody in a cubicle somewhere decided it was more important that the state find a family who would adopt Brandon and me together than to allow me to have a permanent home. The adoption was denied. We both got yanked out of the Millers' home."

"You're kidding."

"Nope. It was not a good time for me. I didn't take it well."

"I can imagine."

"I became a real problem child. I was so angry. I'd lost my mother, I'd never had a father, and my needs always took a backseat to my brother's. I didn't understand why I couldn't be the focus of attention for once or why I had to lose another home and another chance at a family. I had absolutely no control over what happened to me, so I acted out. Started stealing. Skipping school. I ran away and went back to the Millers. The third time I did that, everybody got into trouble. They weren't allowed to have any contact with me after that. Honestly, losing them was worse than losing my mother."

"How old were you then?"

"Eleven."

"Have you ever touched base with them since then?"

"I Facebook-stalked Cerise—Mrs. Miller—for a while when I was in high school, but my art teacher convinced me that wasn't healthy for me. She was right. Cerise had twin girls, and I was getting a little goofy about them."

"Sounds like your art teacher did double time as a therapist, too."

"No kidding."

"I had a football coach like that. He was a great help to me after my father died. Mentors can be worth their weight in gold."

"If not for my art teacher, no telling where I would have ended up. Honestly, there's a good chance I would have followed in my mother's footsteps."

Jake's heart ached for the little girl she once had been. "Seems like someone's priorities got misplaced. Keeping a family together is a fine goal, but circumstances need to be looked at and addressed individually."

"Well, water under the bridge, like they say."

"What happened to your brother?"

"He died when I was twelve."

Jake took hold of her hand and gave it a squeeze. "I'm sorry, Tess."

"I have a lot of guilt where my little brother is concerned. About six months after we left the Millers, he was placed in a special care facility. Those six months cost me my adoptive home. I resented the circumstances, but I did love Brandon. When I visited him, his eyes followed me. I don't know if he knew me, but as a child, I thought he did. I read to him, not that he understood, but because Mom had read to us. I sensed that he liked hearing my voice, but honestly, reading to him comforted me and gave me something to do when I visited. When I'd leave, I'd wonder if he missed me. I loved him as best I could. He was my only family, after all, but at the same time, I resented him so much."

"That's a tough situation. You shouldn't beat yourself up over your emotions. Look, I'm an expert when it comes to brother resentment. You were in a no-win situation."

"Expert, huh?" she asked, in an obvious attempt to lighten the mood. "Are you the resenter or the resentee?"

"I've served on both sides of the aisle."

"Oh wow. Jake!" Distracted by the view as they made a switchback turn headed up the mountain, Tess sat forward in her seat and peered out the passenger's side window. "How gorgeous. You turned off the main road?"

"I did. Remember me telling you about Inspiration Point? I called you from there last week? When I was hiking with my mom? Well, it is all but on our way to Lake in the Clouds. I thought today would be a good time to check it off of our to-do list. Okay with you?"

"Sure."

Jake still had some questions about her childhood, but when she began asking about elevations and topography and other subjects, he took his cues from her and swallowed his questions.

He was sensitive to time and place and pace when revisiting dark memories. What a sobering story she'd shared. It certainly put his own hardships in perspective. Yes, losing Dad so young had been a tragedy, but compared to what Tess had gone through, Jake's path had been paved with rose petals. He and his sibs didn't have a thing to bitch about. What were they doing hating each other this way? Jake was ashamed of himself and his siblings. No wonder Mom ran away to Lake in the Clouds.

All the trials that Tess had to overcome only made her accomplishments more impressive.

"What makes the rocks so red?" she asked, tugging his attention back to the present.

"The rocks? Iron, I think, but I won't swear to it. I've been here a week, Tess. Something tells me I'd better plan to stop by the tourist bureau in town with you before we go adventuring too much."

She grinned. "If they have pamphlets, definitely so. I love pamphlets. I actually did the drawings for the horned toad pamphlet the State of Texas gives away at the Welcome Centers at the borders."

"Seriously?"

"Seriously."

"Tell me about it."

"Another time. Looks like we've arrived?"

"We have." He pulled into the lot where he'd parked the previous week, pleased to see that his truck was the only vehicle in attendance this morning. Upon switching off the engine, he turned to Tess and asked, "Do you want to go straight out to the point, or are you up for a hike first?"

"I'd love a hike."

"Good. Me, too. We have two choices. The short route is about a mile. I haven't hiked it, but Mom said it takes you to a pretty meadow that's covered in early wildflowers. The longer trail goes down to that waterfall. It's a great walk. Nothing too strenuous and some awesome views. Getting up close and personal to the waterfall is a fabulous payoff. The drawback here is that while I have plenty of water, all I have to eat in the truck are apples and some trail mix. If we take the longer hike, it'll be a lot closer to dinnertime than lunch when we reach Lake in the Clouds. So take potential hunger pangs into consideration when you cast your vote."

"I skip lunch all the time. I vote for the waterfall unless you need more than fruit and nuts?"

"Nope. Waterfall it is."

Jake was the point man during the hike, though he had to keep an eye on Tess. She proved to be even more of a looky-loo hiker than she was as a passenger, and he'd easily have left her behind accidentally. But her delight at the natural wonders along the trail proved to be a joy to witness.

Spying a red fox foraging at the base of a tree, Jake put his finger to his lips in a signal for quiet. He motioned toward the action. Tess's eyes went round, and she covered her mouth with her hand. They stood watching the animal for a full minute before the fox took note of them and darted away.

"How cool was that?" she asked. "I wanted to take a picture, but I didn't want to frighten him away. Have you seen a lot of wildlife since you've been here, Jake? That was my first fox. I'm going to start a list."

She tugged her phone from her pocket and navigated to an app. Watching her thumbs move on the screen, Jake realized it was the first time since he'd picked her up at the airport that he'd seen her on her phone.

Seeing her delight when the sound of the waterfall first reached her ears was worth the hike. She picked up her pace and actually took the lead to reach the viewing spot. Tall and narrow, the frothy snowmelt tumbled some sixty feet or so into a pool, more a gushing noise than a roar. Nevertheless, Jake loved the sound. It seeped into a man and washed away the troubles.

Even more, he loved watching Tess experience this little piece of heaven.

Delight made her glow. She was a fairy in the woods,

a bright-eyed leprechaun. "Don't be diving for the pot of gold," he warned.

"Excuse me?"

"Never mind, Sprite." He offered her a bag of trail mix. "Hungry?"

"Not yet. I'll wait until we finish the hike. This is so fabulous. I know it's not summer yet, but how is it that the trail isn't covered with people? It feels like we are the only humans for miles around."

"That's probably the truth of it." He explained to her about the special arrangement between locals and private property access to Inspiration Point offered by the Triple T Ranch as explained to him by his mother. "It's definitely a wilderness area and a hidden gem."

"Thank you for bringing me here." She went up on her toes and kissed him. A friendly-plus kiss, the first overt action on the flirt side of the line all day.

Jake was ready. He'd been holding his cards, waiting for her to make the first post-first-date move. He saw her the friendly-plus kiss and raised her a scorching one.

"You're welcome," he replied, his voice a little hoarse when he released her and stepped back.

Tess stared up at him, then slowly, deliberately, pulled her phone from her pocket. She made a note, then put her device away.

"Let me guess. Your wild animal list?"

"Mm-hmm."

"Whadya write down?"

"Shall we continue our hike?"

"Mountain lion?"

Tess took point, following the obvious trail through the woods. Jake fell in behind her. "Wolf?"

"I love these aspen trees. I'll bet it's beautiful here in the autumn. Isn't it pretty how the sunshine dapples the forest floor?"

"Elk?"

"And the textures. You know, this is really inspiring. I wish I had my sketch pad."

"Eagle?"

"Badger."

He snorted a laugh and then, when she hesitated in uncertainty at an apparent fork in the trail, eased around her to take the lead. Upon reaching the end of the trail, he led her out onto Inspiration Point. She stood at the railing and sighed with pleasure over the view of the valley below, which included Mirror Lake and the town of Lake in the Clouds. "Oh wow. It's fabulous. This is where you were when you invited me to Colorado?"

"Yes. I was inspired."

"It lives up to its name. Hold on a minute. I'm going to grab something from my suitcase. Will you unlock your truck?"

Jack pushed the button on his key fob as she hurried back to his truck. A few minutes later, she returned carrying a sketchbook and a pair of pencils. "Looks like you weren't kidding about being inspired."

"I wasn't. That's twice within a short time I wanted my sketchbook. I've learned to listen to the urge."

She sat beside him on the bench, opened her book, and went to work. Jake watched her with avid interest. "You're good. Did you learn to draw as part of your design training, or is it something you've always done?"

"Drawing led me to design. That art teacher I mentioned earlier? She took me under her wing. I don't know where I would have ended up without her."

"God bless mentors."

"Absolutely. Mine truly changed my life. She nurtured my talents and encouraged my confidence. Without her help, I never would have navigated the way to higher education."

Jake's admiration for Tess had multiplied significantly since learning about the challenges she'd faced. Such strength, determination, and fortitude had the orphaned child so mistreated by the system possessed to become such a strong, successful woman! She had some strong mojo. He tried to recall where she'd gone to college. He'd had her file in front of him when he called Steve at Innovations Design about hiring her. It had been one of the Big Twelve schools. SMU? No, he remembered. Fort Worth. She'd gone to TCU.

Private school. Good design program. Bet she went on scholarship. "You went to TCU, right? But what about high school? Where did you grow up?"

"Around Houston mostly. Mom was never far from a beach. She loved the sand and surf, and her biggest goal was to live in Hawaii someday. She met Gary in Gulf Shores, Alabama, but we were in Houston when she passed. We'd gone there for its medical care for Brandon, but Galveston being so close was a draw for Mom."

Jake nodded in understanding. "My dad was that way with lakes. He loved the lake. Any lake. The Lonesome River ran through my great-grandfather's ranch, so when they built Lonesome Lake, he ended up with some prime lakefront property. My grandfather built a lake house on it, and it was my dad's favorite place on earth. He was a fiend on a slalom water ski. Taught us all how to ski by the time we were six years old."

"That young?"

"Yep. He used to drag us all out of bed at the crack of dawn and have the ski rope in the water the minute it was light enough to be legal. He was one of the most generous men you'd ever want to meet—except on the water. Dad always took the first ski ride of the day. Best water. Of course, after his ride, he'd drive all over hell and back to find good water for the rest of us to ski. The man loved boating."

"And your mom?"

"She loved Dad. She loved her kids. She totally loved the family time we spent together. Time at the lake house *was* time spent together. We didn't have Internet or cable TV there. Our phone was a landline, so no hiding in your room talking to friends. It was one for all and all for one at Lake-at-the-Ranch."

"How many siblings do you have again?"

"Three. Two sisters and a brother."

"Lucky you."

Jake couldn't argue with her, not after the story she'd shared with him today. His lips twisted in a rueful smile as he added, "Yes, well, unfortunately, we're in the middle of a family fracas these days, so right or wrong, I don't think anyone would name themselves as lucky."

"Who? Your siblings?"

"Yeah."

"What happened?"

"It's a long, stupid story. Lots of anger seething among us. My brother and I aren't speaking at all. I'm not sure where things stand with the girls these days. It's been a civil war. Mom is pretty much disgusted with all of us right now."

"Well, you should fix that."

Jake laughed. "Sure. I'll take care of that right after I cure cancer."

"Is there a reason whatever is wrong can't be put right? I mean, something permanent—like death."

"No, but—"

"Everything else is an excuse, Jake. You're a problem solver. Why haven't you solved this one?"

He scowled at her. "What makes you think I haven't tried? That's half the problem. Hell, three-quarters of it. My family doesn't want me to solve any of their problems anymore. Not my job."

"So tell me about it. What happened?"

"Like I said, it's a stupid story." He didn't want to talk about it, either. The entire thing sounded childish and stupid in comparison to her story because it *was* childish and stupid compared to her story. "How did the conversation get focused on me and my family drama anyway? I was trying to learn about you."

"I told you all about me."

"No, you didn't. Why did you choose to attend TCU?"

"I figured out that a design career fit my skills. TCU had an excellent program, and I was lucky when it came to financial aid. Probably the best perk about being in the system—lots of available aid if you take advantage of it."

"As I recall, you came to Bensler right out of college?"

"Yes. I worked a summer internship there between my junior and senior years and then got hired after graduation. And that's the entire story of Tess Crenshaw. Now it's your turn. What caused the family drama?"

Jake popped the stopper on his water bottle and took a long sip. The water tasted good. It was refreshing and reviving and just what he needed.

He wished it were booze.

"Dammit, Tess. It's embarrassing. I'm ashamed. Truly,

after everything you just told me, what's going on in my family sounds infantile. Your mother died. Our dad died. That's where all similarity ends. You scraped and scrabbled and fought and climbed and built. We had everything given to us. Everything. Love. Security. Support. And we grew up to be such a bunch of whiny kids that our mom ran away from home to get away from us."

"I'm pretty secure in the opinion that it isn't that simple."

"No, I guess it's not. From the outside looking in, what's gone wrong in my family is simple. But being in the middle of it, it's damned murky. Are you familiar with the term *When lakes turn over*?"

"I've never heard of it."

"I don't know if it's a real thing or not, to be honest. It's something my granddad used to say. Our lake had some of the cleanest, clearest water in Texas. Every few years late in the summer, the water would cloud up and get smelly and taste nasty. Gramps said the lake was turning over. What was on the bottom was moving to the top, and what was on the sides was shifting to the center. It was remaking itself. I think that is what is happening with my family. We're turning over and in the smelly nasty stage."

"Do you know why it's happening?"

"I know why it started. I don't know exactly how we ended up smelly and nasty. If I could figure that one out, maybe I could come up with that cure."

"Jake, remind me of something. Remember all those plaques hanging on your office wall at Bensler? They were awards, right?"

He watched her slender fingers sketch the roofline of Raindrop Lodge along the shore of Mirror Lake. She was good with perspective. "Yeah."

"Awards for what?"

"Leadership mostly."

"And in order to lead, what must one have? A team. That's what you're missing, Jake. You're too close to the problem to see all the possibilities. Why don't you let me be your team? We work well together. You know we do. Bring in an outside consultant, a new set of eyes to study the problem. Maybe I'll see something you haven't."

"You want me to open a vein and bleed all over you, huh?"

She lifted her shoulders and continued to draw. "I showed you mine..."

Jake slowly filled his lungs with air. Except for his lawyer, who didn't count, he hadn't told anyone his side of the story. Mom—no. He'd never go there. He'd come close to confiding in Aunt Helen once, but he didn't want to put her in the position to take sides, and yet, something about Tess made him want to open up. Exhaling in a rush, he said, "Okay, but if I'm going to do this, I need more than trail mix. Do you care to sacrifice that meat and cheese pack you bought yesterday to take back to the office? We can replace it before you return to Texas."

"Sure."

"I'll go get it. You keep drawing."

He returned a few minutes later with sustenance produced by the Triple T Ranch. She'd finished her sketch of the valley, flipped to a new page, and had begun drawing an elk in the meadow. She must have had a visitor while he was gone. "Did I tell you that the contractor in charge of the renovations on the lodge is a Throckmorton—as in Triple T? Though I gather they have some family drama of their own going on because he made sure my mother and aunt knew his business was in no way connected with the ranch."

"Well, if my budding consulting business goes well with the Prentices, perhaps I can add the Throckmortons as clients."

"Gettin' a little ahead of yourself there, aren't you, Crenshaw?"

"I'm just confident. So spill, what happened to your family?"

Jake reclaimed his seat beside her and offered the tray of sliced meats, cheeses, nuts, and crackers. "In a nutshell, death and taxes."

Tess made a selection. "I'm going to need more than a nutshell."

"Figured you would." He popped some summer sausage in his mouth, followed up with cheese and nuts and half a bottle of water, then continued, "My father had a decent amount of life insurance when he died, so my family didn't hurt for money. That said, Mom was careful with it. She'd been a stay-at-home mom—paying for day care for four didn't make sense—so money management was part of her job. She grew up in a middle-class neighborhood, and she respected the value of a dollar."

He paused, frowned, and added, "Which is one reason why the way she's conducted this Colorado project of hers has thrown me for a loop. But that's another subject entirely. My dad's family has been ranching property in the Hill Country since the 1880s."

"The Lonesome River Ranch. You also had a photograph of it on the wall in your office."

"You remember that?"

"I do. Designers notice things."

"Ah. Yeah. Well, down through the years, the family managed to keep most of the ranch intact, and my great-grandfather bought back parts of it that had been sold off over the generations. He and my grandfather were very proud of that fact. Very proud. They didn't work the entire ranch. They leased a good portion of it to other farmers and ranchers to work, but Lonesome River Ranch owned the land. My grandfather was his father's sole heir. My father was an only child. He predeceased his father, who passed about three and a half years ago now."

She looked up from her page, where she worked on the animal's rack. "Don't tell me your grandfather left you the ranch? Like a British entailment thing?"

"Oh no. He left equal shares in the ranch in trust to my siblings and me. The question we faced was whether to keep it and continue to ranch or cash out. His will setup was red-blooded American egalitarian—one person, one vote with a tie going to the house—keeping the status quo—which should have worked. It would have worked, too, had he not made some late-in-the-game changes to the trust documents because the lady lawyer Lucas was sleeping with thought she'd screw us all."

"That sounds ominous."

"She was a piece of work, I'm telling you. She's the grand-daughter of the attorney who drafted the original documents. He was a good man. A good attorney. There was absolutely nothing wrong with the documents he drafted. After her grandfather died, she reviewed the Lonesome River Ranch's file and managed to convince Lucas, who then convinced my grandfather, that the documents required updating. As usual, my brother was thinking with his di—" Jake swallowed the word, but not quickly enough.

Tess chastised him with a look, then asked, "Was she wrong?"

"Yes. Well, not entirely. The documents could have used tweaking, but not the wholesale restructuring that she gave them. It dissolved the original trust and created a new one. My grandfather never should have signed the papers without having them reviewed by another attorney. The whole thing was a disaster."

"Did it change who inherited the ranch?"

"No. It was more subtle than that. Due to changes in tax law, the structure of the new trust created a significant tax liability. I'll go to my grave believing she did it on purpose. She wanted her grubby little mitts on the land. You know how much property in the Hill Country has appreciated in the past twenty-five years. Never mind normal growth. The ranch is smack-dab in the middle of the Texas wine country."

She set down her pencil. "You had to sell it to pay taxes?"

"We did. In my opinion, we had no effing choice. Lucas about had a heart attack when he finally realized just who was screwing whom. I thought he might kill the lawyer. I truly did. Not that it's a done deal yet—here it is over three years later. One thing after another has delayed the settlement. My sisters wanted to sell from the beginning— as everyone knew they would. Lucas believed up to the very end that I'd vote with him to hold on to the ranch and scrape together enough somehow, someway, to pay our sisters for their shares. The problem is that numbers don't lie. The land is more valuable than the ranch. If we sold enough land to pay the taxes and the girls, there wouldn't be enough ranchland left to work. Lucas didn't agree, but he was thinking with his heart, not his head. I had to do what was best for the family, Lucas included, and voted to sell."

"So the lady lawyer bought the land?"

"Some of it. Or at least, a group she's connected to are attempting to buy it. The sale is now tied up in courts. I swear, I have some choice opinions about lawyers these days. Begging Aunt Helen's pardon. We're hung up in court, and in the meantime, the IRS is talking penalty smack like zebras at a convention of Sunday refs."

"Zebras at a...oh...the two-legged kind. Sorry." Tess flipped her sketchbook closed. "The sport reference came out of left field, so to speak. Who is 'we' hung up in court?"

Jake rubbed the back of his neck and winced. "There are some lawsuits going on."

"Involving?"

"Well, all of us."

"Who is suing whom?"

Jake sighed heavily. "I filed a malpractice suit against Lucas's former lawyer and her firm. Lucas is suing everybody and the dogcatcher for any reason he can come up with. He just wants to delay the sale as long as he can. I suspect that Lucas, Willow, and Brooke are suing me, although I don't have a clue as to what grounds they think they have. I haven't been served, so I could be wrong about that, but it's an educated guess based on the guilty looks I saw when I stumbled upon a meeting between the three of them. As far as I know, Mom hasn't told them I showed up in Lake in the Clouds."

"Oh, Jake. You're running from a process server?"

"I don't know that. It's just a guess."

"Family suing family. Your poor mother. So the bottom line here is what, Prentice? Your grandfather's estate is not settled after...how long?"

"Three-and-a-half years since he died. Three years since the excrement hit the fan."

"What exactly is happening with the land?"

Jake closed his eyes and shook his head. "Understand that we each had a truckload of money coming to us, and then just as we were beginning to realize what bag of crap Lucas had gotten us into, Willow's husband was killed."

"Oh no."

"It was terrible. Andy was a really great guy. They have two young kids, Emma and Drew. After Andy died, Willow had no time or mental energy to worry about the ranch. Brooke was another story. She's my younger sister, and she's married to Travis, who may be the biggest asshole I've ever encountered in my life. None of us could ever figure out what she saw in him, but Mom had learned the hard way with Willow and Andy and kept her mouth shut when Brooke started bringing Travis around. So Lucas and I followed her lead. Travis was always a bit of a wheeler-dealer, but once our grandfather died and the prospect of all that money coming to Brooke, well, I think he made some promises he shouldn't. I don't know for sure, but I suspect they're in a serious financial bind because we're slogging our way through the legal bog."

"That's terrible, Jake. No wonder your mother ran away. I'm surprised she only went as far as Colorado."

"Well, she did get on an airplane with her passport yesterday, so..."

"Back to the bottom line." Tess ticked the points off on her fingers. "Your inheritance is tied up in court. It's tearing your family apart. The only people who will benefit from this will be lawyers and maybe the IRS. You know this, don't you?"

"Yes."

"So why are lawyers still involved? Why haven't you

done your leader thing and found a solution everyone can live with?"

"Because I am not my father!" Jake exploded. "Apparently, I have an identity crisis. Imagine three little kids with their hands on their hips and snotty little voices saying, 'You're not the boss of me.' That's the message I got loud and clear. Even better, they delivered it through my mother."

Jake shoved to his feet. "I'm sorry. I can't do this anymore. Not now. I appreciate the effort, Tess, but…I just get so damned angry."

Tess gathered up her sketchbook and rose gracefully. She studied him, the tilt of her chin signaling that she was carefully considering her words. Inwardly, Jake squirmed a little bit, waiting to see what she'd have to say. Finally, she nodded. "All right. Like they say down in Enchanted Canyon, the road from Ruin to Redemption wasn't built in a day."

Her reference to a Texas Hill Country tourist hot spot succeeded in introducing a ray of light into Jake's dark thoughts. His Bensler team had spent a four-day work retreat at a resort there last spring, a renovated cathouse, saloon, and dancehall built halfway on the road between the thriving small town of Redemption and the ghost town of Ruin. They'd had a productive meeting and a damned good time listening to some fabulous budding Americana musicians, a couple of which had scored hits on the country music charts in the months since.

Conversation during the rest of the trip to Lake in the Clouds revolved around the retreat and the friendship that had developed out of the event between Jake and the three owners of the Enchanted Canyon property, one of whom apparently lived in a small town in Colorado not far from Lake in the Clouds. "I want to get over there to visit

Boone Callahan and his bride while you're here," Jake said. "Eternity Springs is on my to-explore list."

They stopped at a restaurant for a real lunch, then visited the bait shop to purchase a fishing license for Tess. After dropping by Aunt Helen's to feed the cat, they finally pulled into Raindrop Lodge and Cabins Resort a little before four. Jake pointed out his cabin but drove directly to Cabin 12. "I hope you'll have everything you need, but if you don't, just let me know."

He dug the shiny new key out of his truck's console where his mother had left it and handed it to her. "The cabins still use old-fashioned locks, but you don't need to worry that every tradesman and tourist in town has a key. I had all the cabins rekeyed last week."

"Thanks." Tess glanced around, her expression bright and interested. "This is so cute. It's right out of *Little House in the Big Woods*."

"Laura Ingalls Wilder fan, hmm?"

"I lived at the library when I was in grade school. Reading was my escape."

"Nothing beats a good novel when a person needs to run away. And don't forget, there's a hammock outside of my cabin I'm happy to share. But your porch swing is a pretty good reading spot, too."

"I'm so excited!"

Jake chuckled. "Go on in. I'll bring your bags."

He didn't have to tell her twice. By the time he followed with her things from the truck, she had the door open and stood in the center of the cabin's main room with her hands clasped and a smile on her face as she turned in a slow circle. "It's perfect. Just perfect! Cozy and homey. Rustic but not too rustic. Oh, and look. They left fresh flowers."

"Mom is crazy about flowers." Jake carried her suitcase and the shopping bags from yesterday's outing into the bedroom and set them down. "You should see her holiday tables. She goes all out. Well..." He paused and a look of nostalgia flashed across his face. "She *used* to go all out anyway. Think we ruined that for her."

"Maybe you can redeem yourselves."

"Maybe." Returning to the main room, he said, "I think that's everything from the truck. Mom stocked the fridge with basics, and the tap water is safe to drink. I'll head to my place and let you get settled in. I have steaks to grill for supper. Want to wander on over to Cabin 1 about martini time?"

"That sounds great."

"Good." He gave her a quick, easy kiss, then said, "See you later, Sprite."

Jake sauntered toward the door, but at the threshold, he paused. The words that had been churning deep inside him all this time rose from within him and burst from his lips. "It's not the money."

"I'm sorry? What?"

"It's not about the money. Well, maybe with Brooke, it is about the money, but that's mainly because of the asshole Travis pushing her. For Willow and especially Lucas, no. It wasn't about getting rich. It wasn't even about keeping or losing the land. I think that a lot of this is about losing Dad when we did. It's been almost twenty years, but we are all still stuck. It's the traditional versus the burgundy and gold Christmas tree all over again. My family—Mom included—is still grieving, and we're doing a piss-poor job of moving beyond it. We haven't grown up."

Seventeen

I THINK THAT A lot of this is about losing Dad when we did.

Jake's statement echoed through the cabin long after he'd left. Tess pondered it as she unpacked her suitcase and checked out the fridge, the cabinets, and the pantry. She tested the fragrances of the toiletries in the bathroom. "Oh wow, that's nice."

Checking the label, she saw they were made by hand at a shop called Heavenscents in Eternity Springs, Colorado. "Need to make sure we put a stop at the soap shop on our list."

It's been almost twenty years, but we are all still stuck.

Tess checked out the novels on the nightstand, then opened the back door and explored the back porch. What a gorgeous view. Jake had been right about the swing, too. Genevieve had left a throw folded and draped over the back of it. Made a girl want to curl up beneath the blanket with a cup of hot tea and watch the water. Maybe with a chocolate chip cookie, too. Genevieve had left three tubes of cookie dough in the fridge. She'd made a point to mention that Jake had a serious sweet tooth and chocolate chip cookies were a favorite.

My family—Mom included—is still grieving, and we're doing a piss-poor job of moving beyond it.

Tess decided that she'd sat enough for today. While tube cookies weren't as good as cookies made from scratch, they'd definitely do in a pinch. Besides, doing something with her hands would help her think. She needed to think.

How could she best help Jake? Drop the subject? Offer him advice? A shoulder to lean on? What advice did she have to give him anyway? Suck it up, Buttercup? Bottom line, that's how she felt, wasn't it?

He was right. Compared to her, he'd had it made in the shade. And yet...

We haven't grown up.

What did she know about families anyway? She'd never had one. Well, not since her mother died.

Maybe that's what I know. I know about losing a family.

Hmm. Tess made the cookies, her mind whirring. While she sliced and shaped the dough, Tess thought over everything she'd learned about Jake Prentice during the time she'd worked for him. She considered what she'd discovered about the man since that day in November when he'd fired her. She pondered the revelations today had brought.

We haven't grown up.

His family was his blessing. His family was his cross to bear. *Suck it up, Buttercup. Do you know how lucky you are?* He did, obviously. That's why he was so tormented.

Tess sighed. She'd adored Genevieve and Helen when she'd met them. Honestly, it was hard for her to relate to his complaints about his family. She had nothing for him beyond chocolate chip cookies and a sympathetic ear or a comforting hug or all three. She'd start with the cookies, maybe drop off a few warm from the oven rather than wait and bring them for dessert tonight like she'd originally planned. She wouldn't have to disturb whatever he was doing now. Just put a few on a plate and leave them in front of his door. Text him they were there. A nice little surprise. Yeah, that's what she'd do.

We haven't grown up.

When it came to cookies, everybody was still a kid, right?

She'd just slid the baking sheet into the preheated oven when a thudding sound outside captured her notice. She glanced out the window but couldn't see anything.

Turning her attention back to her baking, she set the timer on her phone and tried to decide what to do next. Maybe take a walk alongside the lake after the cookies finished baking? Perhaps she should try out one of the fishing poles she'd spied standing in the corner on the back porch.

Whack. Whack. Whack.

Hmm. Either a really big woodpecker had shown up, or someone was chopping wood.

The sound was coming from the opposite direction of Jake's cabin. That's strange. Maybe the contractors had shown up early.

Curious, Tess decided to check. Situational awareness was always good policy for a woman, whether in the middle of a city or at an isolated lakeside cabin in the mountains.

She grabbed her phone and stepped outside. Following both the sound and a footpath through the woods, she walked along a twisting trail for perhaps a hundred yards or maybe longer to a cabin a little larger than the others she had noticed here at Raindrop Lodge as Jake drove her to her cabin. She spied the marker for cabin 14, and concern washed over her. She knew for a fact that no one else was supposed to be staying at the cabins. Both Genevieve and Jake had mentioned that. Did Raindrop Resort have a squatter?

She'd better tell Jake.

Tell him what? That she'd heard a really big woodpecker? Tess decided to move just a little closer and see if she couldn't gather more helpful information without exposing herself to a potentially dangerous situation. After all, she wasn't one of those slasher movie characters who acted stupidly and earned their bloody demise.

Whack. Whack. Whack.

But then again, that did sound like an ax hitting wood.

In that instant, a number of things happened simultaneously. Something large rustled through the trees in the woods behind her, which sent Tess scrambling forward. She spied the rear end of a vehicle parked behind the cabin.

Tess caught sight of the axman. Her heart pounded, and her mouth went dry.

Jake was naked above the waist. He'd changed into faded jeans that hung low on his hips and hugged his ass. His large hands grasped the wooden handle of an ax. As he swung it back, around, over and down, muscles bulged in his arms, bunched in his shoulders, and rippled along his back. His skin glistened with sweat.

The log split in two. A shudder ran through Tess.

He set another log on the stump. Swung the ax. *Whack.* Wood dropped.

It was raw masculinity in motion, primitive and magnificent. Tess stood watching him. Wanting him.

Beep. Beep. Beep. Beep. Beep. She jumped when the timer on her phone went off. "Shoot!"

Jake checked his motion mid-swing and managed not to

cut his foot off—thank God—as he twisted around toward the noise. Tess fumbled to turn off the alarm.

"Shoot. Shoot. Shoot. Shoot. Shoot." The cookies were gonna burn. She smiled at Jake and waved. "Gotta run. I'm baking cookies. You should stop by my cabin and get some while they're hot!"

She turned to leave, then hesitated just long enough to add, "Hey, Jake? I think it's gonna rain."

He took the fastest shower in history.

The air in Cabin 12 smelled like burnt cookies, but he wasn't the least bit bothered. His senses were too busy feasting on what he found waiting for him in the bedroom.

Damned it if didn't actually rain.

She made another batch of cookies, which they ate in bed fresh from the oven, listening to raindrops patter on the roof's wood shingles. Thunder rumbled across the valley from time to time. Twice, lightning strikes had Tess near to jumping out of her skin. And lovely skin it was, creamy and sweet. Tasty. Addictive.

Lying beside Jake after they'd made love for the third time—nothing like a dry spell to goose a man's stamina— Tess stretched like a cat and purred. "Mm. There's only one bad thing about afternoon rain showers."

Jake would have arched a curious brow if he'd had the energy. Even dry-spell stamina ran out eventually. He did manage to meet her gaze and blink.

"Your wood is all wet."

Okay, for that, he did manage the brow lift. "If not, I wasn't doing it right."

She giggle-snorted. "Firewood. You said something this morning about a campfire beside the lake. I thought that's why you were chopping wood."

"Ah. No. We have a couple of covered woodpiles on the property. I decided to split logs because I needed to beat up on something after thinking about my brother."

Tess nodded her understanding, then said, "I think that the thunder and lightning are over. I'm going to take a nap."

"Excellent idea." Jake drifted off to sleep.

When he next woke up, the mattress beside him was empty, but the sheets where she had been lying weren't cold. She hadn't been gone long. He rolled out of bed, dressed, and went in search of his guest. His friend. His lover. He liked the sound of that.

She was sitting in the swing on the back porch, a mug of something hot in her hands, her legs curled up beneath her and covered by a blanket. The smile she turned toward him warmed him like a five o'clock Friday afternoon martini. Finally, she asked, "Feel better?"

"Like a million dollars."

"Me, too. Water's still warm in the hot pot if you want some tea."

"I'm good. Thanks." He sat in the swing and stole her blanket.

"Hey!"

"C'mere." Grinning, he pulled her against him. "Did you sleep?"

"I did. For a little while. Then I got up and ate the last cookie—"

"No!"

"And came out here to think. There is something I need to talk to you about."

"You know, in my experience, that's never a good thing to hear."

"It's not a bad thing, I promise. But it is a thing. You have good instincts, Prentice. You've always had them."

"Are you going to dim my shine, Crenshaw?"

"I hope not. I don't think so. It shouldn't. But I can't in good conscience go any longer without showing you what I brought tucked into my suitcase." She reached over and plucked an envelope from behind a pillow on the swing. "I've come from Austin bearing gifts of a sort. It's a job offer from Innovations Design."

"Whoa. Whoa. Whoa. What the hell are you talking about?"

"They're offering you a partnership and the CEO designation."

He shifted her away from him. "Wait. I don't understand this. This is coming at me out of left field."

"I know. Here's the deal. Your name came up in a conversation I had with Steve, and one thing led to another. I'm just the messenger. Frankly, I don't think now is the time to discuss it. I don't want to discuss it now. This is our time. We can talk about the job later, at the end of my trip. Shoot, we don't have to talk about it at all. You call Steve and leave me out of it. However, under the circumstances, I couldn't in good conscience let any more time pass without telling you an offer is on the table."

"For me to work with you again."

"Yes."

"As the CEO. Which means Bensler all over again. No…fraternizing."

"No worries. I've got that one covered. I made sure. Read the paperwork. It's all in there. We're organized as a partnership. I'd be a partner. We'd be equals. No sexual harassment among equals."

Jake shook his head. "I don't want to think about a job, Tess. I'm working real hard at not thinking about working, and that's working for me."

"Good. That works for me, too. That said, I do think that when you're ready, you should take a look at it and give the offer serious consideration. I'm going to say one thing about it, then I'm going to shut up. Not only would you be perfect for the job, the job is also perfect for you. After you find a way to end your family's war, you are going to want to go back to work. So there's the envelope. The subject is closed. Do you know that your mother's contractor arrived riding a horse a little while ago? Made me feel right at home."

Jake didn't respond at first. He'd gone from feeling like a million bucks to his personal version of a Blues Brother with the appearance of a single manilla envelope. Except it hadn't been the envelope that brought back the blues, had it?

"What makes you think I'm going to manage an armistice? Do you have an atomic bomb in your pocket you're willing to share?"

"Nope. What I do have is clarity. I have a rope to throw you so you can climb from that murky lake."

"Heave-ho, darlin'."

"It's about what you said earlier. I think you are too close to the situation to see it clearly, but your mother is, too. You said she gave you this big charge about figuring out who you are. Well, the thing is, your mom hasn't seen you the way I have. She sees her son, who stepped up when his father was gone and filled some vital family roles. She doesn't see the managing director of a global business firm Jake Prentice, an accomplished leader and problem solver. You know exactly who you are, Jake, and it's not your father. You are who you've always been. You. A leader and a problem solver. You don't need to change that. You're a man who would make your father proud. A man with the values your parents instilled in you. But you are your own person, and you're a good one at that."

"Tess, I appreciate the sentiment, but it's not that simple."

"I know, and I'm not finished yet. Give me another minute."

"Must I?"

"Yep. Because I'm a pragmatist, and I'm about to throw you that rope."

"Okay, I'm listening. Save me, Tess."

"You're going to save yourself. You'd have done it on your own, but I'm here now. You've always worked well with a team. Right, Mr. Quarterback?"

"You're a hoot." And somehow, she made him feel better even when talking about the thing that bothered him most of all.

"Look at it under the nature versus nurture lens. Perhaps your father's death when you were fifteen fundamentally changed you. Or maybe what it did was accelerate the development of the traits with which you were born. I'll bet you were a leader on the school playground. I know you were the quarterback of the football team. Leading others and solving problems is your nature. I don't think you can change that. You don't need to change it. No one should ask it of you.

"So here's my rope. It's obvious to me that your number one priority isn't figuring out who you are or what job you want to do for the rest of your life. Your number one priority is family, and you are the family fixer. You fix things. The Lonesome River Ranch issue is more complicated than most, so it's taking you longer than you are accustomed to things taking. You haven't lost your mojo, Jake."

He snorted.

"For one reason or another, and I agree that grief is probably a big part of it, you've lost faith in yourself. You can fix this. I know you can. I have faith in you."

"How?"

"I don't know. When you're ready, you'll stop thinking with your heart and your pride, and you'll start thinking with your head, and you'll figure it out."

"What are you, my cheerleader, then?" He waggled his brows. "Is this the place I make a pom-pom joke?"

"Partners, remember? I'm your star receiver."

"We're gonna turn this Prentice Civil War into the Family Super Bowl?"

"And win."

"Hmm. Who's performing at halftime?"

"I think that would have to be the singing nuns direct from the convent in Austria, wouldn't you?"

"That would certainly be a change." He snuggled her back against him, kissed the top of her head, and sent the swing into motion with a push from his foot. He considered what she'd said. Did he buy into her theory? Maybe. The idea did sort of settle on his shoulders like a favorite old T-shirt.

Well, there was no rush to worry over it. He'd let the idea cook for a bit. He was on vacation. He had a woman in his arms and mountains to climb. Trails to hike. Fish to catch. *Watch out, Colorado. Here we come.*

"One thing before I let this go, Tess. Does this theory of yours mean I don't have to figure out what I want to be when I grow up?"

"Exactly! That's lesson number one of successful adulting. A person grows up his entire life."

～⫘

The Bavarian Alps

"I can't believe we're here," Helen said, sitting with her sister at a café not far from where the final scene of *The Sound of Music* had been filmed, cups of steaming hot cocoa before them. "I swear I wouldn't be surprised to see Captain von Trapp appear on that trail right below us."

"It's so beautiful. Breathtaking." Genevieve gazed out at the panoramic view of the mountains and sighed. "It's been a fabulous tour. When we get home, I'm going to send Kimberly a case of her favorite wine."

"I'll admit I thought having a private guide was overkill, but Klaus has been a treasure. We saw everything we could have wanted, and then some. No way would we have been able to twirl our way across that meadow if we'd been part of a tour bus."

"I just hope he doesn't use those photos for blackmail purposes."

"He wouldn't do that." Helen nibbled at her bottom lip a moment and added, "I don't think."

Genevieve gave a little laugh and winced. "I can't believe we actually wore nuns' habits. We really need to find a church and go to confession before we board an airplane to go home."

"We're not Catholic, Gen."

"That's the point, Helen."

"No. The point is we danced barefoot across an alpine meadow while singing at the top of our lungs, never mind that our voices are more Janis Joplin than Julie Andrews."

"You're right," Genevieve agreed. "Oh, Helen. I'm so glad we finally made this trip."

"The trip of a lifetime. Our dream trip. Now we can go home and die."

Genevieve frowned at her sister. "Are you feeling all right? Is your knee bothering you again?"

"Of course my knee is bothering me. My knee is always bothering me. Or if my knee isn't bothering me, it's my hip. Or if it isn't my hip, it's my back. If it's not any of those, I have gas, or the runs, or I can't get the damned international calling card to work. Once upon a time, I was on the cutting edge of technology. Do you remember that? I owned some of the first personal computers of anyone in our acquaintance. Now your grandchildren whip my ass playing Nintendo games. Have you seen the island that Emma has built in *Animal Crossings*? It's magnificent. She's only three, and she has flowers everywhere. Her island puts mine to shame. And don't even get me started on how Drew humiliates me in *Mario*. I'm just the plodding old Auntie H."

"No, you're the cool auntie with a Nintendo Switch who lives in Colorado and plays *Animal Crossings* and *Mario* with her great-niece and great-nephew in Tennessee. Have I mentioned recently how much I appreciate your doing that with the kids? They love it so much. And by the way, Willow helps Emma with her flowers."

"She helps her buy them. Emma plants them all on her own."

Genevieve smothered a smile. "Willow says it's been a real escape for them since Andy died."

"It's fun. I'm glad I can help." Helen's tone sounded somewhat mollified. "I remember what it was like for your kids when David died. A little escape time helped. I was pretty darned good at *Legend of Zelda* back in the day."

"I remember that. You played with the boys."

"I did. I just hate that the technology comes so much easier for kids now. And I *really* hate it when younger people laugh at us about it. Young kids, okay. I'll take it from them, but young adults? Hey, at least we can store a ten-digit number in our heads. Half of them don't even know their own partner's phone number!"

Genevieve carefully smoothed the napkin in her lap. Helen didn't often get in these sorts of moods, but when she did, watch out.

"They think they're so much smarter. They know more than all the generations who came before. Well, excuse the hell me. Knowledge builds upon knowledge. Wonder what percentage of these know-it-alls would freeze to death if they had to build a friction fire to keep themselves warm?"

Helen took a sip of her hot cocoa and returned her attention to the alpine vista. Her voice sounded hollow as she finished, "I can't believe it's over."

"Something has happened, Helen. What is it?"

"We're at the end of our *Sound of Music* tour, that's what. Klaus is taking us back to Salzburg. And then what? Home to die."

"Well, aren't you Miss Cheery and Light?" Her sister's attitude had finally tripped her own mood over to annoyed.

Helen shrugged. "Actually, no, I'm not. I'm sad. We've looked forward to this trip for the better part of our lives, and now it's behind us. Box checked. Just like so many other things. We don't have many boxes left, Gen. Have you noticed? And our chances to check 'em off are getting scarce as hen's teeth and can end like that." She snapped her fingers.

"So we don't waste any more time. *The Sound of Music* tour wasn't our only dream. Let's go ahead and start planning the next box to check."

"Like what?" Helen asked glumly.

"Well, one thing pops to mind immediately. We should come back to Germany. We've always said we wanted to come to the German Christmas markets. We should make plans to do that in December."

"Genevieve, you're not going to do that."

"Why wouldn't I?"

"You didn't have Christmas with your children this past year. You are not going to miss two in a row. I know you."

"Well, you have a point." Genevieve sat back in her chair and folded her arms. "I never would have done that in the past. But this is a new year. A new me. I danced barefoot in an Alpine meadow while dressed as a nun, for goodness' sake. I'm letting go, remember?"

Helen darted a hard look Genevieve's way, then took a long sip of her cocoa. "What about the lodge renovation? We would sort of be bailing on our big project, don't you think?"

"We're not doing the work ourselves. We're supervising. We hire people we trust and follow up to make sure they're trustworthy. We have time to do both, Helen. We are on no one's schedule but our own. That's the blessing of retirement, isn't it?"

"I don't feel like I retired. I feel like I surrendered. As far as being on our own schedule, that's BS, and you know it. We're on our doctors' schedules. Do you think we'd have time to fit all of our doctors' appointments in between the time we get back home and the time we'd need to leave again?"

"Okay, there you have a point."

"At my age, all I do is go to doctors' appointments. I'm about ready to start taking Dad's approach."

Genevieve arched her brows. "Stop going to doctors?"

"They won't find something wrong if you never go." Helen shrugged and added, "It worked for Roger."

Her offhand manner was a Big Fat Clue. "Roger? Would that be Roger Seidel?"

Roger Seidel was Helen's second husband.

"I got an e-mail. He's dying. His doctor says he's got a couple of weeks. Pancreatic cancer."

"Oh, Helen." Now her uncharacteristic mood made sense.

"He had a couple of things he wanted me to know. He said he's happy about the way he's going out." She shrugged, and her eyes filled as she added, "He was a sorry, no-good, cheating asshole, but..."

Genevieve reached across the table and patted her sister's arms. "I know. He was your sorry, no-good cheating asshole for a while. I am sorry, honey. I did like him for a little while."

"About three months, as I recall."

"More like two. It took me some time to work up the nerve to tell you."

Helen sobbed a laugh. "You have tissues in your purse?"

"Of course." Genevieve fished one from her bag and handed it over. "News like this only makes me more determined to come to Germany this coming December."

"Why? Because life is so damned short? You're afraid one of us won't make it to next year?"

"Well, that's always a possibility, isn't it? Life being short isn't a surprise to me. That lesson was driven home when my husband died when I was thirty-nine years old. We aren't guaranteed another moment on this earth, and we owe it to ourselves and those we love to live every day we're given as the gift it is and face the end with as few regrets as possible. I've been doing some thinking, myself, during this trip, Helen. It's time I fix some things."

Her sister gave her a penetrating look. "The kids?"

"Yes." Genevieve sighed heavily. "They are first on my list. I need to go back to being their mom again. Not the old mom, mind you, but a new, improved version. A healthier version. One who isn't so dependent on them for my own happiness. Colorado has done that for me."

"Oh, honey. I'm so glad. I knew Lake in the Clouds would be good for you." Helen reached for Genevieve's hand and gave it a squeeze. "I think there's something special about the mountain air in our part of Colorado. My friend Celeste likes to say it is where broken hearts come to heal."

Genevieve smiled in response. "Maybe it's mountain air everywhere. The Alps have been good for me, too. Something inside of me has healed, Helen, and I'm ready to tackle family life again. When we get home, I'm going to invite all of my children to visit."

"I'm so glad to hear that. I think the mountain air will do them good, too. Who knows, maybe the Prentice family will find peace in Lake in the Clouds."

"From your mouth to God's ears." Genevieve shrugged and added, "But if they don't, I won't let it destroy my peace. That's where the new and improved mom comes in. I have to let them live their lives as they see fit. I need to not be dependent on them for my happiness, and the way to do that is to live my life fully. That's why you and I will go to Germany for the Christmas markets this year. We may have crossed the Alps off our bucket list, but we've got more adventures ahead of us."

Helen sighed with satisfaction. "We climbed every mountain, didn't we?"

"I can't think of one we missed." Dramatically, she added, "And, we'll always have Germany."

Amusement sparkled in Helen's eyes for the first time all day. "Are you attempting to movie quote? I thought it was, 'We'll always have Paris.'"

"Har. Har. Har. That's another movie for another day."

"Ah, *Casablanca*. Bogart and Bergman. Love and sacrifice. No matter how many times I watch that movie, I always hope she won't get on the plane. Why was I never able to find a man willing to sacrifice a darned thing for me?"

"Never say never, Helen. You're not six feet under yet. Who says you have to stop looking? There are some perfectly good, decent, handsome guys our age out there. Gage Throckmorton, for example. If that box isn't on your list, you need to add it."

"Whoa whoa whoa? I'm getting a little freaked out here. This role reversal we are having is just a little too much."

"Helen, it's not role reversal. Are you not paying attention? You are looking at a new and improved Genevieve Prentice, remember? What's to say that I'm not ready for a little romance myself."

"Well, I guess I shouldn't be surprised. You did buy that vagina necklace."

"If you play your cards right, when we get home to Colorado, I'll buy one for you, too. Now, let's go track down Klaus, shall we? We need him to take our photo here in front of the Alps to bookend the Bennett sisters' oh-so-awesome *Sound of Music* tour."

The women rose from their seats, and as they exited the café, Genevieve heard her sister muse, "Hmm. Maybe we could do one where I pretend to be Gretl, and he's the captain. That'd be a really nice way to end the tour."

Genevieve rolled her eyes and laughed at the reference to Captain von Trapp carrying his youngest child, Gretl, up the mountain trail on his back. Helen was back to her usual self.

All was right in Genevieve's world.

Eighteen

TESS SPENT THE NEXT two weeks tumbling head over heels in love with her former boss's boss's boss as they explored Lake in the Clouds and the surrounding area together. During the day, they hiked, fished, climbed, and rafted. They shopped, dawdled, toured, and tasted. They spent their evenings tucked away in Cabin 12, cooking supper, listening to music, sitting beside the fire, talking, laughing, and making love. It had been nirvana.

Because Jake was Jake and owning it, every morning before they left Raindrop Lodge, they checked in with Zach Throckmorton for an update on the previous day's accomplishments. Zach understandably resisted the supervision, but once Jake proved he wouldn't interfere, the contractor took Jake's interest in stride.

Occasionally, they talked about the job offer, and Tess could tell he was seriously considering it. When Tess brought up the necessity of scheduling her return home, he'd rolled out a business proposal of his own. He wanted to hire Tess to do the interior design for the Raindrop Lodge remodel.

He would present the design plan as a gift to his mother, he explained. Not only would that give her an excuse to delay her return to Texas, but it would also be good for the Raindrop Lodge and, as a result, his mother and aunt's bottom line.

Tess wasn't so confident that this was a good idea. Genevieve Prentice and her sister struck Tess as women who wouldn't want unsolicited input on their project's interior design. Nevertheless, at Jake's insistence, they held a conference call with Steve during which they discussed both the lodge project and the offer Innovations Design had extended to Jake. By the time the call ended, Steve had agreed that Tess should prioritize the Raindrop Lodge design and work virtually on her other projects from Lake in the Clouds until the lodge project was completed. Jake had promised a decision on the offer by the time Tess returned to Texas.

After disconnecting the call, he turned to her with a smile on his face that didn't quite meet his eyes. That's when Tess had her first inkling that he wasn't feeling the Innovations Design position the way that she'd hoped.

"What's wrong?"

"Nothing really. I just…" Jake shrugged. "I'm really glad that you are here. I like making plans on the fly."

"I'm glad to be here, too. This has been the best vacation I've ever had. Unfortunately, it is a vacation. I haven't socked away enough to retire quite yet, and even wonderful jobs have limited vacation days."

"I'm not ready for them to end. You know, Sprite, being unemployed has its perks."

"Yes, well, some of us need a paycheck." When his wry grin melted into a frown, she added, "However, the half-day arrangement you negotiated for me with Steve is totally awesome."

"Yeah. I did do a good job with that."

"It might actually be the best of both worlds. Honestly, vacationing with you is hard work, Prentice. I'm sore from that hike we did yesterday."

"Want a massage?" He gave her that slow grin that invariably made her weak in the knees. "Or since you don't officially begin the new schedule until Monday, maybe this would be a good time to make that drive over to Eternity Springs. I understand they have hot springs soaking pools. We could get a room and stay overnight at that B and B my mother raves about. Poke around the shops tomorrow before heading back. That's where the soap shop that you're anxious to visit is located, right?"

"Don't you have the Internet guy scheduled to come back tomorrow?"

"Oh yeah. Forgot about that." Once Jake had conceived the idea to have her create a design for the lodge, he'd immediately set about furnishing Cabin 1 as an office space, which included the installation of Internet service. However, unreliable service had necessitated a callback for the technician. "He's supposed to show up about ten. How about we leave for Eternity Springs after he's done?"

"That works for me."

"Cool. In the meantime, lie down, Sprite, and let me see what I can do about the knots in your muscles."

By the time he was done, Tess was limp as a noodle from head to toe, and when Jake wanted to go fishing, she opted for an afternoon nap. As a result, she walked through the woods alone after awakening from her slumber, heading toward the lake in search of Jake, when everything changed.

Yap. Yap. Yap. Yap.

Tess halted in her tracks, startled by the noise. What wild forest animal sounded like a small dog? None that she knew.

Yap. Yap. Yap. Yap.

This sound reminded Tess of Mabel, the Scottish terrier owned by the Stewarts, the foster family with whom she'd lived the last year before aging out of the system. What if it was a dog making this noise? A lost dog?

She should go check.

Tess took the path that veered toward the sound, the same path that led to the more isolated cabin where she'd watched Jake chopping wood.

Yap. Yap. Yap. Yap.

"Eloise, come back here!"

Tess pulled up short. The feminine voice sounded young and strained. It was not a voice Tess recognized.

"Eloise! Please."

Yap. Yap. Yap. Yap.

A four-legged three-colored ball of fur came bursting through the trees, bounding toward Tess. She was a beautiful dog, a Cavalier King Charles spaniel if Tess wasn't mistaken. Following on her heels was a woman who might have been younger than Tess. It was difficult to tell.

Her hair was blond. Her clothes were stylish. She was tall. She was thin. She had sad, spaniel eyes just like her Eloise.

The woman's face was black and blue with bruises.

Tess couldn't hold back her startled gasp. "Oh my. Are you okay?"

The woman didn't respond to the question. "My dog. Please, will you grab her?"

Tess reached down and took hold of the spaniel's collar.

"Thank you. She doesn't ordinarily run off that way. She's just excitable right now. Misbehaving. Life is in a bit of turmoil at the moment. I couldn't have chased her much farther, I'm afraid."

"How far did you come?" Tess asked, trying to recall what was beyond the trees. Could she have traveled around the lake from the campground? Except she wasn't dressed for camping.

The woman pointed behind her as she limped toward Tess. "Not far. My cabin is just through those trees. I just let her out to pee, and she dashed off."

Her cabin? The only nearby cabin was part of the Raindrop Resort property. Tess knew for a fact that Genevieve had no other guests. Was this woman a squatter? She was definitely injured. Beneath her bruises, her complexion was wan and pale.

Something was definitely wrong here.

"Your Eloise is awfully squirmy. I see you don't have a leash. I have a good hold on her now. Why don't you let me help you get her safely back to the cabin?"

"Okay. Thank you so much. I don't know what I would do if she ran off. My place is this way."

Tess kept a firm grip on the spaniel's jeweled collar and followed the woman, who moved as slow as Christmas. This woman was definitely not okay. It occurred to Tess that she might be doing something idiotic, the equivalent of a foolish girl in a horror movie following the serial killer to her death.

Maybe she should send a text to Jake. Not that he'd have his phone with him while he fished, but he'd know where to look for her body if she didn't return to cabin 12.

"Do you have someone at the cabin who can help you with her?" Tess asked the stranger. "You're not alone, are you?"

"Hmm?"

The woman glanced back over her shoulder and, in the process of doing so, teetered. She looked confused. Not quite all there. Tess feared the woman was about to fall over. She repeated, "Is there someone who can help you at the cabin?"

"I'll be okay," the blonde responded, even as she reached out and balanced herself on a tree trunk. "I just need to rest. It's been a long drive. I just really need a nap."

A drive from where? Who was this woman, and why was she at one of the Raindrop Resort cabins? Eloise made little mewling noises that Tess thought sounded like sympathy cries. Was Eloise a Lassie type of dog, going for help for her Timmy?

When the woman swayed again, Tess decided the time had come to commit. She hurried ahead, dragging Eloise along with her, and wrapped an arm around the stranger's waist. "You look like you're about to fall down. It's obvious that someone hit you. Is he around here somewhere? Do we need to hide you?"

She hesitated a long moment before saying, "That's why I'm here. I don't think he'll find me here. Not right away anyway. I came a long distance."

"Okay, good. I'm going to help you. Are you headed for the three-bedroom cabin up ahead?"

"Yes."

"Okay. I'm going to help you get there. My name is Tess. What's yours?"

"Brooke. I'm Brooke."

"Hi, Brooke. I'll get you and Eloise settled in Cabin 14... wait." Tess put the clues together. "You are J—" She changed her mind at the last minute. "Genevieve's daughter?"

"You know my mom?"

And your brother, Jake. "Yes, I do."

"Yes. I guess that makes sense if you're here. She's in Europe with my aunt. Do you work here?"

Tess thought of the cabin Jake had equipped for her. She could totally answer yes without it being a lie. From what Jake had told her, his siblings didn't know he was here at Raindrop. That wasn't her secret to spill, so she answered by not answering. "Your mother and aunt fixed up one of the cabins for me. I'm in Cabin 12. When you're feeling better, you and Eloise will have to stop by for a visit."

"Sure."

By the time they arrived at the cabin, Brooke was flagging. Upon entering the more spacious structure, Tess immediately identified a problem. Although the resort's housekeeping crew regularly cleaned the cabin, it hadn't been prepared for occupancy. As such, she doubted the beds were made. The wood box was empty, and she'd bet the cabinets and refrigerator were bare, too. The cabin had electricity and water, of course, so she had the necessities, but not the comforts Tess enjoyed upon her arrival.

Even with the office set up, Cabin 1 would be a lot more comfortable for her than here. Although Tess wasn't certain that the woman didn't need to be in a hospital rather than an isolated mountain cabin. "There are no sheets on the bed."

"I don't care. I'll worry about that tomorrow. I'm so tired I could sleep on a bed of nails."

Tess guided Brooke into the closest bedroom. "Well, the mattress looks fluffy and free of nails, so you're in luck."

The closet door stood open, and Tess spied a pair of zipper bags on the shelf. "I do see a blanket and pillows."

"Perfect." Brooke sighed heavily as she sank gingerly onto the mattress. "Thank you so much for being my Good Samaritan in the woods."

Tess retrieved the items from the shelf, removed them from their storage bags, and handed them to Jake's sister. "I'm glad I was there to help."

As Brooke lay down, the spaniel bounded up on the bed and stretched out beside her. "What a good dog you are, Eloise," Tess observed. "Is there anything else I can get for you before I go?"

"No. Thanks. I'll be fine. I just need sleep. I've been driving forever."

"Okay, then. Just…one thing I must ask before I leave. Brooke, have you seen a doctor?"

She turned her face into the pillow. "Yes," came her muffled voice. "This morning. I'm okay. I just need to sleep."

"Then I will leave you to it."

Tess exited the cabin and shut the door behind her. Walking away from the cabin, she added almost beneath her breath, "I wouldn't count on similar consideration from your brother."

⸎

Jake cast his fishing line into the water. He was baitcasting, not having the energy or the concentration for fly-fishing this evening. His mind wasn't on what he was doing. His mind wasn't anywhere near Mirror Lake or Lake in the Clouds or even Colorado. In his mind, Jake was back in Texas at another lake, on this date almost two decades ago.

It had been his father's birthday, and as it turned out, the final one he'd celebrate. It had been on a Wednesday that year, a workday for Dad and a day the boys were enrolled to attend summer day camp. Nevertheless, the night before, Dad had come into their room and told Jake and Lucas to pack a bag, that the three of them were going to the lake. He wanted to spend his birthday fishing. The following morning he'd rousted his sons from their beds at the butt crack of dawn, and they'd taken out the little aluminum boat with its ten-horse Johnson outboard. On it, they could get up in the shallower creeks where they fished for crappie and black bass.

The first cast of the morning, Jake had caught a two-pound black bass. Lucas, too, had hooked a fish right off—a one-pound sand bass. Then Dad completed the trifecta with a three-pound black bass. He'd crowed with delight, and in his mind, Jake could hear Dad's words as clearly as if he'd spoken them.

"Here's a life lesson for you, buckaroos," Dad said. "Never lay up in the fart sack when you can spend a day doing something you love, especially if you have someone you love along for the ride."

Lucas giggled and asked, "So does that mean we never have to go to school or to work again?"

"Afraid not, but it does mean to be smart about the time you have. We have a finite amount of time on this earth. Only the good Lord knows when that time is up. Use what you have wisely, boys. So get your hooks in the water now, y'hear?"

Standing on the shore of Mirror Lake, Jake tossed a topwater lure onto the surface. He allowed it to sit a bit, allowed the memories to float through his head. For so long now, he had been focused on forward. He didn't often allow himself to look back. Perhaps that had been a mistake.

What would Dad have to say about the way Jake had spent his life? He'd be proud. Jake was certain of that. He knew as sure as Granite Mountain that in the wake of David Prentice's death, Jake had acted the way his father would have wanted where the family was concerned.

You grow up your whole life.

He'd been chewing on the point Tess had made ever since she'd said it. He had the sense that some universal truth existed somewhere in the mix with Tess's growing-up observation and in Dad's lying-in-the-fart-sack warning. *Hell, he might as well throw Mom's dire truth in there, too. You are not your father. Who are you?*

Well, he was one lucky sonofabitch, that's what. He could admit that. He wasn't going to deny it, but he wasn't going to apologize to anybody for it, either. He'd had both the privilege and the curse of being firstborn in a family where one was taught the virtues of self-sacrifice, dedication, hard work, family loyalty, and the observance of the Golden Rule. As a result, he'd shouldered a responsibility to his siblings— and yes, to his mother, also—that under other circumstances, would not have been required.

Jake turned the crank to reel the line and pull his chugger to shore. *Be smart about the time you have. Get your hooks in the water. You grow up your whole life. Spend a day doing something you love. Have someone you love along for the ride.*

Softly, Jake said, "Happy birthday, Dad."

"Jake?" Tess called. "Jake? Where are you?"

He turned toward the sound. A peculiar note in her voice caught his attention and made him frown. Something sounded off. Instinct told him to begin reeling in his line. He shouted back. "Here. I'm over here by the bonfire site."

He spied a flash of yellow moving through the trees and concluded it was Tess. She'd been naked when he'd left her earlier, but she'd worn a yellow shirt this morning.

He decided to leave his gear on the bank. After securing the lure's hook, he propped his pole against the stack of logs and began walking in Tess's direction. Upon getting his first good look at her, he made a trio of quick observations. She wasn't bleeding. She wasn't smiling. She was worried.

Well, hell.

He picked up his pace. What could have her troubled? "What's the matter?" he called. "You okay?"

"I'm fine." She wrapped her arms around herself, and the smile she attempted to show him looked a little sick.

Jake wasn't buying it for a moment. He put on a burst of speed and reached her. Clasping her arms below the shoulders, he demanded, "What's wrong? Oh, hell. It's not my mother, is it? I didn't take my phone when I went down to the lake."

"No. It's not your mom." Tess drew in a deep breath, then exhaled in a rush. "I woke up from my nap a little while ago. Forty-five minutes or maybe an hour ago now. I think the sound of a car woke me up. Anyway, I went looking for you, and as I walked through the woods, I heard a dog barking."

"Zach's Lab?" The contractor, Zach Throckmorton, brought his Labrador retriever almost every day.

"No. I knew right away it wasn't King. This was a smaller dog. Turned out to be a spaniel. A very pretty dog. Her name is Eloise, but I may call her Lassie."

Spaniel...Eloise...Jake was putting the clues together as Tess confirmed his suspicion. "Your sister Brooke is here."

"Brooke is here? At Raindrop Lodge?"

"Yes. She's taking a nap. She says she's okay. She told me she saw a doctor just this morning."

"Whoa. What?" Brooke. Here. A doctor?

"Why did she see a doctor? Is she sick? What's wrong?"

Tess grimaced and sighed. "Oh, Jake. I'm not exactly sure. Someone hit her, I think. She's pretty bruised up."

"Wait. What? She's what?"

"Beaten. She's been beaten."

"Travis." For just a moment, everything inside Jake went cold before red-hot rage blasted through him. "What the hell did he do to her? Where is she? Is he with her? I swear I'll kill that sonofabitch."

"She's bruised and moving very slowly. She's alone. Well, she's here with her dog. She's exhausted, Jake. I think she's been driving quite a while and only arrived shortly before I stumbled across her."

"Wait, an hour ago? You didn't come to get me right away?"

"No, I didn't. I decided to give her a chance to get a little of the sleep she so obviously needed. I stayed and watched over her. She's been sleeping peacefully."

He closed his eyes and dragged his hand down his face. "Where is she?"

"Cabin 14. She's fragile, Jake. Be careful with her."

Jake took off running. Arriving at the cabin, he paused long enough to glance into the front window and make sure she wasn't standing there buck naked or something. The room was empty, so he opened the door and went inside.

"Brooke?" In the cabin's master bedroom, Eloise whimpered. Jake followed the sound and spied his sister lying on the bed, her dog curled up beside her. He muttered a vicious curse beneath his breath.

I'm going to kill that bastard. I swear I'm going to tear him limb from limb.

Jake backed away from the door, his fists clenching and releasing helplessly at his sides. He wanted to hit something.

Throw something. Kick something. He could go chop some wood. However, any of those things would make noise, and he could tell that Tess had been right. Brooke needed to sleep.

So he took a seat in the chair in the corner of the bedroom and waited for his baby sister to awaken.

Within a few minutes, Tess had joined him. Gracefully, she sank onto the floor at his feet. He frowned at her and attempted to lift her up into his lap, but she declined with a fierce shake of her head.

The dog hopped off the bed and padded over to cuddle with Tess. She scratched Eloise behind the long, droopy ears, and the spaniel rested her head on Tess's lap. Jake had no clue how long they waited because his thoughts drifted between the past and trying to imagine what had happened to Brooke and fantasizing about what he would do to her husband. He had no doubt that Travis was the scum of the earth who had done this to her. The only question was why, and Jake would bet his share of the ranch that her share of the ranch was the answer.

Eventually, the dog apparently decided Brooke's nap had lasted long enough because she rose, hopped up onto the bed, and licked his sister's face.

Brooke's eyelashes fluttered and rose. "Eloise. Hi, baby. How's my good girl? Do you need anything? Some water?" She went to sit up and groaned aloud.

The sound brought Jake to his feet. "Stinky?"

She looked over and up, her eyes going round with shock. Big and brown like her dog's, they immediately flooded with tears. "Jake. Oh, Jake. How did you find me? Did Willow call? She promised me she wouldn't. You didn't go after him, did you? I need a plan first."

"First, I need the truth. You have seen a doctor? What are your injuries?"

Pain that he pegged to be as much emotional as physical flashed across her face. "I did see a doctor. I'm mostly bruised. I'll heal. Everything will heal. I need time and rest."

Jake crossed to the bed and sat down beside her. He took her hand in his. It was cold, too cold. *Her poor face.* His heart twisted with pain. These bruises were two, maybe three days old. "What happened, Stinky?"

"Stinky," she repeated. "It's somehow reassuring to know that some things never change. I got into it with Travis. He lost his temper."

"He hit you." Jake needed to hear her say it. He wanted no potential of misunderstanding here. "With his fist."

"Yes."

"Did he also hit you with something else? A belt or a stick? Anything? Did he kick you?"

"No. No. Just his fist. A few times. And then he shoved me, and I tripped. I fell. I f-f-fell down the st-st-stairs."

Fresh tears welled in her eyes and spilled down her cheeks. Jake spat out another long line of epithets, then gave his head a hard shake. "Shush, that's okay, honey. No more. You don't have to talk about it anymore."

"No!" Brooke yanked her hand free of his. She swiped at her cheeks, wiping away the tears. "Let me tell you what happened. I need to tell you. I'll tell you everything, I promise. I'm not going back to him. Ever."

"Thank God." Jake released about a million tons of tension on a sigh. "Okay. I'll shut up. You talk."

"Okay. Good. It's a mess, Jake. It's all a mess. It's the stupid ranch and the stupid money. I wish Poppy had given it all to the church. I swear, our family would have been better off."

"I won't argue otherwise."

"Everything goes back to Poppy telling us he was going to leave us the ranch. Travis has made some idiotic financial decisions and business deals. We're way overextended. He basically started spending the inheritance the day Poppy died. I didn't realize it. I was so foolish, Jake. I trusted him. I signed things without reading them, so now I'm afraid I'm in trouble, too."

Oh crap.

"I thought he was cheating on me. I wanted to find out who the woman was and how bad our finances really are, so I went snooping through his desk, looking for the papers I signed. I found them and other things. A doing-business-as form from the county and formation paperwork for an LLC. The names rang a bell, so I went back through some of the early e-mails we got right after Poppy died. Jake, it's like the Russian nesting dolls that Willow had as a girl, but if you keep unwrapping them, you'll find three names at the center. The Harbor at Lonesome Lake, Travis, and Tamra Groves."

Crevasses as deep as the Black Canyon of the Gunnison creased Jake's brow. Was she saying what it sounded like she was saying? Tamra Groves was Lucas's lying lady lawyer. The Harbor at Lonesome Lake was a shovel-ready real estate development planned by the ranch's buyer the moment the sale finally closed.

"Do you mean…"

"I think my husband and Lucas's girlfriend set us up from the very beginning. Even before Poppy died. And it's all my fault."

"Brooke, hold on a minute." Jake rested his elbows on his knees and leaned forward, frowning at his sister. "That's impossible."

"No. Listen. It was the Fourth of July before her grandfather died. She and Lucas had been dating for a few weeks at that point. We'd all been out in Poppy's boat together. We'd been skiing. You were there, too. You and Lucas went up to the house to reload the cooler with drinks. Do you remember?"

"No. No, I don't."

"Well, Travis, Tamra, and I got talking about how gorgeous it was along that part of Lonesome Lake. Then Travis and Tamra got talking about how the ranch's lakefront property was a potential goldmine. One of them—I don't recall who—brought up the fact that Poppy was no spring chicken, that the four of us were going to inherit, and the Lonesome River Ranch might be on the market sometime in the not-too-distant future. That's when I said how much I loved the lake house, and that I really wished we could keep the part of the ranch adjacent to the lake and sell the rest."

"This is the first I've heard of that idea," Jake said.

"Because they told me that wasn't possible."

"Who told you that?"

"Tamra and Travis. See, that holiday weekend, I said I wanted to ask our grandfather about it. She said she'd take care of it, and that provisions could be made in the trust. So I left it up to her. She was Poppy's new attorney, after all. Her grandfather left her his firm. I think that's how this entire mess started, Jake. I think—no, I know—that she and Travis decided they wanted to develop the lakefront land, and they did whatever it took to make it happen. What they didn't plan for were lawsuits that would delay the sale for more than three years."

"To be fair, the three years aren't all because of the lawsuits. The first two years were mostly about the delay in probating the will, which didn't turn out to be as simple as we'd believed, and exploring our options where the ranch was concerned."

Brooke shrugged, then grimaced at the pain the motion caused. "Bottom line is they didn't anticipate the delay. They've been robbing Peter to pay Paul, but they need the ranch sale to close. Jake, that's why Travis had me set up the lunch in Austin that you stumbled upon. He was planning to present the trouble I'm in to Lucas and Willow, and use it as leverage to convince Lucas to end all his lawsuits and allow the sale to go forward. Despite everything, Lucas loves me."

Jake's head was spinning as he tried to rearrange the puzzle pieces after receiving this new information. This was not at all what he'd imagined. "And Willow loves you, too, and she's the one person Lucas has occasionally listened to throughout this debacle."

"That's why we asked her to the meeting. Travis sent plane tickets for her and the kids and arranged for Andy's parents to visit. They took Emma and Drew to the beach house in Galveston for a few days. Travis was betting that Willow would help convince Lucas to see things our way."

"Did she?"

"The meeting never happened. Travis got held up in traffic and ran late. Then you showed up. After that, Lucas was in no frame of mind to talk about the ranch. He was stewing about you. When Travis finally arrived, almost the first thing out of his mouth ticked Lucas off and he left. Travis has been on a slow burn ever since the lunch disaster."

This turned Jake's perception of the event upside down. He'd assumed that Lucas had arranged the meeting that day. Willow and Brooke had looked guilty when they'd met Jake's gaze. Lucas radiated belligerence. It had been a natural conclusion for Jake to draw, especially since Travis hadn't been sitting at that lunch table.

"What did you sign, Brooke?"

"Honestly, I don't know for sure. It's in the stack of papers I found in the desk, but I didn't take time to study it. The other papers I recognized. Jake, there was a copy of Poppy's original will and trust documents. It had Travis's handwriting on it, and Tamra's, and a piece of paper attached with notes."

"You're sure that's what you saw?"

"Positive. Those documents I did take a good long look at. The notes prove Tamra had a conflict of interest at the very least, and maybe even committed fraud, don't you think? Maybe we could get the whole thing thrown out. Go back to the original trust?"

Jake rubbed the back of his neck. *I doubt it. But...* "I honestly don't know."

"I was going to take them to Lucas, but then I heard Travis come home, so I hid them. He found his desk disturbed, and he confronted me. He wanted me to give him the documents. I wouldn't do it. I never dreamed he'd hit me. Shove me. I—I—I fell down the stairs. At least he called 911."

"Oh hell, Brooke." Jake ever so gently touched her face.

"I should have given them to him. If I'd known..." She closed her eyes, shuddered, and swallowed hard.

Jake used the pad of his thumb to wipe away the tear that

trailed slowly down her cheek. "I'm so sorry you're hurt, Stinky. He had no excuse to hit you. None. I hope you filed a police report."

"No. I'm worried about the papers I signed."

"Oh, Stinky. That's no reason not to report domestic violence. Don't worry about the papers. I'll take care of that situation. Where is Travis now?"

A long silence ticked by before she responded. "I imagine he's looking for me. I sneaked away. He might think I went to Willow's or to my college roommate's place in Dallas. He knows Mom is in Europe, so I don't think he'll look for me in Colorado. That's why I came here. He's in full apologetic mode."

"He'd darn well better be."

"I'm sure he's worried this will cause problems with him getting his share of the inheritance."

He won't be touching one thin dime after what he's done to you. With effort, Jake kept his voice gentle. "Texas might be a community property state, but as the legalities stand today and thanks to Lucas's hard head, you haven't inherited anything yet. Technically, nothing has been commingled, and he shouldn't have any claim on anything from Poppy's estate."

"But I signed—"

"I don't care what you signed," he assured her. "Travis won't win this one. That said, we need to get our hands on those documents before he does."

"They're in the laundry room." She described where she'd secreted them and added, "He'll never find them."

Jake gave her hand a squeeze, then rose and paced the room. He identified one obvious solution. "I think I should call Lucas and ask him to go raid your laundry room. Would you be okay with that, Brooke?"

"You would call Lucas?"

"Yes."

"But y'all aren't talking to each other."

"Yeah, well, things are different now. What information is he going to need to get into the house?"

"Gate access number, and the code to disarm the alarm system. Travis might have changed them, but I should have been pinged if that happened, so I think we're okay. I also have a hidden house key. Travis doesn't know about it."

"Do you have anything to write on?" Jake asked his sister.

While she frowned, Tess spoke up and headed toward the kitchen. "I saw some paper and a pencil on the fridge. It's a Lake in the Clouds Market advertising magnet."

A moment later, she handed a pad of paper and a stubby pencil to Brooke, who proceeded to write out the necessary information. While she was busy, Jake took a good look around the cabin and frowned. "This place is awfully bare."

"I think she and Eloise would be more comfortable in Number 1."

"Good idea." To his sister, he said, "It's a cozy little one-bedroom that I fixed up when I arrived. It's much more livable than this. Why don't we move you there?"

"No." Brooke didn't look up from the paper. "I like that this one is back out of the way. Besides, we need the three bedrooms."

We? Jake wondered.

"Willow and the children will be here soon."

"Willow's coming to Raindrop Lodge, too?"

"Yes. I sent up the bat signal."

Jake opened his mouth, then shut it without comment.

Brooke knew him well enough to follow the direction of his thoughts, however, because she spoke with a defensive note in her voice. "I needed help, and I didn't know you were here, Jake. Besides, she is my sister. We're close."

"I know. I'm glad she's coming. It'll be nice to see her and the kids." He hesitated a moment, then asked, "Why didn't you go to Lucas, honey?"

"He blocked my calls after the lunch disaster. I thought about asking Willow to call him, but…" Brooke shrugged. "I had enough to deal with. One crisis at a time, you know?"

"I know."

She handed Jake the long, narrow sheet of paper. "This should be everything he needs."

While Jake scanned the list, Tess asked Brooke, "While your brother is there if he has time, is there anything else you need? Clothes? Medicines? Toiletries?"

"I'd love to have my hiking boots. I was afraid to bring them because I thought if Travis noticed they were missing, he might decide to check Lake in the Clouds whether Mom is here or not."

"Let him check," Jake muttered. "I'll tell Lucas to grab your boots, too. Anything else?"

"That's all."

"Okay." Luke pulled his phone from his pocket and entered the number from memory. The call went straight to voice mail even as a thought occurred to him. Wonder if Lucas had blocked him? He tried sending a text: Travis hurt Brooke. She needs your help. Call me.

Not delivered.

"He's blocked me. The sonofabitch has blocked me." He sputtered a stream of curses, then stopped and sucked in a deep, calming breath. He maintained a steady tone as he asked, "Tess, may I use your phone, please?"

She eyed him warily, but handed over her device. He

dialed the number again. Halfway through the third ring, his brother answered, "Hello?"

"It's me. I need to—" Three beeps signaled that he'd disconnected the call. Jake lowered Tess's phone and stared down at it in disbelief for a long moment before spitting a particularly blasphemous curse. He typed out the same text he'd sent from his phone.

Undelivered.

Jake blew a gasket.

Nineteen

RECOGNIZING THE NEED FOR damage control, Tess sprang into action. She grabbed her phone from Jake's hand before he could throw it and shoved him toward the door. "Go. An angry man is not what your sister needs to see right now. Go for a run or chop some wood. Jump in the lake. Do something—anything—to cool off."

"I don't have time to cool off. I have to figure out a way to get my granite-headed brother to listen to me long enough to finish a sentence."

"Go do your figuring out somewhere else," Tess insisted. "Go get sheets for the beds from the housekeeping carts or go—"

Tess broke off as a ringtone played from somewhere else in the cabin. Brooke said, "That's Willow."

Jake moved toward the sound. "I'll get it."

"Don't answer it. Let's surprise her that you're here. It'll be nice."

That, more than anything, seemed to drain some of his temper. Jake nodded toward Brooke and exited the bedroom.

Moments later, he returned and handed his sister her telephone. "Hello? Where are you? You see a maroon King Ranch?"

Brooke's eyes met her brother's, and for the first time, Tess spied a real smile on her lips. "You're almost here. Stay to the right, and the road loops around. Keep driving until you see our cabin." She listened a moment, then added, "You won't be able to miss it. The truck's driver is talking to me now. I'll ask him to flag you down. See you in about four minutes."

She hung up and said, "There you go, Jake. The floor is yours."

Jake smirked. Tess was happy to see identical sparks of mischief in the Prentice siblings' eyes. She decided to allow the brother and sisters a private reunion, so she slipped away to get sheets for the beds—and give an idea she had about the Lucas problem a try.

She snagged the notes Jake had compiled from the Lake in the Clouds Market pad on her way out. The spaniel followed her, but Tess halted, braced her hands on her hips, and gave the dog a firm look. "No, Eloise. You stay. Play with the children."

Maybe the dog understood her. Maybe Tess's tone made the difference. Nevertheless, she sat and stayed, and Tess hurried on her way toward the lodge. She bypassed the housekeeping cabin and headed straight for the lodge's lobby, where she expected to find Zach Throckmorton. Sure enough, he and another man stood over a set of blueprints spread open on a table placed at the center of the room. Hearing her come in, Zach looked up and smiled. "Good afternoon." Adding a hopeful note to his voice, he questioned, "Are you here to deliver cookies again?"

"I'm afraid not today."

"Now, there is a crushing disappointment."

"Actually, I'm here to ask if I can borrow your phone to make a call?"

"Sure." He reached into his shirt pocket, pulled out the device, and handed it over.

"Thanks. This shouldn't take long. I'll be out on the back porch."

"We'll be right here."

The back door's rusty hinges squeaked loudly as Tess pushed it open and stepped onto the covered porch, which spanned the entire lake-facing side of the lodge. She took a seat in one of the wooden rocking chairs, scrolled to the recent calls on her own phone, then typed a text to Lucas Prentice. My name is Tess. I'm a friend of your sister, Brooke. Travis beat her. She needs your help. I'm going to call you. Please answer.

She sent the text and began silently counting. Her plan was to give him half a minute and call. Zach's phone rang in ten seconds. In a voice that sounded eerily like Jake's, Lucas demanded, "Tess? How bad is she hurt? Bottom line it, please."

"She'll be okay. Now, why don't you let me start at the top? I'll tell you everything that's happened and how she needs your help. When I'm done, I'll answer any of your questions. Okay?"

"Okay."

"One thing before I start. I borrowed a friend's phone to contact you, and I need to return it to him. I'll call you from my own phone, but you need to remove the block you placed on it this morning when your brother called you."

"Whoa. Wait. Jake is involved in this?"

"It's the number with the 210 area code." Tess disconnected the call and rose from the rocking chair, hoping she'd bet correctly. Sure enough, her phone rang before she'd made it halfway to the door.

"Hello, Lucas. Bear with me a moment as I return my friend's phone to him. Zach?" She smiled at the contractor and held out his phone. "Thank you so much. I promise there will be cookies coming your way soon."

"From your oven to my mouth," he replied.

Lucas was spitting out comments or questions—Tess wasn't sure which because she didn't listen until she exited Raindrop Lodge and turned toward the housekeeping cabin. Bringing her phone up to her ear, she said, "We have privacy now. If you can manage not to interrupt, you'll have your questions answered faster, I promise. All right?"

He exhaled heavily. "Go on."

"I used to work for your brother at Bensler, and Jake invited me to vacation with him in Colorado."

Tess shared only enough personal stuff to set the stage for today's events and moved quickly to the meat of the story. Soon, Lucas was muttering a string of curses that once again made him sound remarkably like his brother. Tess finished her tale by saying, "Your sister Willow arrived just moments ago. I think that's everything."

"Willow went to Colorado?"

"Yes. Willow and Brooke spoke yesterday. Or maybe the day before yesterday. I'm not certain when."

"She brought the kids?"

"I believe so, yes. So will you retrieve these papers from your sister's house?"

"Of course. I'll head over there right away. Tell Brooke I'll get her boots, too."

"Will you remove the block on Jake's phone number so he can get hold of you if he needs you?"

Following a long pause, Lucas sighed. "Oh, all right. But tell him not to call unless it's an emergency."

"I'm sure that won't be a problem. Do you have something to write on? I'll give you these codes."

"I'm in the car. Why don't you text them to me?"

"Of course."

"I'll keep y'all posted on how things go here. Tell Brooke I'll be there as fast as I can. If she thinks of anything else she needs, give me a shout. I'll pick it up along the way."

"I will tell her. Thank you, Lucas."

His voice held an edge to it as he replied, "No need to thank me. She's my little sister."

Tess allowed a beat to go by. "Yes. Okay. Well. How about I wish you good luck and safe travels, and maybe suggest you don't kill Travis if you happen to run across him? It won't do Brooke any good if you're in jail."

"Might be worth it, though," he returned.

After what she'd seen and heard today, Tess wasn't going to argue with him.

◦◦◦

Seven-year-old Drew Eldridge erupted from the backseat of his mother's rental car and shot like a rocket toward Jake. "Uncle Jake! Uncle Jake! I didn't know you were going to be here! Uncle Jake, will you take me fishing? I want to go fishing!"

Jake couldn't think of any better medicine than a child's excitement. He caught the boy and swung him up and around in the air. "Hello, Drew Man. I'm so happy to see you. Of course I'll take you fishing."

"Now? Can we go now?"

"No. We'll go at the butt crack of dawn tomorrow morning. You'll need to go to bed early tonight, so you'll be all rested."

"You said butt crack." The boy giggled, and when Jake returned his feet to the ground, he ran back toward his mother, who was unbuckling three-year-old Emma from her car seat. "Mom, Uncle Jake said 'butt crack.' Are you gonna get him in trouble?"

Willow set her daughter on the ground and gave Jake a tentative smile. "That's his mother's job, not mine. Hello, Jake. This is a nice surprise."

"Two great minds, one great thought. You look great, Will."

"Great" wasn't an untruthful choice of words, but neither was it the most accurate. Willow Prentice Eldridge was a beautiful woman whose name suited her. Tall and lithe, she'd scored the Scandinavian lottery of their genetic heritage, with blond hair and blue eyes and the high, prominent cheekbones of a Norse goddess or supermodel. The fifteen pounds she'd lost since her husband's death a couple of years ago had added a gauntness to her appearance that Jake didn't like to see. She looked exhausted—totally understandable under the circumstances.

"Emma, don't pick that up," Willow said to her daughter, who had squatted down and was studying a beetle. To Jake, she said, "I can't wait to hear the story about how you made it here before me, but first, how is Brooke?"

As Jake strode toward his niece to give her a hug and hello, he shook his head and met Willow's worried gaze. "She says she's okay." Keeping his voice low, he added, "She looks awful."

Willow closed her eyes. "I could strangle Travis Sunberg."

"Me, too." Jake gave her a brief synopsis of the events of the past twenty minutes and asked if she'd had any contact with Lucas.

"No. He and I argued after that lunch you stumbled upon."

"About what?"

"You. It's obvious that neither one of you is happy about the way things stand between you two. You've had enough time to get over your snit."

"Our snit?" Jake repeated, offended by the term. He thought *battle* or *war* was more appropriate.

"Yes, your snit. You need to fix it. My intention was to talk to him and then talk to you, but he just wasn't listening that day. I decided to take another run at it in a few weeks. Yesterday I tried to call him and tell him about Brooke, but I think he's blocked my number."

Jerk. "I'll get hold of him somehow, but first things first. You go on in and see Brooke. I'll watch the kids for a bit while y'all visit. I can take them for a tour of the property in the Mule."

"That would be fabulous, Jake. Thank you." After a brief good behavior lecture to her children, she disappeared into Cabin 14.

"We're gonna ride a donkey?" Drew asked.

"No. The Mule is like a golf cart, only for work." Jake hunched down in front of Emma and said, "Hey, sugarcakes. Remember me? I'm Uncle Jake."

"I know. You are in the picture."

Jake sent a questioning glance toward his nephew. "The picture?"

"Nana and you and Mom and Uncle Lucas and Auntie Brooke. The picture is on the dresser in Mom's bedroom."

"Ah. I see. I have that same picture."

"Auntie Brooke has a bad boo boo," Emma said, her eyes round and solemn.

"Yes, she does."

"Uncle Travis wasn't nice to her."

"I know, and that was a bad thing. The good news is that she's going to be better really soon."

"That's what Mommy says."

"Your mommy is right. So are y'all ready for your Mule ride?"

"I want to ride a horse," Drew said. "Mommy said maybe we could go horseback riding while we're in Colorado."

"I imagine that can be arranged, too." Jake lifted the little girl and propped her against his hip, then extended his free hand toward Drew. "This way."

The Mule was kept in the housekeeping cabin's garage. Jake figured he'd likely run into Tess either there or when she was on her way back with the clean sheets for Cabin 14. It surprised him not to find her either on the path or at the housekeeping cabin, so with the children loaded into the utility vehicle, he fired up the engine and went in search of his woman. He spied her seated at a picnic bench, halfway between the lodge and the supply building, talking on her phone.

He headed her way. Seeing the vehicle's approach, Tess gave a little wave, and a moment later ended her call. She rose and waited for their arrival. Gravel crunched beneath his tires as Jake braked to a stop. "Hey, pretty lady. We're taking a tour of Raindrop Lodge. Want to ride along?"

"I'd love to ride along. Thanks."

He introduced her to his niece and nephew. Tess climbed aboard, and they took off. Jake's first destination on the

Raindrop Lodge tour was the section of Mirror Lake's bank where the children could find rocks to throw into the water to their hearts' content. While Emma and Drew gathered and tossed stones, Tess gave him a rundown of her solution to the Lucas problem and the results.

"You are an amazing woman." He grabbed her and gave her a quick, hard kiss. "Thank you."

"Glad to help. Your brother said he'd send a group text following his visit to Brooke's house and give you all an update."

The promised text arrived after the hot dogs had been roasted over the campfire Jake built in front of Cabin 14, but before they broke out the makings for s'mores. Lucas's mission had been a success. He had papers and boots in hand, and he'd seen no sign of Travis. His plans were to pack up a few things and head north. He'd get to Lake in the Clouds as soon as possible, likely sometime the day after tomorrow.

The children and his sisters were ready to call it a night by 8 p.m., and Tess and Jake headed to bed not much later. Ordinarily, Jake drifted off shortly after they'd finished making love. Tonight, his spinning thoughts kept him awake.

Worried that his tossing and turning would disturb Tess, Jake slipped out of bed. He pulled on his jeans and padded into the cabin's main room, where he foraged in the cabinets for a snack. The pickings were slim. He settled for pouring milk into a mug, which he zapped in the microwave. Shoving his feet into hard-soled slippers, he pulled on a jacket and carried his milk outside.

The scent of woodsmoke from the campfire they'd extinguished almost two hours ago continued to drift in the air. Above, a three-quarter moon rose in a starry sky. Jake preferred Tess to join him on moonlight walks beside the lake, but tonight he had plenty of ghosts to accompany him.

He was worried as hell about Brooke. He could tell that Willow was troubled, too. He'd also picked up on the fact that he didn't know everything. Something else was going on here. More than once, he'd spotted Willow exchanging a look with Brooke that sent his antennae quivering.

His sisters having a nonverbal conversation was nothing new. Over the years, he'd learn to interpret much of what they were saying with their shrugs and raised eyebrows and long significant stares. Unfortunately, today's exchange used vocabulary in a language he couldn't decipher. Those two women definitely knew something he didn't, something important that had a bearing on current Prentice family events. Something important that they'd chosen not to share with him.

In the recent past, Jake would have demanded they let him in on the secrets. Now, well, he was reevaluating.

The Mexican restaurant rendezvous hadn't been what it seemed. He'd wrongly assumed that his brother had arranged the event. The anger Jake had nursed toward his siblings, his brother in particular, for that event had been misplaced. He certainly wasn't going to blame Brooke for Travis's misdeeds.

So where did that leave him on the torqued-at-the-family scale?

Ready to compromise.

Was he? Really? Was he ready to throw in the towel and drop his lawsuits? Do whatever it took to settle the estate ASAP? Perhaps. However, this attitudinal change of his might not make a damned bit of difference. Lucas was the one being stubborn as a borrowed mule. Jake could be ready to compromise from here to Christmas, but unless Lucas was willing to get there, the idea was a nonstarter.

Jake shoved his hands into his jacket pockets. The night was quiet, with only a few faint sounds drifting across the water from the campgrounds across the lake. He reached the spot where he and Tess had thrown rocks with Willow's children that afternoon, and he paused to repeat the action now.

And just what this compromise might be, he didn't know. He hadn't given it any thought in months. Truth be told, anger and hurt had created a swim cap of a barrier around his brain that prevented any compromising thoughts regarding the Lonesome River Ranch from seeping into his consciousness. Today's events had yanked that cap off. Was he ready to dunk his head back into the sewer of a family brawl? What would solving the problem do for him?

Set you free.

The idea drifted through his mind like an opium cloud, sweet and enticing.

I'm not David Prentice. I've got it. Understood. We grew up, and roles have changed. They don't need me to be Dad's stand-in any longer.

So who am I?

Tess had a label or two for him. Leader. Problem solver. He wore them comfortably enough. But what if they were more David than Jake? Maybe he'd developed leadership and problem-solving skills not because they came naturally to him but because they'd been an integral part of his father's personality. Maybe the real Jake Prentice would be content to sit back and go with the flow.

He picked up a stone as big as his hand and threw it in a hard, high arc. It landed in the water with a loud *ka-thunk*. One way or another, he needed to lead and find a compromise settlement that his siblings could accept. If he could rid himself of the ball-and-chain that was the Lonesome River Ranch, maybe he'd have the opportunity to find out the answer to the question his mother posed back on Epiphany Sunday. Had she chosen that particular date for a reason?

Of course she had. Why had it taken him until now to figure that out?

Because his thinking had been clouded, that's why. Foggy with grief. Maybe, finally, the haze was beginning to clear.

Tess had helped with that. *You grow up your whole life.* Such a simple way to make a point he'd never quite grasped before. Maybe he'd seen it in himself, accepted it in himself, but he couldn't in good conscience say he'd done that with his sibs. Isn't that part of the reason why he'd wanted to get all the Prentice family *t*'s crossed and *i*'s dotted as the clock ticked toward the day when he'd be thirty-nine years and three months old?

Jake had a, well, *superstition* wasn't the right word. Neither was a *premonition.* A *sense of destiny* maybe? Never mind what the shrink whom Mom sent him to after Dad died tried to tell him, no matter what basic logic allowed, the bottom line was that a part of Jake believed he was fated to follow in his father's footsteps. He figured he'd kick the bucket before the age of forty. Acorns and trees and all that. Like father, like son. Genetics.

Every day up until that red-letter day had been a deadline of sorts. He'd always figured that any day he lived beyond that date damn sure would be a gift.

I'm a head case.

You grow up your whole life.

But maybe he could be a head case unchained.

With the ground beneath him illuminated by silvered

moonlight, Jake bent over and scooped up another handful of stones. One by one, he threw them into Mirror Lake, and with every rock that dropped, years fell away in his memory.

"Look for a flat one, Brookie. Like this. See?" A ten-year-old Willow held up a smooth gray stone.

Brooke, who had just turned six, spoke with the ever-constant whine in her voice. "I don't see any."

"I see one. I see three! Three perfect ones!" Eight-year-old Lucas swooped in and stole the flat stones right from beneath his little sister's nose.

Both girls protested. "Lucas!"

At twelve, Jake was bigger and brawnier than his brother, though not nearly as sneaky. Nevertheless, Lucas wasn't watching him, so Jake could swat his younger brother's hands and capture the stones. "Here you go, Brooke."

"Hey! Those are mine!"

"Finders keepers, losers weepers."

"Asshole."

Willow gasped with intense, offended ten-year-old girl's drama. Brooke looked over her shoulder and called, "Mommy! Lucas said 'asshole.'"

Mom called, "Lucas B. Prentice. Don't make me get up out of this chair and come down there with my bar of soap."

"That's right, boyo," Poppy called as he checked the thermometer on the smoker, where he'd had a brisket going since the middle of the night. "Keep it up, and she'll rip you a new one."

"C'mon, Dad," Dad said, rolling his eyes and smirking as he lifted his bottle of Coors to his mouth.

It was the Fourth of July at the lake house, and as usual, the Prentice clan had gathered. They had boated and water-skied and ridden the inflated tube. They'd fished and kayaked and swum and popped firecrackers. Because apparently having a whole lake to swim in wasn't enough—friends of Poppy's actually had a swimming pool, too, at their lake house. They'd hosted a money scramble and greased watermelon war for the children of family and friends. Jake had scored six dollars and twenty-three cents diving for change in the money scramble, and of course, his team had wrestled the watermelon from the pool to win that war. He wondered if he'd ever get the Vaseline off his body, though. He had the greasy stuff in places where only babies had Vaseline after that event.

Dinner was served at just about sundown. Poppy's brisket wasn't as good as Dad's, unfortunately, but then, nobody's was. Jake almost made himself sick eating Mrs. King's potato salad, it was so good, and Mom's baked beans couldn't be beaten. Homemade peach ice cream finished the meal, and everyone settled down for the big fireworks show to begin. It was while they waited that the Prentice siblings busied themselves skipping rocks across the surface of the lake.

Lucas had held the record with a five-skipper for a whole three days since their contest the day of the family's arrival. Jake was determined to see that record fail.

He'd scooped rocks. Searched for the perfect stone. Thrown over and over and over again. Finally, he found the one. The perfect one. It was black, an unusual color for rocks in that part of Texas. Smooth as butter. It fit in his hand perfectly.

As the first rocket rose into the night sky, Jake drew back his arm and sent it sailing with a sidelong snap. One. Two. Three. Four. Five. SIX! SIX! SIX!

Nobody else saw it, but that didn't matter. Jake knew

he'd done it. He knew. He watched the Fourth of July fire-works that night in Texas, and he went to bed knowing he'd accomplished what he'd set out to do.

In Colorado, decades later, a million family miles beneath his belt, Jake went to bed that night maybe not knowing, but with a glimmer of an idea.

Maybe, just maybe, he'd thought of a compromise.

Twenty

"LET'S PUT LUCAS IN Cabin 4 when he gets here," Jake said to Tess the following morning over a breakfast of bacon, eggs, and toast. "It's the farthest away from us."

Despite his poor night's sleep—his tossing and turning had awakened her on numerous occasions—the man had risen early and taken the children fishing. Tess had chosen to sleep in, and she'd awakened around seven forty-five to the heavenly aroma of frying bacon. Jake explained that a lack of fish on the line meant bored kiddos and a brief stint lakeside. They planned to try again that evening.

Tess mentally reviewed the available cabins and frowned. "You haven't updated the bathroom in Cabin 4 yet, have you?"

"Nope." He smiled. "The showerhead needs replacing for sure. It trickles at best. The warm water heater makes a banging noise, too."

A *warm* water heater? "That's a bit passive-aggressive, don't you think?"

Jake shrugged. "He can sue me. Again. Speaking of which, now it's five after eight, which means it's five after nine in Texas. I need to call my lawyer. Brooke gave me an idea, and I want him to okay it before I present it to the sibs."

"An idea about Travis?"

"No, about the Lonesome River Ranch."

Tess's eyes widened. "Oh, Jake. Have you thought of a way to end the war? It's not an atomic bomb, is it?"

"I don't think so. Maybe. It's no bomb. More like an armistice, I believe. I hope. I'll tell you about it once I know if it's a doable deal or not. I don't want to jinx it."

"Go call the man. I'll have my fingers and toes crossed."

"Thanks."

It proved to be quite an involved phone call. He was still talking and taking notes on a yellow legal pad when Tess finished showering and dressing. She listened for a moment, trying to get a sense of what his idea might be, but they were talking about contract clauses, so she tuned out. When she mimed that she intended to walk over and visit his sisters, he nodded, smiled, and waved her off.

At Cabin 12, things were in a bit of an uproar. Drew had been running in the woods and tripped. He'd fallen on a jagged rock and cut his hand. Willow had just finished a call with the doctor's office as Tess arrived.

Tess comforted a crying Drew because Willow and Brooke were in the midst of an argument. "I told you I saw a doctor," Brooke said, her voice tight.

"It darn sure won't hurt anything to get a second opinion. They said they could fit you in."

"But—"

"But nothing. I dropped everything and spent big money on plane tickets to come to Colorado."

"You didn't have to come."

"Sure I did, and I don't regret it or begrudge it, but I do demand that you do this one thing I ask in return. I'm telling you, sweetheart. I've been there. What you're describing is unusual."

"Everything about this situation is unusual. I won't argue with that...Okay, fine. I'll go."

So Willow convinced her sister to see a doctor. Good. Tess didn't like the way Brooke held herself as she walked. She looked entirely too, well, *tender* was the word that came to mind.

"My hand hurts!" Drew cried. "Look at all the blood, Mama!"

While Willow comforted her son, Tess said, "Jake and I will watch over Emma here for you. We can—"

"No! I want to go to town, too."

"Oh, honey," Willow began.

"I've got a boo-boo." Emma held up her thumb.

"There's nothing wrong with your thumb," Drew challenged.

"I wanna go, too!"

"Emma." Willow closed her eyes and grimaced. "I need to take care of your brother. I can't—"

"How about I take Emma to the library?" Tess suggested. "If I remember correctly, they have story time this morning. If I'm wrong about story time, I'm sure we can get her a library card and check out some books."

The little girl's face lit up. "I love story time and library books."

Relief washed over Willow's face. "Perfect. Okay, then. Thank you, Tess. That'll be a tremendous help."

They took Willow's vehicle since it had the car seat, and

as the registered driver of the rental, Willow drove. Brooke sat in the back with the children in order to comfort Drew. Tess sent Jake an explanatory text and climbed into the front passenger seat.

Willow waited until they'd exited the Raindrop Lodge property and traveled the highway toward town to casually ask, "So how long have you been in love with my brother?"

Tess hesitated. "I don't know that 'love' is the right word. I've crushed on him ever since I started working with him three years ago, but workplace relationships are a no-go at Bensler, so I couldn't even admit my feelings to myself. Then he fired me in November and—"

"Wait." Surprise registered in Willow's sidelong glance. "He *fired* you? And *then* you fell in love with him?"

Yes, well, maybe "love" was the right word, after all. Rather than either admit or deny the charge, Tess told them how he recommended her for the new job, her dream job. Jake had told his sisters yesterday that he'd quit Bensler, so Tess didn't need to explain about that.

In the backseat, Brooke had distracted Drew from the pain of his injury and captured Emma's attention by sharing a story about her dog and a missing television remote. Willow casually asked, "So what's next for you two? How long is Jake planning to stay in Colorado?"

"That I can't answer. I'm staying until I finish my design for the lodge." She explained about the job he'd hired her to do, and Willow gave a long, soft whistle. "I hope you won't take this personally, Tess, but that's a spectacularly bad idea."

Tess winced. "Because it isn't his place to hire a designer for his mother's and aunt's project."

"Yep."

"That's what I tried to tell him."

"This is their project, not his. He's being his buttinsky self by hiring you to create a design."

"I know. He said he's going to give it to his mother as a gift with no expectations that she use it or not. Honestly, he came up with it as an excuse to keep me in Colorado because I needed to go back to Texas and return to work. He worked this deal out with my boss."

"Oooh. That's different." Willow darted her an intrigued look. "So how long has he been in love with you?"

Tess's heart skipped a beat, then began to race. "I don't know for sure that he is. He's never said the words."

"Have you?"

"No, but like I said, we haven't been together that long." She waited maybe five whole seconds before asking. "Why would you say he's in love with me?"

From the backseat, Brooke proved that she hadn't missed the conversation by responding, "The Raindrop Lodge is technically Mom's roof, and Jake is sleeping with you beneath it. Openly and publicly. That is a declaration with a capital D."

"Do you really think so?"

Both Prentice sisters spoke simultaneously. "Yes."

"I don't know. That's subtle, and Jake is one of the most direct men I've ever met. That's one of the things that made him such an effective boss."

"That's work Jake. Completely different animal than lovelorn Jake."

"Lovelorn?" Tess chuckled at the silliness of that idea.

From the backseat, Drew piped up. "Why are y'all talking about Uncle Jake? I'm the one who is hurt. You should be talking about me!"

"Talk about me!" Emma said.

"Nope. We're going to play the quiet game from now until we get there."

Tess was grateful for the strategy because her mind was spinning, and her mouth had gone dry as West Texas in August. Was Jake really in love with her? How could his sisters be so certain of it? Shoot, she'd only figured out her own feelings a short time ago. Sure, she'd known she had a thing for him, but she hadn't known she capital L, forever-'til-the-end-of-time loved him until, well, when? Sometime during these past two weeks?

Sometime during these past two minutes?

Oh, holy moly.

"Can you direct me to the library, Tess?" Willow asked.

Glad for the distraction, Tess said, "Sure."

"And let me give you my phone number. If you send me a text so that I have yours, I'll keep you up to date on how our schedule is looking at the doctor's."

"Good idea." Tess pulled out her device, and Willow rattled off her number. "Do you know where the Lake in the Clouds Medical Clinic is, Willow?"

"I do. I spotted it on the way into town."

"We go to the doctor's all the time," Drew explained to Tess, his tone serious. "I'm always having accidents. I'm an active boy."

"I see."

His lip quivered. "Mommy, my hand hurts."

Willow said, "I'm hurrying, baby."

"Hush, bubba!" Emma said.

Tess slipped her cell phone into her pocket and said, "Turn right at the next corner, Willow. The library is half-way down the block on your right."

Her memory proved to be correct regarding story time, and Tess and the three-year-old passed a pleasant couple of hours searching for books and listening to the day's reading selections, the theme of which centered around love.

Quite appropriate, under the circumstances, she decided.

Willow called to say they were finally through at the doctor's office and on the way to the library. She asked Tess to meet her car out in front. "One of the nurses here recommended a sandwich shop nearby. Apparently, they have exceptional chicken strips, which is Drew's favorite food in the world. We thought we'd have lunch before returning to the lodge if that's all right with you?"

"Sounds great."

The sandwich shop had outdoor seating and was located directly across from a playground. After finishing their meal, the children asked to go play, and their mother went with them.

Tess and Brooke sat at their table watching the trio in companionable silence for a few moments, then Tess observed, "Drew seemed pretty proud of his sticker and his stitches."

"Yes. A little too proud, according to Willow." At Tess's questioning look, she elaborated. "She's worried about him. Drew is a troubled little boy. You know that his father is dead."

"Jake mentioned he passed away a couple of years ago."

"He was killed in a car accident. Drew was in the car with him."

"Oh no."

"Our little guy came through it without a scratch, but he's had this fixation on injuries ever since. Willow has him seeing a therapist. He's doing better, but the accidents haven't really slowed down. How much of it is because he's a normal, rambunctious seven-year-old, she can't tell. He's her older child, and she's cautious about mentioning her worries to other mothers of her acquaintance. In this day and age, she's half afraid that someone will turn her in to Child Protective Services."

Tess couldn't blame her for that concern. "What does your mother say about it?"

Brooke winced and dragged a French fry through a pile of ketchup. "She doesn't, I'm afraid. Willow's relationship with Mom is complicated these days. Willow hasn't confided in her about Drew and his accidents. If Drew tells Mom about them, I don't think she has put the clues together to recognize a problem. She hasn't asked me, and I think she would have because she knows that Willow and I talk."

"Poor Willow. Poor Drew." *Poor Genevieve.* Then, figuring in for a penny and such, she asked, "And how about you? Did the doctor give you a sticker for bravery, too?"

"No. I tried to wheedle a lollipop out of 'em, but they claimed that those went out of favor a decade ago. Made me feel old."

"But you, um, don't need stitches or anything?"

Brooke sighed. "How old are you, Tess?"

"I'm twenty-nine."

"Great. So when Jake marries you, I'll have two older sisters."

"Whoa. Who said anything about marriage?"

"Me." Brooke popped the French fry into her mouth and smirked. "I say he pops the question by the Fourth of July."

Tess thought about it a moment, then shook her head. Jake's sisters might think they knew him well, but she understood something about their brother that they had yet to comprehend. The Jake whom they'd met yesterday in Colorado was not the same man as the one with whom they'd grown up in Texas. "That's a valiant effort at deflection from my question, Brooke. I apologize if I was too nosy."

"No." She waved away the apology. "You're engaged to be engaged to my elder brother. You're allowed."

Tess softly laughed. "I'm not going to change your mind on this one, am I?"

"Nope."

The bright smile she showed Tess suddenly faltered, and her eyes filled with tears. Alarmed, Tess instinctively reached out for her. "Brooke?"

"No." Brooke held up her hand, palm out. "It's okay. I'm sorry. The doctor said that physically, I'm healing fine. Emotionally, I'm a little more beat up than is readily obvious. Honestly, thinking about you and Jake is a nice diversion from my own situation. My brother makes me crazy, but he's not a bad guy. I want him to be happy." She swallowed hard, and her gaze drifted toward her sister. "I just want us all to be happy. Sometimes that seems like an awfully tall mountain to climb."

Tess couldn't argue with her, but she sensed that a change in tone and subject would be welcome. Searching for a way to lighten the mood, she said, "Speaking of climbing mountains, Jake has me a little concerned about a potential issue with the overarching idea of the design I've developed for Raindrop Lodge. Brooke, what can you tell me about your aunt Helen and cuckoo clocks?"

She chortled so loudly that Willow, Drew, and Emma all looked their way. Drew called Tess and Brooke to join them, and they whiled away another hour in the park before loading up the car to return to Raindrop.

Tess's phone dinged with a text when they were halfway between town and the resort. "Jake would like you to drop me off at the lodge," she said to Willow. "He's meeting with the contractor, and they have an idea they wish to discuss with me."

"No problem. I need to ask Jake where the password for the Internet is in Cabin 1. I couldn't find it where he told me to look."

Emma said, "We need the Internet to play *Animal Crossings*. We get fifteen minutes to plant flowers before our afternoon nap."

"I don't plant flowers," Drew grumbled. "I smash rocks."

"*Animal Crossings*?" Tess asked.

"A video game," Willow explained.

"Nintendo," Emma elaborated, emphasizing each syllable. "We play with Nana on the Internet. She has an island named Play Date, and she plants flowers everywhere, but she's bad at catching fish. I miss playing with her. I'll be glad when she gets home from vacation."

"Would you drop me off at the cabin first, Will?" Brooke asked. "I've all of a sudden run out of steam. I need my nap without fifteen minutes of *Animal Crossings*."

"Sure."

Brooke added, her tone oh-so-innocent, "I wonder if Jake's meeting has anything to do with cuckoo clocks?" Brooke asked in an oh-so-innocent tone.

"Cuckoo clocks?" Drew repeated. "Like Auntie Helen has? I love them."

Willow groaned, and Brooke chuckled as Emma asked, "Mommy, what's a cuckoo clock?"

A few minutes later, Willow dropped Brooke off at Cabin 12 before driving on to the Raindrop Lodge. As she pulled into the circular gravel drive, a dusty black pickup truck pulled in behind them. A man climbed down from the cab as Willow and Tess exited her car. Willow exclaimed, "Lucas! Wow! Brooke said you wouldn't be here until tomorrow."

Well, Tess thought as she watched the tall blond beauty greet a man who could have been Jake's twin. Lucas was a bit leaner perhaps. Perhaps a skosh taller. He had the same dark hair as Jake, but Lucas wore sunglasses, so she couldn't tell if he and his brother had the same color eyes.

But as his arms opened wide for his sister's embrace, his stance echoed his brother's. His grin was identical to his brother's. And his laugh sounded so similar to Jake's that Tess actually gasped in shock.

Then Jake stepped outside the lodge accompanied by Zach Throckmorton. Lucas lowered Willow to her feet, removed his sunglasses, and slipped them into his shirt pocket. The brothers' gazes met and held. Jake's green eyes were as cold as a glacier. Lucas's amber ones sizzled and snapped with temper.

Okay then. The next few minutes promised to be interesting.

Twenty-One

HEARING THE CRUNCH OF gravel beneath car tires, Jake said, "That must be Tess now. I think she'll go for your solution, Zach."

"Good. I hope so." Zach Throckmorton flipped his notepad shut and slipped it into his shirt pocket. "I like her instincts. If she thinks it's a good idea, it's likely your mom and aunt will give it a thumbs-up. That'll save us a good two weeks of work."

"I agree." Together, the two men turned toward the door.

Jake walked out into summer afternoon sunshine with a smile on his face. He'd missed having Tess around today. After he'd worked through his idea for the Lonesome River Ranch with his attorney, he had wanted to discuss it with Tess and get her opinion. At the same time, he'd liked the idea that she'd gone to lunch with "the girls," as his sisters had been called in the family ever since Brooke was born. Now he was glad she was back. Zach could tell her about his idea for the change to the kitchen plans, and then Jake could run his own solution for the family—oh.

Jake drew in a deep breath. Lucas. He must have driven almost straight through. Wonderful. Just won-der-ful. He'd be exhausted and not in the best frame of mind for mending family fences.

Well, nothing Jake could do about that now. This was the hand he'd been dealt. Had to play it. *Game on.*

He stepped forward, holding out his hand toward Tess. Just because he had to play his hand didn't mean he wouldn't use every advantage he had. Having Tess in his corner was definitely an advantage. Drew scrambled from the SUV and began screaming Lucas's name. Left trapped in her car seat, Emma started wailing.

The next few moments proved to be chaotic. Drew launched into his tale about the doctor's visit, and Emma decided she needed to pee RIGHT NOW. Willow hurried back toward the vehicle to tend to her daughter. Zach offered to show mother and daughter to a working restroom inside the lodge. Drew decided he needed to go, too, so Lucas set the boy down, and Drew scampered after his mom.

Lucas smirked, shrugged, and muttered, "Guess I'll take a bathroom break, too. Long drive."

He followed the crowd, which left Jake and Tess standing in front of the lodge alone. Jake was glad for the respite, temporary though it may be. "Well, that was a welcome I expect you didn't expect."

"You probably don't want to hear this, but the two of you could be twins."

"You're right. I don't want to hear that." He waited for a beat and added, "I've heard it all of my life."

"I imagine you have."

Jake took hold of her hand and squeezed it, then brought it to his lips for a kiss. "Maybe we should let him get some rest before we tackle anything more serious than a hello. He looked like something the cat dragged in. Where's Brooke, by the way?"

"She's taking a nap."

"Did the doctor visit go okay? Did you find out what the meaningful looks going on between my sisters are all about?"

Tess gave him a sharp look. "So there *is* something? I sensed maybe there's a puzzle piece I'm missing."

"You didn't find out what it is?" When she shook her head, he added, "Damn. Yeah, Willow knows something we don't. I'll get it out of one of them, but in the meantime, Brooke seems all right?"

"Yes. Better than yesterday. She got a prescription for pain medication, and I'm sure that will help her."

"That and rest and clean, cool mountain air, and being away from the King of Assholes." Jake hooked his thumb toward the entrance to Raindrop Lodge and added, "Unfortunately, the Prince just arrived."

"Oh, stop it." Tess elbowed Jake in the side. "You are not being—Jake? What's wrong?"

He'd gone stiff and still as a rattlesnake ready to strike. Another vehicle approached the lodge. Fire engine red Maseratis weren't all that common on Texas roads, let alone Colorado's. He hadn't seen one since entering the Rocky Mountains. Jake knew only one person who drove such a car. His voice soft and dangerous, he said, "Looks like I spoke too soon."

The car pulled into the circular drive going the wrong direction, blocking the egress, and parked. The engine died. Travis Sunberg unfolded from the driver's seat.

At the sight of the man, an ugly emotion rumbled through Jake.

He'd never liked the guy, not since the first time Brooke had introduced them. Travis was a pretty boy gym rat, a smarmy snake oil salesman type who always had a scheme going. He was the same age as Jake, too. Just a couple of months younger. Jake had believed he was too old for Brooke from the start. She'd still had some growing up to do when they'd met, and Jake believed Travis had preyed upon her.

He'd been right. She'd grown up now, hadn't she? Faster than necessary. The bastard.

Travis shut the door and strode toward Jake. "I'm surprised to see you here, Jake. Although maybe you can help me out. I'm looking for your sister. I'm afraid that she and I have had a bit of a marital tiff. Have you heard from her, by any chance? Is she here?"

Travis was tall and buff and ham-fisted, while Brooke was lithe and little, like Tess. Jake pictured his sister's black eye and swollen cheekbone. He remembered the careful way she walked. Rage rumbled through him like thunder in the mountains.

He snapped out a single word. "Sunberg."

The man might be an ass, but he wasn't stupid. He picked up on Jake's temper. "So you've talked to her at least. Is she here? I need to talk to her. Look, this was all a misunderstanding. It was an accident, just an accident. I feel horrible that she somehow managed to trip and fall down the stairs the way she did. I know I shouldn't have left afterward. I should have called for help, but I went for help instead. She's all right, isn't she? Is the baby all right?"

The baby.

With two little words, Jake's blood went as cold as snowmelt at the top of Granite Mountain. Beside him, Tess gasped.

The baby.

Jake hadn't gone snooping in his sister's things, but the opened bag of feminine pads had been lying in plain sight on the counter in the master bathroom in Cabin 14.

Ah, Stinky. I'm so sorry.

"You sonofabitch." Jake closed the distance between him and Travis and put everything he had into a right hook that knocked his brother-in-law on his ass. Unfortunately, Sunberg's gym training included sparring, so he recovered quickly. He came back at Jake fast, launching himself low, taking Jake to the ground.

The men rolled and punched and gouged. Sunberg grunted and groaned. Jake didn't make a sound, not even when Sunberg took the fight down a level and started using his teeth. How long it lasted, Jake had not a clue. He saw red and it was laser focused. He wanted to kill Travis Sunberg, but he decided to stop short of that. He'd settle for breaking bones. Inflicting major pain. Messing up that pretty face of his.

He was vaguely aware of the noise happening around him. Footsteps pounding from the direction of the lodge and the cabins. Shouting. Yelling. Screaming. Hollering. Cursing. Crying. A siren.

Travis had landed some significant blows. Jake tasted blood from a cut on his lip, and he had to blink away blood flowing into his right eye from a wound on his forehead. His ribs hurt. The bastard had bitten a chunk out of his shoulder, and he kept trying to knee Jake in the balls. Luckily, Jake had grown up battling a brother, so he was an old pro at protecting the jewels.

When Jake felt hands pulling at him, he shrugged them off and finally found his voice. "No!"

"Dammit," Lucas said. "Get off him. You're gonna kill him."

"Good. He deserves it. She was pregnant."

Travis grunted. "Was? So she lost it? Figures. Couldn't even do that right. Eff you, Prentice. Both of you. All of you. Especially your worthless bitch of a sister, too. I didn't want a baby anyway. I'm glad it's dead."

At that, Jake lost what little grasp on his temper remained. He went up on his knees, left hand gripping the bastard by the neck. Jake drew back his right fist and swung for Travis's temple. "Rot in hell, Sunberg."

Had the blow landed square, it may well have killed Jake's brother-in-law. Instead, he scored only a glancing jab because his brother launched himself at Jake and knocked him off his perch and onto his back.

Lucas's action didn't calm Jake's fury one iota. In fact, he'd been spoiling for a fight with his little brother for better than a year now. Better than two years. So he slammed a fist into Lucas's breadbasket.

"You asshole!"

As Zach Throckmorton saw to Travis, the battle between the Prentice brothers commenced.

They rolled. They punched. They grappled. Perhaps this fight didn't have the viciousness of Jake and Travis's battle, but it did not lack in intensity. Throughout the scuffle, as the brothers exchanged physical blows, they also reverted to trading verbal punches, the same ones they'd issued under similar circumstances beginning in boyhood.

"You dumbshit."

"Asswipe."

"Turdhead."

And so on. Eventually, Jake's temper began to wane. His hands hurt. His face hurt. His kidneys hurt. His ears hurt from his sisters' shouts. Hell, his heart hurt. So when, once again, a pair of hands reached to separate him from his opponent, he didn't resist. Jake rolled off his brother and lay on his back, eyes closed, breathing heavily.

Hell, he hurt.

He thought he might just lie there for a while. He had a bit of a buzzing in his ears, and he wondered if he might have a concussion. He must be hallucinating.

He could have sworn he heard Aunt Helen say, "What in the ever-lovin' purple mountain majesties has happened to your precious empty nest, Genevieve?"

He opened his eyes and looked. Sure enough, his aunt and mother stood next to his brother's truck. Auntie's arms were folded and her right foot tapped the ground. Mom's eyes were closed as she massaged her temples. She looked tired, travel worn, and unhappy as she said, "Apparently the family feud moved north while we were away."

"Sure looks that way," Aunt Helen replied, her voice tight. "Well, neither one of us has the energy to deal with drama right now. Between the jet lag and the gin, we're liable to do or say something that would make matters worse."

Jake levered himself to a seated position saying, "Hold on. Mom, wait. Let me explain."

"Later, Jake," Aunt Helen snapped. "Lucas, is this your truck?"

Lying prone beside his brother, Lucas groaned as he lifted his head. "Yes, ma'am. What—?"

Helen opened the passenger side door. "Genevieve, climb inside. His keys are in the ignition, and I'm driving you home. Gage, thanks so much for the lift from the airport. Sheriff, you have my blessing to arrest anyone for anything you see fit."

"Auntie!" the Prentice brothers exclaimed simultaneously

as their mother got into Lucas's truck and their aunt slammed the door shut. Jake added, "You don't understand."

Helen's eyes flashed with temper. She'd morphed into protective big sister mode. "What I understand is that your mother spent half of our sisters' trip focusing on her new Prentice Family attitude and planning Epiphany Part Two. Arriving home to this nonsense totally pops her healed-and-hopeful balloon. I'll tell you this much, chickadees. You're flunking adulting."

She marched around to the driver's side of the truck and moments later, spun the tires as the Bennett sisters sped away from Raindrop Lodge.

~⊱⊰~

Tess dragged her attention away from the dust cloud rising from the gravel road in the wake of the truck's departure and focused on the Prentice siblings. "That was terrible timing," Willow said as she watched the departing truck. "Who called 911?"

"I did," Zach said. "I saw some serious slugs happening. Figured we might need the paramedics."

"Good call," Lucas said, groaning.

"What happened here?" Brooke asked as she emerged from the trees.

"Good question," Tess observed.

Genevieve and Helen had arrived in a truck sporting the Triple T Ranch logo directly behind the sheriff's truck and before the paramedic van. Zach Throckmorton had identified his father as the driver of the truck and a man whose habit was to monitor emergency calls on the truck's radio. Zach explained to Tess that he had no idea why

Genevieve and Helen had arrived home from Europe with his dad.

Gage rubbed the back of his neck. "I have their bags in my truck."

"You can leave them with us," Willow said. "I'm going after her to explain."

Brooke said, "I'm going with you."

As the Kevin Costner look-alike strode away, Tess turned her attention to Genevieve's elder son. "Oh, Jake. You poor thing. Tell me what hurts most. Tell me where to start. The paramedics are tending to Travis first."

"I don't need a damned paramedic," he growled.

"Good. Travis does."

From off to Tess's left, Travis's weak voice cried out, "You need to arrest Jake Prentice, Sheriff! He assaulted me. I'm suing. Just wait until my lawyer gets hold of you, Prentice."

"Don't worry." The older man, whose belly strained at the buttons of his khaki shirt, tipped his hat back off his forehead. "Everybody's getting arrested."

On Tess's right, Lucas levered himself to a sitting position. "Hey, I'm not at fault here. I was trying to break up the fight."

"We will settle it all down at the station," the sheriff said.

"Great. Just flippin' great." Lucas dropped back onto the ground and closed his eyes.

The sheriff strolled over to speak with the paramedics, and a few minutes later returned with two chemical ice packs. He handed one to Jake and one to Lucas. Once Travis had been loaded into the emergency vehicle, the lawman addressed Zach. "Want to help me get these men into my truck?"

Jake winced as he held the ice pack against his left eye.

"No. Don't arrest my brother. This was a personal beef between the two of us. Tell him, Zach."

"Don't do me any favors, asshole." Lucas dropped his own ice pack, pivoted toward Jake, and attempted to hit him again.

"Enough!" Brooke exclaimed with a sob. "Stop it! All of you. I can't take any more." She turned to Willow, tears welling in her eyes and overflowing. "C'mon Willow. Let's go find mom." And with that the sisters walked away.

Jake spat a curse and made to stand, and to both his and Tess's obvious surprise, Lucas offered him a hand up. Jake accepted, and then the brothers stood side by side, their stances eerily similar as they watched their sister cry.

Tess heard Eloise barking, and she looked around for the dog, finally spotting her framed in an upstairs window of the lodge. Jake had been charged with dog sitting this morning. He must have taken her with him to the lodge.

Bet she's shut in, or else she'd be down here. Tess glanced around. No one else appeared to have noticed the barking. Recalling the comfort Brooke took in her pup's presence, Tess decided to run up and retrieve the spaniel. Quietly, she turned away and hurried into Raindrop Lodge.

The errand took her a little longer than she'd anticipated. First, wet varnish on the main staircase prevented her from accessing the second floor that way. Then carpenters working in the south stairwell meant she needed to head for the north. When she finally reached the second floor, she thought she had a good grip on Eloise when she released her from captivity, but she thought wrong. The danged dog sprang from her arms and raced for the main staircase—wet varnish be damned. So Tess tracked down the painter to explain and apologize, which took another ten minutes.

By the time she'd returned to the front of Raindrop Lodge, everyone was gone.

Tess was alone.

Genevieve sat in her driveway and stared in dismay at the pots sitting on either side of her front door. Her geraniums were toast. She should have taken Gage up on his offer to store them in his greenhouse.

Then, and only then, did she begin to cry.

She wasn't sure why the waterworks started then. Neither did she understand why she'd allowed Helen to scurry her away from the scene of the…what? Crime wasn't right. Her boys had been pummeling each other almost since birth. Scene of the…family? She had seen Willow and she was almost positive that she'd heard Brooke call her name as she climbed into Lucas's truck. The boys were here. The girls were here, too. Why?

Helen patted her knee. "It's okay, Gen."

"I shouldn't have left the lodge. I shouldn't have run away from them."

"You didn't. I dragged you away. Genevieve, you found peace and a plan in the Alps, and you came home to chaos. I did damage control. You are exhausted. Better for you to come home and gather your thoughts and plan your next move rather than react with pure emotion and say or do something damaging."

"My emotions aren't pure. They're a jumbled mess. On one hand, I'm thrilled to have my family gathered together again. On the other hand, I'm worried that some sort of calamity brought them here. It probably isn't anything too disastrous, or someone would have called. If not me, then you. They haven't come to welcome me home, because none of them knew the date of our return to the States. So why are they all here? Certainly not to tell me they've kissed and made up, judging by the way the boys were going after one another."

"Like Mama used to say, I'd like to snatch those two bald-headed, brawling like they were in the front yard."

"In one way, it was nice." A smile flickered on Genevieve's lips. "Just like the old days."

She swiped the tears from her face. "And, you were right to get me away, Helen. Thank you. Caught by surprise the way I was, I might have reverted to the old me and tossed Epiphany Part Two out of the window."

"We don't want that." Helen reached for Genevieve's hand and gave it a hard squeeze. "You've got this, sis. Go in and take a shower and maybe a nap, and then when you're ready, put on your wimple, hold your head high, and sing 'I Have Confidence' as you go to take care of your family in a manner that's right for you all."

"Helen, what are you thinking? Maria didn't wear her nun's habit when she left the convent to care for the Von Trapp children."

"It's a metaphor. Work with me."

Genevieve laughed. "Okay. You're right." She opened the truck's door and paused. "Do you want to come in?"

"No, I'm dead on my feet. I want to get home and check on the cat and have my own shower and a nap. I'll call you in a few hours. Okay?"

"Sounds good." Genevieve climbed down from the truck, but before shutting the door, she said, "Helen, the trip was…." She shrugged. She didn't have the words.

"I know. It was…! And now, we look forward to Christmas markets! Jingle bells, Gen!"

"Jingle bells, Helen." She shut the door and watched the truck as her sister backed out of her drive. Helen gave the horn a little honk before driving away, and Genevieve turned toward her house. Only then did she realize that she'd left her purse behind in Gage's truck. Thank goodness she had an extra key tucked away.

After retrieving it from its hiding spot near her back gate, Genevieve let herself inside. The scent of lemon oil hung on the air, proof that her biweekly housekeeper had freshened up her home on schedule first thing this morning. It was nice to come home to a clean house. It was nice to come home, period.

And Lake in the Clouds *was* home. Had her children come here in an attempt to convince her otherwise?

The knock on the door suggested she might find out sooner than she'd wished. No time for a shower or a nap, apparently.

This could be the neighbor kid whom she'd hired to care for her plants come to explain why her flowers were dead, but Genevieve knew better. Her kids had come to call.

Okay, Mom. Be strong, but patient. Don't let feelings get in the way.

Hadn't she decided to end the estrangement with her offspring while she was sitting in a meadow in Austria? Hadn't she committed to making an effort to help her family became a happy, loving unit again? Epiphany 2.0. Genevieve didn't regret her actions this past December and January. She'd needed a break from family drama and strife. She'd needed independence, mentally and physically. She'd had her time to herself, and her soul had done its healing. She had a new life not so dependent on her children.

It was time to widen her world.

Genevieve took a deep breath, pasted on a smile, and opened her door. Her smile melted as horror swept through her. "Oh my God! Brooke! Sweetheart. What happened to you?"

"He killed my baby, Mama."

"What?" Horror shot through Genevieve. *Her baby? Oh, no. Please, God, no.*

"He pushed me down the stairs, and I lost the baby!"

"Oh, my love." Genevieve enfolded her youngest child in her arms, and Brooke collapsed against her and started sobbing. "Honey, honey, honey."

"It hurts so bad."

"Oh, baby." Genevieve led Brooke to the sofa and they sat. She tenderly held her daughter, gently rocking, pressing kisses against her hair. As Brooke wept, her mother met her older daughter's gaze. Silently, she asked, "Travis?"

Willow confirmed with a nod.

I'll kill him. Genevieve murmured, "Hush, baby. You poor little thing. It's okay. It'll be okay. We're all here for you. We will help you get through this."

Again, she wordlessly asked Willow for confirmation. Again, her daughter nodded. "Drew and Emma are in the car, Mom. I need to see to them."

"Of course, honey," Genevieve said softly. Despite her despair, she felt a flicker of pride. Her children had rallied in support when it mattered.

We're going to be all right.

⚜

His hands cradling his head, Jake gazed up at the wood ceiling. "When was the last time we shared a room?"

Lucas didn't bother to open his eyes. "A room or a jail cell?"

"Thinking about a cell."

"Key West."

"Oh yeah. That lawyer still sends me a Christmas card."

"Speaking of lawyers…." Lucas turned his head and looked at Jake. "Do you think Auntie will do her thing and get us out of here?"

"Yes. She never stays angry at us for long."

"I hope she hurries. I can sure use a shower."

You're telling me. Jake kept the thought to himself, however, because Brooke's trouble had broken the ice between him and Lucas, and he was treading carefully. Once their little sister fell apart, Willow had taken charge, gathered up her children and Brooke and gone in search of their mother. Jake had no sooner turned around to speak to Tess—who was nowhere to be found—than he found himself loaded into the backseat of the sheriff's SUV with his brother and carted off to the hoosegow.

In the time since, Jake had explained to Lucas how he'd come to be in Colorado and answered to the best of his ability his brother's questions regarding Brooke, Mom's life here in Lake in the Clouds, and Willow's state of mind. When Lucas asked about Tess, Jake surprised them both by saying, "She's the one for me."

Lucas turned his head and studied Jake. "As in, the *one* one? The forever one?"

Jake nodded. "Yeah. She's it."

Lucas whistled. "Wow. That happened pretty fast."

"Not really. We worked together at Bensler," Jake explained.

"Whoa. Better be careful, bro. HR will come after you."
Was that real concern Jake heard in Lucas's voice?

"Past tense. Neither one of us works there now. She's at a
boutique firm. I'm currently unemployed."

"You didn't get fired?" Lucas sounded incredulous.

Jake laughed. "No. I quit."

"When do you start your new and better gig?"

"I don't have one."

"Seriously? That's not like you at all. Oh, wait a minute."
Bitterness colored Lucas's tone as he added, "Let me guess.
You're going to spend your time helping your lawyer think
up more lawsuits to file against the ranch and Poppy's estate
and me."

Jake wasn't ready to do this, but he couldn't have asked
for a better opening. "Actually, I did speak to my lawyer
this morning. I dropped the lawsuit. I had an idea for a
compromise solution that I'd like to pursue if you and the
girls will agree to it. Something Brooke said gave me the
idea for it, and I think with this compromise, if the four of
us presented a united front, we could get those leeches to
go away. I haven't said anything to either Brooke or Willow
about this yet. I figure the compromise hinges on you."

Lucas had gone as still as a coiled cottonmouth before the
strike. "I've never been one to think much of compromise."

"This, I know."

"If I won't even listen, you will reinstate your suit
against me?"

"No. I'm done with lawsuits. Besides, I wasn't suing you
personally. I'm throwing in the towel. Mom has taught me
how to do it. It's time I let go. Y'all are all adults. You'll do
what's best for yourselves. So do you want to hear about my
idea or not?"

Jake waited for a long moment. A long, long, long moment. He'd offered his brother an olive branch. Would Lucas accept it? Would he take it and fashion the end into a spear point and plunge it into Jake's chest? Would he turn away and leave Jake holding the stick?

Jake honestly had no clue. That by itself revealed the extent of the damage to his relationship with his brother. Prior to this debacle, Lucas had always been his best friend.

"What's this compromise?"

"We could continue the court fights, attempt to prove Tamra Groves guilty of fraud and get the revised trust documents invalidated. It's a noble fight and I'll admit that part of me wants that. But it will continue to drain everybody's bank accounts as it drags out. Or, we could go back to square one where the sale of the ranch is concerned. We cancel the sales contract."

"I don't see how that solves anything at this point." Lucas shook his head. "For one thing, Brooke is going to need her inheritance more than ever. And Willow's circumstances have changed. I don't see how we can possibly afford to keep the ranch."

"We can't. But we could save the heart of it."

Lucas shot Jake a sharp look. Jake braced his elbows on his knees and leaned forward. "I propose we carve out the lake house and the land on the peninsula and put it into a family trust. Everything else, we sell. Even with the fees and penalties we'll incur from canceling the deal, we'll probably still come out ahead. Land prices have skyrocketed since we've been embroiled in this battle."

Lucas remained silent for a full minute, then two. Two stretched to three. Hope sparked to life inside Jake. His brother hadn't rejected the idea out of hand.

"What would we do with the peninsula land?" Lucas asked.

Yes! The fish was nibbling. This was where Jake set the hook. "That's up to y'all. Build on it. Don't. I'll go along with whatever the majority wants. I don't want to be part of the decision making."

"What?" Lucas sat up, swung his feet around, and put them on the floor. He met his brother's gaze with an incredulous one of his own. "I'm sorry, but this is a bizarro world. You are always part of the decision making. You make the decisions and then convince us to see it your way. That's how this family rolls."

"Not anymore."

Lucas studied him with a long, intense gaze. "You mean it."

Jake nodded. "I do."

His brother closed his eyes and rubbed the back of his neck. "I, um, I guess...I could live with this compromise."

Yes! "Okay, then. Good. Maybe while we're here in Lake in the Clouds, we can run it by the girls and see if they're on board."

"Okay. Sounds like a plan." Lucas swung his legs back onto his bunk and lay down. He pillowed his head in his hands, fingers laced, elbows outstretched, gazing up at the ceiling. "What about Travis? Will he get half of Brooke's fourth?"

"No. I confirmed that with my attorney. We should be able to protect her against that because inheritance doesn't fall under community property laws. Auntie will make sure Brooke gets the best divorce and estate lawyers available. This is one area in which this delay has worked in our favor. If the sale had been settled and she'd commingled the funds, then yes, Travis would have a claim. As it stands now, especially in light of recent events, Brooke doesn't have to worry.

And, we'll do our due diligence prior to accepting another offer and make sure we're selling to honorable people."

"Amen to that."

The brothers didn't speak again for a good ten minutes. Finally, Lucas asked, "What are you going to do?"

It was an awfully big question. Was Lucas talking about Tess? About a job? About Jake's relationship with the family? About his immediate legal situation considering he'd given their sonofabitch brother-in-law a thorough ass whipping? "Do about what?"

"Next."

Ah. Lucas was asking the big, big question. Okay, he'd give him the big, big answer. "Mom asked me a question at that fun Sunday dinner back in January. I'm going looking for the answer."

Lucas gave a dramatic shudder. "What a day that was. I've tried to block it from my memory. So what was the question?"

"She told me I wasn't Dad, and—"

"Oh yeah. I remember now." Lucas snapped his fingers. "So what are you going to do? Run away and find yourself?"

Jake shot his brother a narrow-eyed glare. "Maybe that's exactly what I'm going to do."

"You? Mr. Responsibility?" Lucas chortled. "Yeah, right. I'll tell you what you're going to do. You're going to take some C-suite position with a fancy office and an even fancier view, marry the lovely Tess, beget a boy and a girl with the option for a third, and buy a home in the suburbs. You'll spend summer weekends at the lake house and have the kids riding a Big Mabel tube at the ripe old age of three."

Jake shifted uncomfortably on the hard jailhouse bunk.

Lucas continued, "Friday nights in the fall are reserved

for high school football. In winter, you'll take ski vacations up here, and in spring, oh, I don't know. You'll probably coach T-ball. Of course, year-round, you'll mentor up-and-comers at the firm, and you and the little missus will spend two Saturdays a month hobnobbing with power brokers at whatever charity social gala is on the docket."

"Eff you, little brother." It was all too easy for Jake to see himself falling into the life his brother had described. It was exactly the future he'd been headed for when he'd been at Bensler. That was not the future he wanted anymore. He knew that much about himself at this point, didn't he? "Or maybe I'll keel over dead from a heart attack at thirty-nine."

"Yeah." Lucas sighed heavily. "I think about that sometimes, too."

Surprised, Jake folded his arms. He and Lucas had never talked about this. "Does it bother you?"

Lucas shrugged. "YOLO, bro."

"That is the point, after all, isn't it? You only live once. You ought to know who the hell is doing the living."

～✦

Genevieve held her injured child for a long time, constantly murmuring words of comfort and encouragement. Finally spent, Brooke drew back and looked at her with sad, big brown eyes. "Oh, Mama."

Genevieve pressed a butterfly kiss against the swollen knot on Brooke's cheekbone. "There. That will feel better now."

"It already does."

"Shall we go see what your sister and my grands are up to? They went somewhere—I heard the car leave earlier. But they returned a few minutes ago."

Brooke gave her mother a little smile. "Willow promised them cookies. I'll bet they made a bakery run."

She'd guessed right. Genevieve followed the beautiful sound of children's laughter to the backyard where Emma and Drew played on the swing set erected by the previous owner. Willow sat in the glider on the back porch. Holding up a white sack, she said, "We brought raisin oatmeal cookies from the Sugar Clouds Bakery."

"Fabulous. I'll make tea to go with them. Would you like hot or iced?"

"Hot, please," Brooke said. Willow nodded her agreement.

Inside, Genevieve's hand trembled as she filled the tea-kettle with water and put it on to boil. She'd fought off tears while tending Brooke, but here in the privacy of her kitchen, she gave herself a few minutes to mourn what had happened to her daughter. Luckily, she already had red, tired eyes, so a few more tears wouldn't give her away. However, once the kettle whistled, she wiped them away, loaded up a tray, and pasted on a smile.

Once they were seated at the patio table, Genevieve asked her daughters to explain how the four Prentice siblings came to be in Lake in the Clouds. Genevieve asked questions to clarify details until she understood the current situation, and then she texted her sister to request that Helen don her lawyer's hat and act as the Prentice men's counsel.

By their second cup of Earl Grey, the conversation had moved on to Tess Crenshaw. Among other interesting de-tails, the girls gave her a heads-up about Jake having hired Tess as a designer for the lodge. Genevieve rolled her eyes at her son's high-handedness, but it didn't make her angry the way it would have six months ago. For one thing, if Jake hired Tess for the job, Genevieve could count on her work being excellent. Also, Genevieve liked the woman, and she liked that her son did, too. Finally, she was a bit worried about all the cuckoo clocks. "Oh girls. Wait until you see all the clocks Aunt Helen bought."

Talk turned to the Europe trip. After Genevieve had told them about playing Julie Andrews and twirling around the mountain meadow, Willow said, "Oh, Mom. I am so happy for you and Auntie. I will never forget watching *The Sound of Music* with y'all the first time."

"Me, too," Brooke added. "I couldn't believe you two knew all the words to every song."

Willow nodded. "And much of the dialogue, too."

"You got to live your dream. Your sisters' trip. That's so awesome." Brooke glanced at her sister and said, "Too bad we didn't bring her *The Sound of Music* commemorative plates with us. We could use them for our cookies."

Genevieve's brows arched. "One of you kept the commemorative plates?"

Her daughters shared a look. "We kept all of your dishes, Mom," Willow said. "For you."

Brooke added, "We kept everything. It's all in storage."

"Everything?" Genevieve frowned. "No, you couldn't have. The estate sale company sent me a significant check."

Both girls nodded, and Willow explained, "Emotions were high. Rather than attempt to divide things up, we boxed them up. We thought that, under the circumstances, you might not welcome the news that your things remained yours. So we let the estate sale company price everything, then we pitched in together and bought it. That was the first thing we'd all agreed on in months."

Genevieve considered it a moment, then said, "You were right. My baggage was baggage at that point."

"And now?" Brooke asked.

"I think…" Genevieve sipped her tea, took a bite of cookie, then drummed her fingers on the table and examined her feelings. "I think next time I come to Texas, I would like to pick up those commemorative plates. We can probably use them at the lodge. And maybe I'll bring back my china, too."

"You definitely need your china, Mom," Willow said. "Drew has already asked if we can spend Christmas here. It's not Christmas at Nana's without the Santa Claus china."

Genevieve opened her mouth to mention the Germany trip, but decided that now was not the right time. Brooke asked, "What about the rest of your stuff?"

"I'm doing fine without it. I appreciate your keeping the things in storage, but you're right. My baggage was baggage. Y'all can get rid of everything else."

"Not the table," Willow said.

"You have to keep the dining room table, Mom," Brooke added.

"I bought a new one. It's gorgeous, very modern. I love it. It's perfect for this house."

Neither young woman looked happy about that. Willow said, "The table in Texas is an heirloom. I'd love to have it, but I don't have a place for it now."

"Me, either." Brooke smiled crookedly, then winced and touched her cheek. "I don't even have a house to go to. No way I'm going back to Travis."

"I'm glad to hear that," Genevieve said. "Tell you what. Let's just keep it in storage. There's no sense rushing to get rid of the unit, is there?"

"No," Willow said.

"None at all," Brooke added. "In all honesty, I'll probably

be sticking some of my things in there, too. Would that be okay, Mom?"

"Absolutely, honey. Absolutely."

In harmony for the first time in what seemed like forever, the three women all reached for a cookie. Willow said, "These are delicious. They remind me of Mrs. Davis's raisin cookies."

"Oh, I remember those. She used to hand them out on Halloween. Mom, do you remember the year that the boys went dressed as peanut butter and jelly? Remember the mess they made in the backyard as they made their costumes?"

"Oh, I definitely remember peanut butter and jelly," Genevieve said. "Their mess attracted that possum, who then got into our attic."

Brooke began to giggle at the memory, and as Genevieve sipped her tea, she decided it was the nicest sound she'd heard in a very long time. For the next hour or more, the three women sat at Genevieve's kitchen table, reminisced, and healed.

∼⊱⊰∼

The sheriff kept the Prentice brothers incarcerated overnight. Helen arrived shortly after breakfast the following morning, babbled an apology for the delay in getting them sprung, then saw to the Prentice brothers' release from jail. Immediately upon exiting the building, Jake asked, "Have you talked to Tess?"

"Tess?" Helen's blank expression lasted only a moment. "Oh. Of course. She was at the lodge when we arrived, wasn't she? Where did she go? I didn't see her when we left."

Jake muttered a curse. He had lost his phone during the

scuffle, so if she'd tried to call, he had no way to know. But then, surely she'd guessed where he'd gone and would realize he didn't have a way to contact her. "What about Willow? Have you talked to her?"

"Well, yes. She and the children and Brooke spent the night at your mother's."

"So you just abandoned Tess? Great. Come on, Auntie."

"I'm sorry. I feel terrible. Everything was chaos, and I was trying to wrap my head around what was going on. I was jet-lagged, too, you know. I missed it. I missed her. I'm sorry."

"Get me out there ASAP." When she hesitated, he narrowed his eyes. "What?"

"We planned to have a family meeting at Genevieve's. Everyone is waiting."

Everyone is waiting.

The whole fam-damn-ly.

"This meeting is for what reason?"

"Well, I understand that Lucas brought paperwork with Brooke's signature that needs to be reviewed. We didn't find it in your truck, Lucas."

"I have a custom compartment built-in. I'll get them."

Helen nodded. "Good. Your mother and I believe that Brooke's tragedy has brought the four of you together again, that you agree that the battle between you has gone on long enough. For everyone's sake, it's time to come to some sort of consensus on the Lonesome River Ranch so we can move forward as a family."

Jake met his aunt's steady gaze, then he glanced at his brother. He and Lucas weren't all hunky-dory, but they were speaking again. "Can I use someone's cell?"

Lucas handed his phone over first. Jake dialed Tess's

number. It went to voice mail. "It's me. I've been locked up. My phone's somewhere on the Raindrop Lodge front lawn. I'm looking for you. I'll keep looking and calling until I find you."

He ended the message and returned the device to his brother. To Helen, he said, "Lucas has this. I'm free, Auntie. For the first time since I was fifteen years old, I'm free to choose. I will not be attending this family meeting, not because I'm angry or upset about anything, but because my presence is not required. Tell Mom and the girls that I love them, but I have something more important to do."

Both Helen and his brother looked shocked. "Didn't believe me, bro?"

Lucas's shock quickly smoothed to a smirk. "Oh, I believe you. I called it, if you remember. You are skipping out on the family meeting in order to ask the lovely little Tess to be your blushing bride."

"No. Actually, I'm not. Auntie, you don't mind if I borrow your car, do you?" He reached out and nimbly plucked the keys from her hand. "Mom or Willow can pick up you and Lucas."

"But…but…but…Jake! You can't do this."

"Sure I can. I'm not my dad."

"What does that have to do with anything?"

"It has everything to do with everything."

"What? What will I tell your mother?"

"Tell her I've gone exploring."

Twenty-Two

TESS WATCHED THE SUNRISE paint the sky above Mirror Lake in a pallet of pinks and purples and promised herself that today would be a good day. Better than yesterday, certainly, and it's reminder of her foster kid years when she'd always been on the outside of family looking in.

She had spent a lonely evening without even Brooke's dog to keep her company after Willow returned to Raindrop Lodge long enough to pick up the spaniel and overnight supplies for herself, her children, and her sister. Willow confirmed that Jake and his brother had been carted off to jail rather than the hospital. "But they should be released any time now," she'd added to Tess.

Tess had waited patiently, but when Jake neither arrived nor called, she'd decided that a little self-care was in order. Tess had grilled a steak for dinner and opened the ridiculously expensive bottle of wine Jake had been saving for a special occasion.

That proved to be a mistake. Alcohol only paved the way

for a good old-fashioned pity party. She'd watched the sunset down by the lake, by herself, feeling oh-so-lonely. Going to bed by herself hadn't helped that situation one bit.

But, today was a new day, and already Tess could acknowledge that her dismay at being left behind yesterday had been foolish. Jake had been carted off to jail. You didn't bring along your girlfriend in such a circumstance.

As for as the rest of the Prentice family, well, why would Tess think that they would include her, considering the chaos? Genevieve had just returned to find all her children unexpectedly in Colorado, and her youngest injured and in crisis. Of course their focus was on family. Tess wasn't family!

She needed to regain and maintain her pragmatism. She needed to keep her head out of the clouds here in Lake in the Clouds. Enough of this fantasyland. Life was no fairy tale and she did just fine on her own, thankyouverymuch. She didn't need a prince who came with a queen and a brother prince and sister princesses. She was a good little worker bee who would be happy by herself or maybe with a frog someday.

She'd gone to bed last night having downed a dose of reality with a chaser of broken dreams.

Today, it was back to the real world, the one where Tess depended upon herself for her own happiness. To that end, she decided to follow through with the plans to visit that small tourist town, Eternity Springs, that Brooke's arrival had interrupted. She really wanted some Heavenscents soap before she returned to Texas, and no telling how long Jake's family matter would keep him tied up. So to speak.

She phoned the B and B that Jake had mentioned and reserved a room for the night, then packed a bag and wrote a note explaining her absence. She suffered only a momentary glimmer of guilt about taking Jake's truck without asking his permission.

The drive was beautiful, if hair-raising at times, owing to the narrow, two-lane road and high mountain passes between Lake in the Clouds and her destination. Nestled in a remote mountain valley, Eternity Springs was a quaint little mining town that had seen a resurgence as a tourist destination over the past decade as an angel investor had taken the town under her wing and brought it back from the brink of economic ruin.

Tess's phone began ringing as she spotted the sign for Angel's Rest Healing Center and Spa. It was Jake. "Hello."

"Eternity Springs is a great idea. Mind if I join you?"

Tess hesitated a moment, then decided to be honest. "Your family is all in town. I'm sure you need to be with them."

"I want to be with you."

"Oh. But your family—"

"Can take care of themselves. Did everyone just bail on you yesterday? I'm sorry. I called as soon as they let me out this morning. I found my phone a few minutes ago in front of the lodge. It fell out of my pocket during the scuffle."

"Scuffle?" she asked wryly.

"Yeah, well." He caught her up on the events of yesterday from his perspective. She realized that he'd genuinely had no opportunity to contact her. In fact, maybe she should have gone looking for him instead of throwing a self-pity party. As far as his family went, well, it had been an exceptionally emotional day. She should be an adult and cut everyone some slack.

Jake finished relaying his tale by asking, "So, Eternity Springs?"

"I'm already here. It would be a lot of driving to come to get you and then turn around and come back."

"No need for that. I have my aunt's car. I need to get cleaned up, but I can be there by lunchtime or shortly afterward. What do you say?"

Tess wasn't one to hold a grudge in the face of a sincere apology. She felt the smile spreading on her lips. "Okay. Yes. I'd like that."

"Great. I'll give you a call as I'm getting close, and we can plan where to meet. See you soon, Sprite."

"Drive carefully."

Tess parked Jake's truck in the lot, removed her suitcase from the cab, and rolled it through a rose garden toward a large Victorian mansion. She might have skipped once or twice. She may have hummed a song. It's possible that when she spied the frog hopping along the path, she visualized picking it up and kissing it.

She wouldn't have done that. Not really. Not at all.

She giggled as she opened the door and stepped into the bed-and-breakfast. An older woman with a stylish bobbed haircut, sparkling blue eyes, and dangling gold earrings shaped like angel's wings glanced up from a reservation book and offered Tess a warm, friendly smile. "Welcome to Angel's Rest Healing Center and Spa. I'm Celeste Blessing, the innkeeper here. How may I help you?"

"I made a last-minute reservation for one this morning. Tess Crenshaw. I've had a change in plans. My, um, guy is going to be able to join me after all, so there will be two of us."

"Oh, excellent. That's just wonderful. Wonderful. Quite a relief for me, to be honest. It obviously was meant to be. We had one room left when you called this morning. One cottage. Actually, it's the castle, the Fairy-Tale Castle."

"The Fairy-Tale Castle." A sunny laugh burst from Tess's mouth. "I love it." Hadn't she been having this Disney princess fantasy since she was in St. Pete?

"It's decorated in a fairy-tale theme. We don't ordinarily put a single there, but I didn't want to turn you away when you called, and I just had a feeling it would be all right to give you the room. I don't ignore my feelings."

"Oh. I love fairy tales."

"Me, too. Of course, we only highlight the good ones. None of those scary ones will do at Angel's Rest." Celeste shuddered. "Now, before I show you to your room, what else may I assist you with? Dinner reservations, perhaps? Outdoor recreation tours and activities? We have a wide variety from which to choose, and despite it being high season, I tend to have good luck at securing what makes my guests the happiest."

"In that case," Tess said with a laugh. "If you could get my guy to say yes…"

Celeste's blue eyes twinkled more brightly. "A 'yes'? Are you planning a marriage proposal? Oh my heavens. I just love me some role reversals."

"What? Oh no. No no no. Not marriage. A job. I want him to accept a job."

That took the wind out from beneath Celeste's wings. "Oh. Well, that's just a waste of a good fairy tale, if you ask me."

"I would appreciate help with dinner reservations."

"Very good. Allow me to suggest The Yellow Kitchen. It's the best Italian food you'll find this side of the Amalfi coast. Sometime around seven? For two?"

"Sounds wonderful."

"Let me show you to your cottage. You can leave your bag here, and our attendant will bring it quick as a minute."

Celeste led Tess back outside and down the porch steps to an awaiting golf cart painted in gold sparkles with the Angel's Rest logo in white. The innkeeper motioned Tess aboard, and then they were off. A consummate hostess, she kept up an informative patter all the way to a miniature castle complete with turrets and a moat. "Oh!" Tess exclaimed with delight.

"It's right out of Disney, isn't it? And it definitely doesn't fit with anything else at the resort. I get these whimsies from time to time. Luckily, my landscape designer is brilliant and knows how to hide discordant structures from one another."

She unlocked the door and gave Tess a quick tour of the luxurious accommodations, ending by saying, "I do hope you'll enjoy your stay at Angel's Rest, Tess. I trust you'll feel like a princess here tonight, and I predict that after a night in the Fairy-Tale Castle, you'll live happily ever after."

"Thank you," Tess replied.

"If you need anything, don't hesitate to pick up the house phone and buzz the desk." Celeste seemed to float toward the doorway, where she paused and glanced over her shoulder. "And about that question…if I were you, I'd give my 'pop the question' suggestion a bit of thought. This *is* the Fairy-Tale Castle. Here, dreams do come true."

She finger-waved good-bye and disappeared.

Tess stared at the empty doorway, reminded herself that she was all about the frogs, and then gave her head a little shake. She went to the bathroom to check out the toiletries. She sniffed the shampoo. "Mm." Wonderful. She couldn't place the scents. Something warm and welcoming and clean. Linen-y. Checking the label, she read aloud. "Heavenscents Soaps. Custom made for Angel's Rest in Eternity Springs, Colorado."

All-righty, then. It was time to shop.

After consulting with the teenager who delivered her suitcase a few moments later, she decided to walk. Her route took her past the restaurant where she'd been told they had reservations at seven twenty. She poked her head in to get an idea of what she should wear and discovered that the aromas were as heavenly as the fragrances in the soap shop down the street. After making her purchases at Heavenscents, she dropped into a clothing boutique. She bought a dress, not anything too fancy, but something she could dress up or down with jewelry depending on what Jake packed. She felt confident he would bring a pair of chinos and a sport shirt like he had for dinner in Durango.

As the boutique owner rang up the sale, she suggested that Tess check out the shop next door. "The jeweler is a craftsman. A true artist. She has some dangling copper earrings that would pick up the threads in the dress and be perfect with your bone structure."

How could Tess say no? She had time to kill. She hadn't shopped for the fun of it in forever. When she walked into the jewelry store, her gaze fell on a display of antique jewelry. The item for sale could be traced to two historical mines in the area, the Silver Miracle Mine, from which Eternity Springs had its start, and a smaller strike, a gold mine named simply the Home Mine.

Tess's gaze zeroed in on a man's plain gold band, simple and strong and beautiful. Classic.

She thought of Celeste Blessing.

She thought about fairy tales.

She thought about frogs and being fifteen and foster homes and families and fate.

Get real, Tess Crenshaw. It was just yesterday…
yesterday…that they left you all alone. Again. Like always.

Nevertheless, her heart began to pound. What did she
have to lose? He would say no? She would be alone? Hello!
Been there, done that. State of being.

Besides, she shouldn't discount the fact that Jake had been
hauled away yesterday. He hadn't walked away. That counted
for something, didn't it?

Could she do this? Really? Role reversal extraordinaire?

Why not? She loved him. She needed him. Why not
reach for the dream? Roll the dice? Live the fairy tale? Kiss
the frog?

Why not ask the prince to be her life's partner?

Why not ask Jake Prentice to marry her and work with
her at Innovations Design? To go home with her to a house
in the suburbs? To make babies with her? To drop them off at
school and sign them up for Scouts and sports and summer
camp? To finally…finally…sink roots deep into the Texas
soil and from that anchor grow a stable, secure life?

Dare she ask the prince to make her family?

Family. Jake Prentice was family first. It was, he was, her
most precious dream.

Tess sucked in a quavering breath. "Excuse me. Could I
look at that ring?"

Jake thought he just might have grown wings.

Here he was headed off to meet his woman, while in his
rearview mirror, the Prentices met to make some of the most
significant decisions in the family's life. He wasn't with them.
On purpose. He'd chosen not to be part of the decision.

And he couldn't be happier about it.

He was free.

What a spectacular feeling.

Not that he didn't care about the ultimate resolution of the ranch issue because he did. However, he'd done what he could to make the best of the situation. Now it was up to the rest of them.

What an amazing concept. *Jake, you are not your father.*

If Mom were here with him right now, he'd give her a big fat kiss—after he pulled the car over. Wouldn't want to drive off the side of a mountain just now when life was getting interesting.

Mom had always been a smart cookie. Why had it taken him so long to listen to her?

Who are you?

This was where the wings came in. The fun part. The exciting part. The YOLO part. He had an idea that he couldn't wait to run by Tess.

He called her when he reached the scenic overlook above Hummingbird Lake, figuring he was fifteen minutes away. She directed him to the resort and added, "Wait until you see our castle."

"Our what?"

"Just wait."

Jake laughed out loud when he saw Fairy-Tale Castle. Zach Throckmorton had told him that Mom and Aunt Helen had come up with lots of wild ideas for Raindrop Lodge after visiting Angel's Rest and talking to the innkeeper. He'd said it had become quite a task to convince them to delay some of them until the next stage of renovations. Wonder if castles had been one of them?

Tess opened the door wearing a sunny yellow dress, her

hair down, her feet bare, and a smile on her face. "Hello, jailbird."

A rush of emotion swept over Jake that he didn't attempt to hold back. He moved inside, picked her up, and twirled her around. His mouth captured hers, and he kissed her. Kissed her. Kissed her.

When he finally set her down, he asked the question that had percolated in his mind all morning. "Tess, I've been thinking. This doesn't have to end."

She stilled. "What?"

"You and me. It doesn't have to end. Run away with me, Tess. Let's explore the world together. Let's explore ourselves and find out who we can become. Let's go to the airport and buy tickets on a whim. Let's climb onto a motorcycle and tour until our butts hurt. Or maybe a boat. How do you feel about sailing? I love boats. You don't get seasick, do you? I'm told Dramamine works wonders."

"Wait a minute." She pulled out of his arms. "What are you talking about?"

"Freedom. It's a powerful word, Sprite. A powerful idea. The freedom train is leaving the station, and I am on board. Come with me. Run away with me."

"You're not serious."

"As a heart attack. Where do you want to go first? I'm thinking maybe north and take advantage of the summer weather. I've always wanted to hike the Grand Tetons. When the season starts to turn, I figure we can, too. We can take those new fishing skills of yours to the Keys or to Cabo. What do you say? Ready to run?"

"Why?" Now she backed away. "Why are you running away?"

He boiled it down to the simplest of concepts. "I've always had my family tying me down. I'm finally free."

"And I've never had a family to hold me," she shot back, her eyes sad, her smile bittersweet. "That's all I've ever wanted."

It put every punch thrown by Lucas or Travis to shame and stopped Jake in his tracks. He blinked, reeled, absorbing. "Wow. That's a pretty powerful idea of its own."

"Tell me about it." Tess wrapped her arms around herself and retreated into the room. "I don't think the two are exactly compatible."

Then she pasted a smile on her face and deliberately lightened the mood. "I thank you for the invitation, Mr. Prentice. It is a wildly romantic fantasy and totally suits our castle, don't you think?"

It wasn't a fantasy, but if that's the way she wanted to play it for now, well, okay. Jake would use the time to think.

"Have you had lunch?" she continued.

"No."

"I thought we could order something from room service and hang out here at Angel's Rest for a while? Does that suit you? There is a lot to do here."

"Sounds great."

"Perfect."

Her smile was cheery, but her eyes were shadowed. Jake's high mood from the morning had plunged like a rock thrown off Inspiration Point.

He'd screwed up. He should have listened to Lucas yesterday. He should have asked her to marry him, not run away with him. Maybe if Lucas hadn't suggested it, that's exactly what he would have done.

And I've never had a family to hold me. That's all I've ever wanted.

Jake Prentice, you're an idiot.

She'd grown up in foster care. She had abandonment issues. Of course, she needed commitment! Jake had allowed his brother to jerk his chain—again—and as a result, he'd screwed up big time. *Run away with me?* How insensitive could he be?

So, how to fix it? He needed a plan. He needed a strategy. He needed to bring that light of happiness back into her eyes.

Ordinarily, Jake had little trouble formulating plans, but the arrival of lunch distracted him. Tess asked the server to set up on the table in the castle "keep." The private courtyard came complete with a small in-ground hot tub. Throughout their meal, his gaze kept straying to the spa. Damned fantasies were getting in the way of his thoughts!

Finally, Tess laughed. "Do you want to soak your sore muscles after lunch?"

More than you can imagine. "Yes, but…" *I stole your joy.* "If you have other plans…"

Tess grinned. "I thought I might seduce you in the hot tub."

"I can eat faster." Jake shoved his sandwich into his mouth.

He was determined to use every sensual trick he knew to make up for his idiotic invitation to run away. Instead, Tess took control. She all but killed him, teasing him, tempting him. Driving him wild. They made love in the spa and then again in the shower. Only after they tumbled into the fit-for-a-princess bed was Jake finally able to slow things down. He took his time making sweet, tender love to Tess and finally, *finally*, saw her eyes smile.

Lying spent next to her in the aftermath, Jake's thoughts cleared. He was able to think. The solution was simple. He didn't have to plan. He didn't need to strategize. All he needed to do was speak from his heart.

Sitting up, Jake took Tess's hand in his and solemnly met her gaze. "Tess, I'm sorry. I screwed up. Badly. I shouldn't have asked you to leave your job for me. I know how much your career means to you. I recognize how talented you are and how hard you've worked to achieve your success. I swept in here today and asked you to walk away from the job you love, for heaven's sake. And to do that with no guarantees. Hell, I rolled out the very opposite of a guarantee, yammering on about freedom. That was downright stupid."

Tess smiled, but it was wobbly. "It's okay, Jake."

"No, it's not. I don't know what I was thinking. Actually, I wasn't thinking at all. I know how much family means to you, Sprite. I was an ass to ignore that. So, let me back the truck up. I need to start over." He took a breath. "Here's the deal. I love you. I am in love you. I'm talking head-over-heels, dippy, sappy, now and forever in love with you."

Tess's eyes had gone wide and round. But he spied no clouds or shadows in their depths, so he pressed on. "It's my first time saying those words to anyone, so I hope you'll be patient with me when I make mistakes. When it comes to family, considering my history, I'm bound to make a lot of them. And family is what I'm talking here."

She whispered the word. "Family."

"Yeah. Family." Jake tenderly tucked a stray curl behind her ear. His voice rough with emotion, he asked, "Let me be your family. Let me promise you that you'll never again be alone. I love you, Tess. Will you marry me?"

For a long moment—a seriously long moment—she didn't react. Jake didn't breathe until her eyes went soft and warm and, yes, happy! A tender smile fluttered on her lips.

"No matter what you think, Jake Prentice, it's clear that a tiger can't change his stripes. You are a problem solver through to the bone. You want to fix my problems."

"No, I—"

She hushed him with a finger against his lips, "I love you, too, Jake. I am in love with you, too."

Whew. He'd thought so, but it was a relief to hear it spoken.

Tess continued, "And I think I might have read in a book somewhere that love is patient."

Jake picked up on her Bible reference. "And it's kind, too." He continued the reference to 1 Corinthians as if making a vow. "It does not dishonor. It always protects."

Tess caressed his cheek. "Always trusts. Always hopes. Always perseveres."

"Love never fails, Tess. I will never fail you."

"I believe you, Jake Prescott." She drew a deep breath, held it a moment, then exhaled in a rush. "That's why I have to say no."

He froze. Did she just say no? "Say what?"

"No. I can't marry you."

Now he stiffened. "Why the hell not?"

"Because you need to go. You need some separation between who you think you were, and the man you are learning to be."

"No, I don't."

She laughed. "Go discover yourself. I know who I am and what I want. I know *who* I want. I'm a confident woman with a busy life and career and goals. I'm not going anywhere." She rolled over, opened the drawer of the bedside table, and removed a silver-colored band. A man's ring.

Tess placed the ring in the palm of his hand and wrapped

his fingers around it. Love and the future gleamed in her brilliant blue eyes as she vowed, "I promise."

She sealed her promise by kissing the fist that held the ring. He blinked, shocked, barely comprehending. "You bought an engagement ring for me?"

She shrugged. Grinned. "A promise ring. You know that I missed out on all that high school sort of stuff. No reason I can't make up for it now, is there?"

Jake's lips twitched. "No." He handed her back the ring and held out his left hand, fingers splayed. "None at all."

Tess snorted. "Geeze, Prentice. Let's do this right." She took hold of his right hand and slid the ring upon his finger. "All things in time. Patience, remember?"

He kissed her again, which led to another round of love-making in the fairy-tale bed. When he was sexually sated, Jake had something more to say. "I doubt I'll be patient for long. I'm going to miss that giggle-snort. And your rose-petal-soft skin. And your kisses. And making love with you. And talking with you. I'll probably call you three times a day. At least."

"No, don't do that," Tess replied, her tone growing serious. "If you call me three times a day, I'll stop answering the phone."

"Why?"

"Because that will make me a tie. A line. An anchor. You're boarding the freedom train, remember? You gotta go."

"What are you going to do while I'm gone?"

"I'll go back to Austin, back to work. I'll earn my way into that partnership despite having failed to land the big fish."

"Well, your fishing license is still good, isn't it? Is there a time limit?"

"Honestly, I don't know." She huffed a laugh and added, "Knowing Steve, I doubt it."

"Okay then. Just remember. You can't land a fish if your hook's not wet, and you can't win the lotto if you don't buy a ticket."

"Now, that is prime advice to keep in mind while you're away and I'm alone."

"Whoa." Jake frowned down at her. "Did I not promise you that you wouldn't be alone? I wasn't kidding. Now that we are engaged to be engaged, my mother—"

"Whoa!" Tess said it louder and followed up with a shove to his chest. "What do you mean, 'engaged to be engaged'?"

"That's what just happened, Tess. I told you I loved you. You told me you loved me. We made vows. Binding, nonbinding Biblical vows."

"Binding, nonbinding Biblical vows," she repeated.

"You gave me a ring."

"A *promise* ring."

"Exactly. You should know my management style well enough by now to understand that I hold people to their promises."

"You're not my manager!"

"True. I'm your beloved." He paused, his brow arched, waiting for her to deny it. Of course, she couldn't, so he continued. "Therefore, I'm afraid you're going to have to deal with my family, Tess. I'm sorry to do that to you, but I know you can handle it. I mean, you baked a Thanksgiving pie and delivered it and everything."

"What are you saying, Jake?"

"I'm telling you that as my official future fiancée, Mom and Aunt Helen and the girls and probably even Lucas are going to clap your dainty little wrists in the Prentice family shackles. You'll be expected to attend the Fourth of July Fam-dango."

"I will?" she asked, her voice heartbreakingly hopeful.

"Damn straight. I know my mom. She might *say* she's done with family holidays, but it's in her DNA. The family rift hurt her badly. And while we're not one hundred percent healed, and I certainly can't promise no drama going forward, the Prentice family is better. Mom might not be ready to pull out the decorations for one of the big guns—Thanksgiving or Christmas—but I'll bet everything I own that she'll tackle the third most important holiday on the Prentice Family Calendar."

"The Fourth of July?"

"Yep. I don't know where they will gather to celebrate, but it'll be a command performance. And everyone will be there. That includes you."

"And that will be okay with your mom? Even though we're only promised? Are you sure?"

"Positive. It'll thrill my mom." He lowered his mouth and gave her a quick, hard kiss. "You can bring a pie."

Twenty-Three

The Lake House
Lonesome River Ranch

THE DINING ROOM TABLE sat dusted and polished and sporting a patriotic centerpiece for this first event in its new home. The classic Queen Anne double-pedestal style in solid mahogany sported a few extra nicks and one unfortunate scratch from the move, new wrinkles on the old grande dame's timeless face.

Genevieve removed a bottle of vodka from the liquor cabinet, paused to adjust the American flag adorning her centerpiece of red and white roses in a blue glass vase, then carried the liquor back into the kitchen, where she mixed a pair of Bloody Marys. After plopping a celery stick into each glass, she carried them out onto the deck, where her sister sat watching the show taking place on the lake.

Both Bennett sisters had gone all out this year with the Independence Day theme. Helen rocked her red, white, and blue attire from her patriotic pedicure to the red-sequined cowboy hat perched atop her head. Genevieve had been feeling Old Glory when she shopped, so she was waving the flag with a floppy hat and matching cotton shirt she wore atop white slacks with red sandals.

"Here you go. Vitamin V." Genevieve handed Helen the drink and sat down beside her.

"Breakfast of champions." Helen took a sip and sighed. "You do that well, Genevieve."

"Thank you. I've had plenty of practice the past few years."

Helen lifted her glass in a toast. "Here's to drinking because you want it rather than because you need it."

Genevieve clinked glasses with her sister, saying, "Here. Here." She took a sip, then asked, "That is good. So how do you think it's going?"

"Well, the day is still early, but so far, so good. I have a confession to make. I came downstairs for a snack late last night, and I heard you talking to Willow. I eavesdropped."

"So you heard her ask if she and the children could visit Lake in the Clouds again before school starts? Did you know anything about this before now?"

"No. Hadn't a clue. She hasn't confided in me since it backfired at Thanksgiving."

"She said Drew was happy during the week they spent in Colorado. She thinks it will be good for him." Genevieve hesitated a moment and added, "She thinks it will be good for the two of us, too. Willow and I need some mother-daughter time without her siblings around."

"Oh, honey." Helen reached for her sister's hand and gave it a squeeze. "I agree. I think it's wonderful. Personally, I'll be thrilled to have Drew and Emma close for a time. It'll be nice to play our video game all together instead of over the Internet."

"You and that game." Genevieve laughed.

"Oh, look. Here they come." Helen nodded toward the lake,

where a twenty-three-foot runabout motored by, towing an inflatable tube shaped like a big chair. Brooke rode in the center with Drew on one side and Emma on the other. Both children were laughing. "Pretty tame for a tube ride," Helen observed.

"Because Emma's having a turn, and Willow is at the wheel. Wait until later when someone else is riding, and Lucas is driving. That's when it gets wild."

"I don't know if you're going to get Lucas that far away from his smoker. My stars, his competitive juices are flowing like brisket drippings. Of course, it's not just the brisket, you know. He's feeling protective of you."

"Protective of me! Whatever for? From who?"

"Those wicked Throckmorton men."

"What?"

The ice in Helen's Bloody Mary clattered as she stirred her drink with her celery stick, grinning. "Let's be honest. You've become close to the family awfully fast."

"I'm not close to them. Zach is my contractor. Gage is...is..."

"Yes?"

"He's a friend who just lost his wife. He's mourning. I know what that's like, and I can relate to what he's going through."

"Still, you invited them to Texas for the Fourth of July. And everybody wants to leave the cool, beautiful mountains for one-hundred-degree heat in July."

"I didn't really think they'd come. But the anniversary of Gage's wife's passing is coming up, and Zach thought it would be good for his dad to have a change of scenery. Plus, this will be a good opportunity for Gage and me to discuss our plans for The Emily."

"The theater is going to be an exciting addition to Lake in the Clouds."

"I'm excited about it. That said, I don't think Gage would have made the trip had he and Lucas not pressed each other's hot buttons talking brisket smack."

"And now we have a barbecue war going on. You'll be the most popular person at the neighborhood potluck this evening."

"It does smell heavenly, doesn't it?" Genevieve grinned.

"Divine. Speaking of the divine, you need to make sure you snag one of those chocolates Brooke's divorce lawyer sent back with her after their meeting yesterday."

"I've already had one of those pieces of heaven. Actually, I had three last night. Brooke brought them to my room because she wanted to talk."

"She did? Oh, honey. That's a good sign, isn't it?"

"Definitely. She's never been one to bottle things up inside her, and that's serving her well now, both where the marriage and the miscarriage are concerned. She told me she's been unhappy for a while, and she knows she'll be in a better place soon. She's so grateful for all the help you've given her with the divorce."

"It's not what you know, it's who you know. I have a good Rolodex."

"I wonder if my children even know what a Rolodex is?" Genevieve questioned.

Helen gestured with her Bloody Mary. "Look. Here comes the boat again." The women watched as the family boat pulled up to the dock, this time with Brooke behind the wheel. Zach helped off-load the inflatable ride-on chair tube, and then he lifted Drew out of the boat. Willow handed Emma in her bright pink life jacket over to Zach. He started up the walkway with the children.

Genevieve expected Brooke to guide the boat into the slip and for the girls to secure the boat with the dock lines. That didn't happen. Instead, her daughters idled at the end of their dock, obviously waiting.

The slam of the upstairs bunk room door offered the first hint. "Ah. I'll bet Lucas is putting on his suit," Genevieve said.

Helen nodded. "Bet they're all going skiing, after all."

The downstairs bathroom door, which was nearest to the outdoor kitchen, banged. "That door is sticking again. I might ask Zach to look at it while he's here." She glanced back at the water. "Perfect time for a ski ride. The wind has died, and the water is smooth as glass. Not much boat traffic out because it's early yet."

"Nothing like a busman's holiday," Helen said with a snort.

"He won't mind," Genevieve assured her as a pair of footsteps pounded down the stairs from the bunk room at the same time the downstairs bathroom door was wrenched open. "Lucas must really want to ski if he's going to abandon his smoker in the face of the enemy."

"No kidding," Gage Throckmorton observed as he joined the sisters on the deck, a Bloody Mary of his own in hand. He'd come from the upstairs kitchen, where the pitcher of drinks was in the refrigerator—not downstairs. "But apparently, serious business is afoot that requires his expertise, and it's even more important than brisket."

"What?" the Bennett sisters simultaneously said in surprise.

"Tess told Jake she wants to learn how to water-ski. He's going to teach her."

"Jake?" Helen asked. "Jake is going to teach her? Today? He made it?"

"Of course, he did," Genevieve said, a smile breaking upon her lips. "He promised the family."

Gage nodded. "He showed up a few minutes ago. He's been on the phone with the boaters. Apparently, Lucas believes he's a superior water-ski instructor, so he's abandoning his smoker in order to help Tess learn. There's been quite a discussion back and forth between your children, Genevieve."

Genevieve's laughter bubbled like champagne. Helen dryly observed, "I'll just bet there has."

Below them, the game room door opened, and like hundreds of times before, Jake and Lucas Prentice jogged out of their grandfather's lake house headed for the dock. With practiced grace, they boarded the boat. As Jake swept Tess into his arms for a kiss, which his siblings accompanied with catcalls, Gage reached into his shirt pocket and removed a folded piece of paper. "Jake was in a rush. Something about the good water being an hour ago."

"Oh…" Genevieve was already blinking back tears at the sight of her family gathered together. The statement almost made her blubber. "It's something his father always used to say."

"He asked me to give you this." Gage handed Genevieve the note.

"Thank you, Gage."

As Brooke put the boat into gear and idled away from the dock, Gage said, "If you ladies will excuse me, I'm going to use this opportunity to add my secret ingredient to my barbecue sauce. Something tells me I might not get another chance."

"Smart man," Helen said with a smile.

Once the women were alone again, Genevieve unfolded the note and read:

I am not my father.
I'm a brother. I'm a son. I'm Tess's husband-to-be.
I'm a family man.

Wordlessly, a lump of emotion hanging in her throat, Genevieve handed the paper to her sister. Helen read it, folded it, then returned it to Genevieve. "I told you he'd figure it out by the Fourth. I win our bet. I get to put cuckoo clocks in the Raindrop Lodge dining room."

"Okay, fine. You win. But I'm not telling Tess about the clocks. You get to spring that bit of design news on her." Genevieve shook her head in wonder. "I really thought Jake would last until Labor Day."

"Was never gonna happen. I was shocked he actually got his passport stamped."

"In Canada. That hardly counts."

"Banff is a beautiful honeymoon spot. In any season. I wonder when the wedding will be? And by the way, speaking of passports, are we all set for the Christmas market trip?"

"We are. Oh!" Genevieve snapped her fingers. "With Willow and the children getting in from Nashville last night, this totally slipped my mind. Kimberly called me yesterday. Guess who had a cancellation? Klaus! He's able to be our private guide, after all."

"Seriously? Well, jingle my bells." Helen clinked glasses with Genevieve and grinned. "That's wonderful. Simply wonderful!"

Out on the lake, Jake floated in the water as he helped Tess put on her skis. Lucas threw out a rope. Brooke captained the boat, and Willow called out instructions for Tess that contradicted her brothers' directions.

"Yes, it is wonderful. It's a wonderful life." Genevieve Prentice rested her head on her sister's shoulder. "You're wonderful, too. I don't say it nearly often enough. Thank you. I don't know how I ever would have managed this growing-up business without you."

"Did I just hear a bell ring?" Helen smiled and used her celery stick to stir her Bloody Mary. "Careful, now, Sister. Don't get ahead of yourself."

Helen winked at Genevieve and added, "We're not dead yet."

Acknowledgments

Publishing a women's fiction novel has long been a dream of mine. Taking my publishing career in a new direction required much more than an idea that percolated in my brain for years. It took a team of people who shared my vision. I want to thank those who have helped bring Lake in the Clouds to life.

First is Amy Pierpont, editor-in-chief of Forever/Forever Yours, Grand Central Publishing. Amy, it's been a joy to work with you again. Thank you so much for your insight and support. Thanks also to Junessa Viloria for her editorial input. Junessa, same sentiment applies. So glad to be working with you again, too!

Also, my thanks to the rest of the Grand Central team, Sam Brody, Associate Art Director Daniela Medina, and Publicity and Marketing Director Estelle Hallick. It's been a pleasure to put my dream in your hands.

Special thanks to Christina Hogrebe and Meg Ruley with the Jane Rotrosen Agency for hearing my wishes on this new direction, helping me hone the idea, and finding it a home.

To Mary Dickerson, first reader, plot rescuer, and friend extraordinaire. I'd be lost without you.

Finally, I must thank my family and make a few public declarations. *The Getaway* is not one of those stories where the names have been changed to protect the innocent. I am not Genevieve. Don't let my multiple sets of china convince you otherwise. Auntie M is not Helen. She never sneaked out of the house at night. I know this for a fact because we shared a room until she left for college, at which point I promptly redecorated. In hindsight, it was wrong of me to get rid of her bed—mainly because I've had to hear about it for decades! The fact that COVID prevented our sisters' trip to Salzburg is only coincidence.

And to my children. You've grown up with a mother who writes fiction, so you know to remember that I tell lies for a living. While some events in this book might strike you as somewhat familiar, unfortunately, you are not inheriting a ranch in the Texas Hill Country. However, any time you want to come waterski, remember that "the good water was an hour ago."

You know I love you more than anything.

Finally, as always, to the readers, whose support allows me to have the best job in the world except at deadline time. I hope you enjoyed *The Getaway*, my labor of love about family. Only, not *my* family. Really. I'm not Genevieve, and I'm not running away to Colorado.

I have another book to write about the Prentice family.

Reading Group Guide

Questions for Discussion

1. In *The Getaway*, emotions frequently run high for the Prentice family and Tess throughout their individual stories. Which of those storylines did you find to be the most powerful and emotional?

2. *The Getaway* had three main storylines—one each for Genevieve, Jake, and Tess. What are some common themes that tie these three plots together?

3. To which character did you relate most strongly? Why?

4. Without Brooke's tragedy to rally around, do you think the Prentice family would have been able to heal their wounds and repair their family? Would stubbornness and pride prevent Jake and Lucas from repairing their relationship?

5. Genevieve's children give her life meaning and purpose following the death of her husband. She

devoted her life to keeping her family close. Do you think the conflict and unresolved feelings of her kids were inadvertently escalated by Genevieve trying to force the closeness they once shared?

6. When his father died, Jake assumed the role as the man of the house and protector of the family. Genevieve calls him out on Epiphany Sunday, which sends Jake into a tailspin of self-discovery. Without the challenge from his mother, do you think Jake would have learned to become his own person?

7. How do you think the loss of his father shaped Jake as a businessman?

8. Why do you think March chose to create the Prentice family dynamic? How does she use the characters to portray the nuances of motherhood and self-discovery?

9. Genevieve places great importance on family holidays, beautiful table arrangements, and her dishes. What are some of your family traditions?

10. Tess did not have a real family since her mom died. If she was not craving that closeness of a tight-knit family, how do you think her attitude toward Jake, his siblings, and their conflict might have changed?

11. Jake, Tess, and Genevieve are the point-of-view characters in *The Getaway*. Why do you think March chose to tell the story through those characters? Were there any other characters through whose eyes you'd like to have seen parts of the story?

12. Helen's love for cuckoo clocks is often mentioned. Do you have any collections or beloved items that your family teases you about?

Genevieve's Ginger Cookies

4 cups flour

2 teaspoons ground cloves

2 teaspoons ground cinnamon

2 teaspoons ground ginger

2 teaspoons baking soda

1 teaspoon salt

1½ cups shortening

2 cups sugar, plus ½ cup for rolling

2 eggs

½ cup blackstrap molasses

Sift dry ingredients (flour, cloves, cinnamon, ginger, baking soda, and salt).

Cream together shortening and sugar. Whisk in eggs, then molasses. Add dry ingredients until just combined—the dough will be stiff.

Form into balls one inch thick. Roll in sugar reserved for rolling. Bake at 350° for 10 to 12 minutes.

YOUR
BOOK
CLUB
RESOURCE

VISIT
GCPClubCar.com

to sign up for the **GCP Club Car** newsletter, featuring exclusive promotions, info on other **Club Car** titles, and more.

 @grandcentralpub

 @grandcentralpub

 @grandcentralpub

About the Author

Emily March is the *New York Times, Publishers Weekly*, and *USA Today* bestselling author of over forty novels, including the critically acclaimed Eternity Springs series. *Publishers Weekly* calls March a "master of delightful banter," and her heartwarming, emotionally charged stories have been named to Best of the Year lists by *Publishers Weekly* and *Library Journal*.

A graduate of Texas A&M University, Emily is an avid fan of Aggie sports, and her recipe for jalapeño relish has made her a tailgating legend.